When The Skies Cry

A Book for Dog Lovers

Steve N Lee

Blue Zoo
England

Published by Blue Zoo, Yorkshire, England.

For those who make the world a better place.
No matter how many legs they have.

Chapter 01

The arm hung over the side of the bathtub, pale and unmoving. Harley nuzzled the hand, its coldness sharp against his nose. Pulling back, he waited for it to reach out and pat his head or scratch under his chin. He stared at it. And stared. And stared. Watching for the tiniest of movements. *Pleading* for the tiniest of movements.

But the hand hung. As loving as stone.

A droplet dripped from the faucet into the gunky gray bathwater, the splash piercing the eerie silence.

Harley gazed at Barney, aching to feel the man pet him and assure him everything was okay. Instead, Barney drilled his gaze into the wall of pale green ceramic tiles straight ahead, his eyes that had once been so blue and filled with love now as clouded as the scummy water.

Harley whimpered. What was happening? Had he been bad so Barney didn't love him anymore?

He nuzzled the hand again. Its fingers still didn't curl into his fur, so he dragged his tongue across the back of it. The fresh salty tang had disappeared, replaced by something stale, moldy, something that didn't taste of life and love but like something Barney had tossed into the garbage after accidentally leaving it out of the refrigerator overnight.

As moonlight slashed the gloom through the blinds, Harley stared at the white-tiled floor and the collection of treasures he'd fetched to rejuvenate Barney: the slippers Barney hadn't put on, the phone Barney hadn't talked into, the can of beer Barney hadn't drunk.

He'd tried. What else could he do?

Resting his head on the side of the bathtub, he stared at Barney's face. It was as if someone had stolen Barney and left behind a fake that smelled like Barney, but also didn't. How was that possible? How could it be both Barney and not Barney?

It was like the stripy brown cat from two doors away; the only thing in the world Harley despised — a mangy fur ball of hisses, claws, and hatred. After a silver car hit it one morning, the thing crawled away and hid under a bush. The hissing stopped. The slashing claws stopped. Everything stopped. Everything except a smell similar to the one in the bathroom now.

Harley whined. He had to bring Barney back so he could hear the man's gravelly voice once more make the most beautiful sound in the world: "Harley."

As the muffled sound of the traffic growling along the darkened street bled in from outside, Harley glanced around the room, desperate for inspiration to help him resolve his dire predicament. The white sink, a can of face foam, a tube of blue mouth gunk, and a mouth gunk brush. Harley's favorite water bowl — into which Barney did all manner of unspeakable things, but for which Harley always forgave him. Rolls of white paper Harley wasn't allowed to play with...

There was nothing.

He whimpered. Barney couldn't stop. He just couldn't.

Harley slumped but then gasped. How had he been so stupid? He knew exactly what would make Barney *Barney* again. Apart from Harley, it was the one thing Barney was never without when home. Stupid dog! Stupid. Stupid. Stupid!

His claws *tap-tap-tapping* on the tiles, Harley trotted out of the bathroom and down the stairs, passing the pictures on the wall of people he'd never met. One of the men looked a little like Barney, but without so many lines on his face, and with much more hair. However, it didn't smell like Barney, so it could've been anyone.

At the bottom of the stairs, Harley stopped. Mired in gloom, the living room was no longer the joyous place it had always been with Barney filling it with his booming voice, his hacking laugh, and a personality as big as the house.

Harley spied the black TV remote control sitting on the arm of the brown sofa that reclined whenever Barney clicked the button on the side.

Harley scampered over. His head at an angle, he opened his jaws and eased them about the TV remote, then padded back upstairs.

With a bounce in his step, Harley trotted into the bathroom, his claws *tap-tap-tapping* once more. This was bound to work. Barney was

6

never more animated than when he watched the pictures that appeared on the big black rectangle in the corner of the living room, and this device played a major part in that activity. How stupid he'd been not to think of this sooner. If he had, everything would have been back to normal days ago.

Bowing his head, Harley prodded Barney's hand with the TV remote. He waited. Any moment, those fingers would clasp the plastic lump, press the little buttons, and Barney would be Barney once more.

Harley gazed up into the man's face. He squinted. Studied every line and wrinkle. Waited for a flicker of movement, a flicker of joy, a flicker of love... Waited for *Barney*.

Any minute now.

Outside, traffic still grumbled through the night. Outside, the world hadn't stopped. But inside...?

Harley waited. And waited. And waited...

Chapter 02

Tick, tick, tick...

With the day's first weak rays of sunlight struggling through the frosted window above the white rolltop bathtub, Rachel stood behind her son, brushing his teeth. She checked their image in the mirror. Too much of the blue toothbrush handle was visible, so she adjusted her grip to hide more, even though it closely matched the blue of his tartan pajamas and robe.

Tick, tick, tick...

After tramping around six different pharmacies while Wes was in school on Friday, hunting for one of the blue toothbrushes she'd used for years, she'd accepted defeat and bought a different blue. For most people, that wouldn't be the end of the world. But for Wes...

Tick, tick, tick...

Luckily, Wes's attention was glued to the countdown timer on her phone on the shelf above the sink.

Rachel finished brushing.

"Rinse." She offered him a glass of water, holding it as close to the bottom as possible so he had plenty of room to grasp it without touching her fingers. Heaven forbid skin should meet skin.

While he rinsed, Rachel put the toothbrush into the chrome stand, it having passed the test, and picked up the wooden hairbrush.

Tick, tick, tick...

She brushed Wes's shaggy chestnut hair while he continued scrutinizing the timer. His lips barely moving, he silently counted down the seconds to when this outrageous physical abuse would end.

His hair hung half an inch beyond his collar at the back. That would need cutting before he realized. Glancing at the timer, she quickened her pace while she brushed his bangs, ensuring the hair hung over his eyes, providing a barrier he could hide behind.

8

Dring, dring, dring, the timer sounded. She switched it off.

"There you go, Wes. Handsome as ever." She smiled at him in the mirror. She didn't expect a reaction — and got none — but she hoped on some level it meant something to him. She reset the timer for 150 seconds.

Counting silently, Wes toddled out of the bathroom.

So his hair was too long and she'd used the wrong shade of blue toothbrush — there'd been no tantrum. Today was going to be a good day.

Checking in the mirror, she dragged her fingers through her straight brown hair as it cascaded over her shoulders. Wes wasn't the only one who needed a haircut.

"Oh, no!" She grabbed her phone and raced after Wes. Today was Monday, not Tuesday. How the devil had she gotten that mixed up? Monday was blue sweater day, and she'd left out a red one. That toothbrush! She'd been so worried about his reaction she'd gotten completely turned around. Today had been going so well, too.

Wes stood beside his bed, staring down at the red sweater and pair of jeans on his cream comforter.

Dashing over, Rachel snatched the sweater away, dropping the phone next to the jeans. She ripped open the second drawer of his dresser, taking care not to jolt his collection of empty cans of different varieties of soup arranged in a pyramid on the top. She rummaged inside and yanked out his favorite blue sweater — a thick ribbed wool one.

Tick, tick, tick...

She scooted across to Wes, who was still standing and counting. Fumbling as quickly as she could, Rachel unfastened his pajama jacket and eased it over his scrawny shoulders and down his spindly arms, ensuring her fingers never accidentally grazed his skin.

It stumped her that Wes wouldn't allow anyone to touch him with their bare hands, yet his favorite item of clothing was the scratchiest thing ever created. Weird. It was likely because his brain was wired differently. Maybe the touch of human skin "burned" him, whereas scratchy wool was like being licked by puppies.

Tick, tick, tick...

She checked the timer. She was cutting this close. Too close.

"Up."

He raised both arms. She pulled his sweater on, then eased down his pajama bottoms.

"Left."

He lifted his left foot and she removed the left leg of pajamas.

"Right."

He lifted his right foot.

Giving instructions, she pulled on his tighty-whities and jeans.

All the while, Wes kept counting and the timer kept ticking.

Tick, tick, tick...

Grabbing his left sneaker, she glanced at the timer: thirty-two seconds. If she screwed this up by running out of time, he'd spend the day walking around wearing only one shoe. Thank heavens he didn't wear socks because they were too fiddly to put on without touching him.

"Left."

He raised his left foot. She eased on his sneaker and fastened it.

"Right."

Wes lifted his right foot.

Fumbling to fit the shoe without touching him, she dropped it. She cursed under her breath, snatched it up, and jammed it on.

Tick, tick, tick...

"Please, please, please." Feeling like she was threading a needle while wearing mittens, she bungled tying the laces and had to start over.

Tick, tick, tick...

She tugged the two ends of the laces tight, looped and wound them, yanked—

Dring, dring, dring.

"Yes!" She thrust her arms into the air, her son fully dressed. "High five to me."

Wes shot a glance from under his bangs so he'd only see her face with his peripheral vision, thus avoiding eye contact, but said nothing.

Through years of experimentation, negotiation, and compromise, they'd developed a system whereby she got to fulfill his personal care needs, while he knew exactly how long such torture would last. It wasn't perfect, but when was anything in life?

Yes, today was going to be a good day.

Her phone rang. She glared at it, unease wrinkling her brow.

A call barely past breakfast time? That never happened, since everyone who phoned her knew the importance of Wes's morning routine. That meant only one thing. Her shoulders slumped. What the devil had gone wrong now?

Chapter 03

Harley woke, squinting as sunlight stabbed through the bathroom blinds. His tail still wagged from his dream of lying on the sofa with Barney scratching behind his ear. Then he remembered where he was, and his tail slapped onto the tiled floor and didn't move again.

No, that wasn't how to think. A new day meant new hope, so he had to be positive for Barney's sake. Yes, today would be the day everything changed.

Harley stretched, then looked at Barney. His jaw dropped.

Yesterday, the man in the tub had been both Barney and not Barney, yet now... Barney didn't just smell different, he looked different – he'd swollen, as if someone had pumped him full of air, and his skin was no longer flesh-toned but a mottled blue-gray. This "Not Barney" wasn't just worrying but outright scary. What was happening? Where was *his* Barney?

Harley's stomach rumbled. No matter the problem, things always seemed better with a full belly, so he wandered down to the kitchen.

Every single morning his food bowl magically refilled while he was relieving himself outside in his special relieving place. Every single day. Until three days ago. However, today was his lucky day. He could feel it.

As he approached his steel bowl on the floor beside the pastel blue cupboards, his tail drooped.

To be certain the bowl wouldn't magically refill, he shoved it with his snout. It scraped across the polished wood floor. Deep down, he expected nothing to happen, but he was still disappointed when nothing did. His shoulders slumped. And his stomach growled again.

Okay, so his bowl was broken, but that didn't mean the plate of ground beef wouldn't have replenished. Barney wouldn't mind if he ate that because it was meant for him. He ambled to the stainless steel refrigerator in the corner and tugged it open with the braided nylon strap attached to the handle. The beef plate was empty too.

A lump of yellow cheese tantalized him with its creamy aroma. His mouth watered. Opening his jaws, he reached for it but jerked away. No! No matter how hungry he was, he was a good dog, and a good dog wouldn't upset Barney by disobeying him when he was so sick. Cheese was a giant no-no because of the small gassy explosions it caused to come from his butt.

Between the bare shelves and goods in containers Harley couldn't open, there was nothing edible.

Or was there?

Harley sniffed. He knew that smell, though he'd never eaten what it belonged to. Pawing at an opaque plastic tray, he eased it open. Something green and leafy lay inside. Harley sniffed it.

Was that edible? If so, why hadn't Barney gobbled down the plants in the park that smelled equally appetizing?

Harley's stomach knotted like some great beast was eating him from the inside out. He whimpered.

A repetitive ringing came from somewhere in the distance, but he was too consumed with thoughts of food for it to register properly. He sniffed the lump of leafy green. Could he eat this? He didn't want to get ill because who would make Barney better then?

Pushing his snout into the tray, he sniffed hard. It did not smell like anything he recognized as food.

The ringing noise gnawed at the back of his mind, but his stomach clenched tighter.

It was no good, he had to be brave — Harley licked the green lump. Urgh!

Tongue dangling, he jerked back, scanning for something to lick to mask the horrid taste. He froze. That noise.

He gasped. That noise!

Harley bolted through the kitchen and up the stairs.

That noise. It was everything he'd prayed for — it was help.

He darted into the bathroom, but the noise stopped.

Nooo!

He stared at the phone on the floor next to the slippers and the can of beer. Whenever the phone made that noise, Barney talked into it and someone talked back.

If Barney talked now, someone could rush to help.

Harley stared at Barney, pleading for just one word so that whoever was on the phone would race to their rescue.

But Barney said nothing. His clouded eyes were still locked on the wall as if he didn't care about anything or anyone.

Talk, Barney. Please. Talk!

A spark of hope clawed its way from the back of Harley's mind. If Barney wouldn't call for help...

Harley leaned down to the lump of black plastic and barked.

He waited, ears pricked for the quietest of replies.

Silence.

He barked again, his gaze burning into the phone, willing someone to realize something was wrong and dash to help.

Nothing.

People talked to Barney on this machine; Harley had heard them. Why wouldn't they talk to him?

He nudged the phone. Barked one last time. Waited.

Silence.

Why wouldn't they talk? Why?

He slumped. No one was coming to their rescue. He was alone. And if he didn't do something soon, Barney might stop forever. But what could he do that he hadn't already tried?

Or maybe he'd already done it. Maybe no one had talked because they'd understood the emergency, and so they were already racing over.

That was it. Someone was coming to save Barney.

Harley darted out and down the stairs. In the hallway, he stared at the front door, tail wagging. They were coming. They were coming now.

Chapter 04

Rachel stood before the window in the dining area near the kitchen, the coldness of the night seeping through the glass. On her run that morning, tiny buds had peppered many of the trees — spring was coming, thank heavens. In winter, it would be so easy to forsake her early-morning runs for an extra hour of coziness in bed, but as she was hurtling toward forty, the day she'd groan rising from a chair or her pulse would jump as she climbed stairs seemed unnervingly close. She had to stave off that day. Had to stay young and fit. Not for her sake, but for Wes's.

She cupped a hand to the glass to see beyond the reflections of the room's interior. A full moon had climbed over the mountain range, its pale light caressing the treetop canopy flowing over the lower slopes.

The corners of her mouth tweaked upward. It seemed a lifetime ago she and Peter had hiked the surrounding hills. They'd thought they were in love — or at least she had. However, once the problems had started, whatever had thrust them together hadn't been strong enough to hold them there. Love? Was there such a thing?

She drew the drapes and turned to the gray leather sofa in the living room. Wes sat at the far right end.

Love? Of course there was such a thing.

Sauntering back, she snagged the bottle of red she'd left to breathe on the granite kitchen countertop and the two glasses beside it. Placing the bottle and glasses on the Indian rosewood coffee table, she sat on the left of the sofa and refocused on the animated movie about a princess trapped in a tower waiting for a prince to save her.

She did a double take. Wes glared at her from the corners of his eyes through his bangs. Something was wrong, but what?

She scanned the room. Everything appeared just as it should be. So was it her?

Looking down, she rolled her eyes. She'd made one of the most elementary mistakes she could. A couple of inches of her right buttock and thigh overlapped the seam in the three-seat sofa that designated where the far left seat ended and the middle one started — she'd encroached on no-man's land.

"Sorry." She shuffled fully onto her spot on the far left cushion, as far from her son as the seating would allow. Wes resumed watching the movie.

Rachel snickered. To Wes, she had to be the most irritating person in the world.

A few minutes later, the front door opened and Izzy strolled in, a tinny screeching leaking from her earbuds.

Without a word or glance, Izzy waltzed to the armchair and slumped into it, her head bobbing in time to the music. It was no wonder Rachel struggled to teach Wes how to socialize when she couldn't even get her tenant-cum-best-friend to say hello when she waltzed in.

Izzy tossed her head back, then raked her fingers through her blue hair, which was cut into a bob. She'd said she was going to change it from purple to blue after she'd sat for Wes while Rachel went running on Friday morning. It looked good. Rachel wished she could be so devil-may-care, but being thirty-six with a kid and a career was different from being twenty-five, childless, and wonderfully directionless.

Around a quarter of an hour later, Izzy said loudly, "Wes won't like the ending."

"You're talking too loud."

Izzy removed one earbud. "What?"

"You're talking loudly."

"Sorry." She gestured with the earbud. "Alter Bridge — it's decent rock, but they're no Monster Magnet."

"Is anyone?"

"Ha, exactly."

Though Izzy was twenty-five, where Monster Magnet was concerned, she was a thirteen-year-old with a monster crush. The only thing missing was a bedroom plastered with posters. Rachel was sure if her tenant agreement hadn't stipulated permissible wall hangings, the apartment above her garage would've become a Monster Magnet shrine within minutes of Izzy's arrival.

Rachel said, "Why won't he like the ending?"

"I streamed it with my niece. A dragon gets killed."

"Doesn't matter anyway." Rachel checked the time on her phone. "There's only four minutes to go."

Izzy stood. "I'll pop to the john."

Rachel showed the screen to Izzy as she strolled past. "Four minutes."

Izzy held up her hands defensively. "No shy bladder here."

"Just saying. I don't want any nasty surprises when I've finally wangled a couple of hours of me time."

"Chill, babe. Everything's cool." Izzy climbed the stairs.

A short time later, Rachel glanced at her phone again: 7:57 p.m. She strained to hear the toilet flushing, but no such sound came.

Wes hadn't looked away from the movie, but Rachel couldn't settle.

She checked her phone again: 7:58 p.m. She turned to the downstairs hallway. No sign of Izzy.

"Come on, Iz."

Rachel rubbed her brow. Wes appeared to be engrossed in the movie, but that would change instantly. This wasn't just about her having a few hours to herself, it was about not having a sleepless night filled with tantrums.

Twisting around again, she stared at the staircase. Under her breath, she said, "Come on, Iz. Come on."

The seconds flew by so fast on her phone she clicked the TV remote to check the time on another device: 7:59:23.

Wes checked his watch.

Oh, no. Please don't say it was fast. She stared at him, willing him not to head to the bathroom only to find the door locked and his routine ruined.

He didn't get up.

Upstairs, a toilet flushed. Rachel sighed. Saved.

Izzy meandered to her seat, as if she had all the time in the world, just as Wes rose from his.

Rachel pushed off the sofa.

"See you in eight minutes," said Izzy.

Rachel nodded. "Pour the wine, if you like. Heaven knows I need a drink tonight — Peter called this morning."

Izzy rolled her eyes.

Rachel found Wes standing at the bathroom sink. She squirted paste onto the new toothbrush that had passed that morning's test and set the timer for 120 seconds. With the first *tick*, Wes opened his mouth.

After the toothbrushing, Wes studied her as she wrapped a couple of baby wipes around her right hand so no skin was visible. Once a week, he allowed her to bathe him; other than that, water was a big no-no. Maybe it was another substance that "burned."

Satisfied, he raised his hands, closed his eyes, and tilted his face upward. She set the timer for ninety seconds and cleaned him.

Finally, Wes sat on the toilet and urinated. That was one thing for which Peter deserved credit — despite the months of scratching, screaming, and scuffling, he'd taught Wes to use the toilet by himself. A small mercy. Or maybe not. Maybe if they'd had fewer problems, and fewer disagreements over those problems, the three of them would still be together.

As Wes pulled up his pants, she couldn't help glancing at his crotch, praying there wouldn't be the first signs of body hair. He'd be twelve soon, so puberty was due anytime. Rachel dreaded the day — life was already difficult, but at least they'd found some form of equilibrium. However, once testosterone kicked in, their peaceful, compromise-laden lifestyle could take a beating.

The time ticking away, Rachel changed Wes into his pajamas and tucked him into bed.

She leaned to within a foot of his forehead and kissed, as if kissing him good night. Despite the distance separating them, he recoiled into his pillow. As it was every night, a knife stabbed her in the heart.

"Good night, Wes." She eased the door closed.

In the living room, Izzy cradled a glass of wine, sitting cross-legged on the sofa in Wes's spot.

"I don't know how you cope with all this, Rach. I really don't."

"Like I have a choice." Rachel snagged her wine from the coffee table.

"Yeah, but all this timer business. Doesn't it drive you nuts?"

Rachel shrugged. "It's as much routine for me now as it is for Wes."

"Don't you ever stick a few extra seconds on to give yourself some breathing space?"

"Yeah, right." Rachel smirked. "I once set 140 seconds instead of 120 for toothbrushing. Did it work?"

"No?" Izzy raised her eyebrows.

"I tell you, I don't know if Wes is awkward, supersmart, or just plain stupid, but once he'd counted to 120, he clamped his mouth shut and no way could I get him to open it again. He spent twenty-five minutes walking around the house with his toothbrush sticking out of his mouth. I had to bribe him with a candy bar to get it out."

Izzy chuckled. "My money is on super smart. I tell you, there's a lot going on inside that head of his. Maybe *we're* just not smart enough to understand *him*." She took a drink of wine. "Oh, and I love — absolutely love — that new image you sent me." Izzy held her phone out displaying a black-and-white illustration of an elf princess and a dragon outside a castle. "It's my new screensaver."

"Thanks." Rachel stared at her feet. She'd been getting paid for freelance artwork for six years, but she still felt like a fraud. How could doing something she loved be work? Especially work people would pay for.

"It's the shading," said Izzy. "It gives it such depth and makes it so dark and brooding."

"I figured readers might appreciate something with a little edge. Something more mature."

Izzy grinned. "Believe me, they're gonna love this. That series is yours, babe."

Rachel snorted.

"Seriously, Rach, this is the best stuff you've ever done."

"Well, let's hope they think so." She sipped her wine. This was a commission for the deluxe edition of a teen fantasy novel, which would feature eighteen plates of scenes from the story. There had been talk of a commission for a number of series *if* she nailed this job.

"You'll get it. Trust me."

Rachel winced. "Maybe. But I still worry I priced way too low. There's no point in fancy commissions if I end up earning less. The whole point is to make life easier. Make things more secure for Wes."

"And so you don't have to work till midnight every freaking day."

Rachel nodded. Something approaching a normal lifestyle would be wonderful. One day.

"Rachel" — Izzy scrunched up her face and shook her head like a disappointed parent — "I know you've got a thing about compliments, but this work is incredible. If they offer you another job, it's because they think it's incredible too, so don't shortchange yourself – negotiate a deal that works for you. You hear?"

Rachel nodded. Sitting with her best friend and a glass of wine, negotiating sounded easy. But alone, facing professionals who thought nothing of publishing multimillion-copy bestsellers, she felt as legit as a three-dollar bill, and just as worthless.

Izzy said, "Seriously, if you don't insist on everything you want, it'll be the stupidest thing you've ever done." She leaned back, cradling her glass. "Anyway, speaking of stupid, what's Captain Doofus done now?"

"Peter?" Rachel heaved a breath. "Oh, only changed the day of the meeting to Thursday, hasn't he."

"But I'm working Thursday."

"I know."

"Did you tell him?"

Rachel shot her a sideways glance. "It seems Claire had a hospital appointment rescheduled that they can't miss."

Izzy leaned closer, a grin spreading over her chubby face. "Is she dying? Oh, please say she's dying."

"Iz, you haven't even met the woman."

"Yeah, but anyone who breaks up a family deserves what's coming to them. So what is it? Accidental Botox overdose? Terminal perky-boob-itus?" She took a swig of her drink.

Rachel snorted a laugh. "I didn't catch everything because I was fuming that he'd ruined our plans. I just remember the words *leprosy* and *clitoris*."

Izzy laughed so hard, she spluttered wine onto her blouse.

Rachel nodded to the stain. "That's going to leave a nasty mark."

"That's what Claire said!"

They both laughed.

"Seriously," said Izzy, "what is it?"

Rachel shrugged. "I don't know and I don't care. As long as the alimony and child support checks continue to arrive on time."

"You're not thinking he wants the payments reduced?"

"Well, I doubt he wants them increased." Rachel put her glass down. "But like he has a hope in hell. And any judge will tell him that if we have to go to court. Wes needs the care he gets, and anything less would reduce his quality of life. No judge is going to side with a high-earning professional and his gold-digging bimbo against a disabled child."

"So what are we doing about Thursday?"

Rachel said, "I left a message for that special needs sitter, so hopefully she'll get back to me."

"I thought she said she'd never come again after Wes bit her."

"So I'll smooth things over."

"You said she needed a tetanus shot it was so deep."

Rachel shrugged.

"What time's the meeting?"

"One forty-five."

Izzy pursed her lips and stared into space. "I'll ask Lucinda if I can take a late lunch, then you can drop Wes off at, say, one thirty. We'll grab a bite to eat or take a walk in the park — he can see the ducks. It'll be fun. A nice change for him."

Rachel topped up Izzy's drink. "You're sure that'll be okay?"

"My tetanus shots are up-to-date, so..."

Rachel smiled. Making arrangements for Wes was a huge weight off her mind. But not the main one — what did Peter want? Obviously it wouldn't be good for her, but why would he think now would be a good time to restructure their financial arrangements? Did he know something she didn't?

Chapter 05

Tinged by the eerie yellow of streetlights, darkness bled through the glass in Barney's front door.

Harley stared at the door, chin resting on his front paws. Rescuers were coming. But when? The stench from upstairs was getting stronger and stronger, so it was obvious Barney was getting no better. If they didn't come to save him soon...

Harley whined. He didn't want to imagine a world in which Barney had stopped. Yet no matter how hard he stared at the door, how much he pricked his ears to listen, how often he sniffed for new scents, no good news shone out of the darkness.

Harley whined again. It was taking way too long.

From behind him, a faint scratching clawed through the stillness. Harley gasped and stared back into the darkened house.

Finally. They were here. But where?

Chapter 06

Harley padded along the hallway into the kitchen, head high, his nails tapping on the wooden floor. Angling his ears independently, he searched for the source of the scratching, which was now closer.

It was odd they were entering through the back of the house instead of the front like people normally did, but that didn't matter — the only thing that mattered was that they were here. Here to save Barney.

As all went quiet, he stopped near the kitchen table. He peered through the shadows.

The scratching came from somewhere back here, but where?

His gaze pierced the blackness, scanning the dark shapes for movement, while his ears were pricked for the tiniest of sounds. Stillness and silence engulfed him.

He frowned. He'd heard scratching. Hadn't he? Or was his gnawing hunger making his mind play tricks on him?

Lifting his snout high, he sucked in a great lungful of air, filtering the aromas drifting through the night and searching for one that shouldn't be there.

No smell fought through the stench flowing down the stairs from the bathroom like a rancid waterfall.

A still darkness enveloped him like a shroud. His head hanging, Harley shuffled away. He was wrong. No one was coming to help. It was the end of the world.

A scratching scraped through the house once more. Harley gasped. Closer to the sound now, he stared at the small room off the kitchen. The de-smelling room was where Barney stuffed clothes bursting with his sweet scent into machines, only to retrieve them later smelling of sterile, fake flowers. Boy, did Barney do some crazy things.

So what craziness was going on now? He and Barney were alone in the house, so what could be scratching in the room that ruined Barney's most fragrant clothes?

Taking a gulp of air, the fluttering hope in his heart turning into an anxious quiver, he plodded toward the de-smelling room.

Scrambling sounds crept through the closed door.

Harley's heart hammered. What the devil was it?

The silver door handle turned. He gasped, freezing with his right foreleg in midstep.

A chunky man in dark clothing stalked out. He whispered, "Geez, what's stinking up the—"

Their eyes met.

Oh, thank heavens. Harley slumped as the nervous energy drained out of him. A rescuer! His tail swished back and forth.

The chunky man glanced over his shoulder. "You didn't say there was a dog."

From inside the de-smelling room came a strained, deeper voice, as if the owner were carrying something heavy or negotiating a tricky obstacle. "There's a dog?"

"Why would I say there was a dog if there wasn't a dog?"

"A big dog?"

Chunky eyed Harley. "Well, it ain't small. It's one of those black-and-white things that herds sheep."

Something heavy hit the de-smelling room floor. "What's it doing? It hasn't bitten you, has it?"

"It's wagging its tail."

"So where's the freaking problem?" A tall man reared out of the gloom behind Chunky. The smell of pepperoni pizza and beer wafted over from them.

A warm glow enveloped Harley. Two rescuers! He barked and scampered for the stairs to lead the way. He leaped up the first few, then looked back.

The men hadn't followed him.

Odd.

What was even more odd was that they were peering around the house with flashlights as if he wasn't even there. Hadn't they seen him? Why were they looking for Barney by themselves instead of letting Harley take them straight to him?

Harley scampered toward Chunky. Six feet away, he barked, then, when the man glanced at him, again raced toward the stairs. And again, Barney's rescuers failed to follow.

He didn't like to think ill of people, especially when they were trying to help out of the goodness of their hearts, but these two men were either very bad at rescuing or just plain stupid.

For a third time, Harley trotted toward Chunky and barked for attention. And for a third time, both men ignored him. However, instead of running for the staircase, Harley stared at Chunky. His jaw dropped as Chunky picked up Barney's glittery old clock and shoved it into a black duffel.

Harley frowned. This couldn't be how rescuers behaved. What was going on?

The tall man snatched Barney's watch off the table beside his reclining sofa and popped it into his duffel.

That wasn't very polite. Barney would be upset when he got better and those things weren't where he'd left them.

Harley barked, but the men continued dropping things into their bags.

Wait... these men weren't here to help Barney but to help themselves to his things.

Harley had never bitten a person. In fact, he'd never bitten anything. He didn't even know if he could. But he was going to find out.

His heart rate rocketed as he stalked forward to protect Barney and the only home he'd ever known.

Curling his top lip, he snarled at Chunky.

This time, Chunky didn't ignore him — the man glared at Harley.

Harley snarled louder, baring his fangs.

The chubby man backed away, so Harley crept closer. He gnashed his teeth at the man. This was Barney's house. These were Barney's things. These men would *not* take them.

Chunky raised a wooden bat Harley hadn't seen. "Just you try it, dog."

Harley lunged. Clamped his jaws around the man's shin. Sank his teeth through denim and into the flesh.

The man wailed and hobbled back, trying to rip his leg free. But Harley twisted his head from side to side, savaging the limb.

Caught fast, Chunky heaved his bat into Harley's side.

Harley yelped, releasing his grip.

Chunky swung his good leg back, then hammered a kick into Harley's ribs.

Harley tumbled across the floor and slammed into the table leg, his left shoulder crunching into the wood. Harley squealed as pain ripped through him.

Tall Man said, "Get rid of that freaking thing."

Harley scrambled up, but his left front leg gave out, and he smashed into the floor again. Chunky thundered toward him, swinging his bat.

"Think you can bite me, huh, dog?"

Harley had to get up. Had to escape. Gritting his teeth against the biting pain, he heaved himself up just as the bat swung at his head. He darted under the table and out the other side. In the kitchen, he cowered in the corner — the refrigerator on one side, the blue cupboards on the other — as Chunky stormed at him.

Chunky raised the bat to pound Harley again. Harley flashed his gaze around the room for escape as the hunk of wood plummeted down to cave in his skull. Had to get away. Now.

He spied one option. One chance of escape.

Harley bolted, and the bat smashed into the refrigerator. He shot through the de-smelling room door. Diving under the shelving unit against the wall, he spun and stared at the door wild-eyed, heart fighting to burst out of his chest.

Chunky loomed in the doorway, his tall friend behind him.

Harley was trapped.

Frantic, he scanned the room for escape as Chunky stomped closer, bat raised to crush him.

There!

Harley shot from under the table, sprang onto the white machine with the circle of glass in the front, and dove through the narrow window that for some strange reason was wide open.

He crashed into the concrete flags outside, next to the raised wooden boxes where stinky yellow flowers sprouted in warmer weather.

Scrambling to his paws, he glanced back at the window, but too late — Chunky flung the bat. It crunched into the side of Harley's head, knocking him sideways. He sprawled across the cold ground. The yard Harley had loved to run across blurred, and the world spun as if he were being swung by his tail. His eyes closed, and silence and blackness descended.

Chapter 07

Rachel strode from her front door through the early-morning gloom, a small light strapped to her forehead illuminating a path paved with flagstones and lined by dwarf conifers. She waved to Izzy, who was cupping a mug of hot chocolate to her chest in the living room window, then clicked the heart rate monitor on her watch as she stepped beyond her white picket fence.

Circling her arms, she marched along the grass shoulder beside the road, alone but for the occasional vehicle rumbling by that bathed her in light. Warmed up by the time she reached a gnarled old oak, she tapped the stopwatch and ran between the road and the bare trees that crept into the woodland, their branches jagged fingers of blackness clawing at the sky.

Six o'clock in the morning was the perfect time to lose herself in a run. It was just her, a path, the trees, and the sky. Almost primal. It stripped away millennia of civilization — all the trappings, the worries, the demands — and allowed her to simply "be."

The toned physique running gave her was a bonus, but the time alone with her thoughts, with no concerns for anyone or anything else, was what coaxed her out of her cozy bed every morning.

Thank heavens Izzy had rented her studio apartment. If not for Izzy's willingness to sit in the living room in case Wes woke early, Rachel's primal paradise could never happen.

Rachel's breath billowed as the road curved upward. She pumped her legs harder to maintain her pace and glanced at her watch — a red heart flashed beside the figure 132. Excellent, she'd hit her target beats per minute.

Relaxing into a rhythm, she let her mind drift as fine rain speckled her face. But a thought clawed its way from the darkest depths of her mind. Something Izzy had said the night before that Rachel had dismissed now stalked out of the shadows to torment her. After all these years, why had Peter decided it was an appropriate time to discuss their financial arrangements?

Her thigh muscles burned as she jogged to the first brow, beyond which the road leveled out before continuing its winding journey up the hillside. She loved that burn. It grounded her in reality and meant she was pushing herself to her limit. She liked to think that attitude defined her whole life.

Easing to a walk, Rachel strolled into a small, deserted parking area at a trailhead. There, she did ten stomach crunches, ten push-ups, and ten squat jumps. She completed three sets, then resumed her run for the homeward leg.

Large water droplets dripped off the trees like monster raindrops. Rachel barely noticed them as the sweat clung to her face and matted her hair. Racing downhill, she glanced at her watch as she passed a mile marker — 6:32 a.m. Dead on schedule.

A hectic day lay ahead. Other than addressing Wes's needs, every spare moment would be spent improving her illustrations for that book. She had to secure those other commissions the publisher had dangled in front of her. Had to. Freelance work supplemented with jobs from a major publisher would be a game changer.

Heading into the home stretch, she shook her head. What the devil was Peter up to? Everything had gone so smoothly for so many years — why rock the boat now? She cursed under her breath. This worry was ruining her alone time. These precious moments of peacefulness were crucial to her well-being and her career. As a distraction from thinking about Peter, she gazed into the trees, peering into the shadows, searching for a spark of inspiration for her illustrations.

At the giant gnarled oak, she slowed to a brisk walk to cool down, then, with only two minutes to go, she completed her stretching exercises on her front lawn. At the stroke of 6:45 a.m., she went inside, jumped in the shower, dressed, and, after saying goodbye to Izzy, was waiting at Wes's door when he got up at 7:00 a.m.

After breakfast, and Wes's washing and dressing routine, they wandered into the study off the downstairs hallway. She sat at a desk facing the front of the house, while he sat at the opposite side.

Rachel took three white plastic cups from a bookcase crammed with teaching resources beside her — books, games, DVDs, CDs, toys...

she held up a yellow jellybean to attract Wes's attention, put it under a cup on the desk, and placed another upturned cup at either side. Like a street hustler, she switched the cups around, quick enough that Wes had to focus, but slow enough that, most times, he could track the jelly bean.

An ordinary person would find the game laughably easy, but for someone with Wes's issues, it was mildly taxing. And that was the key — it signaled it was thinking time.

Wes pointed to the cup on his right.

Rachel lifted the cup to reveal the jelly bean. "Well done, Wes." She smiled. He didn't. With his head angled down, he stared from under his bangs and reached for his prize.

"So what are we doing today, Wes? What color sweater do you have on?"

With a feeble gesture, he pointed to a row of seven laminated cards. Each was the size of a cigarette packet and showed one word printed in a different color. Under his finger, in red ink, was the word *Tuesday*.

"And what do we do on Tuesday?"

He pointed to a large book with numbers in different fonts and sizes spread randomly about the cover.

"That's right, Wes — math. And do you want to choose today's soundtrack or should I?"

After studying the CDs in a small rack, he pulled one out. He clawed at the front of the plastic case, struggling to open it. Rachel ached to help him, but this was an exercise in dexterity, plus practice in following a sequence of events to complete a task.

"Take your time, Wes. Remember how I showed you."

He repositioned his fingers and opened the case.

"That's it."

He clicked open the portable CD player, squashed the disc in place, and pressed play.

Birdsong floated through the air, while a tumbling brook danced around rocks.

"Oh, *Woodland Paradise*. Excellent choice, Wes."

Wes being a huge nature lover, recordings of natural environments calmed him and made the learning experience something to look forward to instead of dread.

She opened the math book to begin.

Many a night, she cried silently into her pillow so Wes would never hear, worrying over the life she couldn't give him. Only decades ago, people like him would've been shut away in asylums and left to vegetate. Living, yet lifeless. Shameful secrets that families never wanted discovered. She couldn't give him the life he deserved, but she could give him *a* life.

He'd never revel in the fun of friendship, never swoon under the magic of love, never know the joy of starting his own family. So many of the things that made life so wonderful would forever be denied him. But until her dying breath, she'd make sure he experienced as fulfilling a life as possible.

Unfortunately, giving him that life consumed most of hers. But what mother wouldn't sacrifice everything to see her child happy?

Her phone beeped, alerting her to a text message. Unless they were using the timer, she turned it off to avoid distractions during lesson and work time, but she was waiting for this particular message.

Izzy: *It's cool with Lucinda. We're on for Thursday.*

Great. Rachel could attend the meeting with Peter.

Yet now she knew she was going, anxiety clawed at her like heartburn. What the devil was he up to?

Chapter 08

Harley's eyes flickered open, then popped them wider; the wooden bat rested on the concrete beside him. Images of it swinging and angry faces clawed away all other thoughts. He yelped and scrambled to his feet, then shot through the yard, his legs pumping as hard as he could make them.

He had to get away. Had to hide. Find somewhere safe.

Harley dove under Barney's blue car in the driveway. Hunkering down, he crawled right under it, his left shoulder throbbing and feeling like it could give any moment. Gulping breaths, he peeked out, praying he was beyond the reach of grabbing hands. His legs shook so much he was certain he'd collapse if he tried to stand.

Yet the terrors of the night had disappeared — darkness no longer engulfed him, no angry faces loomed toward him, no crushing club hurtled at him. He was alone, in the sunshine, in the yard. Safe. Maybe.

Barney!

Barney was still in there. Alone and unable to protect himself.

Harley wanted to run back in and rescue his friend from those monsters, but he remained rooted under the car. Trembling.

He willed his front paws to move forward, to shuffle him from under the vehicle and to Barney's aid. But he didn't move. He couldn't; his legs refused to work. No matter how much he ached to run into the house and save Barney, another part of him didn't want to. And that part was winning.

What kind of friend was he? How could he lie there, safe, when his best friend was in terrible danger?

Harley had always believed he was a good dog — he repaid Barney's love by being his loyal companion and helping the man in every way he could. But Harley wasn't a good dog. No, he was the worst kind of dog — he was a coward.

He whimpered. How could he do this to Barney after everything the man had done for him?

Harley's heart pounded so hard it hammered in his ears. But this time, it wasn't because he was afraid. No, it wasn't fear — it was fury. A gravelly growl rumbled in his throat.

He *was* a good dog. A *good dog!* And now he'd prove it.

He stared at the paws that defied him. They would defy him no longer. He edged his left paw forward, then his right. Inch by inch, quicker and quicker, he shuffled from under the car.

Standing tall in the sunlight, he snarled at the house.

A *good dog!*

He bolted for the window at the back of the house to leap in and rescue Barney.

Harley skidded to a stop, his claws scraping on the concrete. The window was shut.

Maybe because of his panicked escape, he misremembered how things had happened. He was sure that was the window from which he'd jumped, but maybe not. He glanced at the other windows peppering the back of the two-story wood-clad building. They were all closed.

There was no way back in.

Whimpering, he stared up at the place that had been his loving home his entire life. Barney was in there alone. Harley had to get to him, had to be with him as he always had been. But how?

His courage seeped into the cold concrete, and he shivered as an icy wind stabbed through his long fur.

There had to be a way in. Something he'd missed when inside. A door left ajar or a window cracked open. Something!

He slunk to the driveway and studied that side of the house. Nothing. He trudged around to the sidewalk and scrutinized each of the windows on the upper and lower floors at the front of the building. Nothing.

His shoulders slumped. He didn't want to check the fourth wall of the house. If he did and there was no way in, all was lost. But he had to.

Shuffling as if his legs were made of stone, he turned the corner. He closed his eyes.

Please, please, please let there be a way in.

He surveyed the final side of the house, checking every potential entry point. And then he checked them all again. He whined.

Harley lumbered around to the front again. Gazing up and down the street, he prayed he might spy a magical solution to his problem. Maybe someone would see he was in distress and rush to his aid.

The sun shone from a clear blue sky, yet bitterness bit at the world, so the nearby yards were deserted.

Coming toward Harley on the sidewalk, a woman gazed down at her phone while pushing a child in a stroller. On the other sidewalk, a frizzy-haired old lady hobbled along using a cane as a third leg, her free hand clutching the arm of a man with hair as white as his smile.

No one even noticed Harley, let alone saw his desperation.

Harley tramped over to the blue door at the front of his home, shivering more with each step. This was pointless, but he tried anyway; he shoved the door with his snout. Solid.

His world had ended, so he did the only thing a dog could do — he sat down, raised his face to the sky, and howled with all his might.

Howled and howled and howled.

"What's wrong, boy? Have you gotten yourself locked out?" said a woman's voice.

Harley glanced at the sidewalk. The old lady with the three legs and the white-haired man smiled at him. At a loss for what to do, he whimpered and scraped his paw down the door.

The lady jabbed her cane at the neighbor's house. "Billy, try next door. See if they know where the owner is."

"Will do." Billy toddled away.

The old lady hobbled over. Leaning down, she patted Harley's side. "Don't worry, boy, we'll get you home."

She hammered the side of her fist on the door and waited.

Harley gazed up at his savior and she smiled down at him. They were going to get in and save Barney. A warm glow blossomed in Harley's heart, so warm he stopped shivering.

Again, the woman banged on the door. But still, no one answered. "Ellen?"

Harley and the old lady turned. Billy and a woman in thick glasses ambled toward them.

Billy said, "This is Rayna from next door. She says Mr. McCluskey never goes anywhere without his dog."

Rayna shrugged. "He keeps to himself, so I don't really know him, but I never see either of them anywhere without the other."

Ellen's smile faded. "Oh dear, that doesn't sound good."

Billy turned to Rayna. "Does he have any relatives? Or did he leave a spare key with anyone?"

Again, Rayna shrugged. "Sorry."

"I don't know who you call in a situation like this," said Ellen. "Paramedics, police..."

A man in a heavy green coat strolled across the road and shouted, "Is there a problem, Rayna?"

"It's Mr. McCluskey. We think something might have happened to him."

"Hold on" — the man held up the flat of his hand — "he gave me a spare key for emergencies." He scurried back to the house opposite.

A few moments later, he emerged, waving a silver key. Everyone parted to give him access to Barney's front door. The lock clicked and Key Man pushed the door open.

Key Man called out, "Hello, Mr.—" He recoiled, grimacing and cupping his hand over his nose and mouth as the stench from upstairs burst into the street.

Everyone scuttled back from the door, shielding themselves from the sensory onslaught.

"Oh, dear Lord, no." Ellen patted Harley on the shoulder. "I'm sorry, boy. So sorry."

Despite the smell, Harley lurched forward to dash in, but Ellen caught his collar.

"No, you stay with me. There's a good dog."

Billy, Rayna, and Key Man talked in tones as dark as their expressions, then Key Man spoke to someone on his phone.

Meanwhile, Ellen fussed about Harley, stroking and patting him, standing between him and the house. Under normal circumstances, the attention would've been wonderful, but Harley needed to get to Barney. He twisted this way and that to get by the lady and see what everyone was so upset about.

Unable to break free, Harley whined. Why was no one rushing in to help Barney?

Soon after, two men in blue uniforms arrived in a shiny car with an array of lights across its roof and went into the house.

Three more men arrived, two in a white van, one in a silver car. They went in too.

One of the blue-uniformed men came out. He had fur growing across his top lip. He strolled over to the group.

At first, everyone spoke at once, but the lip fur man held up his hands, and as if he had some magic power, everyone stopped talking.

He said, "There's evidence of a possible burglary, but nothing to suggest Mr. McCluskey died of anything other than natural causes."

"Is that definite?" Key Man pointed at his house. "I've got kids, so if there's some nutjob wandering around the neighborhood, we need to know."

Lip Fur said, "When did anyone first notice the dog outside the house?"

Rayna said, "Today. Why?"

"That figures." Lip Fur nodded. "I can't say for certain until forensics and the coroner file their reports, but it's obvious Mr. McCluskey died some days ago. I suspect some opportunist broke in yesterday, figuring the house was deserted, and that's when the dog escaped."

The group nodded, as if they were happy with what had been said.

Lip Fur said, "Do we have details of any children, relatives, next of kin?"

With a pinched expression, Key Man looked at Rayna. "I want to say a son...?"

Rayna shook her head. "Sorry, I barely knew the guy."

Lip Fur pointed at Key Man. "A son?"

"I kind of recall him saying something one day. But they can't be close because he rarely gets visitors."

"We were just passing by," said Ellen, gesturing to herself and Billy. "We only stopped because the dog was distressed."

Lip Fur nodded. "But you live in the area?"

Ellen pointed in the direction they'd been walking. "About—"

Harley smelled Barney closer and barked. He tugged to run to him, but Ellen gripped his collar.

Harley barked again. Barney was coming. He could smell the man getting closer. His scent was still cloaked in that garbage can stink, but underneath, it was Barney. No mistake.

Banging and clattering came from inside the house, as if something bulky and awkward were being maneuvered down the stairs.

Harley wagged his tail.

Finally.

34

They were here. Here with Barney safe and sound.

The two men from the van wheeled a gurney out of the house on which lay a large lump in a black bag.

Everyone stepped farther away as the lump neared, the stench emanating from it clogging the air. Everyone except Harley.

He barked. Barney. That was Barney. But what were they doing with him?

Ellen stooped to him, patting his side. "Shhh, boy. You can't help him now." She looked up at Billy. "No way is this little angel getting dumped in the pound. He's coming home with us, you hear?"

Billy stroked her shoulder. "I wouldn't have it any other way."

The men pushed the gurney to the back of the van, where wheeled-legs collapsed, letting them shove it inside. They then got into the vehicle, the engine started, and the van drove away.

Harley's mouth gaped. Barney? Where the devil were they taking Barney?

He barked and lurched forward, but Ellen gripped him.

The van drew farther and farther away.

Harley barked again.

"Shhh, boy," said Ellen. "Everything's going to be okay. You'll see."

They were taking Barney. Taking him heaven only knew where. Harley might never find him again.

He lurched forward harder, arching his back and bucking against the hand holding him. He writhed, twisting in a tight circle, and broke free.

He shot down the road after the van. Barking. Barking. Barking.

Chapter 09

Harley flew down the sidewalk, pumping his legs harder than ever before. Faster and faster. Faster than he had ever thought possible. Desperate to catch the world slipping from his grasp as the van drew farther and farther away.

He bolted between two people chatting, dodged a woman hauling a foldable shopping cart brimming with groceries, dove through the middle of a group of children...

On and on he hurtled. Yet no matter how he fought, the van shrank, becoming tinier and tinier in the distance.

His muscles burned and his lungs screamed. Normally, he could run for hours and barely feel it, but he hadn't eaten for days and red-hot knives stabbed his left shoulder. Just when he needed it, his body was giving up on him.

But he couldn't stop. He had to reach Barney.

He leaped over a garbage can, scooted over the hood of a parked red car, and launched himself into the road.

Racing down the middle of the street, he hammered his paws into the asphalt as vehicles screeched past on both sides.

Horns blared and cars veered around him. And onward he shot.

Ahead — way, way ahead — the van slowed in traffic. This was his chance!

He gulped air as he rocketed down the road. He was going to make it. He was really going to make it.

A bus crossed from one lane into the other, obscuring the van.

Studying the traffic thundering toward him, Harley waited for a break, then careered onto the sidewalk. But he cut the angle too sharply, his bad shoulder gave under him, and, struggling to stay on his feet, he careered into a store's window. From inside, plastic people with dead eyes stared at him.

Scrambling up, he tore back along the sidewalk, only for a man in blue spandex to wheel a bicycle out of a doorway in front of him.

Harley leaped, high enough to clear the bike with ease, but the man panicked and yanked the machine up toward him.

Harley's hind legs caught the handlebars. He flipped in the air and smashed into the sidewalk, tumbling over and over and over. Finally, he slammed into a wall, his head crunching into the stonework.

Gasping, he struggled to his feet. The man with the bike was a swirling blur as Harley staggered and fell sideways, banging into the wall. His legs trembling, he shook his head and the world came back into focus.

Launching forward again, he bolted to chase down the van but skidded to a stop.

Wide-eyed, Harley stared this way and that. Where was the van?

He scoured the road ahead. It had to be somewhere. Had to be.

Tongue lolling out, Harley dashed to where he'd last seen the vehicle.

The road flowed around a small grassy island with a single tree and a bush, different roads branching off from there. The van had taken one of these roads, but which?

The traffic slowed around the island, so he waited for a break and then darted onto it. Beside the tree, he inched his way around in a circle, squinting in every direction the van could have gone.

Nothing.

He'd lost the van.

Lost Barney.

What was he going to do now?

Chapter 10

Shivering, Harley trudged through the city center. People bustled about, traffic growled by, and shoppers scurried in and out of stores... but little of the city hubbub registered.

Whenever he'd had a bad dream and woken panting and shaking, Barney had been there to pet him and reassure him everything was okay. Who would be there when he woke from this nightmare?

Head down, gaze nailed to the cold sidewalk, he tramped on.

The scent of another dog dragged him from the darkness engulfing his thoughts. Poking his snout upward, Harley sniffed, peering along the sidewalk. Near the entrance to the park he'd been to so many times with Barney, a little brown dog inspected a fire hydrant, then he cocked his leg.

There was nothing unusual about a dog relieving itself on a hydrant, except this dog was little more than a puppy. No way should such a young animal be on the streets alone. Harley glanced around for a mother or other pups, but he and the youngster appeared to be the only dogs in the area.

Very odd.

If the kid didn't have a mother to teach him or an owner to care for him, he'd find the world a strange and dangerous place.

The kid sniffed the hydrant over and over. Harley frowned. It wasn't normal for a dog to spend so much time on one thing after marking it because there were so many other smells to investigate. What was the kid doing?

Harley couldn't find Barney to help him, but maybe there was someone he could help instead. He was good at helping people. It was his superpower. He trotted toward the young dog, but the kid spotted him when he was still a few yards away and bolted. Seeing a strange dog barreling toward him was obviously too much.

Harley slumped. He could easily run the kid down, but that would only terrify the poor pup even more. No, the kid would have to face the world alone. Just like Harley now had to.

He padded over to the hydrant to see what had entranced the kid and sniffed the base and around its curved side.

The fresh marking was clearly the kid's, but there were older markings from a number of dogs too. Harley sifted through the scents. The kid had been here before. He sniffed again. In fact, it seemed like the kid had been relieving himself against the hydrant for some time. The other, older markings belonged to a female dog and two — no, three — pups about the same age as the kid.

Shoving his snout right up to the hydrant, Harley closed his eyes to focus. He drew in a huge breath, breaking down and analyzing each scent to study it further.

The characteristics from the older markings suggested the kid, the female, and pups had all eaten and drunk the same kinds of things. Were they his pack? That was it — he was lost and trying to get back to those he loved.

Harley whimpered. He'd thought he was the only one in the world who'd lost the person he loved. How stupid. Of course there were others suffering similar loss.

He peered down the street in the direction in which the kid had disappeared. If only Harley had known. He'd have approached more slowly, head bowed and submissive, so as not to spook the kid.

Harley shuffled around to another part of the hydrant and squirted a little urine onto it, taking care not to overmark the kid's pack. When the kid next visited, he'd smell Harley's scent, so should they ever meet again, he'd know Harley to maybe accept a few pointers on how to handle the world.

Harley's stomach growled for attention.

Ignoring the cramps twisting his gut, he stared at the city going about its business unaware of the tiny tragedies happening all about it. Maybe he could track the kid now. See he was okay on his own. Or would a big dog following him terrify the youngster even more?

Again, Harley's stomach clenched.

Harley turned away. He couldn't help anyone in his condition. Luckily, he knew somewhere to remedy that.

Chapter 11

Harley tramped through the park's entrance, where a metal man stood on a big stone and asphalt paths led away in three directions. He lumbered down a path curving to the left and through some pine trees, his left shoulder stiff and throbbing. Below, diamonds sparkled on a lake's tiny ripples, stroked into life by the breeze. The water looked incredibly inviting. A quick plunge would normally be fun and exhilarating, but not when the water would be icy and while he was bruised, battered, and half-starved.

Teenage boys laughing and talking loudly drew his attention to a clump of trees. Harley loved children. Some of the best days of Harley's life had been when he'd visited schools to show the youngsters his skills. But then Barney had gotten sicker, so fun times with an adoring audience had transformed into long days of lounging on the sofa with his head in Barney's lap. He loved Barney, but he missed children — young curious minds that smiled and smiled and petted and petted.

A scent wafted on the breeze. Harley's gaze flashed to the source — a wooden bench. His stomach tightened, reminding him how ravenous he was. Wandering closer, he sniffed from twelve feet away to confirm his initial suspicion. And his mouth watered.

Harley tottered over. Beside the bench's ornate iron leg, a hunk of burger taunted him, a good three or four bites big. His stomach clawed at him, like a monster ripping its way out. He stared at the food but didn't move closer. He just stared and stared, drool stringing to the ground.

He wanted to eat so badly. He *needed* to eat so badly. But he couldn't. Not like this. It went against one of the golden rules — unless it was offered properly, food was off-limits, no matter how delicious it smelled.

He whimpered and turned away. He staggered on, pushing himself to move faster than he would have liked to avoid temptation. Barney would be so disappointed in him if he broke that golden rule.

After circling the lake, Harley panted his way up the incline to the far side of the park and an exit to a parking lot. A glimmer of hope warmed him as one of Barney's favorite places beckoned — the shopping mall.

Optimism rejuvenating his weary legs, Harley trotted between the parked cars toward the row of glass doors at the front. As he reached them, as usual, two magically slid apart. He ambled in, a gust of warm air greeting him. He passed the fountain next to the moving staircases, which had seemed scary at first but, thanks to Barney's reassurances, had proven wonderful fun. So much so that occasionally, Barney had let him ride them two or three times.

Along the central avenue, people milled about carrying plastic bags, boxes, drinks, ice cream cones, candy... Harley gazed into the store in which Barney had bought a big box. He'd bought one in the next store too. And the one farther along. In fact, Barney had loved buying boxes. Much more so than bags, which seemed by far the most popular choice. It was strange, because Harley had never seen Barney's obviously extensive box collection at home. Maybe Barney considered it so special he kept it private, even from Harley.

A fat guy gobbling a candy bar did a double take when he saw Harley. As if that wasn't enough, he turned and stared as Harley strolled down the avenue. That wasn't very polite.

A young man with his arm around a young woman stared at him too, then said something to the woman, who stared as well.

Harley stared back. People weren't usually so rude. What was wrong with them? Hadn't they ever seen a dog before?

Before Harley even reached it, he smelled it. Once again, gobs of saliva formed in his mouth.

The avenue opened onto a huge space littered with tables and chairs. From the number of people cramming all manner of food into their mouths, most of the town had come to the food court today. He hoped there was a table free for him.

Weaving through the crowded seating area, Harley spied an empty table. A gray-haired couple pointed at him and said something he didn't catch. At another table, three children sitting with a woman pointed too, all smiles and laughter. After he'd eaten, he'd come back this way and say hello.

Finally, he reached the free table, so he sat and politely waited. What delights would one of the green-apron people bring him today? After the one he'd seen in the park, a burger would be nice. But some fries with lots of salt would be lovely too. Ohhh, a hot dog!

Drool strung to the floor.

On the next table, a woman who was so wide she looked like two people squashed together sneered. "Oh, that's disgusting."

Harley glanced behind him to see what was upsetting her. A greasy-haired man brushed crumbs off his blue sweatshirt, stood up, and loped away, leaving a half-eaten pizza on his plate. Yes, the woman was right to be upset — such waste was appalling.

A young man draped in a green apron wandered past, carrying a tray of dirty plates. On seeing Harley, he did a double take.

What was it with all these people staring at him? Or maybe the man was simply wondering what food to bring him. How thoughtful.

Harley licked his lips. He liked surprises.

The green apron man talked to an older woman behind a counter, pointing at Harley. The older woman's eyes popped wider.

Oh good, oh good, oh good. Harley wagged his tail. They were obviously discussing which delicacy to tempt him with.

Barney ate here often and always slipped something under the table to Harley — a strip of steak smothered in gravy, a chunk of meaty sandwich, a juicy bit of pie. Harley's mouth watered even more, and his tail swished across the floor faster in anticipation of the banquet heading his way.

He was ravenous. Anything would be welcome. Okay, maybe not something green, but any other color.

Okay, maybe not cheesy pizza either. He loved hearing Barney say "Harley," but not with the tone of voice he used while holding his nose because Harley had eaten cheese.

Three men in matching dark blue pants and pale blue shirts approached the woman at the counter. She pointed at Harley, and they all looked over.

Whatever they were bringing him, it had to be enormous for so many people to be involved. He licked his lips again.

The three blue men separated: a bald man headed straight toward him, a skinny one moved left, and a man with a limp moved right.

Odd. What were they doing?

Despite going in different directions, they all seemed to be stalking closer to him. Harley sniffed toward the bald man as he crept nearer, then the other two. None of them had a scrap of food. But that was okay because he enjoyed meeting new friends. He wagged his tail, gazing into the bald man's eyes.

A few yards away, Bald Man held up his palms, his voice wavering. "Good dog. You stay right there." He smiled.

Harley's tail stopped wagging. He stood and shuffled a couple of steps backward. The man was showing his teeth, but it wasn't a genuine smile. And the wavering confirmed what Harley's nose was telling him — the man stank of fear.

Why? Did he think Harley was going to attack him? Outrageous! Harley had never bitten a single per—oops. He couldn't say that now. Okay, so he'd bitten Chunky for taking Barney's watch. But, boy, had that guy deserved it.

He flashed his gaze left — *sniff* — then right — *sniff*.

All three men were pretending to be happy, yet the smell of anxiousness and fear was overwhelming.

Harley shuffled farther away until a seat jammed into his butt.

Bald Man gestured for Limpy Man to close in on Harley, then did the same to Skinny Man.

Harley gasped. They weren't bringing him food, nor wanting to be his friend — they wanted to catch him.

He barked. He knew this place and this place knew him. Why had it now turned against him?

He had no idea what these people intended to do, but someone stinking of fear certainly wasn't intending to give him a loving pet.

Bald Man lurched, grabbing at Harley.

Harley ducked under his arms and leaped. He crashed onto the fat woman's table. A giant cup of cola splattered her chest. She wailed as Harley jumped to the next table, fries and burgers showering a family of four.

Screams erupted as he dove off the table and bolted away between the diners.

He glanced back. The three men scrambled after him.

Head down, he shot for the nearest exit just as the doors magically opened, and a couple sauntered in hand in hand. They leaped out of the way as Harley tore past.

Outside, cars, vans, and trucks zipped up and down the road alongside the building. Rocketing along the sidewalk, Harley didn't look back. He didn't need to now — in the open, there wasn't a person in the world who could beat him in a race. He hurtled down the roadside, traffic on his left, a tall metal fence now on his right.

But a truck pulled out from an entrance in front of him, blocking his way.

Harley was fast. Unbelievably fast. He tore at the truck, determined to dive under it and through to the safety of the other side. The giant truck growled and jerked forward, black wheels eating the black asphalt.

That thing was big, but Harley would make it. Make it easily.

But as he hunkered to thunder through the low gap, his bad shoulder wobbled, about to give.

With the massive wheels aching to crush him into the ground, Harley skidded and turned and shot through the entrance. He was fast; however, that truck was so, so big, and he was so, so tired.

In a square enclosure, two trucks and a van were reversed up to a loading dock on his left, while another truck had reversed to the dock at the back. On his immediate left, a van was parked next to the fence. Harley raced over and dove underneath it.

Panting, he lay on the cold, damp asphalt, tongue lolling out, as a squat one-man car with a huge metal fork sticking out of the front drove into the back of the nearest truck.

He'd escaped the men, but how was he going to escape from where he'd ended up?

Chapter 12

In the study, Rachel worked at her rosewood desk, moonlight illuminating the room together with a red articulated desk lamp. Like a mirror image of the teaching side of the room, beside her stood a bookcase crammed with art books covering everything from Monet, Gauguin, and Dali to Dean, Capullo, and Banksy.

She stroked her pressure-sensitive stylus over the dragon's left wing on her angled drawing tablet, making the delicate veins a fraction more prominent. She glanced at the desktop clock: 11:52 p.m. Eight minutes to clocking-off time.

Leaning back, she studied the image, then opened a version of the same picture from thirty minutes earlier. She squinted. Even she had a problem spotting the difference.

She slung her pen down. "Come on, Rach, the thing's done. Send the freaking file."

The only "free" time she got was a couple of hours in the afternoon when Wes had a nap and after 8:00 p.m. when he'd gone to bed. In those six hours a day, she had to earn an income, clean and maintain the house, pay the bills, grocery shop... everything and anything.

After Peter had left, when everything was up in the air, not least her finances, she'd lived by the rule "another ten minutes won't hurt." Yeah, right. That philosophy regularly saw her still peering at her screen at 2:00 a.m. Starting each day with only four hours' sleep had set her on the road to burnout, not to mention damaged Wes's quality of life because she lacked the energy to do everything he needed. That midnight clocking-off time was now set in stone.

This job had been finished before she'd even picked up her stylus today, but it was so important, she couldn't resist tinkering. And therein lay the problem — tinkering was all it was. The improvements were so negligible it was *Where's Waldo?* at a microscopic level.

She maximized her browser to upload the files for the publisher to access first thing in the morning — the deadline she was working to. As usual, her inbox was bursting. A quick scan of the subject lines confirmed most could be deleted immediately, but halfway down the screen, she frowned.

"Claire? Why's Claire sent me two messages?"

The subject line of the earliest one was "you have to read this," while the second said "don't read that!!!"

Had Claire sent something she shouldn't have, then regretted it, so she was desperately trying to make sure it wasn't read?

Saying "don't read that" made her want to read the other message even more, so she opened it.

I didn't want to have to tell you what's happened like this, but I don't want to do it face-to-face because it'll be too awkward. The link will explain everything. Call me when you've read it.

"What the...?" Rachel's eyes popped wider.

Below was a blue link to a Facebook post.

What the devil could it be? Had Peter been unfaithful and Claire was out for a vicious public shaming on social media?

Rachel smirked. Talk about chickens coming home to roost. She clicked the link. And waited.

And waited.

Nothing happened.

Obviously, it hadn't registered the click properly, so she clicked it again.

Nothing happened.

She scratched her head.

A pop-up appeared on her screen. Below a skull and crossbones, it said: *I now own your computer, having locked it with military grade encryption. You cannot do anything — feel free to try. To access your files and use your computer again, you need a 28-character password. To receive this password, visit my darknet page by following the instructions below and deposit $10,000 in bitcoin.*

"Nooo!"

Mouth gaping, Rachel stared, eyes all but popping out of their sockets. Ransomware? That was an urban myth, wasn't it? This was a joke. It had to be. A sick freaking joke!

She wiggled her mouse, but the pointer didn't move.

"No, no, no, no, no."

She hit the power button and rebooted the computer. She'd once had a virus on her old PC and gotten rid of it simply by accessing Safe Mode and taking the machine back to its last clean backup. If she could do that now, problem solved.

Just before Windows loaded, she pressed Shift and F8, but the desktop opened with the pop-up still showing.

Rachel cupped her face. "No! Please, no!"

Holding Shift, she hammered F8 over and over, staring at her screen, willing her normal desktop to appear.

She raked her fingers into her hair and tugged. Could clicking that link have downloaded a virus?

She grabbed her phone, turned it on, and called Claire.

A groggy female voice said, "Hello?"

"Claire, what the devil is this email you've sent me? Is this a joke, because it's not freaking funny!"

Claire cursed, then said quietly to someone at her end, "Someone else has opened that email."

Rachel said, "Someone else? This is Rachel — you know, as in Peter's ex-wife. How many people have you sent this email to? Because it's not funny, it's not clever, it's not—"

"Rachel," said Peter, "please say you didn't click the link."

"Just tell me what's going on, Peter, and how to get rid of this thing."

"Didn't you get our message?"

"What message?"

"Claire's account was hacked. We emailed everyone that message had gone to."

"I didn't see another message before clicking this one." She'd been nosy, expecting to find something she wasn't supposed to, but she wasn't going to tell him that.

"So didn't you get my voicemail either?"

"What?"

"I left a voicemail the moment we learned this was happening."

She checked her phone. Sure enough, there was a message waiting. "But you know I turn my phone off when I'm working. Why didn't you use the landline?"

"You were working? At this time? Why?"

"Seriously? Because I have a kid and my freaking husband ran off with his freaking secretary!" Grimacing, she pounded the side of her fist into her desk. She hated being part of such a cliché.

"Rachel, I'm trying to help, but if you're going to be like that—"

"Like that? You sent me an email that's locked my PC unless I pay ten thousand bucks!"

"We didn't send the email. I told you. Claire's account was hacked."

"How?" She threw her free hand up. "What's she use as her password? 1-2-3-4?"

"Look, we tried to rectify the situation as soon as humanly possible, but if you're going to get aggressive and insult Claire, this conversation is over."

The line went dead.

"Peter? Peter!"

Rachel clenched her fists and screeched.

She glared at the pop-up. Even if she was a millionaire, she wouldn't pay some scum-sucking scammer $10,000 to access her own PC. She'd rather pay a hitman to hunt down the vermin and bury him.

But the ransom wasn't her immediate problem.

The commission. What was she going to do about sending her files before the 9:00 a.m. deadline?

Chapter 13

Harley woke under the van, shivering in the darkness. He had to move. Had to get warm or he'd freeze.

The trucks had disappeared, as had the car with the fork on the front and all the men who'd been bustling about earlier. Now, only gloom filled the enclosure.

He shuffled from under the vehicle and scanned the area for a way out.

All the roll-down doors on the loading docks were closed, as was the entrance gate.

Now what?

A tantalizingly meaty scent dragged his gaze over to two dumpsters in the farthest corner, set back in an alcove where the raised part of the loading dock ended. Was that food?

He sniffed. It was. And a lot of it. Maybe his luck was changing.

His tail up, he trotted into the empty, dark expanse. Halfway across, rooftop floodlights drowned the area in bright white light.

Harley froze, ears flat to his head, tail down. He squinted in the sudden glare, barely daring to breathe, let alone move. Finally, he glanced around to check no one was rushing to grab him, then he bolted for safety.

The dumpsters too far, he made for the nearest cover — the left-hand loading dock where the trucks had been reversed. He cowered against the dock wall, praying it hid him from spying eyes.

Heart pounding, he scoured the enclosure for an escape route, ears pricked.

Without any warning, the floodlights shut off and darkness returned.

Wide-eyed, Harley gazed into the gloom. Waiting. Hoping he was safe again.

Again, no one rushed to catch him.

Still wary, he rotated his ears, listening for pounding footsteps.

Nothing.

He sniffed, scouring the chilly night air for new smells.

Nothing.

Content there was no impending danger, he trotted back into the expanse toward the far corner and the promise of dumpster food.

The burning bright lights nailed him again. And again, he froze, only daring to move his eyes in the hope of spotting his tormentor. But no one was there.

Picking up his right hind paw, he tentatively stepped back. Slowly, he shuffled to the dock wall and waited for something to happen.

Once again, the lights cut out.

Okay, it sounded crazy, but maybe he was putting on the lights. Twice he'd walked into the expanse, and twice the lights had come on. He didn't know how he'd done it, but only a fool argued with logic. So, if he stayed out of the expanse, maybe the lights would stay off and he'd be safe.

He crawled, hugging the wall below the level of the left-hand loading dock. Halfway along, he stopped and scanned the area. Nothing but shadows and stillness. Good.

His belly all but scraping the ground, he crawled on. He paused at the corner and checked the area again. Still clear.

He crept along the wall below the rear loading dock, still low, still slow, still wary. Intoxicating scents drew him onward as if he had a ring through his nose and was being pulled by a rope. He slunk faster.

At the end of the wall, two dumpsters loomed, and a meaty smell drifted out of the shadows. Harley's mouth watered.

As if he needed a reminder, his stomach twisted, dragging his insides into a giant knot. He grimaced and hunched over.

The food was so close now. If he could just make it.

But what would Barney say? Harley hadn't been offered the food and had no idea whose food it was. Eating it broke one of the golden rules.

But he was sooo hungry. Barney would understand. He had to.

He reached out with his right forepaw to take another step but yelped and pulled back, his insides feeling like they were gnawing on him.

He could see the dumpsters. Almost taste the food. He was so close.

With a whimper and pain grinding his insides, he took another tottering step.

On the dock above him, a door opened and an arc of light flooded out.

Harley froze, one paw off the ground in midstep.

Footfalls clomped across the concrete dock and a flashlight beam sliced through the night.

Harley cowered against the wall, screwed his eyes shut, and prayed he wouldn't be discovered.

Chapter 14

Rachel stood in her front doorway, light flooding out onto the lawn. Izzy shuffled toward her, sporting a blue puffer jacket and animal slippers — the left a cat, the right a dog.

Izzy held up a tablet. "The cavalry's here." She yawned as she handed the device to Rachel.

"Thanks, Iz, you're a lifesaver." She let Izzy in, then stepped outside.

"Can't you do it on your phone?"

Rachel shook her head. "The files are too big. Listen, Wes rarely wakes up in the night, so you should be all right, but you never know. Okay?"

Izzy frowned. "You're not doing it here?"

"I don't know if viruses can infect routers, so I was going to use yours. That's okay, isn't it?"

"Like I'm going to say no." She waved Rachel away. "Go."

Rachel scurried along the gravel path toward her garage.

With one big room and a bathroom at the back, Izzy's apartment had been built for Peter's aging mother, but Rachel had learned about Claire before the old lady had moved in. Now it served as a welcome source of income — not to mention providing a babysitter on tap.

Entering into the kitchen, Rachel rolled her eyes at the collection of clean and dirty kitchenware scattered everywhere, suggesting Izzy had just hosted a dinner party — which she appeared to do every day.

Rachel scooped a pile of crumpled T-shirts, leggings, and underwear to one end of the gray sofa, then logged in to her online backup storage and downloaded the commission files to the tablet. These were versions from around 3:00 p.m., meaning the entire night's work was wasted, but it was these or nothing.

Uploading the files to a file-sharing site, she shook her head. Like many people, everything she did was digital. Everything. Because of that, she used alphanumeric passwords, off-site backup, and a VPN. She did everything possible to protect her digital world — yet her safeguards had been shredded by her own nosiness. Talk about dumb. What would be next? Disclosing her bank details to a Nigerian prince?

The upload complete, she sent the publisher a link to the files and fell back against the sofa, closing her eyes. "Thank heavens."

All the stress melted away. Muscles she didn't even know had been tense relaxed, and for a moment, the relief felt like she was luxuriating in an essential oils bubble bath. For a moment...

With a groan, she opened her eyes. That problem was dealt with, but what the devil was she going to do about the $10,000 ransom demand?

Chapter 15

On the loading dock above Harley, a man's voice said, "Perkins to Control."

"Control," said another male voice, sounding distant with a slight metallic crackle.

"We got no action here."

"You've checked all along Dock A?"

"There's nothing. Hit the floods for a sec."

The rooftop lights bathed the area again.

Trembling, Harley cringed. They were going to catch him. Catch him and punish him for being bad and being somewhere he shouldn't.

He squashed himself into the angle between the wall and the ground, hoping it would swallow him. He closed his eyes, trying to block out the blinding light. Trying to picture lying on the sofa with his head in Barney's lap, and Barney stroking his back over and over.

Harley screwed his eyes shut. Tight. So tight, he thought they might never open again. If he couldn't see them, they couldn't see him. If he couldn't see them, they couldn't see him...

Footsteps thudded closer and closer.

Harley held his breath. If he couldn't see them, they couldn't see him...

"Nope, nothing," said Perkins.

"Well, something tripped that motion sensor."

"Could be the wind," said Perkins.

"Microwave detectors aren't affected by the wind."

"Look, if you're that bothered, review the security footage, because it's freezing out here."

Footsteps clomped away and a door slammed.

Harley peeked from one eye just as the floodlights clicked off and darkness once more descended.

He'd been right. If he couldn't see them, they couldn't see him. Logic was a beautiful thing.

Panting, he slumped to the cold, hard ground as if he'd been running for hours, the nervous energy draining from his muscles. He lay, struggling to summon the strength to go on.

Was this day never going to end?

But then, did he want his last ever day with Barney to end, knowing that every other day of his life would be spent without his best friend? Harley whimpered.

He heaved up and shuffled on, staying close to the ground, clinging to the wall. Finally, he reached the dumpsters.

He ached to leap straight in and devour everything inside, but only a fool would leap into the unknown — the way his luck was going, he could leap straight onto broken glass. While being in the open was risky, maybe just a second wouldn't hurt.

Harley leaped onto the loading dock, muscles tensed to dive into the dumpster.

Dazzling light burst forth, revealing two black corrugated plastic lids covering each dumpster.

Harley glanced back at his safe place under the van, then at the nearest lid. Should he risk it? Or should he bolt for cover?

His clawing stomach decided for him.

He stuck his snout under the lip of the nearest lid and nuzzled it up. Sticking his head in to raise the lid even higher, he checked for danger, then wriggled inside. The lid banged down after him.

In the gloom, he cowered, glaring at the jagged streak of light bleeding in around the rim, praying the lid wouldn't lift and the flashlight man wouldn't grab him.

The floodlights clicked off, plunging Harley into darkness.

Safe.

Relaxing, he sniffed the discarded bags and boxes surrounding him. He ripped open a cellophane bag and chomped into a bread bun but relaxed his jaws and let the bun drop from his mouth.

He slumped back on his haunches and glowered at it.

That was food. And he needed food so, so much. But could he really eat without being given the go-ahead? Break one of the golden rules?

He glared at it. Aching to eat, but determined to be the good dog Barney was so proud of.

His mouth watered and his stomach screamed.

He wanted to eat so much. He *needed* to eat so much.

Harley whimpered, staring at the bread. He hoped Barney would forgive him for what he was about to do. He snatched it up and chewed.

Heaven. It was the only word for it. He'd almost forgotten what it was like to eat. He wolfed down another, but even as he devoured it, another scent drew his attention.

Digging his snout into the debris, he pushed various packs aside, rooting for something his nose said was there.

He wagged his tail. There it was. He snagged the corner of the packaging in his jaws and tugged. Lodged under something else, it wouldn't come free. He braced himself, digging his claws into the surrounding debris, and heaved.

A white tray covered with a plastic film came away. He stamped a forepaw onto it, then ripped the film off with his teeth. A slab of ground beef stared up at him.

He pressed his nose to it and sniffed hard. The tiniest hint of decay caressed his nostrils, but it was nothing his stomach couldn't handle.

Leaning forward, he scoffed the lot, then licked the white tray clean.

Harley jammed his snout back into the mound, pushing this way, pulling that way, digging farther and farther down. After a few seconds, he yanked free another tray of beef. He gobbled every scrap.

With a heavy breath, he sank back onto his haunches. That was a mighty big meal. Especially considering he'd had nothing for days.

He shivered. Okay, he'd solved his hunger problem, but how was he going to get warm? Where would he be safe from the people out to catch him?

Harley nuzzled up the dumpster's lid. Peeking over the rim, he scanned the enclosure. Three solid concrete walls with no exits and a tall fence with a closed gate. Maybe the question wasn't where he could go but how he could go anywhere.

A low hum caught his attention. He twitched his ears, angling them to home in on the sound. He leaped out of the dumpster and once more hugged the low wall of the loading dock as the lights lit. A narrow gap lay between the corner of the dock and the dumpster. Harley stuck his nose in and sniffed.

That was promising.

Air gushed toward him. It was fusty, dry, and old, as if it had been used for too long. But above all, it was warm.

Harley squeezed along the gap. Behind the dumpster, a metal vent stuck out of the building wall, from which warm air flowed. Harley shuffled closer. Next to the vent, he lay down, heavy with food and caressed by warmth.

He closed his eyes. He didn't want to believe this might be his last day with Barney, but he was at a loss for what else he could do. However, one thing was certain — after a day like today, tomorrow could only be better.

Chapter 16

Beep... Beep... Beep... The shrill sound sliced through the air as sharp early-morning light bathed the enclosure.

Cozy lying beside his personal heating system, Harley opened one eye and shot a cursory glance underneath the dumpster. A vehicle reversed to the loading dock opposite, far enough away not to be a bother.

He'd woken when the sun had first cast its feeble rays over the area, but still satisfied after his midnight feast, and with no idea of what he was going to do next, he hadn't left his vent.

Trucks came and went all morning, unloading all manner of goods. The endless stream of boxes being taken inside had both cheered his heart and made him want to howl the world to pieces with sadness — Barney loved boxes. What a spectacle the man was missing.

Harley whimpered. He didn't mean to, it just slipped out, his heart hurting as if someone had reached into his chest and squeezed. He was lost without Barney. Lost. Being Barney's friend had been Harley's sole purpose. Now? What point was there to life if it had no purpose?

No, he couldn't think like that. Barney would hate it. He had to move. Find a reason to go on.

He stretched his forepaws out in front and pushed his butt into the air, his tongue curling as he yawned.

Yesterday, he'd been so famished, he'd thought his insides were going to grind themselves to mush, but now, he wasn't even remotely hungry. However, he didn't know when he'd find food again, so it would be wise to have a bite in his private pantry before he left.

Scraping against the wall and the dumpster, Harley squeezed around to face the way he'd come, then crept along the gap to the end. He peeped out.

A red truck pulled into the enclosure and *beep-beep-beeped* its way backward to a section of the loading dock yards from Harley.

Fantastic. If he timed it right, he'd be able to scoot from his hiding place, jump onto the dock and nuzzle the lid up, then dive into the dumpster, all while hidden by this truck.

His luck really had changed. But then it had to. No way could it have gotten any worse.

He prowled out of the shadows and, without even glancing around, leaped onto the edge of the dock, eased up the dumpster lid with his snout, and wriggled in.

With the unloading commotion drowning out his activities, he pawed through the garbage.

In the background, the truck at the other side of the enclosure revved and pulled away like vehicles had all morning. Harley paid it no heed.

Harley munched a bread bun from the pack he'd opened the previous night while he nosed packages aside. Various edible items lay buried, but the scent of more ground beef was tantalizingly close.

He dug junk out of the way and shoved his snout as deep into the gap as he could. He sniffed. Yes, it was meat. Beef. If he could only reach it.

Using both front paws, he fought to dig a hole in the waste. But digging through garbage proved far harder than digging soil — some lumps wouldn't budge, others slid back in, and some broke when he yanked on them.

Another truck growled into the enclosure. Harley ignored it, intent on reaching his prize. The meaty aroma driving him on, he shoved his head right, made a small hole and nuzzled his snout into it, then shoved left to create even more space.

The new engine sound drew closer. Good. The trucks didn't appear to stay in the enclosure long, so if this one was parking near him, it would hide him leaving the dumpster. He hadn't intended on being this long, but then he hadn't figured on reaching the meat being such a problem.

He rammed a paw into the hole beside his snout and pulled back, widening it.

Yes!

Wiggling his snout to make room, he clamped his jaws about a cardboard package that smelled like beef burgers. He pulled, but the package remained wedged.

Tensing his muscles, Harley yanked on the package, pushing with his strong forelegs. Bit by bit, it worked loose. He shook his head to loosen it even more. This beef was *his*.

The truck revved so close it sounded to be on top of him.

It didn't matter. The dumpster lid hid him from view, so the closer the truck was, the more it would conceal him when he jumped out.

He tugged and tugged on the package. Finally, it jerked free, and he stood with it triumphantly clasped in his jaws.

He was getting good at this. If he came back later, he'd check the second dumpster — if there was so much treasure in this one, there had to be some in that one, too.

The dumpster shook as if something had prodded it.

Harley jumped and dropped his beefy package. Someone was out there.

He cowered. If he stayed still and quiet, he might go undiscovered.

He waited, flashing his gaze around the rim of the dumpster lid for signs of someone lifting it. He tensed his muscles, ready to spring out and run for cover.

The dumpster jerked forward. Harley gasped.

His heart racing, he eased up the lid and peeked out.

The cab of a white truck moved past him, as if it was sinking into the ground.

Harley's eyes popped wide open. The truck wasn't sinking; he was rising. He had to get out. Now!

Harley braced himself, readying to surge upward — to thrust open the dumpster lid and leap out in one bound. He pushed with his hind legs, but the dumpster jolted and he fell against its front wall.

He struggled to his feet, but the dumpster tipped over.

The lid swung open, and Harley plummeted into a metal cell. All the garbage he'd been standing on tumbled out. It buried him.

Chapter 17

Harley twisted and writhed to escape, gasping for breath under the crushing piles of garbage. Buried in the darkness, he wasn't even sure which way was up.

He pushed with his hind legs to thrust up and out of the mass, but whatever was underneath his back paws shifted, so he didn't move.

Fighting for air, he wiggled left, then right, creating a small pocket of space around him. He kicked and squirmed and flailed and lurched. Inch by inch, he battled through the junk.

Between a soggy cardboard box and a bulging black bag, a speck of blue sky teased him.

He bucked with all his might, heaving against the crushing pile. Clawing and biting, he hacked a hole in the mess and gulped fresh air.

With oxygen once more powering his lungs and providing a glimmer of hope, he lashed out with his forelegs and pounded his hind legs into the junk below. Writhing and kicking, he burst through the debris, battered aside a white bag, and clambered to his feet.

Free.

Sort of.

Four metal walls imprisoned him. He searched for any sort of platform to pounce on so he could escape through the open ceiling.

A mechanical whine screeched outside his metal compartment. The second dumpster reared over him. Its two lids swung open, and another pile of garbage plummeted down.

Harley dove for the side of the compartment to escape the falling trash, but the mound engulfed him.

Buried once more, at least Harley knew which way freedom lay this time. Pushing against the metal wall, he lowered his head and jammed his shoulders upward, heaving with all his might to shove through boxes and bags and packets and wrapping...

He dug with his front paws, ripped with his teeth, and kicked with his back legs. Bit by bit, he scrambled through the mountain of garbage. His head and forelegs broke through the surface. Relief flooded his body; just another almighty push and he'd be free.

A loud mechanical humming shook the compartment. The metal wall behind the truck's cab scraped toward him, squashing the garbage mountain and him back toward a metal cave.

If he didn't escape right now, this thing was going to eat him alive!

Harley heaved with his back legs, kicking and kicking and kicking. He had to get out. Get out now before he was buried in the cave forever.

With shallow pants and wild eyes, he flailed his forelegs, battering debris away, struggling to keep his head above the wave of trash. But the wave swept him toward the dark, stinking cave.

He clawed at the wall, fighting against being shoved farther, but his nails only scraped along the metal, gaining no purchase.

He was going to drown. Drown in a sea of unwanted junk. And no one would ever know to be able to tell Barney.

The metal wall crushed tighter and tighter.

Harley kicked harder and harder.

But the garbage wave dragged him to the cave's entrance.

He flung his right foreleg up and latched his claws onto the edge of the cave's metal mouth. He heaved. Heaved with all the strength of his love for Barney. Kicking his hind legs into the moving mass, he hauled himself back inch by inch.

But his hold slipped. His claws raked the metal as the wall crushed the garbage farther into the cave, dragging him with it.

Battling against the tide, Harley clung on by one last claw, struggling to save himself from being eaten by the machine. But that last toe bent back — another second and he'd lose his grip...

The metal wall crushed a bulging white bag, bursting it with a *bang*. Polystyrene beads flew into the air like a foamy fountain. The space left behind created just enough room for Harley to rip a hind leg free and plant it on the top of the moving mound.

He flung his other foreleg up. Claws scraping on the metal lip, Harley heaved himself upward and pounded his back paws into the moving mass.

With one almighty thrust, Harley leaped free and scrambled onto the roof of the garbage truck.

He raced across the blue metal, dove off the end and into the middle of the enclosure, and shot through the open gates onto the sidewalk outside.

Hurtling down the roadside, he scanned frantically for a safe place. There had to be one. Somewhere without crushing machines. Somewhere without chasing people. But where?

Chapter 18

Rachel struggled to focus on the morning's class in the study while jungle insects and birds chirruped, cheeped, and cawed from the CD player. English and communication skills was the worst session of the week because it demanded Wes speak. She usually encouraged him by being more upbeat, but with her computer held ransom, and with it her livelihood, she was fumbling for words as much as he was.

With the timer ticking away so he could monitor how much more torture he had to endure, she turned her tablet toward him and clicked play: an emperor penguin waddled across an ice field to its colony and shuffled a large gray egg onto its feet from its partner's.

Rachel said, "Okay, Wes, spin the Wheel of Questions." Years of trial and error had proven engagement came through fun and interactivity. Her solution was unorthodox, but worked.

Wes spun a roulette wheel. Numbers one through thirty-six had been sectioned into groups of four, each labeled with a word highlighted in either blue, red, or green: What, Where, When, Why, Who, If, How, Name, and Describe. The two zero pockets were marked Mystery.

"Now the Ball of Wisdom."

He dropped in a white ball. It bounced and clattered around before landing in "Name" highlighted in blue.

"You know what that means, Wes." She placed a molded strip of modeling clay over the pockets in the "Name" section so the ball couldn't land there again, then pushed an oversize blue die with large white numbers painted on it toward him.

Wes rolled a three.

"Name three things you saw in the video, Wes."

Keeping his head down so as to avoid eye contact, and with a mutter as opposed to clear, confident vocalization, he said, "Penguin."

"Good."

"Egg."

"Yes. And?"

"Penguin."

"No cheating, please. You know you can't use the same name twice, even if there's more than one of them in the video."

He paused for a moment, then said, "Beak."

"Well done." She pointed at the wheel again. "Go ahead."

He spun and the ball landed on "What" written in red.

Rachel pushed a red die marked with higher numbers across the table.

Wes threw a twelve. He rolled his eyes.

Rachel said, "In no fewer than twelve words, describe what the penguins were doing."

He stared at the paused screen. She wasn't sure if he was thinking of an answer or how he might get out of using so many words.

He said in a monotone, "One penguin walked slowly to an other penguin and moved an egg."

"Sorry, Wes, but that's only eleven words. Try again."

His lips moving, he counted off the words to himself on his fingers, then furrowed his brow, but still didn't meet her gaze. "Twelve."

"The word 'another' isn't like 'an egg' where it's two words. It's all one word with 'an' and 'other' joined together. Do you remember?"

He shrugged.

"Okay, now try again, please."

He heaved a breath as if being asked to recite the Gettysburg Address from memory.

"One penguin walked slowly to another penguin to move a big egg."

"Excellent, Wes. Now, do you know why they were moving that egg?"

He shook his head. He squinted at the frozen image through his bangs.

"Think about it, Wes. Where do penguins live?"

"Marineland."

"Okay. Yes, but where is their real home in the wild?"

"I like Marineland."

"I know, Wes. And one day we'll go again. But now we're in the middle of a lesson." She pointed at the screen. "Look. What's all that white stuff?"

"We could go again now."

She tapped the timer. "You know we can't go, Wes. The alarm hasn't sounded to end the lesson yet, has it?"

He heaved another breath.

Again, she pointed to the screen. "Penguins live somewhere cold, so what could all this white stuff be?"

Before he could answer, her phone rang. She normally let it go to voicemail during lesson time, but today she was thankful for a break. She answered it.

"Hi, Mom."

Her mom's gravelly voice said, "Morning, sweetheart."

She looked at Wes. "Two minutes. It's Grandma."

Wes gazed about as if looking for another person.

Rachel pointed to the phone. "Here. On the other end."

"Is Wes with you? Say hi from me."

"I told him it's you. Didn't you hear?"

"So say I said hello."

"He won't get that, Mom."

"So I can't say hello to my only grandson?"

Rachel rubbed her forehead. As if she didn't have enough problems. "Wes, Grandma says hello."

Wes frowned, peering about the room.

"Wes says hi back, Mom."

His brow knitted, he stared at her. She'd told him Grandma was there, when she obviously wasn't, then she'd said he'd said things he hadn't. The world was a confusing place when taken literally.

Grandma said, "Was that so difficult?"

"Sorry, Mom, but it's not a good day today."

"Then it's a good thing I called, because this is going to cheer you up."

Rachel doubted it. "Yes?"

"You know the Clintons next door and their son Tad?"

Rachel winced. Oh, please don't say she was trying to matchmake.

"Well, his wife is opening a restaurant and needs someone to do the menus, so I suggested you."

"Me?"

"No need to thank me."

"Mom, I'm an artist, not a graphic designer."

"Artist, designer... It's all creating stuff on a computer."

Rachel pinched her nose and drew a slow breath. "No, Mom, they're different disciplines. It's like asking a plumber to decorate your living room — you wouldn't do it, would you?"

"My handyman changed my bathroom taps *and* wallpapered my kitchen."

"Okay, bad example. I'm just saying that I, as an artist, don't design restaurant menus."

"So now I have to go back and tell them you're not interested after I built you up to be this great designer?"

"It's not that I'm not interested, Mom. It's a different skill set."

"It can't be that different from designing a book cover."

"But I know what works for book covers. I don't have a clue what works for restaurant menus."

"Okay. Sorry I tried to help."

Rachel sighed. Did all adult children have such problems with their parents? Surely pushing kids to do things they didn't want to was something parents grew out of, especially if their children weren't just independent but had children of their own.

Or did they?

She'd be a parent until the day she died because Wes would need care his entire life. Maybe that was how all parents felt — their offspring were always their "children" no matter how old they were, so it was their duty to look after them as best they could. Maybe she should go easier on her mom.

"Mom, I appreciate you thinking of me, so thanks. Maybe next time will be a better fit."

"So why are you having such a bad day? Didn't you get that work you wanted?"

"Computer problems. But I don't want to bore you with that."

"So speak to Tad."

Rachel slapped her forehead. "Mom, please, I'm not doing a restaurant menu."

"Yes, I got that message, thank you. But that doesn't mean you can't talk to him about computers."

She paced into the kitchen. "Why would I want to talk to a restaurant owner about computers?"

"Because, little Miss Grumpy Pants, as I said, it's his wife who's opening the restaurant. He works in IT."

Was this a plumber doing a decorator's job again?

"When you say IT, do you mean someone who just uses a computer or someone who takes them apart?" The last thing she needed was an "expert" advising her to turn off her computer, wait thirty seconds, then turn it back on.

"He put a new power supply in my laptop when the old one blew."

"Do you have his number?"

Chapter 19

Wandering through the park, tail down, Harley puzzled over what to do next. No matter what he tried, it all went wrong.

He tramped down to the lake. A man with gray hair offered a bag of sliced bread to a chubby boy in a red coat. The boy took a slice, ripped it up, and threw it in the lake. Ducks with shimmering green necks glided over, causing barely a ripple, quacking their appreciation.

This boy and old man obviously liked animals. And Harley liked boys and old men. It was perfect. After the morning he'd had, meeting new friends was just the tonic.

His tail up, Harley trotted over. Being the polite dog he was, he didn't interrupt the pair but sat on the path directly behind them. His tail wagged as he pictured how events would unfold – the pair would notice him, see what a polite dog he was, then smile and pet him.

He waited.

After a few seconds, the boy sniffed loudly. He curled his top lip and twisted to the old man. "What's that stink?"

The old man sniffed, too.

The two of them turned, and the boy jumped when he saw Harley.

Harley wagged his tail all the more, tilting his head to one side. People seemed to like it when he did that, which seemed odd, but then, people were odd.

Clutching his nose and mouth, the boy tottered back. "Ewww, that dog stinks like a garbage can."

Too close to the edge, the boy's foot slipped off the stone edging and splashed into the water. He toppled backward, but the old man grabbed his arm and yanked him to safety.

Shrieking, the boy lifted his foot, his shoe and pant leg sodden.

It was lucky Harley was there, because nothing turned a bad day into a good one more than a lick from a loveable dog.

Harley bounced over and licked the boy's arm.

The boy shrieked again and jerked away. The old man swung the bag of bread like a cosh, clonking Harley on the head.

Harley yelped. Not because it hurt, but because of the shock of his good deed being repaid with such impoliteness.

He scampered away, glancing back only to make sure the horrible man wasn't chasing him.

What was wrong with these people? He was a good dog. Why was everybody treating him like he was some freak?

He whimpered. He couldn't go home because there was no way in, and even if there was, it wasn't home without Barney. He couldn't risk the shopping mall again — the chasing men and the crushing machine made that a no-go area. So where could he go?

Maybe one of the bistros on the main street Barney occasionally visited. Or the movie theater. Oh, yes. That place was always warm and dark. He'd had some of his best naps there.

But there were people in all those places. With Barney, people were all smiles and stroking hands. Without Barney? People were monsters.

No, he had to find a place without people.

He trotted up the path curving through some bushes that sometimes bore blue flowers but were now only a mass of green. At the other side, two black wooden benches sat beside a tree with limp branches that drooped to the ground — Barney's favorite spot.

Harley whined. They'd sat there together for hours, watching the world go by. Not saying anything. Not doing anything. Just being. Together.

He plodded over, sniffing the ground, then the nearest bench. He whined again — there wasn't a trace of Barney anywhere.

At the other side of the drooping tree, a group of teenage boys talked loudly.

People. He'd had enough of people for one day.

Harley shuffled under the bench where he wouldn't be disturbed and collapsed in a heap, chin resting in the dirt. Nestled under the wooden slats, he closed his eyes and drifted back to those far-off hours with his best friend. He could almost smell Barney, almost feel his warm hand on his back, almost hear his voice.

A scent blowing on the breeze dragged him from his daydream. A scent he recognized.

70

Pricking his ears, he opened his eyes and sniffed, gazing toward the drooping tree and the grassy slope beyond.

Harley wasn't the only one staring out across the grass — the gang of boys stared too.

A little brown dog, tail up, sauntered across the slope — the kid. After the catastrophic day Harley had suffered, seeing his young friend enveloped him in a warm glow, even if they weren't actually friends yet. He lifted his head out of the muck and raised his tail.

A boy in a black leather jacket muttered something and the other boys laughed. Stooping, he held something toward the kid. The youngster wagged his tail and bound toward the gang.

Squinting, Harley leaned out from under the bench and sniffed. Was that... a cookie?

Awww, so the kid had friends after all. Great. Everyone needed at least one good friend in their life.

The kid ambled up to Leather Jacket and grabbed the cookie. But, before he could eat it, Leather Jacket fired a kick into the little dog's side.

The dog squealed and tumbled across the grass.

Laughing, Leather Jacket grabbed a pebble from the ground. "Stupid dog, get out of here." He threw the stone.

The kid scrambled up and, tail between his legs, shot into a bush covered in thorns.

Harley's jaw dropped. Had that really happened?

Leather Jacket snatched up another stone, then pointed to something lying in the grass. "Get that stick, Jonesy. Let's have some fun."

They stalked toward the thorny bush, Leather Jacket hurling the stone into it.

A rumble simmered in Harley's throat, exploding into a growl as he parted his lips to bare his teeth. Hackles raised, he prowled from under the bench. If people weren't going to be polite, neither was he.

He charged under the drooping tree and across the grass. As Leather Jacket joked with the boys, Harley leaped. He soared through the air and slammed Leather Jacket in the back.

The boy crashed to the ground. Harley lurched at the boy sprawled on the grass. Gnashing his teeth and barking as loud as he could, Harley shoved his snout so close he showered the boy's face with spittle.

The boy flung his hands up to shield his face and wailed. Wailed like a tiny girl who'd fallen and hurt her knee.

As the boy rolled away, Harley lunged, baring his fangs and snarling.

Leather Jacket clambered to his feet and bolted.

Hackles still raised, Harley snarled at the other boys. They scurried away too, fleeing up the slope and disappearing over the brow.

The danger passed, he peered through the bush's thorny branches.

Trembling in the shadows, the little brown dog stared up at him with huge brown eyes full of fear.

An ache welled inside Harley. Not like hunger or tiredness, but kind of like how he felt without Barney. Like something precious had been ripped away to leave a gaping hole.

Harley tilted his head at the pathetic creature cowering in the rotting leaves. Poor little fella. What kind of an introduction to life was he having? Without a guardian to protect him and teach him the ways of the world, his life was going to be a miserable one, and probably a short one, too.

Since losing Barney, Harley had longed to have meaning back in his life. Maybe he'd just stumbled upon it.

Chapter 20

Quaking, the little brown dog stared at Harley from behind his protective shield of spikes. Harley yipped to encourage him out, but the kid ignored him.

Harley glanced about for inspiration. Where Leather Jacket had smashed into the ground lay a shiny plastic pack. Harley sniffed — cookies!

He darted over and snatched the packet up. While the kid's gaze drilled into him, Harley shook his head and four cookies fell from the pack. He munched one to show the kid it was safe, then stepped back to give the youngster space. Sitting on his haunches, he waited.

The kid didn't move.

Harley shuffled farther away and lay on the grass, his chin on his front paws. After such a traumatic ordeal, the kid was understandably wary of strangers, and unfortunately, Harley was one. While he could leave the cookies so the kid could eat in peace, that wouldn't solve the kid's real problem — how to get by in the world. Harley had believed himself an expert on how the world worked, yet since he'd lost Barney, it was obvious the world worked far differently without his old man by his side. However, he still knew vastly more than this pup.

Harley waited. And waited.

Brittle leaf litter crunched underfoot as the kid crept through the thorny branches toward the cookies. So as not to spook him, Harley remained lying down.

With puppy eyes as big, brown, and round as bowls of beef stew, the kid reached a trembling paw out of the bush and placed it on the grass. Through the leaves, he stared at Harley, obviously waiting to see if he should dash back into the bush.

Harley didn't move.

The kid scanned the area, then finally thrust his snout through the

73

branches and emerged into the open, his tail wedged between his legs.

Hobbling, he padded over to the cookies. Gaze fixed on Harley, he gobbled down the first one, then the second, and finally, the third. All the while, his tail hung between his legs and his ears remained pulled back. Tiny nicks from the thorns covered his back and sides.

Harley wagged his tail.

The kid leaned forward, pushing his snout as close to Harley as he could without actually moving. He sniffed as if to assess if this was another trick or if Harley could be trusted.

Still Harley stayed put. The kid was trying his best. If Harley gave him enough time, things would work out.

The youngster took a teetering step toward Harley. From the age of the scents on the hydrant, the kid had been alone for a good few days. He'd done well to keep going the way he had, but it was obviously more through luck than savvy. Harley could help with that.

Another faltering step.

An intoxicating sense of hope gushed through Harley's veins. He felt more alive, more invigorated, than he had for days. In losing Barney, he'd lost his purpose. Maybe now, he'd found a new one.

The little dog tottered toward Harley, stopping a few feet short. He craned his neck to get as close as he could while still leaving as much space between them as possible in case an escape was needed. He sniffed.

Slowly, so as not to rattle the kid, Harley craned his neck as well. They gently touched noses and sniffed each other's scents.

As if wanting to test Harley further, the little dog picked up his right forepaw and swatted Harley on the snout.

When Harley didn't react aggressively, the kid stretched out his forelegs, with his chest almost touching the grass and his butt in the air. A play bow stance. The kid barked an invitation — *arr-rufff!*

Harley pushed his butt in the air, keeping his forelegs where they were to mirror the kid.

With another bark, the kid raced away across the grass. Harley darted after him.

Harley chased down the little dog and nudged him in the side, sending him sprawling into the grass. The kid yipped, scrambled up, and lunged at Harley, so Harley turned tail and ran up the slope. The young dog bolted after Harley, yapping and yapping.

74

Harley ran slow enough for the pup to keep pace, then dashed around a tree and back down the hill. The kid followed, yapping all the way. At the bottom, Harley spun around and play-bowed, and the kid mirrored him. Harley barked and leaped to the right. The kid leaped too, then sped across the grass, glancing back only long enough to check Harley was in pursuit.

In the glorious sunshine, the pair chased around the park, weaving in and out of the trees, flying through bushes, running over desolate brown flowerbeds. The years melted away from Harley as quickly as the plants flew by; he felt young again.

With the kid panting and his tongue lolling out, Harley took him down to the lake, where they both lapped water. The kid spotted the ducks and toddled around the bank, barking at them. That wasn't very polite, but no one had taught the kid, so it wasn't his fault. Harley nuzzled him away from the water and over to a patch of grass, where they lay down, the kid licking the tiny wounds from the thorny bush.

Finally, the kid nestled against Harley's stomach, as if he wanted to feel another dog breathing, another dog's warmth. There, he fell asleep, obviously beat after all their fun. Harley licked his head. It felt wonderful to have someone to look after again. To have meaning in a world that had taken so much from him, a world that no longer made sense.

They lay on the grass until the long shadows cast by the dying sun crawled across them and the air turned chilly. The little dog stretched, mouth gaping, then clambered to his feet. He tottered toward the far trees and the city street that lay beyond, then looked at Harley and barked.

They needed somewhere sheltered and warm to sleep. The vent had been ideal, until the garbage truck had tried to mangle him. Maybe going late in the day and leaving early the next morning would avoid such dangers. However, the vent was in the opposite direction from the one in which the kid wanted to go.

Harley trotted a few steps toward his vent, then beckoned the kid with a bark. But the kid barked back, scampering another couple of steps his way. Was it possible the kid had stumbled upon somewhere even better than Harley's vent? He'd stayed safe alone up to now, so maybe he knew something Harley didn't. Harley followed the kid up the grass slope toward the park exit near the fire hydrant.

The kid led them along numerous streets, all the while the air getting crisper and the sky darker. By the time they plodded along the sidewalk
beside a brick wall daubed with graffiti, streetlights cast an eerie yellow glow over the darkened buildings.

Harley frowned, his stomach churning, gaze darting through the shadows. He slunk along, head down, ready to run or fight. Strangely, the kid bounced along without a care, as if the area conjured happy memories.

At a corner, the kid barked at Harley as if announcing they'd arrived. Harley ambled into an alleyway, scanning the area for a warm vent or a secluded alcove. The only thing he saw lay a few feet from the alley's mouth — a moldy old box on its side.

Surely that wasn't...

The kid scampered inside and gazed at Harley as if proud to invite him into his home.

Glancing around, hoping there was more to the box than was immediately apparent, Harley wandered over, sifting the scents washing over him. He recognized them instantly — an adult female dog and three pups around the kid's age. The kid's pack.

Harley sniffed the box's interior. The scents were as old as the ones on the fire hydrant. It had been days since the pack had been here, but if a protective mother returned and caught a strange dog sleeping in her bed next to her kid...

No, he'd have to find somewhere else. Maybe trail back to his vent.

Harley nuzzled the kid, then left. If the kid didn't turn up in the park again tomorrow, Harley would find him. Though the kid had made it this far alone, as Harley had discovered, everyone's luck ran out sometime.

Chapter 21

Rachel strolled out of Digital World onto the main city street, clutching a brand-new ten terabyte hard disk in one hand and the five-foot-long blue strap to the harness Wes wore in the other. Because he wouldn't hold hands, the harness kept him close and safe.

A woman in a fake fur coat sauntered by with a toddler wearing a similar harness. She frowned at Wes, who was around three times older than her son yet still wore the same device. Rachel ignored it. Over the years, she'd become immune to the stares and snide remarks.

Luckily, a chat with Tad had promised to solve her digital woes — instead of paying one cent in ransom for her computer, she'd install this new drive following the video Tad had sent, transfer the mirror image of her system setup from backup, and download her files from her cloud storage. It would be a boring process, but she'd enjoy flipping the digital bird to that thieving hacker scum.

As they passed the park entrance, Wes pulled to go in.

Rachel eased him away. "Sorry, Wes, not now. But Izzy might be taking you later, which will be fun, won't it?"

She strolled on, but he stopped, yanking the harness strap.

"Wes, please. I'm pressed for time."

He ignored her, watching a black-and-white border collie sniff a hydrant, squirt urine on it, then turn away.

"Wes!"

He didn't appear to hear her for staring intently into the dog's eyes, while the dog stared back, head tilted.

"Wesley, please." Delicately, she placed her hand on his arm and eased him around to continue along the sidewalk.

She waited for the inevitable wail as she'd had the audacity to violate him so. But it didn't come. How strange. Ambling alongside her, he gazed back as the dog meandered into the park and disappeared.

When they finally arrived at the store where Izzy worked, Izzy shot them a smile while a chatty customer with a braided beard paid for a dream catcher.

Rachel waited by a table of new book releases: the law of attraction, alien abduction, karma, astrology, angels... She checked the time — fourteen minutes to get to the meeting. She glared at the bearded man. She hated customers who didn't just make a purchase and leave but insisted on chatting with the clerk and delaying everyone behind them.

Finally, the customer left and Izzy wandered over.

"Hi, Wes. Ready to have some fun?"

Rachel handed her the strap. "Thanks, Izzy. You're a lifesaver."

"You're welcome." Izzy smiled. "Though, nothing says thank you like a rent reduction." She winked.

Rachel snickered. "Yeah, right. Because Peter's bound to have good news, so there's no way the rent will need to go up."

Izzy's smile dropped. "What?"

Rachel smirked. "Man, you should see your face. Like he has grounds to reduce his payments. Look, I've got to run. I'll meet you where we said in an hour. So long. Bye, Wes."

Wes stared at a wall of books.

"Good luck," said Izzy.

Ten minutes later, Rachel poured herself a drink from a jug of water in the middle of the conference room table, taking care not to let the lemon slices or ice cubes splash onto the highly-polished dark wood.

Taking a sip, she scanned the individual photos of the partners lining the far wall. There seemed more than the last time she was here. Good. That meant the accountancy firm was flourishing, so maybe she could turn the tables and wangle even more money out of Peter.

The door opened and in waltzed a blonde woman whose legs seemed to stretch up to her cleavage.

Rachel said, "Claire."

The woman said hello with equal warmth.

Peter ambled in. "Hi."

He'd lost his paunch and shaved his thinning hair. Was he anxious about holding on to his younger woman?

They each took a seat opposite her.

Rachel gestured to the open door. "You don't mind everyone hearing our business?"

"No, it's— ah."

A man with graying temples to match his gray suit strolled in and sat beside Peter, putting a black leather briefcase embossed with gold lettering on the table. Rachel recognized him from a previous encounter without needing a hint from the initials on his case — Greg MacNamara.

"What the...? You said an informal meeting, Peter." She stabbed a finger at Greg. "*Informal.*"

"It is. Greg is only here in case we needed any legal clarifications."

Rachel slammed her glass down, water sloshing out. "How is it informal when one of the parties has representation?"

"I assure you, Ms. Taylor," said Greg, "I'm here more as a bystander than in a strict legal capacity."

"A bystander?" Rachel glared at Peter. "Seriously?" She shook her head. "Of all the stunts you've pulled, this one's right up there."

She glared at the door. She was out of here.

Peter said, "Before you storm out, Rachel, why don't you listen to what I have to say?"

Tapping her foot under the table to try to clear some of the nervous energy coursing through her, Rachel glowered and folded her arms.

He said, "I'd like to reduce my payments to you."

Rachel scoffed. She'd feared this was coming for years but never dreamed it would actually happen. Not like this. Not on his own son. What had she ever seen in this worm?

He continued. "Your personal income is far greater than when the alimony and child support were decided, so it's only right that this should be reflected in the amount I pay now."

"You mean the personal income I have to work till midnight to earn?"

"Rachel, believe me—"

"Yeah, right."

"—I'm not trying to ambush you. I'm simply asking you to be open to discussing a reduction."

Biting her lip, she stared at the wall to her left. She couldn't bear to look at him. She clenched her fists under the table.

Peter said, "A thirty percent reduction in alimony and a ten percent—"

Rachel snapped her head around and glowered straight into his eyes. "Are you freaking kidding me?" Her heart hammered as adrenaline flooded her body, preparing her for fight or flight.

"The way I figure it, with your increased earnings and the rent you get from the apartment, even after these reductions, you should still be clearing more than you were four years ago when the amounts were set."

"You'd do this to Wes, would you? Your own son?"

Claire spoke with a nasal whine that made Rachel want to hit her every time she opened her mouth. "Peter gave you the freaking house. We had to start out with nothing. *Nothing!*"

Rachel prayed there spontaneous combustion was real, but no matter how much she wished for it, Claire refused to burst into flames.

With dead eyes, Rachel stared at the woman. "That wasn't generosity, that was guilt. I got the house because some skank lured my husband away from me and his disabled son."

Peter held Claire's hand as she leaned forward to say something. He said, "Please, Rachel. If we can keep this civil, it will be much easier for all of us."

"Civil?" Rachel snorted a laugh. "Have I missed something? Because last I heard, your pay had gone up too, not down."

Peter glanced at Claire who nodded to him.

He said, "Look, I didn't want to tell you like this, but Claire and I are expecting, and to support our new family, I need to lower my payments to you. I'm sorry, but I'm sure you understand, considering the circumstances."

"Expecting? Well, let's pray this time you're lucky and get a keeper. Or does Claire appreciate that she and her kid are disposable assets if they aren't perfect?"

Claire nudged Peter. "Are you going to let her speak to us like that?"

Peter held a finger up for her to wait. "Greg?"

"Ms. Taylor, if you'll allow me. The alimony you receive is based on an agreement ironed out between you and Peter, not something upon which a judge ruled. Should this go to court now, in light of Peter and Claire's altered circumstances, I believe you'd find any judgment vastly inferior to that being generously offered by my client. Not least because you now seem to be developing a successful career of your own. A court may even rule that you need no support whatsoever."

Rachel repeatedly clenched and unclenched her fists underneath the table. Finally, she gulped hard. "Well, my thanks to the" — she sneered — "'bystander' for sharing his wisdom. Now, if you'll allow me to respond..."

Greg said, "Of course."

Rachel felt jittery, as if her whole body was shaking. The last thing she wanted was to show weakness, so she drew a long, slow breath. She stared into Peter's eyes. "After careful deliberation, it seems you've left me with little choice, so I'd like to accept your suggestion—"

Peter smiled. "Excellent."

"—of seeing how a judge will rule under the" — she glanced at Greg — "Uniform Marriage and Divorce Act, was it?"

He nodded.

She drilled her gaze into Peter again. "We'll see how a judge will rule when the amount of full-time care needed to look after *your* son is taken into consideration."

Rachel stood. "See you in court." Forcing herself not to run wailing from the room in floods of tears, she strode for the door. "Oh, and congratulations, by the way." Glowering at Claire, she added, "Fingers crossed there's no horrendous tearing." She grimaced. "Things are never the same down there after that."

As she reached for the door, Peter said, "I'll give you full custody."

Rachel froze. That would make life so much easier.

She didn't even turn around. "That's very big of you, Peter, considering how much you care for our son."

"One-time offer, Rachel."

She stared at him with the same dead eyes. "Tell me, how old is Wes? No, forget that. That's way too difficult. What color are his eyes? Have a guess. You've got more or less a fifty-fifty chance."

When they'd split up, Peter had fought for equal custody rights. She'd thought it strange that after fighting so ferociously, he'd taken so little interest in his own flesh and blood. Had this been his plan all along? To use Wes as no more than a bargaining chip to screw her over at some point?

Peter nodded to Greg, who opened his briefcase and slipped a document across the table. "In return for a thirty percent cut in alimony, plus a ten percent reduction in child support, my client is prepared to waive all rights, giving you sole custody."

She stared at the document. She'd never again have to run to Peter with any of Wes's medical issues, never have to consult him concerning the boy's education, never have to consider his opinions on Wes's future...

Chapter 22

Rachel hurried along the main street past a food truck displaying a giant glowing hot dog. Full custody was the proverbial dream come true. Not only because it meant Wes's future was completely in her hands now, but because it delivered two incredible blessings: no more Peter, no more Claire. However, it had come at a hellish price.

When she'd joked with Izzy about a rent increase, it had been met with complete horror. Not surprising – working in a New Age store in a small town didn't bode well for Izzy's financial situation. The trouble was, Izzy was her best friend. Rachel snickered. Her life was so consumed by work and Wes, Izzy was her only friend. If she lost Izzy, her world would crumble. She'd be as cut off as Wes.

Her phone rang. Caller ID: unknown.

She ducked under the red awning of a clothes boutique, the window mannequins presenting items she didn't – and now probably never could – have in her wardrobe.

Rachel answered it, "Hello."

"Hi, Ms. Taylor? This is Kate Branigan from Gold Cloud Press."

Talk about timing. If this was good news about the commission, it would solve everything.

"Oh, hi. And, please, it's Rachel."

"Hi, Rachel. Is this a good time to talk?"

Izzy had been due back at work ten minutes ago. "Yes, fine."

"Well, first, let me say what a fabulous job you've done in bringing *The Dragon Princess* to life. I mean *wow*."

Rachel caught her reflection in the window – she was smiling from ear to ear. "It's a great book, so I'm pleased you're happy with how I interpreted it."

"Anyhoo, I just wanted to touch base, since it will be me giving you notes."

"Notes?" Her smile vanished. Notes was a polite way of saying "this isn't right, fix it."

"Don't panic. There's nothing drastic. Just minor revisions."

Rachel gave a nervous laugh. "Oh, thank heavens. For a moment, I was worried you were going to say you'd reconsidered those other commissions."

"Other commissions?"

"When I showed Mike my portfolio and some drafts for *The Dragon Princess*, he said if this project went well, there'd be a number of others we could discuss."

"Mike's no longer with Gold Cloud."

Rachel gulped. "No?"

"No, he landed a gig with HarperCollins. Great, huh?"

She slumped against the window. "Yeah. Good for him."

"Anyhoo, I wanted to introduce myself so when you get the notes, you know it's not some heartless monster criticizing your work but a person who genuinely believes in you and your talent."

Rachel fought to sound upbeat, but even to her, her voice sounded thin. "Very considerate. Thank you."

"You're welcome, Rachel. Be in touch. *Ciao.*"

The line went dead before Rachel could say goodbye.

She heaved away from the glass. The woman in the reflection looked so drawn, so beaten, so lost.

Ninety minutes ago, she'd been financially secure with a lucrative future with a respected publishing house. How had it all gone so wrong so quickly?

Stumbling along, she tramped over a crosswalk, passed a fire hydrant, and entered the park through the black wrought-iron gates. She felt like she was in a nightmare where she had to run from something bad, but her legs wouldn't work. Her future was slipping from her. Hers and Wes's. Yet no matter how hard she ran to catch it, it was always just beyond reach.

Rachel trudged along a gently curving path. Ahead, Izzy and Wes sat on two black benches near a willow, its bare drooping branches like streams of wooden tears. Holding the harness strap, Izzy lounged on one bench while Wes hunched over a burger and fries on the adjoining one to give him the space he demanded.

Izzy met her gaze. As if sensing something was wrong, she hooked the strap over one of the bench's slats and met Rachel halfway.

"I'm sorry I'm late, Iz, but..." Rachel's bottom lip trembled, so she clenched her teeth to hold in the tears.

Izzy hugged her. "Hey, come on. Things can't be that bad."

Rachel's chest jerked as she stifled her sobs, resting her head against Izzy's shoulder.

Izzy rubbed her back. "Forget Captain Doofus and whatever he's done — you've still got me and Wes."

"For now." Rachel gripped Izzy, her fingers clawing into her friend's black jacket. What if she had to increase the rent, so Izzy moved out?

"For now? Hey, I'm not going anywhere, Rach."

"Thanks, Iz. Look, you're already late, so you should get going."

"I don't like leaving you like this."

Rachel dragged the back of her hand across her eyes. "I'll be okay. Go."

Walking backward, Izzy said, "We'll talk tonight, yeah?"

"Yeah. Thanks for everything."

"Later." Izzy called out, "So long, Wes."

Wes didn't even look up.

As Izzy disappeared up the path, Rachel plodded to the bench and picked up the strap. "Hi, Wes. Sorry it took so long, but I bet you had a good time with Izzy, didn't you?"

He munched on a fry. When he took another from the container, instead of eating it, he appeared to place it on the side of the bench Rachel couldn't see. He then took another one, which he ate, while the next he put beside him.

Rachel groaned, rubbing her forehead. She had enough problems without Wes developing another weird quirk she'd have to live with for the next fifty years.

She stood and peered over. Wes put a fry in his mouth and then dropped the next one between the bench's slats. Rachel took a step to get a better angle.

A filthy black-and-white dog lay under Wes's bench. Oh, no.

She calmly said, "Wes?"

Ignoring her, he fed the stray again.

"Wes?"

Still nothing.

84

She spoke through gritted teeth. "Wesley."

Immediately, he looked toward her, keeping his face down to avoid making eye contact. His full first name was a safe word — he knew whatever she was saying was so important it demanded his full attention.

She beckoned him. "Wesley, stop feeding the dog and walk over here."

"He's hungry." Wes dropped another fry to the dog.

Rachel tottered back, clutching her mouth. Wes had flouted the golden rule — to do whatever she said when using his full first name. But more than that, what he'd said showed empathy for another living being. Every therapist he'd ever seen had sworn he'd never be capable of that.

She laughed. She ached to hug him, to whoop, to grab a passerby and dance, but she simply stared, smiling at her incredible son.

Unfortunately, she had no choice but to cut short this beautiful moment — the last thing she needed was a stray dog latching onto them because they'd fed it. The sooner they escaped, the better.

"It's wonderful you're concerned about the dog, Wes, but we have to go. However, if you'd like to leave it the rest of your burger so it won't be hungry anymore, I'll buy you another one on the way home."

Wes laid his half-eaten burger and fries on the ground and shuffled to her.

"Thank you, Wes." Holding his strap, she guided him along the path. "And I'm sure the dog says thank you, too."

Ahead, four teenagers emerged from the trees and swaggered along the path toward her.

She glanced back. The dog had crawled from under the bench and was wolfing down the meal.

As the teenagers closed on them, a tall one in the leather jacket pointed and laughed at Wes. His friends laughed, too.

Sauntering over, Leather Jacket said, "Taking your pet for a walk, huh?"

Blocking the path, his friends laughed, thereby, egging him on.

The blood drained from Rachel's face. Gripping the strap, she stepped onto the grass to guide Wes around the gang.

Leather Jacket blocked her way.

Avoiding eye contact, she said, "I'm sorry, but can I get by, please?"

She gulped. She ached to yell at anyone who made themselves feel big by picking on someone like Wes — scum — but instead, she stared at the ground, her knuckles white on the strap.

"Get by? Of course. After you tell me where you bought your pet, because my sister loves animals and her birthday's coming up."

Rachel stepped back, ensuring she was between Wes and this teenage thug. Her legs shook so much, she feared they'd give.

She swallowed hard. "Look, I don't want any trouble. I just want to take my son home."

Leather Jacket smirked. "Who's looking for trouble? We aren't. Are we, guys?" The boys backed him up. "See. There ain't gonna be no trouble... so long as you've got a license for that thing." He stabbed a finger at Wes.

Rachel wanted to snap it off and feed it to him. She glanced at his friends, hoping one might do the decent thing and call off their attack dog. But none of them did.

Her mouth so dry she couldn't swallow, she turned to leave the park by another exit but froze.

The dog had crept up behind them. In the middle of the path, it snarled, baring its fangs as though it was going to tear her to shreds.

Under her breath, Rachel said, "Oh, dear Lord, help us."

Without a word, the thugs backed away. She drew a sharp breath as realization hit her — the dog wasn't snarling at her and Wes but at these teenage delinquents. This was her chance to escape.

With a stern glare, she said, "Wesley, move. Now."

She guided him past the gang, who, after their initial fright, surged forward. They shouted at the dog, cursed at it, surrounded it, and kicked at it. The dog gnashed at them as they lurched around it, just beyond reach.

When she and Wes reached the trees, she glanced back. Leather Jacket swung his backpack off and pulled out an alloy baseball bat.

"Don't look, Wes." She hauled him into the trees and out of sight.

A heart-wrenching yelp sliced through the park.

The dog would run. It would run, so it would be okay. Besides, it wasn't her responsibility. She had enough problems.

Another yelp. She cringed.

Clutching her head, she stopped. She couldn't do this. No way.

She unlatched the strap from Wes's harness. "Wesley, you are not to move from this spot. Promise me. You are not to move. Understand?"

He nodded.

Gasping huge breaths, her heart rate rocketing, Rachel stormed back down the path.

The thugs had gathered around a bench, kicking under it and stabbing with sticks. Stooping, Leather Jacket jabbed his bat into the shadows. The dog yelped again.

Rachel rooted in her purse, then ran over. She shouted, "Hey!"

Leather Jacket turned.

She sprayed hairspray into his face. He dropped his bat and clutched his eyes, wailing.

Flashing her hand in front of them, she swung a small can of hairspray, hoping none would realize what it was.

"Anyone else want to be maced?" She glowered at them.

They backed off, dragging their spluttering, blinded friend away.

Rachel reached under the bench. "Bite me and I'll let them loose on you again."

She clicked the strap to the dog's collar, hauled him out, and scurried away. She prayed Wes had stayed where she'd left him. If he'd wandered away, God forbid near that road...

She shook her head. This was crazy. Putting her son at risk over some mangy stray.

Whether the animal knew she'd rescued it and was appreciative or it was simply too frightened — or stupid — to do anything else, she didn't know, but it meekly trotted alongside her into the trees.

"Oh, thank God." She clutched her chest. Wes was exactly where she'd left him.

Together, they dashed through the town to her car. Once there, she belted Wes into his usual place in the right back seat, then laid a plaid picnic blanket over the rest of the seat. Heaven only knew where the dog had been, because it stank like week-old garbage. Satisfied she'd done all she could to protect her car, she patted the seat.

The dog jumped in and politely sat, as if traveling by car was an everyday occurrence.

From the driver's seat, she leaned over and fastened the strap to the back door armrest to ensure the dog couldn't jump on her while she was driving.

"Are you okay, Wes?"

No answer.

Considering the strange circumstances, he was being surprisingly calm. In fact, too calm. Especially with the dog encroaching on his personal space. She'd seen this behavior before. It was the eye of the storm — Wes suffered something traumatic, was perfectly calm for a while, then suddenly exploded.

"Wesley, are you okay?"

Without looking at her, he nodded.

"I'm sorry the dog is so close, but I can't risk having it in the front because it could panic and cause a crash. Understand?"

He nodded again.

She slumped in her seat. She ran three miles every day and barely broke a sweat, yet the last ten minutes had drained her as if she'd run a marathon.

They set off.

Every few hundred yards, she checked the rearview mirror. Each time, she was amazed to see Wes calmly gazing out of the window as if it was a perfectly normal day.

Pulling up to a red light, she glanced at him and gasped — he was smiling. She hit the brake and twisted around. The dog had laid its head in his lap.

"Wes, are you okay?"

He said nothing. Did nothing. Except beam from ear to ear.

Rachel swallowed hard as tears welled at the joy on her son's face. A horn blared behind her, the light green, so she hit the gas.

She could barely stop checking on her son as she drove. Her smiling son. She couldn't remember the last time he'd smiled. Not the occasion. Not the year.

Another horn blared. She shot her gaze to the road — she was straddling the line dividing two lanes. She swerved into the correct one but couldn't resist another glance in the mirror.

A thought brought her crashing back to reality — when Wes was so happy, how was she going to break the news that they weren't keeping the dog?

Chapter 23

Back home, Rachel clicked through the TV channels. "Come on, come on."

She didn't like leaving a strange dog in her car — it could be chewing or peeing or heaven knew what. Finally finding a wildlife documentary for Wes, she slung the TV remote into the armchair and dashed outside.

The dog wagged its tail when she opened the car door.

She grimaced, unfastening the strap tied to the armrest. "Eeew, I don't know where you've been, but good grief, you reek."

Leading the dog in, she said, "You better enjoy having a bath because no way are you staying inside otherwise."

The dog calmly strolled in and up the staircase beside her, gazing around at its new surroundings but appearing unfazed. He seemed way too comfortable indoors to have lived on the street for long, so maybe dealing with him wouldn't be a problem.

In the bathroom, he remained calm, politely standing and looking at her as if expecting her to do or say something.

"Any chance you're going to get in on your own, boy?" She patted the bathtub.

The dog clambered in.

"Wow." She sniggered. "I did *not* expect that. Are you going to shampoo yourself, too?"

The dog wagged his tail.

Taking the shower hose, Rachel waited for the water to reach a suitable temperature, then shampooed him. He stood politely, as if he was enjoying the massage.

Washing him, she found a name tag on his collar that had been hidden by his long fur: *Harley, 612 Ridgemount Drive, 555-7542.*

"Harley, huh?"

He barked and beat his tail, splashing water.

She ruffled the fur on his head. "Pleased to meet you, Harley."

He barked again.

"Like hearing your name, huh? Well, Harley, I'm sure you'll like it even more when you're back on Ridgemount Drive with your owner saying it."

As she washed his left shoulder, he flinched as if in pain. Thank heavens she'd rescued him in the park when she had or it could have been much worse, the poor thing.

Shampooing done, she rinsed him, being extra careful with his left leg.

He'd defended her and Wes in the park, so the least she could do was get him home. And the sooner the better. The last thing she needed was Wes getting the impression he was staying. Forty-eight hours max. Then the dog was gone, one way or another.

She smiled, thinking of how happy Wes had looked in the car. With the boy's personal space issues, his demands for a regimented routine, and a whole host of likes and dislikes, she'd always believed the problems of pet ownership far outweighed any benefits, but maybe not. Though a pet as large as Harley was out of the question. Maybe a hamster.

After drying Harley with a cream towel as best she could, she leaned in and sniffed — coconut. "Well, that's a big improvement, boy, I can tell you."

She patted the rim of the bath again and Harley jumped out. He shook himself, spraying water everywhere.

Rachel recoiled, shielding herself with her arms. She laughed. "Smart, Rach. Real smart."

When she turned back, Harley was sitting on his haunches and gazing up at her, as if awaiting instruction.

She opened the door. "Come on."

Harley ambled out.

On the living room TV, three female lions ran down a wildebeest. Wes didn't look up when she strolled in, but when Harley meandered across and sat beside the coffee table, he couldn't take his gaze off the dog. Harley glanced at him, then peered around the room as if studying the place.

Rachel looked on the coffee table for the TV remote to turn the volume down so she could call Harley's owner, but it wasn't there. She checked her place on the sofa, picking up the pillow to make sure it hadn't fallen behind it, then scoured the floor.

"Wes, do you have the TV remote?"

No answer.

"Wes, TV remote?"

He didn't take his eyes off the dog.

"TV remote. Wes, have you seen the TV remote?"

No response. Until...

Harley padded to the armchair, then padded back with the TV remote in his mouth. He sat on the floor in front of Rachel, head up, as if presenting the remote as a gift.

Her mouth agape, Rachel stared at him. "What the...?"

Wes laughed and clapped, as if he'd seen an amazing magic trick.

Rachel looked at the dog with the TV remote in its jaws, then her son with a beaming smile. What was happening? It was like something out of *The Twilight Zone*.

She didn't want to touch a remote slathered in dog saliva, so took a tissue from her pocket and used that to hold one end. Once her fingers closed around it, Harley let go.

She inspected it – no tooth marks, no spittle. Frowning, she said, "Thank you, Harley."

Harley wagged his tail.

Rachel looked at the TV remote, then the dog, then the chair, then back to the dog. It had to be a fluke. Surely.

She strolled over and tossed the device into the chair again, then returned to the sofa.

After a few moments, she said, "TV remote."

Instantly, Harley retrieved the device and presented it to her.

Wes giggled and again applauded the feat. Rachel laughed too. This was unbelievable. Possibly the most incredible thing she'd ever seen.

"Shall we try him again, Wes?"

Wes nodded, grinning.

Waving the remote in the air so Harley got a good look at what she was doing, Rachel placed it on the island in the kitchen and returned to her seat. "TV remote."

Harley trotted into the kitchen, limping slightly on his left foreleg. So it was hurt. He rose onto his hind legs, took the remote in his mouth, then trotted back and sat on the floor to present it.

Rachel and Wes laughed. And the more he laughed, the more she did. She couldn't remember a time they'd shared laughter like this. Ever.

She took the device and offered it to Wes. "Do you want to try?"

His eyes popped wide and he beamed. He nodded.

Wes wandered into the kitchen and did a figure eight around the island and the table. He meandered back to circle the living room armchair before heading to the kitchen again and placing the remote on the top of the stainless-steel trashcan.

Retaking his seat, he said, "TV remote."

With no hesitation, Harley retrieved the device and presented it to Wes. Wes clapped, giggling and giggling.

Rachel cupped her face, laughing. She hadn't intended to tell Wes the dog's name because keeping the animal anonymous was a way to stave off attachment, but maybe she was missing a trick — before returning the dog, she could test how well Wes would cope with a pet.

"His name is Harley, Wes. Harley. He has to be the smartest dog in the world, doesn't he?"

Wes nodded.

"You're a smart boy, Harley, aren't you? The smartest I've ever seen." She turned to Wes. "Do you think he could fetch me a beer?"

Nodding, Wes laughed.

"Harley, can you fetch me a beer, huh? Fetch a beer?"

Harley wandered to the kitchen.

Rachel pointed, eager to keep the fun going with her son. "Look, Wes, he's going for one."

Harley clamped his jaws around the refrigerator handle and opened it.

Her jaw dropped. "No freaking way."

He stuck his head inside.

The open door blocked what he was doing, but no way on earth could he be looking for a can of beer. That was beyond freaky. That was entering the realm of... miracles.

Harley shuffled backward out of the refrigerator, nudged the door with his shoulder, and wandered over to her. He sat before her and presented her with a cool can of beer.

Rachel froze, mouth agape.

***

Three hours later, Rachel peered from her front door. A blue bus rumbled past, and a minute later, Izzy trudged toward the house.

"Iz!" Rachel beckoned her. "Quick."

Izzy sped up. Approaching the door, she said, "Someone's feeling a lot happier."

"You've got to see this. We've been testing him all afternoon. It's unbelievable. Seriously. Un-freaking-believable."

Izzy shot her a puzzled glance. "What's going on?"

Rachel pulled her inside. "You've just got to see it for yourself."

Harley was sitting in the living room, all manner of things dotted around him: slippers, books, a landline phone, cans...

"Awww, you've got a dog?" Izzy smiled. "You never said you were getting a dog."

"I haven't. Well, I have kind of, but not really. Look, it's a long story." She pushed Izzy toward the armchair. "Sit."

"Okay, okay." Izzy took her seat, frowning. "What's wrong with Wes?"

"What?"

"He's smiling. What's going on?"

"That's part of it. But I can't tell you. You've just got to see it."

Izzy shrugged. "Okay, so let me see it."

Rachel took her seat and turned to Wes. "Shall we let Izzy have a turn?"

Wes nodded.

Rachel snagged her phone from the coffee table. "I'm sending you a text, Iz. When you get it, say exactly those words, and nothing more, in a clear, loud voice."

"A text? Can't you just tell me?"

"No, because then it will happen. Seriously, you have to see it for yourself."

"Okay."

Rachel sent the text. "Those words, Iz. Nothing more."

An alert sounded on Izzy's phone. She checked it and then, looking at the dog, said, "Harley, fetch a beer."

Harley sauntered into the kitchen. Izzy looked at Rachel.

Rachel pointed at the dog. "Watch."

Using the scarf Rachel had tied to the handle to give him a better grip, Harley opened the refrigerator, retrieved a can of beer, and trotted over to present it to Izzy.

Izzy clutched her mouth. Her eyes as big as saucers, her gaze shot to Rachel, then to Wes, then back to Harley.

Finally, she said, "Are you freaking serious?" She laughed — a belly laugh like a drunken sailor at a comedy club. Taking the beer, she scrutinized it, shook it as if to see if it was real, and then laughed again.

Calming down, Izzy said, "That's the most amazing thing. Can he do it again?"

"Try."

Izzy chuckled, wiping her eyes, then composed herself by sitting up straight and clearing her throat. "Harley, fetch a beer."

Harley fetched another beer.

Presented with her beer, Izzy shrieked with laughter, slapping her thigh with delight.

Izzy gazed about the room. "Am I being punked?"

Rachel rolled her eyes. "Yeah, that's what's happening. I get so bored with all the free time I have, I couldn't resist spending years training a dog in secret just to dupe you like this."

"Can he do anything else?"

"He made Wes a PB&J sandwich."

Izzy's eyes widened. "Really?"

"Nooo. He's a dog. Come on."

"You say that, but have you tried? Until today, I'd have said dogs couldn't fetch beer from a closed refrigerator."

Rachel said, "He's fetched a book, my phone, the TV remote, and all sorts of stuff that we've shown him or he knows the name of. Wes, do you want to show Izzy what Harley can do?"

Wes didn't look at her, but he turned toward her. "Can I?"

"Of course. Why don't you leave your footwear behind the sofa."

Wes moseyed behind the sofa.

Izzy frowned at Rachel, mouthing, "He's talking?"

Grinning, Rachel nodded.

Wes shuffled off his sneakers and picked them up. "Harley? Sneakers. Sneakers."

The dog studied Wes.

Wes put them behind the sofa and returned to his seat. "Harley, fetch my sneakers."

Wagging his tail, Harley ambled around and brought the sneakers back. Wes beamed as if he'd achieved something spectacular, too.

"Well done, Wes," said Rachel. The boy's smile widened, but he didn't look at her.

"Yeah, that's amazing, Wes." Izzy shook her head, gazing at Harley. "So where did he come from?"

"He was a stray. Some teenage thugs decided to pick on Wes in the park, and Harley came to our rescue. The least we could do was rescue him."

"A stray?"

"Well, a stray or just plain lost. There's contact info on his name tag."

"Have you phoned yet? There must be a doozy of a reward for a supersmart dog like this."

"I got a machine, so left my details."

Izzy ruffled the fur on either side of Harley's neck. "Wow. What a dog you are, Harley."

Rachel said, "I just don't get how he can do it. Unless he was a circus dog or something."

"Aliens."

"Oh, you blame everything on aliens."

"Well, what do you want me to say?"

Rachel held her arms out. "I don't know. I just don't get how I can say 'TV remote' or 'beer' and a dog magically brings me those things. How is that possible? It's like he has superpowers."

"Maybe he developed powers after being bitten by a radioactive bug."

"He's a dog, Izzy, not Spider-Man."

"So he's the next step in evolution. Some mutated gene has heightened his abilities."

Rachel shook her head, smirking at her friend. "That's the X-Men. Izzy, do you do anything except stream movies on the weekend? But seriously, how can he do it? He's just a dog. A great dog, but, come on, a dog's a dog. They do dog things. They don't..."

"Act as your butler?"

"Exactly. Who has a dog that fetches them beer?"

"I'm gonna stick with aliens."

Rachel glared.

"What? It's the only logical explanation."

"Logical?"

"Well, it's more than you've got!"

And it was.

"Oh, I know — he escaped from a secret lab after being given some experimental treatment," said Izzy.

Rachel slapped her forehead. "That's *Planet of the Apes.* You ever think of picking up a book, Iz?"

"I tell you, if your days were crammed with shamanism, Kundalini energy, Zen Buddhism, cosmic ordering, Wicca... you'd crave some light relief on weekends, too."

"Fair point."

Izzy leaned forward and sniffed. "For a stray, he smells gorgeous."

Rachel laughed. "He does now. You should've smelled him when we found him. I'll be lucky if my car doesn't reek for weeks."

"So what are you going to do with him?"

She shrugged. "Wait for the owner to get in touch."

"And if they don't?"

Rescuing Harley had been something of a knee-jerk reaction, being the only decent thing to do in the circumstances. Then, when she'd found a collar with a tag, his future had seemed sealed. But what if the owner didn't phone?

Izzy said, "You could keep him."

Rachel snickered. "Yeah, right. Like I don't have enough responsibilities already. No, if I hear nothing in the next couple of days, I'll contact a shelter about having him rehomed. He's a handsome dog with some amazing talents, so someone's going to love him."

Izzy arched an eyebrow and gestured with her eyes. "I think someone already does."

With a delicate touch and a beaming smile, Wes stroked Harley's head.

Forty-eight hours. That was it. Any more than that, and the wrench would be too much for Wes. And maybe not only Wes.

Chapter 24

As Wes scratched Harley's head, Harley gazed into the boy's eyes, which were partially hidden by long brown bangs. He liked Wes. Not just because the boy had given him food but because he seemed the type of person who'd have needs. And nothing provided a better purpose than fulfilling someone's needs.

Harley tipped his head, so Wes scratched behind his ear, just how he liked it. From the corner of his eye, he glanced at Rachel. He liked her too. She'd saved him from those nasty teenagers, but more than that, she seemed a genuinely caring person. Maybe it was because of how patient and protective she was with the boy. She obviously liked having a purpose too.

Twisting to let Wes scratch his other ear, Harley eyed Izzy. He'd only just met her, but already liked her — when she laughed, she roared just like Barney.

On arrival, he'd wondered why they'd brought him here, but over the past few hours, the reason had become clear — they were incapable of looking after themselves. He'd lost count of the number of items he'd retrieved for them. Sometimes he'd found the same thing over and over because they'd put it down and instantly forgotten where it was. He must have fetched more things today than he did in a week for Barney.

Yes, these people were nice. Dim, but nice.

Chapter 25

Fifteen minutes earlier than she usually got up, Rachel yawned, wandering down the hallway to the internal door to the garage. She turned the handle, cringing at what would be waiting on the concrete floor: chewed tools, broken patio furniture, puddles of urine — or worse.

Crossing her fingers, she peeked in and clicked on the light.

She raised her eyebrows. "Oh."

Other than the black stain from an oil leak, the floor was clean. Her tools hung on the pegboard, her exercise bike stood in its usual spot, and the decorating supplies she'd bought for Wes's room sat in a neat stack. Everything was in its place.

"Well, aren't you a good boy, Harley?"

Harley wagged his tail, sitting on the folded brown blanket she'd laid on the floor as a makeshift bed.

She clicked the harness strap to his collar, then opened the back door.

"Do you need to pee, Harley?" She stood aside for him to go out. The security light illuminated a small paved area where she kept her trash cans, sectioned off from her yard by a stone wall.

He looked at her.

He'd eaten Wes's food in the park, plus some ground beef she'd bought for chili, washed down with a bowl of water. He'd definitely need to relieve himself. So why wasn't he?

When she'd given him the beef last night, despite gazing at it and drooling, he hadn't touched it until she'd given him the go-ahead by patting the plate, saying, "Food, Harley. Food." He seemed to love following instructions.

"Pee, Harley. Pee."

Nothing.

"Harley, wee. Wee."

Still nothing.

He was a supersmart dog, but was he super literate as well? It was worth a shot. "Urinate. Urinate, Harley."

He couldn't look less interested.

Rachel cringed, hoping it wasn't something vulgar she was going to have to say. "Whiz. Whiz."

No response.

"Peepee," "number one," and "piddle" all drew a blank too.

"Leak, Harley. Do you want to take a leak?"

Harley walked over to the stone wall and peed against it.

Mystery solved.

As he toddled back, she had another idea.

Twenty minutes later, after reminding Izzy to pick up some kibble on her lunch hour, Rachel activated her watch's heart rate monitor, then set off for her morning exercise. Harley trotted alongside at the end of two straps latched together so he wouldn't get under her feet.

At the oak, she started her stopwatch and broke into a run. Harley matched her speed but frowned at her, seemingly delighted, yet confused. From his physique, it was obvious he'd been exercised, but maybe his owner had only thrown stuff, never run with him.

Harley barked, then put his head down and shot forward, as if testing her. So much for having a bad leg!

"Are you calling me slow, dog?" She kicked up a gear. "I'll show you slow."

As she ran alongside, he once more barked up at her, as if to say, "Nice one, girl."

They raced down the side of the road, the light on Rachel's forehead illuminating their way.

At the incline, Harley barely seemed to notice the extra effort needed, maintaining his pace while appearing to breathe no harder. It was as if his breed was built to run. Her thigh muscles burning, she dug deep to push on with him. Two-thirds of the way up, she slowed, gasping for breath and desperate to give her screaming legs a break.

Harley tugged on the straps, begging to run on. Rachel grimaced, gritted her teeth, and drove for the crest of the hill.

Sweat running down her face, she broke over the brow and punched the air with a gasped, "Yes!"

Harley barked and spun in a circle, as if he knew there was something to celebrate.

Panting, she strode into the rest area. While she did her sets of push-ups, stomach crunches, and squat jumps, Harley ran around her, yipping, as if offering encouragement.

The route back was always easier, being mostly downhill. The cold air biting her face, Rachel pumped hard, refusing to coast down the incline when her partner was so eager to run. On the flat final leg, she pushed all the more, desperate to finish as strongly as she'd started. She sprinted. Together, they flew past the oak tree she used as a finish.

She clicked off her stopwatch and slowed to a fast walk. Her chest heaving, she checked the time.

"Whoa." She froze, gazing at her watch. She'd slashed two minutes thirty-eight seconds off her best time.

In her driveway, she did her stretches, then went inside.

"Was it okay with the dog?" said Izzy, kicking back on the sofa with a magazine and a glass of OJ.

"Okay?" Still breathing heavily, Rachel said, "Man, we had a fantastic run. Didn't we, boy?" She patted Harley.

Harley licked her hand.

Izzy arched an eyebrow. "We? Aren't 'we' praying the owner calls and collects him today?"

"Yeah. Why?"

"At this rate, it won't just be Wes's heart that's broken when Harley leaves."

"Don't be silly."

"So you're not getting attached already? Because it kinda looks that way."

Rachel held her arms wide. "We had a run, is all. No big deal."

"I hope not, Rach. It's not like you're having the best of weeks as it is."

"So it can only get better." Rachel headed for the shower. So she'd enjoyed running Harley. So she and Wes had shared a special moment yesterday because of Harley. All that proved was that having a pet one day was something to consider. *One day.* Not today.

After she showered and got Wes up, they dawdled into the living room.

Harley was stretched out on the blue rug near the coffee table. In the armchair, Izzy said, "He hasn't moved, so there was no need to worry."

"It's good to know he can be left alone. Thanks, Iz."

"You're welcome." Izzy headed for the door. "Later."

"Don't forget that kibble, please."

"The biggest bag I can find, or one that'll last just a few days?" Rachel tilted her head.

Izzy smirked. "Just checking." She left.

Wes couldn't take his gaze off Harley while eating his cornflakes and toasted muffin, so breakfast took twice as long as normal.

After, they completed their usual early-morning routine and then took their places at the lessons desk. Harley moseyed over and sat at the side between them. Rachel had hoped he'd go back to the rug so as not to cause a distraction.

She gripped Harley's collar. "I'll put him in the garage for a couple of hours."

"No!" Wes lunged to grab her wrist but pulled away before making contact.

If Wes felt so strongly already, it might be wise to separate them as much as possible.

He said, "He'll be lonely in the garage."

Empathy again. She pursed her lips. This might be the worst mistake of her life, but...

"I... er, I suppose he can stay. But you have to promise to work and not look at him all the time. Okay?"

Wes nodded.

To the sound of waves shushing on a beach while gulls cawed overhead, she lined up three cups, showed Wes a green jelly bean, placed it under the middle cup, and switched the cups around. Wes watched, but his gaze drifted to the dog.

"Wesley."

He snapped back to her.

"Wesley, if you want Harley to stay, you must concentrate on the lesson. If you don't, he has to go in the garage. Understand?"

Wes nodded again.

"Okay. Let's try again." After showing him the jelly bean, she shuffled the cups.

"Which one?"

Wes moved his hand toward the far-left one but then pulled back. He leaned forward as if believing closer scrutiny would help.

Harley craned his neck and shoved the cup on the far right.

Wes pointed to that one.

Rolling her eyes, she lifted the cup, revealing the jelly bean. "Thank you, Harley."

Wes laughed and took the candy. Instead of eating it, he offered it to Harley, holding it between his thumb and forefinger.

Instinctively, Rachel caught his hand. "No!" Letting go, she cringed, waiting for an outburst because she'd dared to touch him, but it didn't come.

She placed a jelly bean in her palm and offered it to Harley. "You have to do it like this so he doesn't nip you by accident."

Harley gobbled it up.

"Do you want to try?"

The boy nodded, put the candy in his palm, and offered it to Harley, who again obliged.

Wes giggled as the cold nose and wet tongue caressed his hand.

"Another one, please." Wes held his hand out.

"What...?" She arched her eyebrows. "Er... of course."

Worrying over Harley being present wasn't misplaced, it was outright stupid — he could prove to be an excellent teaching aid.

She placed another jelly bean under a cup. "If you can find it, Wes, you can give it to Harley."

He straightened his back and slid his seat closer to pay as much attention as he could.

After shuffling the cups, she said. "Which is the jelly bean under, Wes?"

He hovered his hand over the cups while deciding, but Harley nudged the middle one.

Rachel slapped her forehead. She picked up the cup to reveal the candy, making Wes laugh again. A grin spread across Wes's face as Harley licked the candy from his palm.

Rachel rubbed her chin. Wes had never interacted like this. Never. If she played things right, it could elevate his education to a whole new level.

"Wes, shall we see how good Harley really is at finding jelly beans?"

He nodded. Rachel upturned two more cups, showed a candy to Harley, then put it under one and switched them around as quickly as she could. When she finished, she had no idea where the jelly bean was.

She lined the cups up along the side of the desk. "Harley."

He needed no more invitation; he nuzzled the second from his left. Sure enough, the candy was there. Wes clapped, then gave him the jelly bean.

"He's too good for me, Wes. Do you want to see if you can fool him?"

Wes's mouth gaped as if he didn't believe her.

"Really. You can do it."

She lined the cups up for him and handed him a candy. "Show Harley what he's looking for, then put it under a cup and mix them up."

Grinning, Wes showed the candy, then hid it. His hands moving slowly and jerkily, he switched the cups around. He squinted, focusing hard on doing the job well enough to trick Harley. Finally, he lined the cups up.

Rachel said, "Now say his name so he knows it's time to do his job."

"Harley."

Without hesitation, Harley nudged the middle cup.

"Is that the right one, Wes?"

The boy scratched his head, then lifted the cup. The candy was underneath it. He threw his hands up, then giggled, giving the candy to Harley.

"I'll tell you what, Wes, how about every time you get an answer right today, you can play the cups game with Harley?"

His eyes lit up and he nodded.

Rachel placed the roulette wheel before him. "Okay, then, spin the Wheel of Questions."

Wes's spin landed on "Describe" highlighted in green, so he rolled a large green die with an unusual numbering system, each side displaying not one number but two. It rested on "3 & 3."

Rachel said, "Good job, Wes. Now, describe three things about Harley using three different words each time."

Wes looked at the dog and, with barely any hesitation, said, "Wet black nose. Floppy, furry ears. Long waggy tail."

Rachel applauded. "Bravo. That was excellent, Wes. And so fast."

But he didn't care about compliments. He grabbed the cups, hid a candy, then shuffled the cups, sticking his tongue out as he concentrated.

Satisfied he'd shuffled enough, he said, "Harley."

Harley nudged the far-right cup. Wes cupped his hands to his mouth and giggled.

"Is that the right one?" asked Rachel.

He nodded and revealed the candy, which he gave to Harley.

"Good job, Harley." Wes leaned down and hugged him.

"Awww." Rachel clutched her chest, looking at them.

Her phone rang. She checked the caller ID — unknown number. Her heart leaped into her throat. What if it was Harley's owner? She was supposed to protect her son but had gotten so drawn in by him opening up. To lose Harley now would break Wes's heart.

Her stomach roiling, she glared at her phone. She did not want to answer it.

Chapter 26

Harley gazed through the car's window, raindrops spattering it. Behind a black metal fence sat a four-story red brick building surrounded by asphalt. A blond-haired woman standing under a red umbrella said something to Rachel and Wes. Harley couldn't hear what because of the distance and the children swarming about, laughing and chattering.

He whined. He loved seeing the joy in children's faces as he nuzzled and licked them. Air wafted in through a narrow gap at the top of the window, so he pawed it, but couldn't open it wider.

As if that wasn't bad enough, the blond-haired woman guided Wes toward the double glass doors at the front of the building.

Where was she taking Wes? The boy and Rachel were hopeless by themselves, so Harley should be with them constantly. Especially Wes.

Wes disappeared inside.

Harley whined. He had to find a way out. He lurched to squeeze between the front seats, but the strap tied to the armrest yanked him back. Pawing the window again, he whimpered. He'd only just found a new pack and a new purpose, yet already he was losing both. Why did everyone abandon him?

Rachel emerged through a gap in the fence and strolled toward the car. So he wasn't being abandoned? He wagged his tail. Though Rachel appeared to be the pack's alpha, she'd proven she needed his help almost as much as Wes. Harley yipped with excitement. Maybe he had a job to do and a purpose to fulfill after all.

Or maybe they were going for another run.

Harley barked at the thought of it.

Barney had let him run in the park but had never run with him. Harley had never known that people could run like Rachel. He'd seen kids run in the park, often falling over, and he'd seen people on the street attempt to run, only for their faces to turn red as they gasped for breath after barely going anywhere.

But Rachel? Running was like her superpower. And when he'd suggested it, she'd even run faster. She obviously loved it as much as he did. He barked once more. This could be the best day ever.

Sliding into the driver's seat, Rachel said, "Okay, let's see if we can get you home, Harley."

She pressed some buttons on the center console and a picture appeared on a small screen. The engine revved and the car moved off.

Barney had liked Harley to travel up front beside him, but Rachel seemed to like him in the back. Harley liked the back. People would probably think he was important to be lounging across this wide seat while his driver sat alone in the front.

Maybe that was why everyone had stared on the streets and in the mall — they'd recognized that he was special. He wasn't one to brag, but... he'd never seen any other dog do any of the jobs he did. They were all too busy running after balls, jumping for Frisbees, chasing birds, sniffing each other's butts... Okay, all that was great fun, but realistically, it was meaningless. It wasn't like his life would be empty without it. Well, except for the butt-sniffing — he was sophisticated, not crazy.

A woman's voice said, "At the traffic island, take the third exit."

Who was talking? Harley glanced about, but there was no one else. Rachel seemed completely oblivious to it. He sniffed, sifting through the scents for a person possibly hiding in the car.

Nothing.

Strange. Maybe it was someone outside.

A short distance from the red brick building, the bodiless voice said, "Take the third exit."

That woman again! And again, Rachel didn't respond, so obviously hadn't heard.

He gasped. Crazy. He must be going crazy. It was the only logical answer. Why else would he hear someone who wasn't there? Maybe the garbage truck had crushed his head and caused serious damage. Or the strike from the baseball bat had. Either way, something was horribly wrong.

As the car turned right, a small island with a single tree and a bush in the middle caught his eye. He gasped again, twisting to the rear windshield, where it was disappearing into the distance. Harley's jaw dropped.

That island!

He stared at Rachel. He'd thought he was helping her, but was it really her helping him? Was she taking him to Barney? His tail beat loudly against the seat back.

Rachel glanced in the mirror. "Seen something you know, Harley? Are you getting excited, boy?"

A familiar smell all but slapped Harley across the face. He sniffed the gap at the top of the window, then scanned the buildings lining the street. There! Inside one decorated in shades of blue, people sat at tables eating. Yes, that was where he'd gone with Barney for plates of meaty balls and pale yellow strings all smothered in red-brown sauce.

And there — a place Barney had bought one of his beloved boxes. When they'd gotten home, another silver box had magically appeared inside that box. Barney had put the silver box in the kitchen and stuffed food in it that came out warmer, but Harley had no idea what he'd done with the original.

The voice spoke again. "In 100 yards turn right."

The bodiless voice didn't speak a lot, which was good because she didn't sound much fun, her voice so emotionless. Thank heavens he'd found his purpose in helping Barney. To be so passionless, the bodiless person had obviously never done anything or met anyone to give their life meaning. What an awful existence that must be. The poor bodiless person.

"Turn right."

Again, Rachel didn't react. Why? She was caring. How could she be so cold to the bodiless person? Well, he'd let them know someone was listening. Make them feel they were worth something. Harley barked.

Rachel said, "We're getting close, are we, boy?"

Yes, when he and Barney visited his new friends, he'd help Rachel with her social etiquette and communication skills.

The car turned right. Harley pressed his nose to the gap again and savored the memories: the streetlight where the male German shepherd relieved himself ... the flowerbed in which the black-and-white cat buried her poop ... the maple where tiny black birds tweeted after the leaves appeared ... the bush under which the brown tom stopped...

Harley gasped. Home. Home. Home!

Chapter 27

"You have reached your destination," said the bodiless voice, just as the car stopped.

Rachel twisted to look at him. "Well, Harley? Is this home?"

Harley wagged his tail so hard it moved his whole body. Barney was going to love Rachel and Wes. Love them! He yipped.

Rachel laughed. "I take it that's a yes." She glanced at Barney's blue car in the drive. "Looks like they're home, Harley."

Her smile faded as she stroked him and her voice faltered, "You'll never know what you've given me, Harley. I hope your owner loves you as much as we would have."

Sniffling, she turned away. She stared into space in silence, then turned the car key partway. Letting go, she muttered under her breath.

Without warning, she slapped the steering wheel over and over and then slumped over the wheel, shaking her head.

Her voice quiet as though she wasn't talking to him, she said, "Get a grip, Rach. Just rip the Band-Aid off."

After wiping her eyes with her fingers, she glanced at him in the mirror. "You stay here and be good, Harley, while I see if someone's home."

Rachel got out and strode up the paved path that divided the lawn. At the front door, she gave the brass doorknocker three raps.

Sniffing through the gap, Harley studied the scents. He could smell the compost pile from across the street, someone cooking spiced chicken two doors down, and cold pizza the neighbor had tossed in the garbage yesterday. The scent he'd prayed for was missing: Barney hadn't been back.

He whimpered.

What if Rachel didn't want him and was abandoning him here? This wasn't a home anymore. It was just a box. A box both he and

108

Barney had loved, yes, but only because the other one was in it. Without Barney, the box was just a void.

Rachel peered at the windows. No light or sound came from within.

She banged the doorknocker again.

No one answered.

Rachel ambled back along the path, paused to slip an envelope into the ornate black aluminum mailbox standing on a pedestal, then headed for the car.

Oh no, she was coming for him. Coming to drag him away from his new life and strand him outside this deserted box. He whined and curled up in the corner of the seat. If he made himself small, maybe Rachel would forget he was there and take him with her.

Rachel yanked the door open. "Sorry, boy, but it's not your lucky day."

She clambered in. The car revved and pulled out.

He wasn't being left here? That meant Rachel wanted him to fulfill his purpose with her and the boy!

He barked.

Rachel glanced in her mirror. "Awww, I'm sorry, Harley. No one's there, and I can't just dump you on the sidewalk, can I?" She smiled. "Oh, I know what might cheer you up."

As if by magic, his window lowered with a gentle hum. Harley stuck his head out. The wind ruffled his fur and rain splattered his face with cold freshness. A never-ending tidal wave of smells washed over him — bird poop, pizza, a tree, oil, grass, a sweaty man, candy...

Tongue lolling out, he yipped.

After a few minutes, Rachel said, "Okay, Harley, that's enough. I don't want you catching a chill."

The window rose a couple of inches, so he pulled his head in. The window hummed all the way. Harley shook himself, water droplets spraying from his head and shoulders.

Rachel wailed, holding her right hand up to shield her face.

The rest of the ride back to Rachel's house was a joy after the trauma of believing he was going to be dumped in a house filled with nothing but memories. He hoped he could fetch lots of things to show how much he appreciated being there, but Wes wasn't home and Rachel busied herself in the study. She eased a metal box from under her desk, took the side off, and poked about inside. So she liked boxes as well.

Harley frowned. Maybe she and Barney knew each other. Maybe on those few occasions when Barney had gone out without him, he'd gone to a box collectors' club. That would explain why Harley never saw any of Barney's special boxes — they were so precious, Barney kept them in a secure location.

People were so strange. They filled the world with an endless array of magical things, and yet they were never more delighted than when someone gave them a new box to open. Sometimes they were even happy at what was inside the box, though not every time. Yes, nothing made people smile like being given a box.

But why were they so fascinating? Was he missing out on one of life's great pleasures?

He wandered over and stuck his nose in the metal box. He rolled his eyes — more tiny boxes. Lots of them. And wires. Lots of them too.

Rachel pushed him away. "Harley!"

He cringed. He loved hearing his name, but not when it was said with that tone. People only said it like that when they thought he'd been bad. And of all the things he tried to be, bad was never one of them. He devoted his life to being good. To helping anyone who needed help. That was his purpose. Wasn't that why Rachel had brought him back here?

He whimpered and shuffled away, tail between his legs. If he couldn't help people, he was worthless. He trudged out and plodded down the hall to the garage. Pawing the handle, he opened the door and sloped in and over to his blanket. He curled up. And whined.

Maybe that was why other dogs were content to do nothing but chase balls and jump for Frisbees. If people didn't believe in them enough to have them do jobs like he did, didn't appreciate the value a good dog could bring to their lives, then what else was there to do other than fritter life away on the most trivial of things? Maybe if he did that, people would love him instead of abandoning him.

A voice drifted down the hall. "Harley?"

He pricked his ears.

Closer. "Harley?"

Head on the blanket, he looked from the corner of his eye. Rachel peeped in.

"Awww, are you feeling sorry for yourself because I pushed you away?"

110

She'd just scolded him seconds ago, yet now she was using her happy voice. Why? Did her happy voice mean she was pleased he was upset? Or was she using it to make amends? Talk about mixed signals. People were such strange animals to understand.

Crouching, she stroked him. "I'm sorry, Harley, but my computer is fragile, and the last thing I need is you swallowing something and ending up at the vet."

She continued stroking. He was almost sure she was making amends. Almost.

"I know what will cheer you up." She stood. "Harley, TV remote."

He jerked up, muscles tensed for action. Had she just asked for help? He nuzzled her.

"TV remote."

A job! His claws scraping on the concrete floor, he shot out of the garage and along the hall. Gaze flashing around the living room as he ran in, he spied the TV remote on the coffee table. Angling his head, he eased his jaws around it.

What a day it was proving to be. A real roller coaster of emotions. This was going to be a wonderful place to live, if he could prove his worth to Rachel so she'd let him stay.

Chapter 28

"Harley, light switch," said Rachel, standing by the sofa.

Harley scampered over to the wall near the entrance, pushed onto his back legs, and swatted the light switch with a forepaw. Again.

Rachel crouched as Harley padded back. "Good boy."

Harley wagged his tail.

She scratched his chin. He seemed to get as much pleasure out of doing these little chores as ordinary dogs did out of chasing a ball. It was odd. But so endearing. Not to mention potentially useful, should she ever spend a day lying on the sofa in her PJs. Yeah, right. Like that was ever going to happen.

She patted his back. "Okay, boy, that's it. My computer isn't going to fix itself."

Harley trotted beside her as she ambled to the study. If she didn't complete repairs today, her work could grind to a halt for days. That was the last thing she needed after Peter's bombshell.

It was 11:45 a.m. That gave her barely three hours before she had to leave to pick up Wes from his class.

Following a video on her tablet, she fitted the new hard drive, screwed on the side panel, and slid the machine under her desk.

Sitting beside her, Harley watched as she reconnected the cables.

Crawling out from under her desk, she said, "Fingers crossed, Harley."

She hit the power button. The usual LEDs flashed on the unit, the fan whirred up to speed, and the boot-up screen appeared on her monitor.

She grinned. So far so good.

Now to install the operating system and essential software from her backup before downloading her files from the cloud. Easy, though boring and time-consuming. Still, it was infinitely better than paying some hacker scum thousands of dollars to use her own property.

To be sure she wouldn't lose track of time, she set an alarm on her phone for 2:40 p.m. before turning it off.

This was her one full day when someone else took care of Wes. Initially, she'd been a control freak, believing no one could give him the level of attention she could — even a class for special needs students. Talk about a rod for her own back. Unrelenting care, morning, noon, and night, was utterly draining. These days, she loved her Friday break, even if it consisted of dashing around to complete all the tasks she couldn't do with Wes present.

The benefits for her aside, however, it also wasn't healthy for Wes to be alone with her day in, day out. Prisoners serving life saw more people and more places than Wes did on an average day. While his personal space and social skills issues prevented him from interacting as much as she'd like with the other special needs kids, at least he was around them, seeing different faces and new things.

"Oops." She grabbed her phone and turned it back on — it was so ingrained to turn it off whenever she was at her desk. Most people had her landline number, but she'd only left her cell phone for Harley's owner.

Her being so anxious at seeing "Caller ID: unknown" the other day — which had been Tad recommending a brand of hard drive — had shown how attached they were already to Harley. She couldn't afford that.

Most people would consider hers and Wes's lifestyle unbearable, yet it had demanded years of hard work for them to come this far. Harley had coaxed Wes further out of his self-imposed isolation in a day than she'd managed in a decade. But when his owner took him away, what mess would she be left with to clean up?

Rachel connected her external hard drive to her machine and clicked through the options to reinstall her operating system.

Logically, the sooner Harley went, the better, yet emotionally... That morning, in her car outside Harley's home before going to knock, she'd almost driven away. It had taken all her strength to trudge to that front door.

She'd known she was doing the best thing, but her heart wanted to cling onto the dog for dear life. The problem was they'd had all the joys of dog ownership without any of the concerns. How many people got a dog on Christmas Day and thought it the greatest gift ever, only for the poor thing to be homeless by New Year?

Her heart would recover. So would Wes's. And both would recover quicker the earlier the "problem" was removed. The best option for everyone was to return Harley during this honeymoon period. Maybe one day they'd have a pet. But only after extensive planning and research to ensure they got the most appropriate species *and* individual to fit their unique lifestyle.

She nodded to herself. She was doing the right thing.

A progress bar on the monitor crept along incredibly slowly.

She tickled Harley behind one of his ears. "You're a worry, aren't you, huh? What are we going to do if no one calls?" She sighed. And what was she going to do if someone did?

Chapter 29

Outside, Rachel waited near the school doors as Jess, a female teaching assistant, guided Wes through the hordes of swarming children. He shuffled along, a little blue backpack slung over his right shoulder and his arms wrapped around his chest to hug himself. His head stayed down, so all he'd likely see would be the ground and other kids' feet dashing by.

A dark-skinned woman wearing glasses with round blue lenses strolled behind them — Consuela, Wes's special needs teacher. Rachel groaned. It was never good news when a teacher wanted to see a parent.

"Hi, Jess, Consuela," said Rachel. "Hi, Wes. Had a good day?" She didn't expect a reply, so she wasn't disappointed when none came.

Consuela lightly touched Rachel's arm. Turning away from Wes, she said, "Is there anything happening at home? Any major changes?"

Rachel slumped. "Why, what's happened? Please don't tell me he's bitten someone else."

"No, nothing like that. He's talked more today than ever before."

Rachel involuntarily widened her eyes. "Oh!"

"Obviously, it's wonderful if we've made some sort of breakthrough, but it would be great to know what sparked it so we can build on it."

Rachel grimaced, rubbing her forehead. "It's, er, a long story..."

Consuela nodded, waiting, eyebrows arched.

"We got a dog." She raised her hand to add stress to her next words. "Temporarily. *Not* permanently. Just for a few days."

"Okay." Consuela nodded again. "Is there any chance it could become permanent?"

"No. The owner might even come get him today."

"In that case — and this is only a friendly suggestion — it might be worth considering getting your own." With a pinched expression, she said, "Would that be an option?"

Rachel heaved a breath. "It's not that simple." She gestured to herself. "Single mom" — she gestured to Wes — "special needs kid."

"Hence the" — Consuela made air quotes — "'friendly suggestion.' Seriously, if this is the difference a dog makes, we could be looking at a game changer."

Rachel smiled politely. So no pressure.

Rachel took Wes's strap from Jess and, after saying goodbye, guided him across the schoolyard. He flinched as a small boy accidentally brushed his arm while scooting past for one of the yellow school buses. Wes hugged himself even tighter, clawing his green parka. As he walked through the throng of children, he jerked left or right whenever he imagined someone was too close.

Beyond the buses, fewer children crowded the sidewalk, so Wes relaxed, his knuckles pink again as he unclenched his fists on his jacket.

"We're here, Wes," said Rachel, reaching their car in a line of parked vehicles.

Wes raised his face for the first time, saw their car, and shot around the back toward the traffic zipping by.

"Wes!" Rachel braced herself and yanked him back just as an eighteen-wheeler rumbled past.

"Oh, thank the Lord." She always had to be vigilant because it was impossible to predict when he might bolt.

Seemingly oblivious to his near-miss, he peered into the car through the rear windshield, as if looking for something. Or someone.

Rachel waited for a break in the traffic, then guided Wes to the only door he'd use — the right-hand rear.

Peeking in the door, he checked the back of the car, then the front. He plonked into his seat and stared at the floor.

Rachel knelt backward in the front passenger and clicked Wes's seatbelt in. It was a hassle, but the passenger seat created a barrier so Wes didn't become distressed because she was too close.

Once he was secure, she said, "Wesley, what have we agreed about running off the sidewalk?"

He shrugged.

"We agreed not to do it, didn't we?"

He shrugged again.

"We did. So why did you do it? Were you rushing because you thought Harley was in the car?"

116

He flicked his gaze up for a moment. If he'd been playing poker, he'd just lost that hand.

She drew a long breath. As signs went that Harley should go, that was a pretty freaking big one. Rachel climbed into her seat and started the car. Once underway and far from the trauma of hordes of people, she glanced in the rearview mirror, aching to ask a question. Wes was still staring at the floor. Communicating was always problematic, but when he was gazing at the ground? A nonstarter.

By the time they reached home, Wes had at least raised his head to look out of the window.

In their driveway, Rachel reached between the front seats and released Wes's seatbelt. She strolled around and opened the door for him, then stepped back to give him space.

Finally, she asked her question. "I hear you had a good day today?"

He got out in silence.

"Mrs. Hernandez said you had a very good day. It sounds like you were her star pupil."

No answer as he scuttled toward the house.

"She said you were surprisingly chatty."

Still nothing.

Rachel unlocked the door and swung it open. "Is there any reason you were in such a good mood?"

He scanned the entranceway and staircase, then scurried into the living room and through to the kitchen.

The house was empty.

His shoulders slumped, he tramped to his spot on the sofa and collapsed onto it.

Taking her jacket off, Rachel said, "You know, there's someone in the garage who'd probably love to see you."

For a fleeting moment, their eyes met. Wes leaped up and bustled to the garage. Swinging the door open, he clutched his mouth.

"Harley!"

The dog barked and bound over. Wes knelt and cuddled him. Harley licked Wes's face. Instead of being repulsed and running away screaming at the touch of another being, Wes laughed.

Rachel stood in the hall, tears welling in her eyes. How could she ever get rid of Harley? But more importantly, how could she ever keep him?

Chapter 30

Sitting on the edge of the sofa, Wes said, "Harley, TV remote." Harley scampered to the garage door and returned with the device in his jaws.

Wes laughed and clapped as if seeing the feat for the first time, even though it was the twelfth time in the last hour. Rachel couldn't help but grin. It was like a dream. Like having the son she'd always imagined. Every therapist she'd ever met had told her to accept Wes as Wes, that he'd never change, that he'd never form relationships, and that hoping for anything different would only bring her anguish. Every single one.

It was a miracle.

After taking the remote from Harley, Wes scampered into the kitchen, waving it for Harley to see. He crawled between the dining table chairs and left the remote there, then returned to the sofa.

He said, "Harley, TV remote."

Dutifully, Harley trundled away, leaving Wes beaming ear to ear.

Rachel's cell phone rang on the coffee table.

Oh dear Lord, not the owner. Please no.

She gulped, staring at it. Her heart rate rocketed as an emptiness swelled in the back of her throat.

Under her breath, she said, "Just another few days. Please."

She reached for her phone. Slowly. So slowly.

The caller ID washed a wave of relief over her.

"Thank heavens." She slumped back, answering it. "Hi, Iz."

"Hey. Just checking to see if we need more kibble."

Harley presented the remote to Wes, who collapsed in a fit of giggling.

"What do you think?" Rachel held out her phone for Izzy to hear the laughter for a couple of seconds.

Izzy said, "I'll get a big bag this time. See you soon."

"Thanks, Iz. See you."

A big bag. Was that a mistake? Should she just bundle everyone into the car right now and take Harley back? Get it over with?

Her sole purpose was to care for and protect Wes. Was she failing? In fact, was she not just failing but actively setting him up for a trauma it might take him years to recover from?

She leaned forward, elbows on her knees, face in her hands. If only she had someone to share this burden with. Someone who'd know what to do for the best. Surely the longer they had Harley, the worse the wrench would be when he was taken away. That meant there was only one thing she could do — return him. Right now. Even if that meant tying the poor thing to his owner's front door handle and driving away.

She put her hands on the sofa to push up.

Wes leaned over and rested the TV remote on her hand. "Your turn."

She screwed her eyes tightly shut. It was as if everything was conspiring against her. Even her own son. How could she fight that?

An hour later, Izzy waltzed in, cradling a twenty-pound bag of kibble. She looked at Rachel and Wes sitting at either end of the sofa, then around the room. "Am I too late? Did the owner finally show?"

Harley's claws tapped on the wood floor as he trotted back in from the hallway with the landline phone in his mouth.

Nodding for Izzy to follow, Rachel meandered to the kitchen. Izzy dumped the kibble on the dining table.

Rachel cupped her hands over her face then pulled them down until her fingertips rested on her chin. She shook her head. "I don't know what the devil to do, Iz."

"So there's been no word from the owner?"

"Nothing."

"And you tried the house? Left a note?"

Rachel nodded. "What am I supposed to do?"

"Maybe they just don't want him."

Rachel scowled. "How could *anyone* not want Harley?"

Izzy shrugged. "Maybe they're out of town and he was with a sitter, but got out."

"Do you really think so?"

"No. But it's all I've got."

The owner had to know Harley was missing. Even if they were on vacation, whoever had been caring for him would've informed them. Why on earth was no one crawling over glass to get him back?

"So what am I supposed to do? Every second he's here, Wes gets more attached to him."

"So keep him."

Rachel snickered. "What? How?"

"Just don't give him back."

"So I've stuffed a note in their mailbox and left umpteen voicemails, all saying I've got their dog, but when they ask for him back, suddenly, I don't have him? How the devil is that going to work?"

Izzy smiled. "That's exactly why it *will* work. You've done everything a decent person should, so if they finally get around to phoning you, why would they suspect you're lying if you say you let the dog out to pee and he ran away?"

In the living room, laughter erupted once more as Harley presented Wes with a can of soda.

Izzy said, "Look at it this way — if you lost a great dog like Harley, what would you do to get him back? Hand out flyers, offer a reward, plaster his photo all over Facebook... But it's too much trouble for his owner to make one simple phone call?" She shook her head. "An uncaring idiot like that doesn't deserve Harley."

Rachel frowned. She couldn't steal Harley. Could she?

Chapter 31

The next morning, Rachel studied her phone as she crept downstairs so as not to disturb Wes and ruin the day by disrupting his routine. She scrolled through the results of a local search on Facebook for lost dogs. There wasn't a single mention of a dog resembling Harley. Twitter either. Why hadn't Harley's owner plastered pleas for help all over social media?

She opened the garage door. "Har—oh." She pulled back with surprise.

Instead of being curled up on his blanket, Harley sat two feet away looking up, as if expecting her.

She squinted at him. Harley was smart, but come on — he was just a dog. She'd been as quiet as possible, so how had he known she was coming?

Okay, she hadn't showered since after her run yesterday, but did she really stink so bad Harley could smell her through a closed door and concrete wall? Ewww.

She bent her neck and sniffed her armpits but couldn't smell anything.

No, it had to be a fluke that he was waiting like that.

She let Harley out for his morning toilet break, using both "pee" and "leak" in the hope of weaning him off the latter because she didn't like it. Once Izzy arrived to sit for Wes before heading off to work, Rachel and Harley went for their run.

They powered along the flat. At the incline toward her trailhead, Rachel's breath came harder and her thighs burned as they pushed for the top. Alongside her, Harley ran with such ease, she felt like an asthmatic geriatric. Even for a dog, his stamina was incredible.

But what was she going to do about him? She'd done everything she could to return him, but nothing had worked. It was as if the owner had forsaken him. Could that be the case? Could she legitimately claim Harley on the grounds of abandonment?

She snorted a laugh. Yeah, right. This wasn't the Wild West in the 1800s, and Harley wasn't a plot of land she could lay claim to because no one else appeared interested. If the owner called in a day, a month, or a year, they still owned Harley, *not* her.

Izzy's comments wouldn't quit swirling around her head. *You've done everything a decent person should ... but it's too much trouble for his owner to make one simple phone call?*

Yes, she'd done everything a decent person could because she was a decent person. What had Harley's owner done? Squat. In fact, less than squat. She'd done all the hard work, so the owner had barely had to lift a finger, yet even that had proven too much effort. However, could she lie and steal for her family's sake?

As she completed her exercises on the ground, Harley ran rings around her, occasionally barking, as if he was her personal cheerleading squad.

Racing back down the hillside, she finally faced the truth — deep down, she'd always known what she had to do. What she *needed* to do. For Wes.

She ran along the grassy shoulder, cycling through various conversational exchanges in her mind. By the time she was stretching on her lawn, she knew exactly what she was going to say.

Under her breath, she said, "Oh, I'm so sorry, but I let Harley into the yard to pee yesterday and he jumped the fence. I haven't seen him since. Please let me know if he makes it home okay."

She nodded to herself. That was detailed enough to be believable, yet not so complex that she might panic and stumble over the words. Izzy was right — with everything she'd done to return Harley, why would anyone suspect she was lying?

She was good to go.

After breakfast, Rachel packed a flask of hot tea in a red backpack, with some tuna fish sandwiches and a plastic container of kibble — it was time for Wes's weekly workout.

Seeing the backpack, Wes bounced up and down with excitement. Whenever they went into the city, he had to wear his harness, but for his workout, he was allowed to roam free — to a degree — which appeared to be one of the highlights of his week.

With Harley on two of Wes's linked straps and Wes untethered in his parka and walking boots, they strode across the scruffy back lawn toward a gate in the wooden fence that enclosed the area to keep Wes safe. Beyond the gate, they wandered into a wood, where the tree branches were speckled with shoots and tiny leaves bursting with the freshest green. The scent of pine hung in the air.

Rachel gave Harley enough slack to stay ahead while Wes ambled immediately in front of her so she could monitor his every step.

The boy approached a mass of exposed roots creeping across the ground from an aged sycamore. Rachel readied to grab him should he stumble.

His head down, checking his foot placement, Wes stepped over one root and placed his feet side by side between that and a second root, then stepped over the next.

Harley seemed fascinated by Wes and his progress through the wood, scrutinizing the boy as if wanting to ensure he was safe.

Farther along, Wes misjudged a clump of grass the size of a melon and stubbed his toe. Rachel lunged to catch him but pulled back as he recovered his footing. He continued on.

To an average person, a leisurely stroll in the countryside was little more taxing than walking across their backyard. However, to Wes, it was an assault course littered with all manner of obstacles, providing excellent balance, coordination, and strength challenges.

The trees opened out onto a shale shoreline, where a glistening lake stretched away to snowcapped mountains. A breeze rippled the water's surface, below which gray depths hid secrets only the fish shared.

Rachel dumped her backpack at the base of an outcropping of rocks that marched forty feet into the ice-cold lake.

Wes confidently strolled toward the water, fewer obstacles along the shore compared to the wood.

Sitting on a rock, Rachel said, "Wesley, not too close to the water. Remember."

Harley whined, bouncing up and down in the same way Wes had at home.

"What? You want to be off the leash?" Rachel grimaced. He'd pulled the strap taut only twice in the last hour. If he was going to make a break for it, surely he'd have tried it already.

She sucked her teeth. "Can I trust you, Harley?"

This would be the first time he'd been off the leash since they'd found him. What if he took off and she never saw him again?

Everything about him said he wouldn't.

She held the clasp attaching the strap to his collar. He yipped with excitement, obviously guessing what she was about to do. Rachel stared into his eyes. "Please don't make a fool of me, Harley."

She released him.

For moments, their eyes locked.

With a wave of her hand, she said, "Go. Play, Harley."

Harley bolted down the shore, slivers of shale kicking up behind him.

She smiled. Boy, how he loved to run. Maybe almost as much as she did.

Rachel shouted, "Harley, not too far!"

He bound on. Head down, legs pounding.

Her smile faded — he wasn't stopping. "Oh, no."

She stood, cupping her hands to her mouth. "Harley! Come back! ... Harley!"

Harley shot farther and farther away.

"No, no, no." Rachel froze, clutching her mouth as the dog became a speck in the distance.

What had she done?

Chapter 32

The wind howled in Harley's ears as he flew along the shoreline. Two big gray birds lounging on the shale honked and splashed into the lake in their haste to escape. Harley had no interest in waterbirds; he just wanted to run. Run and run and run.

The walk through the wood had been interesting, but frustrating — all the new smells had tormented him. He'd have loved to investigate them, but he'd had to watch over Wes. It was wonderful to be fulfilling his purpose again by having someone to help, but a new scent was a new scent. Period. An object didn't smell for no reason, but for a very specific one — it wanted to be smelled. If it wasn't, it lost its purpose, and Harley knew how crippling it was to lose the meaning of one's life, so it pained him to deny that honor to other things.

His tongue lolling out, paws pounding into the loose gray ground, he stormed along the waterline to a group of boulders beside an ancient fallen tree. He leaped onto one boulder, sprang to another, and jumped to the trunk. He strode along it as it sloped down into the murky depths.

Dipping his head, he lapped water. Icy cold, it tasted like a nighttime winter walk — sharp, dark, biting.

Harley gazed over more water than he'd ever seen and giant hills climbing so high they touched the clouds. It had to be the biggest park in the world. In the city, men in green coveralls cut the grass and tended the plants. There had to be an army of them in a park this big. Strangely, he couldn't smell any of them.

Overwhelming everything else was the scent of fresh water. He sucked in more air, reveling in fir trees, rotting leaves, fungi, and...

He sniffed. Dropping his head to his forepaws, he homed in on the source.

Yep, bird poop. He must have trodden in it when passing those flapping birds.

To his right, the shoreline arced around below craggy slopes, while to his left, the shale shore led back to Rachel and Wes. Back to his purpose.

Harley tore back along water's edge toward his new life, hoping they hadn't gotten into too many difficulties while he enjoyed his break.

He loved his early-morning runs with Rachel because she really tried, bless her. And considering how disadvantaged she was having only two legs, she did an admirable job of moving quickly. But running — real running — was something else. Barney had told him "Play, Harley" in the city park and let him run and run, so it was nice Rachel appreciated his need to spend some time wild and free too. Very nice.

But then, his new pack was nice. Coincidentally, Rachel appeared to have the same purpose he did — to help people, especially Wes. Unfortunately, her propensity for losing things seriously hampered her efforts. But a purpose was a purpose. Harley would take her as his apprentice. After a few years of training, she could be quite a good helper.

Wes was another story. He was wonderful at laughing, but unfortunately, that didn't qualify as a purpose. Plus, he'd picked up his pack's bad habit of misplacing things. Luckily, he was still young, so with Harley's guidance, he might yet grow out of that. But his purpose? That required further investigation.

Harley careered through the shallows, splashing up water.

What would his pack be doing now — swimming in the lake, running along the shale, chasing water birds? Oh, he'd bet they were having just as wild a time as he was.

As he neared where he'd left them, he slowed. What were they doing?

Six feet apart, Rachel and Wes sat hunched over, each gazing at the ground as if lost in their own worlds.

They had a weird way of enjoying themselves. Thank heavens he was there. Harley barked.

In unison, Rachel and Wes jerked their heads up. Their eyes widened and their mouths dropped open, then together, they shouted, "Harley!"

So that's what they'd been doing — perfecting a little choreographed performance to entertain him. How sweet. And he'd thought they'd just been slouched over wasting their time. That illustrated how difficult spotting a purpose was. Sometimes digging deeper was the only way to reveal one because, while they were wonderful things, they could be mighty tricky little devils to grasp. He barked his appreciation of their skit and raced over.

Wes fell to his knees and hugged him, while Rachel crouched and scratched his head. Barney had never greeted him like this when he'd come back from running in the park. Maybe he should run alone more often.

He licked Rachel's hand, then licked Wes's ear so hard the boy wouldn't stop laughing.

Rachel picked up a stick as long as her forearm. "Wes, do you want to play fetch with Harley?"

"Fetch what?" Wes frowned.

Rachel held the stick out. "A stick."

Standing, Wes took the stick and gave it to Harley.

Laughing, Rachel took the stick back. "Let me show you."

Wes scratched his head.

"Harley." She waved the stick, then threw it. It clattered to the shale sixty feet away.

Harley tore over the shoreline, grabbed the stick, and tore back to drop it at her feet.

"Yay!" Rachel clapped. "Well done, Harley."

It was sweet she was so easily impressed. However, easily pleased people usually had very low standards, and that wouldn't wash if she was to be his apprentice. He hoped she wouldn't think badly of him and his rigorous training regimen.

"See, Wes? You throw the stick and Harley brings it back. It's fun. Want to try?"

Wes nodded and took the stick. He twisted sideways and pulled his arm back at waist height, but instead of using his shoulder to throw, he jerked his body forward while barely moving his arm. The stick flew about fifteen feet.

Harley gazed at Wes. So throwing definitely wasn't the boy's purpose. He darted away and retrieved the stick, dropping it at Wes's feet. He was meant to help Wes, so maybe training him to throw was part of his purpose.

Before Wes picked up the stick, Rachel said, "Wes, do this with your arm." She swung her right arm vertically backward, then forward and up to shoulder level.

Wes copied her.

"And again."

Wes repeated the action a few times.

"Now do it with the stick, but when your hand is here" — she held her arm at forty-five degrees in front of her — "let go of the stick."

The boy picked up the stick and threw it as instructed. It soared through the air twice as far as his previous attempt.

Wes grinned, eyes wide.

Harley raced after it.

"Wow, Wes," said Rachel, "well done."

Harley dropped the stick before Wes. The boy had already improved dramatically. If Harley worked with him, Wes might yet make throwing his purpose.

Wes hurled the stick again. Off target, it sailed through the air and sploshed into the lake six feet from shore. He cupped his hands to his face as if he'd done something wrong.

Harley dashed after it and splashed through the shallows, the water refreshingly cold on his legs.

He scampered back and dropped the stick. Wes clapped and laughed even more than usual.

Fetching the stick was kind of fun. Not fun in the way that doing his job was fun, but in a mindless sort of way. Maybe the dogs that chased balls in the park didn't have it wrong after all, though he could never tolerate this as his full-time purpose.

Wes wound his arm back to throw again, this time standing square to the water.

"Don't throw it too f—" Rachel slumped as it soared away. "And there it goes."

The stick splashed twenty feet from land. Harley shot after it, wading out until the water was up to his throat.

When he returned with his prize, Rachel took three or four steps away from Wes. The boy clapped as Harley presented the stick.

Harley shook himself, his wet fur whipping through the air, spraying water everywhere.

Wes gasped, then shielded himself behind his arms, giggling.

Rachel laughed too. "And that's today's most important lesson, Wes — don't stand close to a wet dog."

Harley trained Wes in stick throwing for nearly an hour. After the boy's dismal first attempt, Harley was pleased with his progress. The boy was a slow learner, but a tireless one. Harley liked that. With such a never-give-up attitude, the boy was bound to go far.

Relaxing on the rock, Rachel called them over. She and Wes dug into sandwiches while Harley wolfed down a portion of kibble.

After eating, they sat in silence, each gazing at the sight before them as the water lapped at the slivers of stone on the shore.

Harley liked this place. The stillness. The silence. The biting freshness. He still hadn't seen any men in green coveralls, but they were doing an excellent job of making this park earthy and wild.

Wes picked up the stick. "Can I?"

"May—" Rachel rolled her eyes. Under her breath, she said, "Save it for the classroom, Rach." She smiled. "Of course, Wes. But stay where I can see you."

Wes dawdled away, swinging his arm back and forth to practice throwing.

As the sun arced across the sky, the boy's stick-throwing abilities got better and better, though the one time he tried it with his other arm, the stick somehow went backward. Being the polite dog he was, Harley fetched it as if he believed Wes had intended to throw it in that direction.

Later, Rachel ambled over. "You've done well today, Wes. I'm really proud." She picked up a flat, round stone. "Next time we come, I'll show you how to do this."

She leaned sideways, her right forearm parallel to the ground, and hurled the stone at the lake.

Instead of plopping into the water and sinking, it hit the surface and magic happened — it bounced.

Harley's jaw dropped. So did Wes's.

The stone hit the surface again and bounced off. It bounced twice more and then disappeared into the icy grayness.

In unison, Wes and Harley turned to gaze at Rachel, even though it wasn't a choreographed performance they'd rehearsed.

That stone trick defied the laws of nature, which meant either Rachel or the water was magic.

If Rachel had magic powers, she wouldn't constantly misplace things that he had to find but simply magic them back. That left only one solution. A solution with a tantalizing possibility – if stones could bounce on magic water...

Harley shot across the shale and leaped onto the rock on which Rachel had been sitting. If stones could bounce, so could he. Logic was a beautiful thing. He just had to get as far out from the shallows as that stone. He sprang from one boulder to another until he reached the top of the massive rock formation, then he bolted along its crest as it arced out into the lake.

"Harley! No!" shouted Rachel.

Paws pounding into the rock, he flexed his muscles as the lake raced toward him. Bounding into the air with all his strength, he launched himself at the water. He was going to bounce. He was going to bounce. He was going–

Harley crashed into the lake with an almighty splash. Shockingly, he didn't bounce but sank. Bubbles exploded about him, shooting water up his nose and in his mouth, choking him.

Flailing his legs, he fought his way through the murk and back toward the light. He broke the surface, spluttering for air.

He swam to shallows and waded out, as drenched as he was mystified. So stones could bounce on water, and birds and sticks could sit on it, but he sank? Sometimes the world just made no sense.

Shaking his head to get the water out of his ears, he tottered toward Rachel and Wes. They both scurried backward for no apparent reason. He shook himself, showering water everywhere.

"Okay, Harley, no more gymnastics, please." Rachel slung her backpack on her shoulder and gestured for the wood. "Who's up for pizza? Wes?"

Wes nodded.

"Don't tell me – ham with extra cheese, extra mushroom, no pineapple."

He smiled and toddled in the direction in which she'd pointed.

Harley scooted past them. If they were negotiating the treacherous ground again, he had to be where he could watch over Wes.

Heading back into the wood, he glanced over his shoulder at Rachel. She wasn't so hopeless after all. In fact, there was far more to her than he'd first imagined. True hidden depths. This was the second time he'd been reminded to dig deeper to find a thing's real purpose, so what was he going to discover next about his new pack?

Chapter 33

Rachel placed a plate containing a gnawed strip of pizza crust on the coffee table and took her glass of water. She lounged back on the sofa and blew out her cheeks.

"Well, I don't know about anyone else, but I'm stuffed enough to burst. Wes? You had enough?"

He nodded, chomping into a slice of pizza heavy with cheese, ham, and mushroom.

"Harley?"

On the floor between them, Harley licked the last scraps off the pizza box.

"I'll take that as a yes." She wasn't sure pizza was good for dogs — or jelly beans for that matter — but the way Harley had wolfed down two slices suggested it was. However, she'd research canine dietary requirements to ensure he stayed healthy. Not that takeout was going to be a problem — this would be their last for a long time. Thanks to Peter's bombshell, belts would be tightened. And collars.

She clicked on the TV. "What do you feel like, Wes? Animals? Cartoons? A movie?"

That was another thing she'd have to look at — paring down her TV subscription package to leave only the essentials for Wes.

"A movie."

"A movie it is." She clicked for the on-screen channel schedule.

"About a dog."

"Oh." Many dog movies involved the dog dying at the end, so she steered Wes away from animal movies until she'd vetted them. She scanned the schedule for *Beethoven*, *Turner and Hooch*, or *101 Dalmatians*.

"Oh, it's your lucky day, Wes. Look" — she pointed at the screen — "*Lady and the Tramp* starts in ten minutes."

She threw the pizza box away and washed the dishes they'd used. When she returned, Wes was grinning and peering down. Harley had clambered onto the sofa and was lying across the middle seat, his head in Wes's lap.

"Awww." Rachel snapped a photo on her phone. She prayed Harley would stay with them, but even if he did, there was no guarantee Wes wouldn't revert to his old withdrawn self. In years to come, such moments would feel like false memories if they went undocumented.

Placing her phone back on the table, she squeezed into her seat, shuffling Harley's rump farther into the middle.

No sooner did a lovable pooch appear on the screen than her phone rang. Rachel's heart rate rocketed. An unexpected call could be a friend with good news... or Harley's owner.

She hovered her hand over her phone, not wanting to answer.

What was it she'd decided she was saying? *The dog ran away because—* No, that wasn't it. It had sounded natural and honest. What the devil was it? *The dog went out for a pee and—* No. *She let the dog out for a pee yesterday and it got over the fence and ran away.* Yes! That was it. Sort of.

Drawing a faltering breath, she grabbed her phone.

She sighed, seeing the caller ID: Mom.

"Hey, Mom." She mouthed to Wes. "It's Grandma."

Wes scanned the room and frowned. She shook her head. One day, she hoped he'd get that.

Rachel moseyed into the kitchen to leave Wes with his movie.

Mom said, "Hi, sweetheart. Just checking in to see if you got your computer fixed."

"There's still stuff to do, but, yeah, it's working again, thanks."

"So I do have good ideas sometimes, do I?"

Rachel rolled her eyes. The repair advice had come about through pure luck, but...

"Yes, Mom, you do."

"How have things been since the dog went? Is Wes okay?"

"That's, er, a funny story."

Rachel could picture her Mom's disapproving glare. "Oh shoot, don't tell me you've still got it."

"Him, Mom. Harley is a he."

"He's a massive mistake is what he is, Rachel. I'm telling you. He's a nightmare waiting to happen."

132

Rachel paced to the window overlooking the valley and hills. "Mom, you haven't seen him with Wes. It's incredible. Wes is like a different person. He talks, he interacts, he smiles. He even breaks from his routine, for heaven's sake, and you know how important that is to him."

"That may be, but you know what a litigious world we live in. What if the owner decides you haven't returned the dog because you've stolen it?"

"I've tried to return him. I've left voicemails, notes, and been to the house. What more am I supposed to do?"

"I'm just saying. I think you're opening a huge can of worms here, so my advice is to get rid as soon as possible."

"Okay."

"Are you saying 'okay' because you agree, or to shut me up? I only want what's best for you, sweetheart."

"I know, Mom. Thanks. I'll let you know what happens. Speak soon."

"Give my love to Wes. Bye, sweetheart."

Rachel crumpled over the granite top of the island. Izzy said to keep Harley, Mom said to get rid of him. Like she didn't have enough worries already.

She slouched back to the sofa and slumped down, squashed into the corner by Harley's butt.

Closing her eyes, she inhaled deeply through her nose and exhaled slowly through her mouth. In and out again. And again. The muscles in her neck and shoulders eased as if she were made of wax and under a hot lamp.

She opened her eyes. It had been a wonderful day. If only the smiles and laughter could have continued a little longer. But that was everyday life for most people — ninety percent struggle and ten percent joy. She'd had a lot of fun today, using way over her quota, so now came the struggle. How long would it be before their turn for fun came around again?

She heaved out a breath and folded her arms.

Harley broke wind — *pfffuuurrrb.*

A smell like burned cabbage smothered in rotten eggs enveloped her.

Wincing, she recoiled, wafting her hand in front of her face.

She glared at Harley, but Wes stared at her, clutching his mouth to stifle his laughter.

"It wasn't me, for crying out loud!" She pointed at Harley.

Wes giggled.

"You think it's funny, Wes Taylor? A dog farting on your loving mom?"

Harley broke wind again.

Wes belly-laughed, holding his stomach and rocking forward.

"Harley!" said Rachel.

Harley glanced at her with an innocent "Who, me?" expression.

"He—" Laughing uncontrollably, Wes pointed at Harley's butt, then at her. "He—" The boy just couldn't get the words out.

"It's so funny, is it? Your loving mom being abused like this?"

He nodded, clutching his stomach and howling with laughter.

Rachel slipped her hands under Harley and shuffled him around so his butt rested on Wes's thigh.

"No!" Wes threw his hands up, squashing himself into the corner of the sofa, as far away as he could get.

"It's not so funny now, is it?" She massaged Harley's stomach. "Come on, Harley. Let's have a big one."

"Ahhh!" Wes wailed, tears of laughter streaming down his face.

He moved his hands toward the butt on his leg but pulled back before making contact. He tried again, only to again chicken out, like someone who knew nothing about munitions or trying to defuse a bomb.

"Ohhh, I can feel one coming," said Rachel. "And it's a big one. Absolutely huge."

Roaring with laughter, Wes stamped his feet and waved his arms.

Rubbing Harley's belly, she said, "It's coming. It's coming. It's coming."

She'd no idea if it was, but Wes's look of pure horror mixed with pure joy was such a sight.

As if wanting to play his part to perfection, Harley cut loose a third time.

Rachel burst out laughing. She hadn't wanted to gas her son, only to continue the joke, but having Harley perform at just the right moment was too much to take. They rocked back and forth in hysterics, tears rolling down their cheeks.

As the laughter subsided, Rachel wiped her eyes. "Okay, let's neutralize this deadly weapon, shall we?"

Still chuckling, Wes nodded.

Rachel shuffled Harley around so his butt was squashed against the back of the sofa.

She patted his back and rested her hand there. Dairy could cause flatulence in lactose-intolerant people, so maybe cheese could do that in dogs. She'd check on that too.

Wes leaned sideways and cuddled Harley, his arm over the dog and his head on the dog's shoulders. The side of his chest brushed Rachel's hand.

Instinctively, she tensed to pull it away and give him the space he always demanded, but stopped. Instead of withdrawing it, she eased it so it lay against him.

She held her breath. Waited for him to realize and scream his outrage at being so violated.

But he did nothing. Nothing but hug Harley.

Grinning, Rachel closed her eyes and basked in the joy of touching her son. Tears once more ran down her face.

Chapter 34

His head lolling over the edge of the sofa, Harley sighed. It had been a wonderful meal to end a wonderful day. And so much delicious cheese! Okay, there'd been small explosions from his butt, but that was a small price to pay. Especially when his new pack seemed so entertained by those explosions. In all the time he'd been here, this was the happiest they'd ever been. They should have cheese every day!

He closed his eyes and basked in the warmth of the boy lying across his back, Wes's breath on his head making his left ear twitch.

Yes, thanks to his hard work, his new pack was happy. Which was a considerable triumph as Rachel and Wes were so broken. Broken in a different way from how Barney had been broken, but broken nonetheless — they seemed to have a problem simply being together. Maybe that was why he'd been brought here — to help them love each other.

From deep inside his chest, a glow spread through his body. The stresses and hardships of the last few days drained away, allowing tense, aching muscles to melt into the sofa like heated cheese.

For longer than Harley could remember, he'd helped Barney. It had been the best job in the world, so without it, he'd feared his life was meaningless.

Pfffuuurrrb.

Laughter erupted once more.

Meaningless? He couldn't have been more wrong. He still had a job to do. Still had people to help. Still had a purpose.

Chapter 35

Monday Wes squinted, the tip of his tongue sticking out as he concentrated on switching around five cups on their lessons desk.

Sitting on the floor beside them, Harley yawned.

The corners of Wes's mouth tweaked upward as he leaned back in his chair, obviously convinced this time he'd beat Harley's magical senses.

Wes gestured to the row of cups. "Harley."

Instantly, Harley nudged the second from the right.

Wes grinned, eyes sparkling as if he knew a secret no one else did.

"Is that the right one?" said Rachel.

He shook his head.

"Got you, Harley!" He ruffled the dog's head. "Got you."

He held the top of the middle cup. "It's this one."

Triumphantly, he swept the cup away. "Ta-da—oh."

Wes's smile vanished as quickly as his brow knitted. There was no jelly bean under that cup.

Wes looked inside the cup he was holding, then peered under the table. He scratched his head.

Trying not to smirk, Rachel said, "Do you think we should check the cup Harley chose?"

Wes stared at Harley's cup, then into the one he was holding. He rubbed his chin. Laying his head on the desk, he tilted Harley's cup just enough to peek under it.

Rachel couldn't see what was underneath, but she didn't need to — Wes's gasp gave the game away. He snapped the cup back down to hide what was inside, checked the empty cup in his hand once more, then tilted Harley's again to peek underneath.

He burst out laughing.

"So does Harley get his prize?"

Rocking back in his chair with laughter, Wes nodded, and Rachel gave Harley the jelly bean from under the cup.

She said, "Do you think we've found a magic dog?"

Wes nodded again. Tears streaming down his cheeks, he shuddered with laughter and spluttered a few words. "That's the … that's the only … explan … explanation."

The cups game had been created to focus Wes's attention in preparation for learning, but learning had a sole purpose — to allow someone to better interact with the world around them. Harley's arrival had elevated the game to heights Rachel had never imagined. Heights that gave new meaning to Wes's life. New meaning to them as a family.

*****

Wednesday

Shrouded in early-morning darkness, Rachel raced down the home stretch with Harley bounding at her side.

The gnarled oak tree that acted as her finishing line loomed out of the gloom. Gritting her teeth, she shot forward to end her run on a high note. Harley needed no encouragement — he bolted with her.

Her breath coming in sharp gasps, she darted across the line. She checked her watch, easing into a brisk walk.

Hands on her hips, chest heaving, she smiled as she sucked in air. "That's another fourteen seconds off, Harley. A week ago, I wouldn't have believed I could make times like these. Maybe you are magic."

She patted him. He barked and bounced about as if they'd had nothing more than a leisurely stroll.

"Sorry, boy, but that's it for today."

Back at home, she showered, thanked Izzy, then, at 6:59 a.m., waited at Wes's bedroom door. His wind-up alarm clock sounded, so she waltzed in to get him up, clicking on the light.

"Good morning, W—" She stopped in midstride.

Wes was not in bed as he always was but standing beside it. Nor was he in his pajamas — he'd dressed himself.

The two bells of the alarm ringing duller as the device wound down, she flicked it off. A clock radio would have been more pleasant to wake up to, plus more accurate, but an old-fashioned clock had been how Wes had learned to tell the time, so his routine being everything, that was what he had. But what had happened to his routine today?

"You've dressed yourself."

He nodded.

He had on one white sock and one blue, which was odd not just because he didn't usually wear socks, but because she always matched them before balling them. His jeans were fastened, but the belt was left hanging, and his green sweater was inside out and the label stuck out under his chin. For a first attempt, it was remarkable.

"Wow. Great job, Wesley. Great."

Even with his head down and bangs hiding his eyes, he couldn't hide the smile teasing his face.

No one else would see how he was dressed to belittle his accomplishment, so there was no value in pointing out any mistake. For the first time in his life, he'd dressed himself — this wasn't an opportunity for learning but for celebration.

"Ready for breakfast, my clever boy?"

He nodded. They ambled down the hall to the stairs, she hugging the wall on the left, he the one on the right so they were an arm's length apart.

"Is there a reason you dressed yourself today?"

"Harley."

"Because if you're dressed early, you can spend more time with him?"

Wes nodded.

In the kitchen, Harley was politely sitting beside a brown ceramic dish on the floor next to the refrigerator.

"Harley!" Wes dashed over.

Wagging his tail so much his whole body swayed, Harley waddled over.

Wes knelt and hugged Harley, who reciprocated by licking Wes's cheek, making him squirm and giggle.

For his entire life, Wes had lived in self-imposed semi-isolation, withdrawn into a largely silent, unfeeling world of his own creation. He never left it and never invited anyone in. It was his sanctuary. A place he called home. But now?

Rachel wiped away a tear. If just a week with Harley could achieve all this, what could a year do?

She flinched as her cell phone rang, wrenching her out of her joyful thoughts. She glared at it on the counter. Who the devil was it at this time in the morning?

Wes and Harley still hugged, ignoring the ringing.

Don't let it be Harley's owner. Please. Not now.

Feeling like she was battling against the tide in a raging ocean, she trudged over. She swallowed hard as she reached for the phone, her hand shaking. She was supposed to describe Harley going for a pee and jumping the fence, but could she go through with it? Could she steal someone's precious pet?

She looked at Wes and gulped again. What was she going to say? What was she going to say?

Picking up the phone, she saw the caller ID. The nervous energy drained from her body so quickly she slumped onto her elbows on the counter.

"Hey, Iz. What's up?"

"Did I leave my..."

Barely listening, Rachel covered her eyes and shook her head. What was she going to do when that call finally came? Because it would. How could it not? Harley was a remarkable dog. So remarkable, she was considering breaking the law to keep him. If she could do that, how far would his owner go to get him back?

**

Thursday

Darkness.

Stillness.

Silence.

An odd sensation clawed its way into Rachel's mind as she lay in bed. Half-asleep, she moved her head back as something cold and clammy touched her cheek. The clammy thing nudged her again.

She groaned and rolled to the other side of her king-size bed. The world once more slipped into the darkest stillness.

Cold and clammy touched her cheek again.

She moaned and jerked away, but it prodded again. Warm air caressed her neck and face. Warm air with a particular scent. Half-awake, she frowned – dog food.

Her eyes flickered her eyes open.

A shadow loomed in front of her face. A dog-shaped shadow.

"Harley?"

Something beat rhythmically against her nightstand, like a dog wagging its tail.

She clicked on her nightstand lamp. Harley's tail beat quicker.

"How the devil did you get in here?" Rachel stretched. "Sorry. Stupid question. For a dog as smart as you, I suppose I should be surprised you didn't make it up days ago."

She rubbed her eyes and checked her digital clock: 5:34 a.m. Eleven minutes before she usually went to meet him in the garage.

Ruffling the fur on his neck, she sniggered. "Are you telling me it's time for our run?" She shook her head. "Smart? Calling you smart is like calling Einstein slow, isn't it, boy, huh?"

Clambering up, she used the bathroom, then dressed in the clothes she'd draped over the curved wings of her black 1960s swivel chair. Once Izzy arrived, they had their run, followed by breakfast with Wes. After that, they jumped into the day's lesson: math.

Forsaking many of the resources she'd developed over the years in favor of the new resource with the cold, clammy nose, Rachel gestured to the Wheel of Questions.

Wes spun "How" written in green, so threw the oversized green die, rolling "2 & 5."

Rachel said, "Okay, Wes, take the number of legs Harley has, multiply that by two and add five. Take your time."

Wes stared at the die, his lips moving as he talked himself through the equation.

Rachel always ached to offer encouragement, but she'd learned saying something was more of a distraction. However, she couldn't help willing the answer to him. *Come on, Wes, Thirteen. Thirteen. Just say thirteen.*

Wes's lips stopped moving and he raised his head slightly. Instead of his usual muttering, in a clear, confident voice, he said, "Thirteen."

Rachel clapped. "Well done, Wes. Excellent."

Whether it was the clapping or Harley could smell the release of endorphins from the pair of them at their success, he barked as if he were happy with the answer as well.

"See, Harley says well done, too."

Wes grinned.

Rachel gestured to the Wheel of Questions again. "Right, let's see if you can do as well on the next question."

Wes's spin landed on "What" printed in red. Without any prompting, he rolled the red die. He scored ten.

"In no fewer than ten words, describe what Harley does with the TV remote."

Wes stared into space, then, counting on his fingers, said, "When I ask Harley he can fetch the TV remote—"

That was ten words. "Well d—" Her hands wide apart to clap, Rachel froze.

"— even if I put it somewhere difficult to find." Wes stopped counting. "He can even fetch it from a different room, if he's seen it there, because he's a magic dog with magic powers."

Agog, Rachel stared, unsure whether or not he'd finished. He hadn't.

"Harley is my friend. I never wanted one before, because why would I? But now he's our family, and I love him."

Rachel gulped. Her breath shuddering, she rummaged through the resources so Wes wouldn't see her cry.

She wasn't prepared for this. All the experts had told her this was impossible and that Wes was the way he was — withdrawn, unfeeling, isolated — and always would be. Why would she prepare for the day he'd reach out with love in his heart?

Her cell phone rang.

"Oh, for the love of God." Rachel threw her hands up. "Seriously?"

She brushed her fingers over her eyes. Beside her on the desk, her phone taunted her with "Caller ID: unknown."

As if a hand had reached into her chest to squeeze her heart and drag it down into her stomach, her world imploded. She could let the call go to voicemail; it was probably a sales pitch, or Izzy using her work phone, which never displayed, or Tad following up...

But what if it was a time-sensitive job offer, or her bank reporting suspicious activity on her account, or a hospital calling to say her mom had fallen?

Her mouth dry, Rachel accepted the call but then waited a moment before she spoke, praying to hear some automated message.

A woman said, "Hello?"

Her voice thin and lifeless, Rachel said, "Hello."

"I'm calling for Rachel Taylor."

Rachel strained to swallow, her throat all but seized. "This is she."

"Oh, hi, Rachel. This is Kate from Gold Cloud Press. Sorry, you sounded a little strange there."

142

Rachel collapsed over the desk. "Sorry, I've, er, had a few crank calls recently, so I'm wary of unknown caller IDs."

"Ah, my fault — I'm on an extension line. Anyhoo, I just wanted to let you know the sample revisions you've submitted are excellent. Just what we wanted. If the remaining artwork is of the same quality, you'll have one very happy editor."

"Great. Thank you, Kate."

She ended the call and heaved out a breath. "Oh, dear Lord."

She couldn't go on like this. The way things were going, she'd have a coronary if she answered a call and a strange voice mentioned Harley. There had to be a way out of this situation. A way out that didn't break Wes's heart. But what was it?

Chapter 36

Tuesday
Driiinnnggg!

Rachel waited outside Wes's bedroom, his alarm clock sounding inside. The ringing muffled, then finally stopped. He was up. Over the last week, this would be the fourth time he'd been dressed and waiting for her.

She pulled on a sweatshirt inside out and back to front and, after ensuring the white label stuck out under her chin, entered the room.

"Morning, Wes."

His nightstand lamp was on, but his alarm clock was missing. A small bulge suggested it was under his pillow. Later, she'd again show him the silver latch that stopped the bells from chiming.

Today his socks matched and his belt was fastened. However, his blue sweater was inside out and back to front, its label sticking up under his chin. How did he get it so wrong so often?

She threw her arms up. "Would you look at me?"

Wes's gaze flicked to her.

"I've done it again, haven't I?" She tugged the white label underneath her chin. "I keep forgetting this thing goes at the back on the inside."

She yanked the sweatshirt off, turned it the right way, and pulled it back on.

Turning her neck, she said, "Oh, that's much better."

Without saying a word, Wes looked down at his sweater, then pulled the white tab sticking out. He laughed.

He said, "I did the same."

"Well, aren't we a real pair." Rachel rolled her eyes. "Who'd have thought it was so difficult to keep the tag inside at the back? Would you?"

He shook his head. He pulled his sweater off and corrected how he wore it.

144

"Breakfast time?"

He nodded. "And Harley time."

The moment they entered the kitchen, Harley wagged his tail. He and Wes met halfway, Wes dropping to the floor and flinging his arms around his best friend. His only friend.

Rachel took eggs and bacon from the refrigerator. As nonchalantly as she could, she said, "You know, if you want to give Harley his breakfast today, that would be a big help."

Wes's eyes widened. "Really?" For a moment, their gaze met.

A chill ran down Rachel's spine as her son looked at her. She'd had a whole speech planned, but she blanked with the shock. "Uh-huh."

He said, "*Really?*"

"Well, if you don't want to, I—"

Wes dashed to the cupboard where they kept Harley's kibble. He plonked the bag on the island, then retrieved the brown casserole dish from the floor.

"Not too much mind. We don't want him getting fat, do we?"

Wes shook his head.

"Have you seen how I measure it?"

He stared into space.

Rachel slumped her shoulders. She'd pushed him too far. It had been a gamble, but giving him a little responsibility would've given him a sense of achievement and self-worth, things sorely lacking for Wes, so it had seemed a goal worth pursuing.

"Don't worry, Wes. I can—"

He ducked down and fished inside the cupboard. Beaming, he stood up, grasping a transparent plastic measuring jug.

Rachel said, "Halfway. No more."

Putting the jug on the island, Wes bent so his eyeline was on the same level as the jug's markings. He tipped in some kibble, then stopped and studied the markings, even though it was barely a quarter full. He added more. Still not half. More. Still not half. More...

He scrutinized the amount, tilting his head left then right to check the level from different angles. Finally, he dropped in dried pellets one at a time, squinting at the halfway mark.

Nodding, he said to himself, "Halfway."

He replaced the bag, tipped the contents of the jug into the bowl, then gave Harley his breakfast, filling up the water bowl, too.

Rachel grinned. She couldn't have been prouder if he'd graduated summa cum laude from Harvard.

"If you're going to be feeding Harley, Wes, maybe we should get him proper dog bowls. What do you think?"

"Okay."

"Are you going to choose them?"

Under his dangling bangs, his eyebrows rose.

"As Harley's best friend, you know what he'll like, right?"

He nodded.

"Good. That's what we'll do, then."

With breakfast and Wes's bathroom routine done, Rachel stood in the living room and held up her tablet. "You could choose Harley's bowls at the desk, but it'll be comfier on the sofa with the tablet on the cushion between us so we can both see it. Shall we try that?"

"Okay."

Rachel took her seat on the far left, but as Wes shuffled around to sit in his spot, Harley jumped up and took it.

Rachel grimaced. Under her breath, she said, "Oh, jeez. Just when things were going so well."

Wes dithered, shuffling from side to side and peering at Harley from different angles as if looking for a way to squeeze in, even though it was impossible.

Rachel screwed her eyes shut and waited for the screaming to start. She'd gotten away with disrupting his routine by having him feed Harley and delaying his class to choose bowls. But losing his seat would tip him over the edge.

Gritting her teeth, she waited for the aural onslaught. But no one screamed. And something lightly brushed her right thigh.

She opened her eyes. Wes was sitting beside her in the middle seat.

With the tiniest of gasps, she froze.

Wes looked down at the tablet in her lap, then up toward her.

She gulped. "Er... what, er..." For a moment, she closed her eyes again and drew a deep breath. The corners of her mouth tweaked upward as shock morphed into joy, but she forced them back down. She had to downplay what was happening, stay calm, and move slowly. Like a lepidopterist who'd stumbled upon a rare butterfly, she wanted to leap for joy but knew that might make this delicate creature take flight. Only by stifling her feelings would the moment linger.

Careful not to accidentally nudge him, she surfed to a pet supplies website and browsed to the section for dog bowls.

Wes leaned over her lap to peer at the selection of metal and ceramic bowls. Rachel held her breath. Every day she was this close to her son to help him dress and wash, but every day, the ticking of the timer reminded her of how distant they truly were. Today, the silence cocooned her in warmth. Tears welled in her eyes.

She ached to run her fingers through his hair or sling her arm around his shoulders and hug him. However, that would spook him, so she froze, drinking in her beautiful boy.

Easing her head to the left, so she could see around his, she scrolled through the products. "Tell me when you see something Harley will like."

Wes nodded, fixated on the screen. Bowls with bones, paw prints, or embossed words on them scrolled by. Some came with nonslip mats, some were paw-shaped, and some had raised indentations inside to compartmentalize the food and thereby stop a dog from eating too quickly.

"That one." He pointed to a plain white ceramic bowl.

"You're sure?"

He nodded.

"You don't think he'd like one with paw prints or its own special mat?"

Shaking his head, he said, "Harley is special. He doesn't need anything to prove it."

"Well, you know best." She added two to her cart, but as she did so, an emptiness clawed its way up from her stomach. Once she bought these bowls, normal life would resume because there would be no reason for Wes to remain beside her. As if to prove that, Wes leaned forward to leave the sofa.

Trying to sound casual while gripped by desperation, Rachel said, "And what about a bed for Harley?"

Wes leaned over her lap again. Rachel beamed. No birthday, Christmas, or anniversary held a candle to this moment.

But her phone rang.

"Don't worry, I'll" — she slumped as Wes stood and meandered away — "get it later."

Rubbing her forehead, she took her phone from the table, disappointment replaced by trepidation. Her heart no longer fought to burst out of her chest whenever her phone rang — she'd had so many false alarms since Harley had arrived — but there was still a Pavlovian response at the thought that, at any moment, Harley could be snatched from their lives. Her mouth dry, she checked her phone.

Caller ID: unknown.

Her pulse jumped twenty beats per minute. She prayed it was Izzy calling from work. "Hello?"

Izzy's voice made her slump with relief. "Pat's Pet World on Bleaker is running a special on kibble. Should I get a couple of bags or we still thinking Harley's leaving?"

Buying bowls had been a tool to engage Wes, but forking out for perishable dog food she might never use when she was trying to economize was one luxury too far.

"Thanks, Iz, but—"

Wes retook his seat next to her.

"But what?" said Izzy.

Wes half-turned. "A blue bed. Harley likes blue."

She bit her bottom lip. It was good Wes avoided eye contact or he'd see her cheeks glistening with tears.

"Rach? You still there?"

"You know what, two would be great. Thanks, Iz." Unless someone held her at gunpoint, Harley was going nowhere.

**

Thursday

Cold and clammy. On her cheek. The sensation half-registered as Rachel lay sleeping. She moved her head and warm air caressed her neck, as if someone was breathing on her. Then...

Cold and clammy. On her cheek. Again.

Through flickering eyelids fighting to stay closed, a dark shadow moved in her bedroom. A dog-shaped shadow.

Inhaling a refreshing breath, she glanced at the clock: 5:31 a.m.

Her voice groggy, she said, "Morning, Harley."

His tail beat against her nightstand.

For the eighth day in a row, Harley had woken her before her alarm, each occasion within fifteen minutes of the time she'd regularly woken him in the garage. He had an incredible body clock.

Rachel canceled the alarm on her clock. "Shall I get rid of this thing and use you instead?" She patted him.

148

They had their run, after which she showered and once more found Wes dressed in his bedroom — with all his clothes on properly. However, no sooner had they gotten their early-morning routine out of the way and sat at their desk than her phone, lying facedown beside her, rang.

The unknown callers had given her palpitations so often, she now left the device facedown so when it rang, her first reaction was not to check the ID because it was so unreliable.

Without a sigh, without a spike in her heart rate, without her hand trembling, she answered. If it was the owner, it was the owner. But like that person was ever going to call now.

"Hello."

"Hi, Rachel. This is Consuela Jimenez from Jefferson High."

Wes's special needs teacher. What could she possibly want so early in the day?

She continued, "Sorry to call so early, but something's happened that I need to act on as quickly as possible."

"Hi, Consuela. Is there a problem?"

"Quite the contrary. I don't know if you're aware, but I run a Wednesday group for high-functioning students."

"Okay."

"One of my Wednesday group has broken his leg, so he won't be attending for three months. That leaves a vacancy."

"Okay." Where was she going with this? Wes went to the Friday class.

"Now, none of the autistic students are as far along the spectrum as Wesley, but because of his incredible improvements over the last few weeks, I was wondering if you'd consider having Wes join us this coming Wednesday."

Rachel grimaced. "That's an interesting idea, but disrupting his routine so much and thrusting him into a new situation with a bunch of strangers... I think it's too much too soon. But thanks, all the same."

"I hear what you're saying, and under normal circumstances, I wouldn't even suggest something so radical, but I've spoken to the county health department, and as long as it's only for an hour to test if Wesley will settle in, your dog can accompany him."

"Harley can come to school with Wes?"

"For the first hour — though you'd think it was for a year if you saw the paperwork. But that's my problem. If Harley can help Wes settle, this could be a wonderful opportunity. What do you think?"

There was no denying that Wes had made gigantic leaps forward and that it was all because of Harley. Classes that were more stimulating, with students who were more outgoing? All she worked for was to give Wes as rich a life as possible, but changing so much so quickly could come back and bite her big-time.

Rachel said, "But what if it doesn't work out? Does he lose his Friday session?"

"Oh, heavens, no. He'll keep his Friday session, and if Wednesday works out, he'll have that as well for the next three months. Then, if he flourishes the way I'm imagining he will, we can look at a whole new school schedule for him in the next academic year."

There were moments in life that completely change a person's future. Sometimes these opportunities flew by so quickly that a person never saw the golden future lying within their grasp. But other times, the signs were as clear as if they were written in ten-foot-tall neon letters.

"What time on Wednesday?"

Chapter 37

Stretching across the car's back seat, Harley rested his head in Wes's lap. He wanted to sniff out of the window to figure out where they were going to prepare for any job he'd have. However, any future job could wait, because he had an urgent one right now.

Wes rocked back and forth, back and forth, back and forth, muttering incomprehensibly.

Driving, Rachel said, "Wesley, everything's going to be fine, kiddo. You'll see. I know it's unusual for us to be going somewhere today, but you've got me and Harley for help, so everything's going to be just fine. Promise."

Back and forth, back and forth, back and forth.

Harley nuzzled Wes's stomach. He didn't know with what the boy was struggling, but whether Harley had to lick it, bite it, or pee on it, he'd be there for Wes, and he needed Wes to know that.

He nuzzled again.

Back and forth, back and forth, back and forth.

Wes wasn't getting any better. He'd been in a weird mood earlier, so Harley had looked to fetch the TV remote and make the boy smile, but he hadn't found it. This was all his fault. Stupid dog. Stupid.

Back and forth, back and forth, back and forth.

Harley licked Wes's hand but got no response, so he wiggled his head under the boy's hand. Still no response. He couldn't fetch anything to make things better, couldn't lick anything better, couldn't even make any butt explosions because they hadn't had any cheese. He couldn't do anything right today. He whined. Stupid dog.

Rachel said, "Wesley, Harley's upset. You have to help him."

Back and forth, back and forth, back and forth.

"Wesley, Harley is frightened. He doesn't know what's happening. He needs you. He needs his best friend."

Back and forth, back and—

Harley closed his eyes as Wes stopped muttering and stroked him. Job done.

"That's it, Wesley. You help Harley. Show him there's nothing to be afraid of."

The rest of the journey, Wes didn't mutter and didn't rock; he simply sat stroking Harley. It was a genuine job, but Harley always felt he was cheating by doing nothing except letting someone pet him. Any fool could lie there and do nothing. However, it was obviously soothing to Wes, so Harley indulged the boy. Though, truth be told, it felt nice to be the one being pampered for a change.

Without looking out the window, Harley guessed where they were once the car stopped. He hadn't seen the grassy island with a single tree and a thorny bush, but he'd smelled it. He hadn't seen the red brick building, but he'd smelled children. Lots of them.

Harley's tail beat against the seat. He loved kids. They were always so fun to be around. And talk about pampering. He couldn't do a lot of math, but he knew his favorite equation — however many kids there were, there was always double the number of petting hands.

Rachel made a quick phone call, and no sooner had she gotten them both out of the car than a dark-skinned woman ambled toward them.

Harley glanced about. He could smell hordes of children but couldn't see one — all of their scents disappeared into the building.

"Hi, Rachel."

"Hi, Consuela. Thanks for organizing this."

"Wow! What a great dog, Wesley." Consuela petted Harley. "So this is the famous Harley, is it?"

Wes nodded.

"Well, aren't you a handsome boy, Harley?" Consuela scratched him around the ears with both hands.

He turned his head so her fingers could claw different parts. It was always a joy to meet new friends. Especially those who seemed to have exquisite taste in dogs. Being petted wasn't such a bad job after all.

Still petting Harley, Consuela looked at Rachel. "Any problems?"

Rachel said, "Harley was upset earlier, but Wes calmed him, didn't you, Wes?"

Again, Wes nodded. "He's a good dog, but he was frightened, so I helped."

"Your mom says he's really smart, too. She said you might show me and some of the other children. Could you do that?"

He shrugged.

Rachel dug in her purse and revealed the TV remote.

Harley gasped. That was why he couldn't find it this morning! How was he supposed to do his job without the proper tools?

Wes smirked, taking the TV remote.

Consuela said, "So you'll come in and show my class how special Harley is?"

Wes nodded. "He's very special. The most special dog in the whole world."

Consuela led them through the double glass doors at the front of the building and along the cream-walled hallway. Gray metal cupboards lined either side, broken up occasionally by a door or a brightly colored poster. Consuela and Rachel talked, but Harley barely heard a word because the place was bursting with more scents than he could count — so many new friends to meet.

Harley wagged his tail so hard his body wiggled when he walked.

They ascended stairs that doubled back on themselves, then turned left into another hallway. Halfway along, Consuela pulled some black material from her pocket and handed it to Rachel. "I borrowed this from a colleague. You're sure he'll be okay with it?"

Rachel winced. "He's the most laid-back animal I've ever come across, but..."

"It's only until we're certain he's safe around a group of children, then it can come off."

Rachel crouched, holding a muzzle. "Be a good boy, Harley. This won't hurt."

Harley didn't like muzzles. Not least because they made it impossible for him to do his job properly. But if Rachel wanted him to wear one...

He raised his snout and closed his eyes.

Rachel fitted it and snickered. "What did I tell you? He's just full of surprises."

Consuela frowned. "And he was a stray you found?"

"In the park. Some teenagers were abusing him."

"Awww, the poor thing." She clapped. "Okay, I'll go remind the students what's happening, then bring you in. I only have one teaching assistant today, but this is a good group, so I can't see any problems."

153

Consuela entered the classroom. A short time later, she ushered them into a room with three rows of four desks; the desk on the far right of the second row was the only one unoccupied. Gaudy paintings plastered the left-hand wall and a blackboard covered most of the wall on the right, a flag beside it. Windows on the other two walls overlooked the street and the side of the building.

Harley trotted in with Rachel and Wes. From behind the desks, faces smiled and eyes sparkled. New friends!

Harley wanted to yip and yip with joy. Wanted to lick each person. Wanted to nuzzle and sniff and jump and run and bark and chase...

But he knew his purpose.

Ever the professional, he strolled in as casually as he could, though he was sure his tail was giving him away – the thing just would not stop wagging. At times, it felt like the thing had a mind of its own. He'd punished it with a bite on more than one occasion, but pain always stabbed his back end as if it were biting him back – the vicious little thing. He'd come to the conclusion that, though it didn't seem to be good for anything other than annoying him, he was stuck with it. So like living with a naughty younger brother, he just had to suffer the inconvenience and get used to rolling his eyes at its antics.

"Okay, everybody, this is Rachel, Wesley, and Harley." Consuela gestured to each of them in turn. "I'm hoping Wesley will like us enough to want to visit again soon. Ben" – she gestured to a bearded man in a blue sweater – "will bring you up one at a time to meet Harley."

Ben pushed a girl in a wheelchair over to Harley.

Harley felt Rachel tighten her grip on his leash, as though she was worried he might run or jump. Why on earth would he do that? It had been years since he'd had an audience like this.

Consuela said, "Bianca, this is Harley. Be gentle because he's had a rough time living on the streets, so needs people to be nice to him."

Bianca beamed and petted Harley on the shoulders so delicately he hardly felt it.

She smiled at Wes. "He's so soft."

Wes peered from beneath his bangs. He nodded, then scratched behind Harley's left ear. "He likes this."

Bianca scratched Harley as she'd been shown.

Wes said, "Good job."

154

Harley tilted his head closer. That was more like it. He glanced around at his tail. Yep, there it was, flailing about like a lunatic. Just once it would be nice if it gave him a little privacy and didn't reveal his feelings to the whole world.

Next, Ben brought over a boy who wobbled when he walked, despite having a cane in each hand. After came a boy with thick glasses whose mouth seemed twisted, coming out of the side of his face instead of the front. Then a girl approached who appeared perfectly ordinary. Each of them, and all those who followed, scratched Harley behind the ears, just as Wes had demonstrated, then looked to Wes as if seeking approval. The boy nodded to each one.

More than once, Harley caught Rachel dabbing her eyes with a white tissue. People were such weird creatures. Here he was having the time of his life and there she was crying. The only people he'd ever seen do that had all been in pain, yet no one was hurting today. People were such a puzzle. Thank heavens for Wes — a person who was emotionally open and eager to engage with those around him.

When the last student had petted Harley, Consuela said to Rachel, "Looks like the muzzle was overkill. Do you want to take it off?"

Rachel removed the muzzle and unclipped Harley's leash.

Harley drew a deep breath. So much better. What now?

Rachel said, "Wesley, do you want to show the class what makes Harley so special?" She pointed to the TV remote in his hand.

Wes held the device above his head for everyone to see and toddled up the wide aisle between the desks. He placed the remote on a table at the back on which sat a Swiss cheese plant.

Harley couldn't help but bounce up and down. He had a job. A job. A job!

Wesley returned to the front.

Harley gazed at him. He knew what was coming but being the professional, he had to wait for those magic words.

Wes said, "Harley, TV remote."

With all eyes on him, Harley trotted to the back of the room, pushed onto his hind legs, gently took the device in his jaws, and trotted back. He sat in front of the boy and presented his prize. Wes took it.

All the students clapped.

Wes hung his head, trying to hide behind his bangs, but he couldn't hide his smile.

Rachel said, "Show them something else." She nodded to the wall.

Wes said, "Harley, light switch."

Harley gasped. Wonderful. A proper challenge.

As eager gazes scrutinized him, he surveyed the room. Where would he find a light switch? Switches were always on a wall, always higher than his nose, not usually on windows — he gasped again — but often near a door!

He spun to the only door in the room. Yes!

Whispers flitting through the air behind him, he padded over, pushed onto his hind legs, and swatted the switch with a forepaw. The room's lights extinguished.

The students laughed and clapped.

Harley trotted back to Wes to await his next assignment.

Instead of issuing a command, Wes ambled over to Bianca. He placed the TV remote on her desk. "Your turn."

Rachel clutched her mouth, Consuela's jaw dropped, and Bianca beamed with excitement. She whispered to Ben, who wheeled her to the side of the room while she held the device aloft. She left the device at the foot of a small bookcase below the windows, then returned to her desk.

She scratched her head. "I've forgotten what to say."

Rachel scooted over and whispered in her ear.

Bianca said, "Harley, TV remote."

Harley looked at the girl, then Wes, then Rachel. Was no one capable of remembering where they put stuff? How did these people ever function without him?

He retrieved the remote and presented it to Bianca. Everyone in the classroom cheered and applauded.

Harley rejoined Wes and faced the class. Which memory-impaired person needed his help now?

Outside, as if in agony, a dog howled the most mournful howl Harley had ever heard.

Consuela said, "What the devil's going on outside?"

Chapter 38

Like everybody else, Harley scrambled to the back of the room and peered out of the window.

Alone, a small brown dog sat in the middle of the asphalt yard. He raised his head to the sky and howled with all his might.

Harley shivered. It was the most harrowing sound he'd ever heard.

He gasped. Wait... Pressing his nose against the window, he squinted, studying the dog.

It couldn't be...

He checked the nearby windows. The one to his right was cracked open, so he sniffed as hard as he could and closed his eyes to focus on the scents drifting in on cold air.

He snapped his eyes open. It was the kid!

Again, the kid howled. It was filled with such sorrow; it felt like someone was reaching into Harley's chest and crushing his heart with ice. What could have happened to the little guy in such a short time that he was suffering such horrendous loss?

Two men darted outside, followed by a handful of children.

One man dashed to confront the kid, the hair combed over the top of his head flapping in the breeze. Brandishing a flat stick with markings on it, he lunged. "Get out of here, stupid dog!"

The kid dodged the angry man with ease. The youngster was a brown ball of speed, while the man was all elbows and knees. Foolish man. Like he had any chance of catching a fit young dog.

It was a pity Harley hadn't had longer with the kid to teach him more about the ways of the world, but this man needed to give him a break — having been abandoned on the street, how was the kid to know how to behave?

As the dog and the man faced off against each other, another voice sliced through the air, a young girl's voice.

"Kai!"

A girl with flowing black hair raced toward the dog, and he raced toward her.

Angry Man shouted, "Please don't tell me this is your dog, Mia Dubanowski. You do know it's against regulations to bring pets to school, don't you?"

Crouching, she flung her arms around the kid, who licked and licked her. She laughed so much she couldn't get the words out to reply to the man.

Harley's heart glowed for the kid. The youngster had found somebody. Somebody incredibly special if the way she was lavishing her love upon him was anything to go by. Just like Harley had. Okay, the kid had a thing or two to learn about not creating a scene in public, but dogs weren't born with wisdom; that was something they developed as they learned how to cope with the weird ways of people.

Consuela clapped. "Okay, everybody, the excitement's over. Back to your desks, please."

Rachel guided Harley to the front of the class, but Harley's mind was on anything but another job. The kid had found a pack, so he would have a fantastic life. That was the best news ever. Harley hoped they'd meet again one day and could swap stories of the things they'd fetched, the things they'd sniffed, and the best things on which they'd peed.

Chapter 39

With Wes seated at the spare desk, Rachel led Harley into the hallway with Consuela.

Rachel said, "I can't believe Wes handed the remote control to another student like that."

"I know." Consuela's eyes widened. "He's never shared anything in class before. If this is a sign of things to come, it's going to open a whole new world for him."

Rachel covered her eyes and turned away. Seeing Wes interact with complete strangers was overwhelming.

Her voice faltered. "I'm sorry. It's just..."

Consuela laid her hand on Rachel's arm. "Wes has taken a huge step forward today. You must be so proud."

Rachel nodded, dabbing her eyes with a tissue.

Consuela said, "And it's all because of this guy." She patted Harley. "Who'd have thunk it?"

"It's incredible. Like we're living in a dream."

"I'm guessing he might've been a service dog before finding himself on the streets."

"You mean like a seeing eye dog?" Rachel arched her eyebrows. "Oh. I figured someone had trained him for fun."

Consuela chuckled. "For fun? Are you kidding me? To do what he does, Harley must've had months of intensive training and years of experience in helping people with physical or mental issues."

"Seriously?"

"You think it's easy for a dog to learn those skills? It would take months. Literally. And cost maybe twenty or thirty thousand dollars."

Rachel gawked. "What?"

"Oh, yeah. Thirty thousand easy."

"Wow."

"And he was a stray living in the park?"

"Yeah. I called the number on his tag and left a note at the address, but no one's gotten back to me."

Consuela raised her eyebrows and shook her head.

"Why?" said Rachel. "Is that a problem?"

"Well, it's not a problem if he was abandoned. But after spending so much money to train him, why wouldn't his owner want him back?"

Rachel shrugged. "It's not like I haven't tried. It's been three weeks now and we've heard nothing."

"For Wesley's sake, let's hope that's how it continues."

Consuela went back to her class and Rachel meandered along the hallway, Harley back on his leash. Thirty thousand dollars? That was like someone leaving their keys in their new car and walking away to let someone else take it. No one would ever do that, so why had someone paid so much to train a dog but wasn't desperate to get it back?

Still, it wasn't like she'd found a valuable dog and kept quiet about it. She'd done everything imaginable to return him, so on moral or legal grounds, surely there could be no repercussions.

She rubbed her brow. Just to be safe, maybe she'd call the lawyer who'd handled her divorce.

"Just my luck." That was all she needed when she was cutting back — legal expenses.

At the car, she secured Harley in the back and sat in the front. Dog ownership was an emotional roller coaster, with the incredible joy and wonder Harley brought being counterbalanced by horrendous anxiety and fear.

What could possibly go wrong next?

Her phone rang.

She sniggered. Talk about timing.

Averting her gaze so, if it was displaying, she wouldn't see an unknown caller ID to send her stress levels rocketing, she answered, "Hello."

"Hello. Am I speaking to Rachel, please?"

"This is she."

"Great. This is Jordan Stein, senior partner at Harvey, Stein, and Pollock Attorneys at Law. I understand you're in possession of a dog belonging to Barney Whitlock of 612 Ridgemount Drive."

Rachel's jaw dropped as her world imploded. She stared through the windshield but saw nothing and heard nothing. The world was suddenly silent, still, and very, very gray — as if she was trapped in an old black-and-white photograph.

Wes. What would happen to him now?

"Rachel?"

She pictured Wes at the far end of the sofa, silent, isolated, cringing if she encroached a fraction of an inch into the no-man's-land of the middle cushion. They'd lived in a gray world where life merely existed, then Harley had arrived and their world had burst into dazzling technicolor.

"Hello? Rachel?"

Having let Wes glimpse the wonders of companionship and love, how could she push him back into a lonely, gray life?

She did the only thing a loving mother could do — she hung up, threw the phone onto the passenger seat, then slumped over the steering wheel. And sobbed.

What was she going to do?

What the devil was she going to do?

Chapter 40

As the car wound along the tree-lined road, Rachel dragged her hand across her puffy red eyes, smearing tears.

Harley strained against the leash tied to the rear armrest. Rachel was in such pain. He had to reach her, had to help her. But he couldn't. Being kept from his purpose was torture. He whimpered.

His mouth fell open as a horrific realization dawned.

Maybe she was upset over something he'd done.

He whimpered again. Had he been bad? Had she been disappointed in the jobs he'd done for the children? That would explain why she hadn't said a word to him since leaving Wes.

He curled up on the back seat, trying to make himself as small as possible to disappear into the cushion so he'd no longer be a burden. He trembled. This was his fault. What else could it be?

Back at home, he hid under the dining table, peeping out to watch over Rachel as she sobbed on the sofa. He ached to run to her and lick everything better, but how could he — he was the cause of her anguish. He'd be lucky if he wasn't back on the street by the time the darkness came.

He whined. He'd tried to be good. Tried so, so hard. But obviously some dogs were deep down bad no matter what they did. That was probably why Barney had stopped. Bad, bad, bad!

Rachel picked up her phone.

A moment later, Izzy's voice came from the device. "Hey. Do you know dogs can smell time?"

Rachel sobbed.

"Rach? What's happened? Is Wes okay?"

Blubbering, Rachel struggled to get the words out. "They're" — sob — "taking" — shuddering breath — "Harley!"

"What? Who? Who's taking Harley?"

162

"Some lawyer."

"What did they say?"

"I don't" — snort — "know."

"You don't know? You mean you haven't actually spoken to anyone yet?"

Rachel wiped her fingers over her cheeks. "No."

"So this lawyer doesn't know if you still have Harley or not?"

"No."

"And the only information you gave the owner was your first name and cell phone number?"

Rachel threw her free hand up. "What's that matter? They're taking Harley. What am I going to—"

"Rachel, listen to me. You know what you have to do because we talked about it. You have to do what any mother would do for her son — lie your freaking butt off!"

Rachel shook her head. "I can't."

"Sorry, Rach, but you're going to have to grow a pair. Good grief, you took in a lost dog, phoned the owner, and even trekked to their house to return it, and they thank you by setting some shark of a lawyer on you? Listen, you lie. You hear? They don't deserve a dog like Harley."

"I can't." She slapped the arm of the sofa.

"Yes, you can."

"Izzy...!" Burying her face in her hands, Rachel heaved up and trudged a couple of steps. Finally, all hunched up, she said, "Iz, you don't understand. Harley's worth thirty thousand dollars."

"So? His owner is scum to treat you like this. Listen, they don't have your last name, address, or landline. If you dump your cell phone, they have no way of contacting you, let alone finding you. So you lie, girl. You hear? Lie your freaking head off and give Wes the life he deserves."

Rachel straightened up, her arms and shoulders relaxing. She sniffled. "Okay."

"Promise me you won't do anything stupid."

"I promise." She sank back into her seat.

"Okay. I'll get home as soon as I can and we'll talk. So long."

"Bye."

Harley dared to lift his head. If Rachel was talking to Izzy, maybe she was starting to feel better, and if she was feeling better, maybe she'd forgive him for being bad.

His tail between his legs, head hanging, he slunk from underneath the table. He crept forward, gaze drilling into Rachel for the slightest indication he should run and hide again. Her sobbing had stopped and her breathing had smoothed out, so he crept another step. She didn't shout at him, or glare with bitter disappointment, so he dared take another step. Then another. And another.

If he could reach her, maybe there was a chance he could put everything back to the way it had been yesterday, when they were a happy, loving pack.

Finally at her side, he whimpered, head down, gazing up at her from the corners of his eyes. He didn't want to be a bad dog. If she gave him another chance, he'd promise to try harder, promise to do his jobs even better.

"Harley." Her voice was so quiet, it was almost a whisper.

Through smeared tears and a puffy red face, his friend smiled. Smiled just for him.

Harley knew it was against the rules, knew it was unprofessional, knew it was what a bad dog would do, not a good one, but he just couldn't help himself — he leaped into Rachel's lap and licked and licked and licked her.

As if by magic, his licking made everything better — Rachel laughed and flung her arms around him.

He nuzzled her.

He was home. Home.

Chapter 41

Rachel hugged Harley. Izzy was right — the owner had to be an absolute monster to set a lawyer on her instead of simply calling. She squeezed Harley. He was going nowhere. He was home, and that was where he was staying.

Peter had walked out four years ago. There'd been no one in her life since, and because of Wes's no-touching rule, the closest she came to human contact was birthday hugs from Izzy or a Thanksgiving cuddle from her mom. Rachel had told herself it didn't matter, that she was better off alone, like Wes. She'd told herself opening up to another person ultimately led to only one thing — pain. But now, enjoying the warmth of another being, sensing them breathe, feeling their heart beating...

Wes hadn't just withdrawn himself from the world, he'd withdrawn her too. Well, no more. It was time for them both to reemerge. Like butterflies from chrysalises. She wanted to feel. She *needed* to feel.

She kissed Harley on the forehead. "You've only been here a few weeks but, boy, I don't know what we'd do without you. I hope what I'm about to do will show you how grateful I am."

Checking her phone, she found a new voicemail. Unsurprisingly, it was the lawyer asking her to call him. His voice was light, soothing, and trustworthy — like a daytime TV host who'd talk about cancer one minute and the next, the best way to peel a potato. Not at all like a shark. But she wasn't going to let that fool her.

She knew what she had to do. And she'd practiced it enough in her mind to be able to do it. She phoned before she chickened out, hoping the lawyer wasn't already suspicious after the earlier call.

A perky female voice said, "Good afternoon, Harvey, Stein, and Pollock Attorneys at Law, Jordan Stein's office. How can I help you?"

Her hand shaking, Rachel said, "Hello, I'm returning Mr. Stein's call. My name's Rachel."

"Rachel...?"

They were getting no personal information that might enable someone to identify her. "He'll know what it's about."

"One moment, please."

That soothing voice said, "Rachel, Jordan Stein. I'm sorry to be contacting you so long after you reached out to Mr. Whitlock about his dog, but I can assure you of a speedy resolution to the matter now. And of course, any incidental expenses will be reimbursed in full. You do still have Harley, I take it?"

This was it. This was a moment on which Wes's entire future hinged.

Her mouth was so dry it felt like she'd been gargling sand.

"I'm sorry, Mr. Stein, but I let Harley out for a pee last week and he jumped the fence. I haven't seen him since."

The tension melted from her shoulders. It was done. Harley was hers.

"Last week?"

"Yes."

"Which day last week?"

She said the first day that came into her head. "Thursday."

"About what time?"

She swallowed hard. What was he doing? He wasn't supposed to ask questions, just accept her story. If she wasn't careful, this shark would eat her alive.

"Look, I'm sorry, but I called the owner, visited his house, left a note — did everything I could to return the darn dog. It's not my fault he took too long to get in touch."

"Again, my apologies for that, but without going into specifics, which I can't because of client confidentiality, all I can say is it's vital we find Harley as soon as possible."

"Why? Is he valuable?"

"He's not a mutt, but he's not a show dog, if that's what you mean."

Typical lawyer — dodging the truth at all costs.

"Well, I don't get why the owner didn't call me after I left the first message but weeks later has an attorney call instead."

"I wish I could proffer some explanation, Ms....?"

She left him hanging.

He continued, "... but again, client confidentiality. I'm sure you understand."

"And I'm sure you understand, Mr. Stein, I did all I could to return the dog, but now it's out of my hands."

"I don't like to press you on this, Rachel, but where did—"

"I'm sorry, Mr. Stein, but I don't like how I'm getting the third degree as if I've done something wrong. Unlike you, I'm not getting paid for this call, and I have work to get back to. I've told you everything I know, so goodbye."

She hung up. She clutched her heart. "Oh Lord." She dropped her head back, exhaling loudly. "Thank heavens that's over."

Closing her eyes, she replayed the conversation. She hadn't given any information that could identify her. Excellent. Harley was hers and Wes's.

So why was a sickness clawing at her insides? The deed was done. No one could find her. She'd done the right thing for Wes.

She slapped the arm of the sofa. She might've done the right thing for Wes, but she hadn't done the right thing.

"Oh, for crying out loud." It was done. It couldn't be undone. She should be celebrating, not chastising herself.

Harley was still sitting in her lap. She hugged him, reveling in the togetherness, then took him to the study, where he sat at her feet while she dove into her work in the hope it would clear the doubts from her mind.

By the time evening rolled around and Izzy waltzed in, Rachel had subdued her pangs of guilt.

Izzy held up a bottle of wine in her right hand. "Are we celebrating" — she held up another in her left — "or commiserating?"

Rachel smirked, pointing to Izzy's right hand.

"Hey, the girl done good." Izzy cupped a bottle under her arm and raised her free hand, and they high-fived. She sauntered toward the kitchen. "I'll get glasses."

Izzy nodded to Wes dozing on the sofa with Harley sprawled beside him. "How was the new gig?"

"It was a shaky start, but his teacher thinks he'll fit right in. All the stress and excitement wiped him out."

"So gold stars all round." Izzy held up a corkscrew. "We are cracking this open now, I take it?"

"After the day I've had, you better believe it."

Izzy inserted the corkscrew. "Any problems with the shark?"

"Nuh-uh."

"He didn't manage to wheedle any information out of you?"

"He tried, but I stuck to my story, so what could he do?"

Izzy grinned. "Look at you, all waterboarding-won't-work-on-me."

Rachel rolled her eyes. "Yeah, right. I almost had a coronary when he started firing questions at me."

"Doesn't matter now. You did what needed doing." Izzy popped the cork. "You do know you shouldn't take Harley out in public for a few months to play it safe."

"I know."

"I mean, your morning runs should be fine because who in their right mind even gets out of bed at that time? But anything else is off-limits until people have moved on and Harley's forgotten about." She took a couple of glasses from a cupboard.

"Yeah."

Izzy stared into space. "Unless there's such a thing as dog dye. Well, either that or a fake moustache? For Harley — yours is coming along quite nicely."

Rachel slapped her arm. "I do not have a mustache." She snickered. "I waxed it last week."

"Oh, yeah?" She poured the red wine. "Are you thinking about putting yourself out there again?"

"Yeah, right. Because I don't have enough stress already."

Izzy checked to make sure Wes was sleeping, but she still leaned closer to Rachel. "Don't you ever get an itch you can't scratch by yourself?"

"It was getting an itch that got me into this situation."

"Really?"

"A weekend away and some fool forgot her pills. I did a quick calculation in my head about where I was in my cycle and..." She shrugged.

"So it's safe to say math isn't your strong suit?"

"Hence the art."

Izzy laughed, sliding a glass to Rachel. "So Wes is only here because you couldn't resist doing the juicy Lucy?"

Rachel shook her head. "The juicy Lucy? Where the devil do you get these phrases?"

"From my homies in the hood." She raised her hand to fist-bump.

Smirking, Rachel held up her wine. "So is it time for a gangsta rap or a drink?"

"To the newest dog owner in town."

They clinked glasses and drank.

Rachel swirled the wine around in her glass and gazed at it.

"Hey," said Izzy.

"Hmmm?"

"What's done is done. You need to flush that gleaming moral compass of yours down the john before it gets you into serious trouble."

Rachel nodded. Izzy was right. But she couldn't shake the feeling that this was going to come back and bite her. Bite her big-time.

Chapter 42

The next day, Rachel couldn't concentrate on Wes's lesson, so even with Harley present, he became irritable, mumbling answers and glaring from under his bangs.

During his afternoon nap, Rachel stared at a blank screen. The creative part of her mind was overwhelmed by the emotional part, which heaped more and more pangs of guilt upon her. Finally, she collapsed over her desk and wept. How was it possible she'd done both the right thing and the wrong thing?

The problem was Harley wasn't a stray she'd found but a service dog who helped someone with physical or mental issues. Someone just like Wes. Maybe even less able than him. If she returned Harley, she'd ruin Wes's life. If she didn't, she'd ruin someone else's. Whatever she did, how could she live with herself after? It was one thing to joke with Izzy about stealing a dog worth $30,000, but the reality of doing it, knowing it could strip someone of their life, was too much. The maggots of guilt were devouring her from the inside out.

That night, she lay in bed, staring at the ceiling and hoping an answer would magically manifest. It didn't.

The next morning as she drove home having dropped Wes at school, Rachel determined what she had to do — the only thing she could do if she wanted to look at herself in the mirror without cringing.

Sitting on the sofa, Harley lounging with his head in her lap, Rachel wiped away her tears and forced herself to smile. If this was going to work, she had to sound upbeat. She petted him. "I'm sorry, Harley. I don't know if this is the right thing for you, but I have to do it."

She phoned the lawyer.

"Hello again, Rachel," said Stein. "I must say, after our last conversation, I'm surprised to hear from you. Does this mean you have some news?"

She bit her bottom lip, as if part of her wanted to hold in the words she was about to say.

"Taylor. My name is Rachel Taylor."

It was done. And now it couldn't be undone.

"Is there something I can help you with, Rachel Taylor?"

She forced another smile, the change in her facial muscles changing the tone of her voice so no one would guess she'd been sobbing.

"Yes, I have good news, Mr. Stein. I've been putting out dog food every day, just in case, and last night, Harley came back."

His light tone transformed, as if he'd been slouching in his chair but had leaned forward to give something his full attention. "You mean he's there now? You actually have him?"

She screwed her eyes shut as the civil war raged inside her. Wes versus a stranger? Wes versus a stranger? Wes—

"Yes. He's sitting with me now." She gritted her teeth as tears ran down her cheeks.

"Oh, that's wonderful. And it couldn't be better timing."

She held the phone away for a moment while she drew a shuddering breath, then forced another smile.

"I hoped you'd be pleased. Though that might change when you see my invoice for all the food he's eaten."

Stein laughed. "I'm going to have to up my billable hours to cover it, am I? Listen, I hope this isn't too much of an imposition, but it would be great if you could bring the dog by the office this afternoon. Would that be a possibility? I should add, there's a reward involved for having found him."

She was going to be rewarded for breaking Wes's heart and destroying his future?

"It depends on the time. I have to pick my son up from school later."

"Your son, huh? I don't want to pry, but how did your family get on with the dog? Any problems?"

"No, he's a great dog. Any family—" Her chin trembled, so she cleared her throat to stall and give her a moment to compose herself. "Excuse me. Any family would be thrilled to have him."

"It's not going to be a problem giving him up, is it?"

She screwed up her face and gulped, forcing down the emotion. "You still haven't" — she cleared her throat again — "said what time to bring him."

"Sorry. One thirty would be great."

"One thirty. Okay."

After Stein gave her directions to their offices, she hung up and collapsed over Harley, sobbing.

"I'm sorry, Wes. I'm so sorry. Please, forgive me."

Chapter 43

At 1:25 p.m. Rachel shoved the smoked glass door on which was emblazoned in gold-and-black lettering Harvey, Stein, and Pollock. She and Harley approached a red-haired woman at the reception desk. The woman phoned Stein's secretary. Seconds later, instead of the perky-voiced woman appearing, a man strolled over with a shaven head and gray suit that fit him so perfectly it looked like part of him.

He held out his hand. "Ms. Taylor?"

"Rachel, please."

"Jordan Stein, counsel for Barney Whitlock. Call me Jordan." He crouched, grinning as he ruffled Harley's fur. "And here's the little troublemaker. I haven't seen you for a while, have I, Harley?" Harley turned his head to have his neck scratched.

Rachel squinted at Jordan. "You know Harley?"

"Sure. I represented Barney for years, so we go way back. Don't we, fella?"

He smiled up at Rachel, his expression unchanging yet seeming like he was studying her. She glanced away, anxious her makeup wouldn't hide her puffy red eyes under close scrutiny.

She said, "If it's okay, can we just get this over with, please?"

He stood. "Of course. Come this way, please." He gestured in the direction from which he'd come.

His office was the size of her living room, with windows on two sides. On the back wall hung a forty-inch TV, below which sat a glass cabinet housing four rows of shelves that displayed twenty baseballs, equidistantly spaced, each grubby and appearing to have something scrawled on it.

Two chairs were occupied at the far right of his desk, while just one was empty at the far left. He gestured to the single chair.

Rachel looked at it, then at the couple gawking at her from the other seats. Slouched in the farthest chair, a man with a big nose and more stubble on his chin than on his head glared at her. "And who the devil is this now?"

Beside him, a woman wearing more makeup than Rachel owned looked her up and down as though she'd smelled something unpleasant.

Jordan said, "This is the star attraction we've been waiting for, Mr. Whitlock — Harley and his friend, Rachel."

"I know who Harley is. But why's she here?"

Whitlock? That was the name Jordan had used — the name of Harley's owner. She stared at the scruffy, chubby guy. Oh no, what had she done?

Jordan leaned back in his chair and steepled his fingers. "Now that's a great question, Mr. Whitlock." Again he gestured to the single chair. "Please, Rachel, have a seat."

She held the leash toward him. "Look, I've returned Harley, now I just want to be on my way, if that's okay."

Jordan smiled. The kind of smile it was hard to say no to. "Indulge me."

She plonked back down, folding her arms. As if ruining Wes's life wasn't bad enough, now she had to suffer this pompous idiot's games.

Whitlock leaned forward and jabbed a stubby finger at Jordan, a black line embedded under the nail. He was either a manual laborer who'd come from work or a slob. Rachel didn't like to judge people, but...

Whitlock said, "My dad paid you good money to handle his estate, so quit the games and tell me when I get the house."

Rachel frowned. What was going on here? If this guy's father was dead and he was waiting to get his hands on the house, what did it have to do with her?

Wait... his father would be named Whitlock, too. And if the house was passing to the son, that meant it was empty, so no one would be there to get phone messages or a note left in a mailbox.

With an emotionless expression, Jordan looked from her to the couple, then down to Harley. "I'm afraid, Mr. Whitlock, it's not so straightforward."

Whitlock turned to the woman and shook his head. "What did I tell you? This is when it all starts."

Jordan frowned. "When what starts, Mr. Whitlock?"

Whitlock sneered. "The legal shenanigans." Without looking at Rachel, he nodded at her. "And the vultures crawling out of the woodwork."

Rachel held the arms of the chair to push up. "I should go."

Jordan didn't even look at her; he just waved her back into her seat. "Mr. Whitlock, if you feel you've suffered any legal shenanigans, by all means, please feel free to her report me to the state bar. In the meantime, however, I'll let your father answer your questions." He gestured to the TV and clicked a remote control.

A haggard man with a shock of white hair appeared on the screen. "Hello, Denzel."

Harley sat bolt upright, fixated on the TV, ears pricked. He yipped.

Barney's tone lowered, suggesting he didn't care for the person he next addressed, "Moira." He grimaced. "I'd always hoped we'd reconcile our differences, Denzel, but if you're watching this, that's proven not to be the case, which I am genuinely heartbroken about, believe me. That said, I was a stubborn old goat, so I don't deny the burden is on me as much as anyone else."

"What the devil is this?" said Denzel.

Jordan paused the video. "Barney Whitlock's last will and testimony. If you want the house, I suggest you continue watching." He clicked play.

"Now, Denzel, I know the only thing you're going to care about is the house." Barney shook his head like a parent who'd continually encouraged a child to do the right thing only to be continually disappointed. "Me? All I care about is the little guy sitting there with you." He broke into a wide smile, his aged yellowing eyes sparkling like a child's at Christmas. He waved. "Harley? Harley?"

Standing, Harley barked and wagged his tail.

"How you doing, boy?" said Barney. "I'm sorry I left you, but I hope you're being well looked after. I'll be waiting when your time down there is done." He sighed, his eyes welling up. "But back to business. Denzel, I want to do what I couldn't do in life — I want to give you the best thing I possibly can, the only thing of true value I've ever owned."

Denzel and Moira smirked at each other.

Barney said, "Now before you ask, the house is already spoken for, and that's nonnegotiable, so I'm going to give you my most treasured possession — Harley. There are some provisos, which I'll let my friend Jordan explain."

"The dog?" Denzel threw his hands up. "I get the freaking dog? Are you kidding?"

Moira said, "So who gets the house?"

Jordan pointed to the recording. "We'll get to that, but the first priority is establishing ownership of Harley."

Denzel held his arms wide. "What do I want a dog for? Can we just get to the important stuff?"

Rachel gripped the arms of the chair again. Maybe all wasn't lost yet. If Barney's next of kin didn't want Harley, maybe they could make a deal.

"As I said, we'll get to the" — Jordan made air quotes — "'important stuff' shortly. So are you confirming you do not want legal ownership of Harley, Mr. Whitlock?"

He shrugged. "What am I gonna do with the dog?"

"I need a definitive yes or no, please."

"No, I don't want the freaking thing."

Moira cupped her hand to his ear and whispered something. Jordan took that opportunity to drill his gaze into Rachel, as if willing her to say something.

Rachel gulped. "If, er, Mr. Whitlock doesn't want Harley, maybe I–"

Denzel held his hand up to Rachel. "Now just hold your horses there, Harley's friend. I never said I didn't want the dog."

"Yes, you did, Mr. Whitlock." Jordan pointed to a recording device on his desk. "I can play it back for you, if you like."

"Yeah, but I haven't signed anything yet, so it's not legal, right?"

"Correct."

Denzel smirked, shooting Rachel a sideways glance. "Yes, we want the dog."

Jordan said, "Okay. Thank you for clarifying that point."

Rachel crumpled as if a boxer had slammed a hook into her gut. It was done. And what was done couldn't be undone.

Jordan slipped a paper from a file and slid it partway toward Denzel. The man reached for it, but Jordan pulled it back at the last moment.

Jordan said, "You are aware it cost just shy of $28,000 to train Harley as a service dog, and as such, he's a very valuable piece of property."

"I can't say as I was aware of that, no."

"Now you're aware." Jordan shoved the paper over. "Bear that in mind as you read the contract of ownership."

Denzel snatched the contract and leaned back, reading. He glowered. "I don't eat prime beef every day, but I'm supposed to feed it to a dog?" A moment later, he squinted at something. "Seriously?" He tutted, then glanced up at Jordan.

Jordan did nothing but raise an eyebrow.

Denzel returned to the contract. Moira gasped and pointed at something.

"This is a joke, right?" said Denzel. "We can't ever sell the dog? What's all that about?"

"Those are your father's wishes. And should you sign to take the dog, they are legally enforceable."

Denzel snickered and pointed to a section. "And one of us has to quit our job to be at home with him every day! Why?" He put on a baby voice and glared at Harley. "So he won't be lonely?" He flung the paper onto the desk. "Do what you want with the thing. Make it into burgers for all I care."

Jordan unscrewed the top of a fountain pen. "That's your final decision — you do not want legal ownership of Harley, former service dog to Mr. Barney Whitlock of 612 Ridgemount Drive?"

Denzel smirked. "Do you need it in blood, or can I use that pen?"

Jordan slid a second sheet over and pointed. "Sign here" — he flipped the page — "and here."

Denzel signed. "Now, can we get to the house, please?"

Rachel said, "Excuse me, could I see the contract of ownership, please?"

The tiniest of smiles flickered across Jordan's face. "Certainly." He passed it.

"Hey, she can't sell it if I can't."

Jordan nodded. "The same contract applies to any interested party."

Rachel scowled at Denzel. "Why would I want to sell him?"

She scanned the document. Everything Denzel had mentioned was there and more, including an annual visit to ensure that the terms of the contract were being adhered to.

Jordan said, "As I said to Mr. Whitlock, this is a legally enforceable contract. His dietary requirements, health insurance, and sundry expenses would be a considerable monthly expense."

Denzel chimed in. "Especially when you quit your job."

Rachel didn't even look up. "I work from home. And I live on a bus route, so I'll sell my car to cover things, if I have to."

"For a *dog?*" Denzel snorted and shook his head.

She said, "Can I borrow your pen, please, Jordan?"

He let her and she signed. She placed the pen and contract on the desk and stood. "Thank you for your time, Jordan. Now excuse me, but I have to take *my* dog home." She glared at Denzel.

Jordan said, "Indulge me a moment longer, please, Rachel." He gestured to her chair.

She'd been happy with her exit line. It was polite, yet cutting. The last thing she wanted was to sit and endure more of this odious Denzel Whitlock. But Jordan hadn't steered her wrong yet, so she sat.

"As requested, Mr. Whitlock" — Jordan clicked play — "let's get to the *important stuff.*"

Barney said, "Though I sincerely hope I'm wrong, Denzel, I'm guessing you've just thrown a hissy fit because you didn't see the value in Harley. Outside of the monetary value, that is." He sucked through his teeth. "Well, be prepared for another hissy fit. My house and all my worldly possessions, I leave to Harley..."

Denzel leaped up. He jabbed his stubby finger at Jordan. "This is bull. Complete bull. You can't do this."

Jordan slipped another piece of paper from the folder. "I can and I have. Take it to any law firm in the country and they'll tell you the same — Harley is the proud owner of 612 Ridgemount Drive and everything therein."

Denzel grabbed the paper, ripped it to shreds, and threw it in the air.

Jordan glanced at Rachel. "Dang, if only we'd thought to make a copy." He glared at Denzel. "Now, are you going to pull on your big boy pants and discuss this like adults, or is your father right and we're going to see another hissy fit?"

Denzel glowered, nostrils flaring. "Who the devil do you think you are talking to me like that?"

Unflustered, Jordan said, "I'm *your father's* attorney, not yours, so I'll speak to you any way I darn well please. You want to act like a little princess, then that's how I'll treat you."

Eyes wild, Denzel slapped his palms down on the desk and reared over Jordan. "Think you're a big man behind your big desk, with your big law degree, huh?"

178

Jordan rose, his voice icy calm. "I might sit behind a big desk during the day, but four nights a week you'll find me at Urban Warrior training Krav Maga. Now, do you want to discuss things here like responsible adults, or in the parking lot like a couple of street thugs?"

Moira yanked on Denzel's arm. "Come on, baby, we'll find another lawyer and fight this."

Denzel backed away, again stabbing his finger. "This ain't over."

"Believe me, it is," said Jordan. "But if you want to blow your money whining to another lawyer, don't let me stop you."

The couple stormed out, Denzel slamming the door behind him.

Jordan sat back down and, for the first time, let his game face slip — he grinned.

"I'm sorry you had to witness that," he said, "but sometimes I can't resist having a little fun when some moron wants to play the big man."

"Thank heavens you practice Krav Maga to know how to handle someone like that if you have to."

He chuckled. "After work, I unwind by playing Schubert on my baby grand." He held his hands up. "Do you think I'd risk Krav Maga damaging these?"

"You were bluffing?"

"I like to think of it as reading people. Not just what they say, but how they say it. And of course, what they don't say." He pointed at her. "Which is why I had high hopes for you."

"Me?"

He held his arms out. "Refusing to give your name? Harley running away? Complaining about being given the third degree — which was a nice touch, by the way?" He arched an eyebrow.

Rachel opened her mouth, but if he could read her so easily, what could she say? "You didn't believe any of it?"

"Just don't go in for any high-stakes poker games." He winked, then smiled and tapped the contract. "But don't panic. It's all legal now. I couldn't take Harley off you if I wanted to."

"So what happens now?"

"Now? Now you and your son go and have a great life with the great dog."

"But how can Harley be a homeowner?"

"Don't worry, that's all organized already. I'll send you the paperwork and walk you through the trickier parts, but essentially, the property will be sold and the funds will be held in a trust for the entirety of Harley's life."

"So how soon do I have to sell my car?"

He laughed. "You really haven't caught on, have you? You really do want Harley for no other reason than because you love him."

She folded her arms. "And that's so wrong, is it?" Talk about an arrogant, pompous blowhard.

"No. It's beautiful." He slipped an envelope across his desk.

She opened it. Inside was a check for $5,000 made out in her name. She squinted at him. "What's this? The reward you mentioned?"

He shook his head.

"Then I don't get it. I get Harley *and* $5,000?"

"Every month."

"Every month what?" Why was he being so cryptic? Man, this guy was infuriating.

"Every month, the trust will deposit $5,000 into your bank account to cover Harley's expenses and enable you to be at home with him instead of going out to work. So no one's selling any car."

"But I don't go out to work."

"Do you think Harley cares? It's his money, he can do what he likes with it."

"$5,000? Every month?"

He nodded once.

"Just to take care of Harley."

He shot her with a finger gun. "I had it cut after your phone call. Like I said, I'm good at reading people."

She shook her head. "No. Nothing's so easy."

"This time it is. Harley changed Barney's life, so Barney's last wish was to change his as a thank-you. Barney was determined that Harley would have as happy a life as possible, so he made these provisions to ensure Harley would be placed in a good home with good people and not left alone all day every day. Your turning up was just happenstance. Otherwise, there'd have been a lengthy interview and vetting process."

She nodded.

"And I'm sincerely sorry it took so long to reach out to you," said Jordan. "Barney lived on his own, which, you'll appreciate, complicated matters, so we only became aware of the situation when the real estate agent stumbled upon your note. But things have worked out as Barney would've liked, which is all that matters."

"$5,000." She smiled. Even saying it again didn't help it sink in. A giddiness bubbled in her gut, like she was a schoolgirl who'd just been asked to the prom by the quarterback.

"And though I hope it doesn't happen for a long time, should Harley, shall we say, be reunited with Barney — due to natural causes or a verifiable accident, I'm legally obligated to add — every cent passes to his guardian, i.e., you."

Chapter 44

Drool strung from Harley's mouth as he sat beside the kitchen island, the scent of succulent raw beef and bloody juices wafting down. It had been weeks since he'd had such a glorious meal.

He'd enjoyed seeing Jordan again, but not so much Denzel. And hearing Barney say his name? He wagged his tail as the warm glow once more enveloped him. Barney was still out there somewhere, so if Harley was good and fulfilled his purpose, one day they'd be reunited, and he could introduce his old friend to his new ones. What a day that would be!

More importantly, Barney sounded well, suggesting Harley no longer had to worry about him. Maybe this was Barney's way of giving his blessing for Harley to help Rachel and Wes, because, boy, did they need it.

Izzy screwed her face up, leaning against the island. "This Denzel sounds a complete sleaze."

"The worst." Rachel chopped the slab of beef with a cleaver.

"And this lawyer guy believes there's no way Denzel can come after you for the money?"

"Jordan says his contract is so ironclad, if Denzel is stupid enough to challenge it, he'll represent me and pay any costs out of his own pocket."

Izzy smirked over the rim of her wine glass. "That's very good of *Jordan*. Does he do that for all his clients, or only the ones with boobs to die for and buns of steel?"

Rachel raised an eyebrow.

Izzy wiggled the fingers of her left hand. "Was he at least wearing a ring?"

"I don't know. I didn't look."

Harley watched Rachel prepare the food. It was clear everyone trusted her whenever a tough decision had to be made — the sign of a true alpha. She was an accomplished runner, too. For a person. So she had leadership skills and physical prowess in abundance. Mental prowess? That was another story... She constantly misplaced things, always dithered over answering her phone, and boy, did she need some poking to wake up in the morning. She was a wonderful alpha, but only because she had such a crack team to cover her shortcomings — Wes and Izzy.

Rachel called to Wes, who was watching TV, "Wes, it's time to feed Harley."

He trundled over. Rachel pushed the stained chopping board in front of him and handed him the cleaver. "Very careful. Remember how I showed you."

Being overly cautious, Wes scraped the hunks of meat into Harley's bowl, Rachel watching his every move. He then put the bowl on the floor near the blue dog bed.

Harley stared at it but didn't move.

Wes said, "Harley, eat."

He dove into his meal, filling the kitchen with munching and slobbering while Wes ambled back to his seat. Boy, he'd missed this taste, but before he knew it, his bowl was empty. He sat back on his haunches and licked his nose clean.

Izzy shook her head. "It's amazing that he won't eat until you tell him."

"He's an amazing dog." Rachel washed her hands.

"Anyway, what do you mean you didn't look? How does an available woman not check out an attractive guy's left hand?"

"There's your answer: I'm not available. I've told you, there is no itch to be scratched. This" — she waved her hand over her body — "is an itch-free zone."

"Yeah, right. And what happens if Wes continues to improve and eventually gets a degree of independence? With Harley on the team, who's to say what the future holds?"

Rachel opened her mouth to say something but didn't.

"I knew it." Izzy wagged a finger. "Itch-free zone my eye."

Rachel frowned. "Oh, I almost forgot. What was it you said today when I called?"

Izzy shrugged.

"Something weird about dogs? Uh... oh, something about time."

"Yeah, I found this great article — I'll send you the link — all about dogs and their amazing sense of smell. It said it's so acute they can smell time."

"Seriously?"

"It doesn't mean they can sniff and think, 'Oh, it's five eighteen and twenty-three seconds.' No, it's like the environment they're in changes over the course of the day — as things like heat, humidity, and pressure affect it — and their noses are so sensitive that, say, two o'clock smells completely different from three o'clock."

"Wow. That must be how Harley can wake me up every day around five thirty."

"I guess so. He must have figured out what five thirty smells like, so he just waits until he senses that same smell, and bingo."

Rachel shook her head. "Unbelievable."

The doorbell rang.

"That'll be the food." Rachel answered the door and accepted a pizza delivery. She opened the box on the coffee table. "Okay, dig in."

They did.

Harley wandered over. He sniffed the pizza on the table — ham, mushroom, and more cheese than he'd ever known on a pizza. Delicious. A piece of that would be worth the butt explosions that would inevitably follow, but... he followed the golden rule and lay on the floor.

Izzy ripped a chunk out of her slice, lounging with one leg over the arm of the chair.

Apart from being fun and friendly, Izzy was the hunter of the pack, being the one to bring back supplies most often. Unfortunately, those supplies invariably consisted of little more than kibble for him and red wine for everyone else. He didn't know how long a person could survive on wine alone, but he was sure Izzy would know down to the second.

Izzy gestured to the pizza on the table. "Is that safe from Harley?"

Rachel nodded. "You've seen for yourself. He won't eat unless he's told to."

"So he wouldn't take this unless I said he could?" Izzy held out her slice of pizza.

Rachel and Wes lurched forward, both shouting, "No!"

Izzy jerked back. "Okay. I was only asking."

"It's not that," said Rachel. "He gets the most diabolical wind you've ever smelled."

Wes laughed. "It's so funny, but it's so horrible. Mom made him do it on my leg."

Izzy nodded. "As any loving mother should. I hope you called the police, Wes."

Wes shook his head.

"Next time, call them. Tell them your human rights have been violated."

"Wesley, do not call the police," said Rachel. "Not unless there's a serious emergency like the ones we discussed." She shook her head at Izzy. "You know he takes things literally."

"Sorry. My bad." Izzy winced. "So is it nice having money again?"

Rachel snorted. "What do you think?"

"Do you know how much yet?"

Rachel shrugged. "The house has only just gone up for sale. Jordan gave some rough figures, but then started talking about trusts, power of attorney, investment bonds, hedge funds... honestly, I lost the will to live."

"Surprising, considering your devastating math skills."

Rachel rolled her eyes, chomping on her pizza. "The scary thing is that if I hadn't come clean about having Harley, I wouldn't have gotten a cent. And that money's going to change everything."

Harley jumped onto the middle cushion of the sofa. The atmosphere was far more relaxed tonight. Over the last few weeks, there had been moments like this, but much of the time, a sense of anxiety, even dread, had hung in the air like the stink from rotting fish. But this? This was more like home. If only someone would give him a job to do, it would be perfect.

He looked at Rachel, but she didn't ask him to fetch anything, so he nuzzled Wes as the boy munched on pizza. Wes would have a job for him, he being the brains of the outfit, the one Rachel turned to whenever a puzzle needed solving. It was a pity more people weren't the strong, silent type like Wes — a person who expressed his feelings clearly instead of hiding behind a mask, who was direct in everything he did, who didn't make endless noise but only spoke when he had something worth saying. What a refreshing change that was.

Wes hadn't inherited Rachel's athleticism, but boy, did he make up for that with mental prowess and emotional stability. He was the perfect example of what a person should be. As people went, he was the closest to a dog Harley had ever encountered.

With no jobs, Harley curled up and basked in the smell of cheese and the warm conversation of his pack.

Izzy said, "You're not going to do anything dumb like ask Captain Doofus for financial advice, are you?"

"Oh, yeah, that's top of my to-do list," said Rachel.

"Thank heavens for that."

"Jordan can hook me up with a financial advisor if I want one, but there's no point at this stage with everything already in place. The only time I'll need help is if anything happens to Harley. So we're good to go." She prodded the coffee table. "Knock on wood."

Chapter 45

Cold and clammy. On her cheek.

Dozing, Rachel turned her head.

Cold and clammy again.

A jumble of images and thoughts coalesced as her groggy mind forsook the world of dreams for her darkened bedroom, thanks to her four-legged alarm call.

Dangling her arm outside of the bed, she patted Harley. "Five minutes, Harley."

She hadn't been drunk last night, but after all the stress of the past few weeks, culminating in getting more than she'd ever dreamed possible, she'd had a glass or two more than intended.

Harley's warm breath stroked her neck. He whined. He didn't usually do that, but she didn't usually stay in bed once he'd woken her, so maybe he was frustrated.

"Just five. Promise."

He whined again.

"Okay. Okay." He was probably right — the fresh air would clear her head, while the exercise would burn off the alcohol.

She shoved her comforter aside but stayed on her back with her eyes closed.

Harley whined again.

"One more minute, boy."

But Harley refused to wait. He leaned across and nipped her right breast. She shrieked, rolling away from him, then bolted upright, clutching her chest.

"What the...?" She sucked air through her teeth and massaged the area, it stinging like she'd been prodded with a hot poker.

She stabbed a finger at the bedroom door. "Get out, Harley! Now!"

Harley whimpered.

She clicked on her lamp. Big brown eyes gazed up at her. If she ever had to draw a picture of pure sorrow, this would be it.

"Out!" She stabbed at the door again.

He reached to nuzzle her. She shoved him away and clambered out of bed. Grabbing his collar, she hauled him toward the door.

"You are *not* going to bite people. Bad dog!"

He didn't fight her, didn't snarl or snap, but allowed her to drag him down the hall, down the stairs, and to the garage door. She pushed it open.

"Get in there!" She jabbed at the cold black garage.

Standing with his tail between his legs and his head down, he gazed up at her, pleading.

"In."

Creeping forward with the tiniest of steps, he shuffled into the darkness.

She pointed at him. "Think about what you've done."

She slammed the door and stormed away, the sound of whimpering dying behind her.

Twenty-three minutes later, she gasped for air, heaving up the steepest part of her run. Alone. The dark sky shrouded by heavy cloud, gloom all but pinned her down, making the run not a joy but a slog.

Her legs like stone, she crested the incline, but instead of running to her trailhead to perform her strength exercises, she collapsed forward with her hands on her knees, wheezing. Having caught her breath, she staggered away from the road and plonked down on the damp ground.

She shook her head. So she'd been a few minutes late getting up —that was no reason to bite her. Had she made a dreadful mistake taking Harley in? Was he only now revealing his true nature? Whatever it proved to be, for now, she couldn't allow him to be alone with Wes. All she could do was pray this was some horrendous anomaly and not a sign of things to come.

A lone tear dribbled down her cheek. Last night, everything had been perfect — she had a relationship with Wes, plus an active future for him. Now? How had everything started falling apart so quickly?

She clambered to her feet and ran home.

"Any problems?" she asked Izzy, dreading hearing that Harley had barked and whined constantly after being shut in the garage, bolstering her worries of behavioral problems.

"Not a sound."

"You haven't been in to see him?"

"No. Like you asked." Izzy squeezed Rachel's arm. "You know, he's been through a lot — losing his owner, living on the street, getting used to you guys. A few teething problems are only to be expected."

"There's no excusing biting someone, Iz."

"It wasn't a *bite* bite, was it? It was just a little nip. My guess is he was overexcited about another fun day with you guys, that's all."

"Maybe."

"Listen, Harley's such a smart dog, he'll have figured out why he was punished and that will be the end of it. Trust me."

Izzy was right — Harley was probably overexcited. He loved his morning runs. Maybe it was a sense of freedom because this was his time, a time when he didn't have to worry about helping anyone else. She got that totally. Behavioral problems? Maybe she was overanalyzing the situation. Harley was a supersmart dog, but he was just a dog. And dogs, like kids, could be mischievous and naughty without any sense of responsibility or maliciousness. After all Harley had given her, he deserved some slack.

She hugged Izzy. "Thanks, Iz. I don't know what I'd do without you."

Izzy left, and after showering, Rachel strolled to the garage door, praying she'd find Harley sleeping peacefully and not a chaotic mess where everything within reach was smashed or chewed.

Her hand on the handle, she drew a steadying breath, then opened the door so an arc of light sliced in from the hallway. The blanket on the floor was empty. Where was Harley?

She clicked on the light. Everything was in its place except one thing — Harley. Huddled in a pathetic ball in the farthest corner, the dog trembled. Head down and turned away, he peeked at her from the corner of one eye, as if terrified that looking directly at her would incur her wrath.

She cupped her face. Look at what she'd done. He'd given her so much, yet because of one tiny nip that she couldn't even feel anymore, she traumatized the greatest gift she'd ever received.

She crouched. Her voice broke as she said, "Harley, come here, boy."

Like a fountain of joy erupting, Harley burst out of his huddled ball and dashed to her, all wagging tail and lolling tongue. She wrapped her arms around him and squeezed, while he licked and nuzzled her.

"I'm sorry, Harley. But you can't nip. I hope you've learned that."

He'd been punished immediately after nipping, so hopefully he'd made the connection and realized it was unacceptable behavior.

Rachel kept an eye on him throughout the day, but he was back to his usual self, suggesting the nip had been an anomaly that would never be repeated.

Once Wes went to bed, Harley curled up on the sofa beside her with his head in her lap and they watched a movie together.

It was as if the nip had never happened.

***

Sunday was an altogether brighter day, both inside the house, because all had been forgiven on both sides, and outside, because the heavy cloud had disappeared, leaving a glorious blue sky.

When they got back from their weekend ramble, they ate, then settled on the sofa to watch cartoons. Harley jumped up into his middle seat, and Rachel automatically rested a hand on his shoulders. Wes leaned down across Harley, with his head turned to the TV while resting against the side of her hand. She waited for him to realize and move, but he didn't.

He laughed as an elephant tripped over its own trunk. Still he didn't move. Either he was too engrossed in the cartoon or he didn't care, yet both reasons were equally puzzling. For years, he'd had a sixth sense regarding the proximity of other people. On the sofa, as little as half an inch could mean the difference between a pleasant evening of TV viewing and glares and agitation, which, if ignored, led to him storming to his room.

It was as if Harley was a buffer between them. Without the dog, they were two sides caught on the verge of civil war — separate, desperate, hostile. With Harley? He acted as a treaty that brought peace, prosperity, and harmony to people more similar than they'd realized.

A thought wove its way out of the dark depths of her mind, from the dark place where she'd buried so many hopes so deep they could no longer hurt her.

No. She banished it back to the darkness.

Just as Harley had learned nipping led to punishment, she'd learned dreams of an ordinary mother/son relationship led to pain. She'd learned that the hard way. Many, many times.

She focused on the TV.

190

But the thought wouldn't remain buried.

What if she moved her hand and touched her son? Would he run screaming to his room? Or would the magical influence of Harley allow her a moment of motherly intimacy?

No. She couldn't risk it. Not when they were already so cozy together.

Could she?

With the lightest of touches, so as not to scare the delicate butterfly, she brushed his hair with her pinkie. She waited for a reaction. None came, so she brushed again. And he let her. As gentle as a butterfly's wing beat, she drifted her fingertips over his hair.

The elephant on the TV squeezed into a tiny car, only for its butt to burst out of the trunk. He laughed.

Again, she drifted her fingertips over Wes's head. And he let her.

With a ridiculous grin and tears rolling down her cheeks, Rachel stroked her son's head. Over and over. And thanked God for bringing Harley into their lives and making the impossible possible.

By 8:00 p.m., Wes had watched hours of cartoons, but she hadn't seen a single one. Though her tears had long since dried, her smile remained. She gazed at the back of his head as she caressed it.

Unfortunately, even Harley's magical touch couldn't change some things. Wes lifted off Harley, kissed him on the head, and said, "Good night, Harley."

After helping Wes with his bedtime routine, she returned to the sofa. She'd dreamed of mother/son closeness, dreamed of a simple touch that meant both nothing and everything, dreamed for so long, and hurt for even longer, yet now it had come true. It was possibly the greatest night of her life.

She kissed Harley on the head too. "Thank you for coming into our lives, Harley."

Harley stretched and shifted around to snuggle up beside her, so she draped her arm over him, allowing him to nestle his head against her waist. With big, round brown eyes, he gazed up as if to say, "Thank you."

She blew him a kiss.

And he nipped her.

Grimacing, she leaped off the sofa, clutching her breast.

"Bad dog!" She raised her hand to lash out.

Harley cowered, trembling.

Resisting striking him, she flung her arm toward the hallway. "Garage. Now!"

Harley whimpered, sadness and confusion oozing from his gaze.

As she lunged to grab his collar, he cringed and screwed his eyes shut, as if expecting to be hit, yet having no intention of defending himself with his teeth or claws. Rachel yanked him off the sofa and hauled him toward the hallway. She released him.

"Garage!"

Ears tight to his head, hindquarters so low they all but dragged on the floor, Harley crept toward the hallway. He glanced back with pleading eyes.

Rachel stabbed her finger again. "Garage!"

Harley scuttled down the hall. She marched after him, shut him in the darkened room, and locked the door.

Cupping her breast, she winced as she pressed on the spot he'd nipped. She stomped to the bathroom, pulled off her sweatshirt and bra, then turned sideways and lifted her right arm to examine herself.

A red mark had already appeared on the lower part of her breast. That would bruise and be tender for days.

"Freaking great!"

Yanking open the medicine cabinet, she rooted inside and found a tube of aloe vera gel. She squirted a little onto her fingers and massaged it into her breast. What the devil was she going to do about Harley? He'd transformed their lives, but she couldn't allow such behavior. No way. Maybe a dog psychologist? If that didn't work... She stopped massaging and stared into her eyes in the mirror.

Could she really get rid of Harley? The money was wonderful, but incidental. It was how he helped Wes and the family dynamic that mattered. However, if he bit Wes just once, it would traumatize her son so badly that, apart from possibly never going near another animal ever again, he might shut down completely. She couldn't risk that. No.

Moving her fingertips in small circles, she rubbed in the gel. Harley had left her no choice. If she couldn't correct his behavior, he—

She gasped, gazed down at her breast, then at herself in the mirror.

Gently, she kneaded the red area Harley had bitten.

"What's that?"

She gulped, then probed the area with her fingertips. Again, she gasped. "Oh, no."

Chapter 46

Curled in his bed, Harley peeked over his tail as someone knocked at Rachel's front door. When no one answered, they tried the handle. Izzy waltzed in. "Hey."

Rachel sat hunched up on the sofa, elbows on her knees, head in her hands.

Izzy sauntered to the chair and flopped down. "Did you watch that cat video I sent yet? Man, I swear I laughed so much, I peed a little."

Nothing.

"You're not running today?"

Rachel shook her head without lifting it.

"What's happened? Is Wes okay?"

Rachel nodded.

Izzy frowned. "Is it your mom? What's happened? You're freaking me out."

Harley whimpered. Why was Rachel shutting him out like this? He loved his new pack and only wanted the best for them. Why was he being punished for trying to help? If he didn't fulfill his purpose by helping those he loved, what use was he?

"Is it Harley? Has he done something?"

Rachel nodded.

Izzy shifted to the sofa and slung her arm around Rachel. "Whatever he's done, it can't be that bad, can it?"

Rachel lifted her head, her eyes swollen and red, and her face pale and drawn from having spent the night staring into space on the sofa.

"Rach, what is it, babe?"

"Harley bit me again."

"Oh no." Izzy rubbed her brow. "So you're thinking you have to—"

"No, no. That's not it. He bit me here" — she touched her breast — "and when I checked if he'd bruised me, I found a lump."

Izzy gasped. "Oh, dear Lord, no."

"I don't know what to do."

"Well, obviously have it checked. Some clinics have walk-in mammograms. My mom—"

Rachel grabbed Izzy's hand. "I don't mean about me. What happens to me happens. But what do I do about Wes?"

"Wes will be fine. It's you we have to worry about."

"But he won't. If he's left alone, he'll be dumped in some state-run facility and forgotten about. Left to vegetate. What kind of life is that?"

Izzy cupped Rachel's hand in hers. "Listen to me, Rachel. Nothing's going to happen to you, you hear? You're going to get checked out as soon as possible, and if anything's wrong, you're going to get treatment."

Rachel didn't move.

"My mom went through the same thing — all the worry and anxiety — and it was just some harmless cyst. There's no point in getting worked up until we know what we're dealing with. Okay?"

Rachel nodded.

"So when did you find it? Just now?"

"Last night."

"Last night?" Izzy threw her hands up. "And you didn't come and get me?"

"I didn't want to bother you."

"Bother me? Rachel, you're more my family than my family. Promise me you'll never do anything like this again. Promise."

"Okay. I promise."

Izzy looked at Harley, cowering in his bed. "Do you think somehow he knew and was trying to tell you?"

Rachel shrugged. "He's smart. I mean, so smart it's unnerving at times, but when all's said and done, he's just a dog."

"Still, you've got to admit, it's some freaky coincidence."

They both looked at Harley.

He cowered even lower. Had he done something else bad? Not the garage. Not alone in the cold dark. Please!

"Awww. Poor little fella," said Izzy. "Where did he nip you the first time?"

Rachel hesitated, then pointed to the exact same spot.

"Are you kidding me? Rach, he's not a smart dog, he's a freaking guardian angel."

She shrugged.

"So you'd have found it without him, would you?"

Rachel sighed, then turned back to him. "Harley. Come here, boy."

He pricked his ears. She was using her kind voice, not her horrible one. Did that mean he'd been forgiven, or was it a trick? The last time she'd shut him in the dark when he'd tried to help, she'd come to him and used her kind voice, so he'd thought everything was okay, and then what? She'd shut him in the garage again later. How was he supposed to do his job when she kept changing the rules?

"Harley." Rachel patted her thigh. "Harley."

Cringing, he padded out of bed, tail wedged between his legs.

"That's it. Come on, boy," said Rachel.

He padded a little quicker, staring at the floor and only flicking his gaze up momentarily to check she wasn't scowling.

She patted her thigh again. "Come on, Harley."

He slunk over and sat just out of reach. He didn't want to be bad by sitting so far away, but he didn't want her grabbing his collar and hauling him into the dark again.

"Awww. He's traumatized, the poor thing," said Izzy.

Rachel shot her a sideways look, then slid off the sofa to sit on the floor. She covered her breast with one hand and reached the other toward him. "Harley."

His tail daring to rise, he toddled closer. He was pleased she was holding her breast because it meant she now knew what he knew — something wasn't right. He didn't know exactly what, but his nose was never wrong. Now he'd done his job and told her, she could go eat grass, or lick herself, or do whatever it was people did when they needed something fixed.

She hugged him with one arm, her other across her chest as a shield. "I'm sorry if you were trying to help, Harley. In the future, I'll try to look at things from your point of view before sticking you in the garage. Please forgive me."

Anxiety and fear oozed from Rachel, but also love and kindness. He wagged his tail. When he'd first started helping Barney, they'd had problems because Barney was set in his ways. However, once he'd realized the burden Harley could lift, they'd fit together like two parts of a puzzle. Harley hoped Rachel would let him stay because there was a puzzle here too. He was trying his best to fit, but he needed time.

If only they'd find him some proper jobs instead of fetching the TV remote twenty times per day, he might have a chance to prove his worth.

People were so confusing. It made them unreasonable in their expectations of others. Not like dogs. A dog didn't demand much — to eat, to sleep, to play, to pee. Nothing confusing there. Uncomplicated expectations meant uncomplicated lives. And what better route was there to happiness than keeping things simple? Wes got that. Why couldn't the world be more like Wes?

Maybe that was Harley's purpose in this pack: Rachel was the alpha, Izzy the hunter, Wes the brains, and he...?

He licked Rachel and she hugged him tighter. He'd struggled to grasp why he'd been brought into this new pack, so it was wonderful to finally have the answer — he was the voice of reason.

Chapter 47

Rachel sat at the side of the desk in the small white examination room decorated with floral prints. Sitting at the other side in a blue uniform, an imaging technologist called Marie scanned Rachel's file on her computer while twiddling a pen in her short, curly brown locks.

Wearing a pink-and-white hospital gown and her jeans, Rachel picked at a sliver of skin alongside her left thumbnail. She'd never imagined being in such a predicament — potentially making life-or-death decisions. In her sixties or seventies, okay. At a push, maybe even in her fifties. But thirty-six?

A sickness roiled in her stomach, as if she was on a boat pitching in high seas. She desperately wanted to hurl, but she couldn't even if she allowed the feeling to overwhelm her because she hadn't eaten all day. Since her doctor had confirmed the lump was suspicious enough to warrant investigation with a diagnostic mammogram and not merely a swelling caused by Harley's nip, control of her life had been wrestled from her grasp. She was in freefall, desperately snatching at a parachute falling just beyond reach.

Marie said, "So your doctor has referred you after you found a lump in your right breast through self-examination."

"Yes."

"Have you ever had a mammogram before?"

"No."

She smiled. "It's nothing to stress about. There may be a little discomfort because we'll need to compress each breast, but there will be no pain or aftereffects. Any questions before we continue?"

"Is it true breast cancer kills more women than any other disease except lung cancer?"

"Ah, I see you've been googling."

Rachel shrugged. "I wanted to know what I was getting into."

"Perfectly understandable. However, the problem with researching online is that much of the information is anecdotal, taken out of context, or just plain wrong." She wrote on a piece of paper and held it up. "This is the statistic I'd like you to focus on."

"Twenty percent? Twenty percent of what?"

"For every woman we see because she's found a lump, only twenty percent of those lumps are cancerous."

"Really?"

"Yes." Marie nodded. "Out of one hundred women, eighty will have suffered all that stress for nothing, and they can get on with their lives as if it never happened."

"So eighty percent of lumps are harmless?"

"Exactly. But it gets better. Of those twenty women who are unlucky enough to have a lump that is cancerous, the condition is so often curable that eighty percent will live another thirty years or more."

"Eighty percent?"

"See? Not so scary when you have the right information, is it? So the secret at this stage is not to panic. Okay?"

Rachel nodded. "Okay."

Marie collected more details, then showed Rachel over to a white machine that was taller than she was and looked like a giant F.

"As I said," — Marie rested a hand on the machine — "it won't be painful, but you may feel some discomfort because I'll need to compress your breast tissue to obtain the correct image quality. Okay?"

"I've had a couple of aspirins because I read that can help."

"Great. Now, are you wearing deodorant, talc, body lotion... anything like that on your upper body?"

"No. My doctor mentioned it, so I showered."

"Excellent, then it looks like we're all set. If you'll stand here, please" — Marie gestured to the front of the machine — "slip your right arm out of your gown, and rest your right breast on this plate, we'll do that one first."

Rachel followed the instructions, letting her breast sit on a black plate that protruded partway up the machine. She flinched at the coldness.

Marie said, "Let your arms hang loose to relax the chest muscles."

Helping her at each stage, Marie guided Rachel into the perfect position and lowered a transparent second plate, gently squashing her

198

breast until the plates were about three inches apart. It felt like she was trapped in a vise, which was uncomfortable, but not painful.

"That's looking good. In a moment, I'll ask you to stop breathing for a few seconds while the machine completes the scan. Please don't take a huge breath and hold it because that will move your breast, okay?"

"Okay."

Marie strolled to the control panel a few feet away. "Okay, stop breathing, please."

Rachel froze. The top part of the F moved in an arc above her to scan her breast from different angles.

"Okay, you can breathe again." Marie strolled back. "That was great. Just a few more views, and before you know it, we'll be all done."

After a few minutes, the process was complete. Rachel dressed and took a seat in the pastel blue waiting area while a radiologist reviewed the images. She checked the time on her phone: 3:14 p.m.

Rachel pawed through the magazines on a glass-topped table: recipes, fashion, health advice, fat celebrities who'd become thin, and thin celebrities who'd become fat... nothing to distract her. She gazed around the room — lush green plants dotted about, more floral prints, a small aquarium with brightly colored fish flitting about. She checked her phone again: 3:15 p.m.

She sighed. She'd never been good at waiting. The time Wes had needed gas for dental work, she'd sat in the waiting room and wolfed down a tube of Pringles and two candy bars.

Tapping her foot, she scanned the room again.

A woman in a business suit caught her eye and smiled. Rachel winced a smile back, then looked away to avoid being drawn into a pointless and potentially uncomfortable conversation.

3:17 p.m.

Eighty percent. She wasn't a gambler, and her math skills weren't great, but any fool knew eighty percent was a good percentage to have in her favor.

But what if it wasn't in her favor? What if she was in the remaining twenty percent? If her time was up, her time was up — that she could live with, for want of a more appropriate phrase. But if her time was up, so was Wes's, and that was unacceptable.

Maybe this was a good thing. Whether she was in the eighty percent or the twenty percent was utterly incidental. She might be in the eighty

199

percent, then walk out and get splattered by a bus. Whatever the result, this was a wake-up call. She planned for Wes's future in days, weeks, and months, but that was useless — she had to plan in decades.

Talk about a silver lining. She was lucky to have this opportunity.

That meant she needed two plans: one for if she was going to be around, and one for if she wasn't. Luckily, Peter had insisted they each take out decent-sized life insurance policies, and though she'd considered canceling hers on many an occasion when money was tight, she hadn't. Thank heavens.

It might be worth asking Jordan about that financial advisor, not least to learn what happened to Harley and the money if she wasn't around. She needed to secure Harley's future. If Wes lost her *and* Harley at the same time...

"Oh, dear Lord."

The businesswoman glanced at her.

"Sorry." Yes, hope for the best, but plan for the worst.

"Ms. Taylor?"

"Hmmm?"

An Indian woman with dazzling white teeth said, "Hello, I'm Dr. Chatterjee, your radiologist. This way, please."

Oh God, this was it. Rachel's heart hammered. She swallowed hard as she stood. The next few seconds could completely change the course of hers and Wes's lives.

Her legs shaky, Rachel followed Chatterjee to a consultation room. The woman's hair graying at the roots didn't suggest only that it was dyed but that she was old enough to have considerable experience in her occupation. Exactly what Rachel needed.

Rachel bit her bottom lip as she lowered into a blue-cushioned chair in front of a desk with two monitors.

Chatterjee said, "I've reviewed your images, which clearly show the small mass you discovered. Please don't take this as a bad sign, but as is often the case, I'm afraid, the findings are inconclusive."

"What do you mean 'inconclusive'?"

"Unfortunately, it isn't always possible to judge what a mass is from images alone, especially with regard to whether it's cancerous or noncancerous. In such cases, we run one or more further tests."

"So you don't know if it's a harmless cyst or a..." Rachel gazed at her lap, unable to get the word out. Saying it might make it real.

"A tumor that needs removing?"

Rachel nodded.

Chatterjee smiled without parting her lips. "Even some tumors can be perfectly harmless."

"But you don't know what I've got?"

"We categorize mammograms using a standardized rating system. In simple terms, we grade the results on a score of zero to six, with one being the optimal result, meaning we found nothing to worry about. The mass you have is what we call a suspicious abnormality, so your results have been classed as 4B."

Four? That was a long way from one! Rachel clawed her fingers around the chair's armrest.

"That rating means that while the findings don't definitively indicate cancer, they don't confirm it isn't either. Unfortunately, I believe there's a moderate suspicion that the mass could well be cancerous."

"Oh God." The walls closed in, and Rachel felt like she was falling even though she was sitting down.

"I'm sorry it isn't the news you were hoping for, but further investigation could prove the mass is indeed harmless."

Her mouth dry, Rachel dragged her tongue over her lips. "When you say 'moderate suspicion' that it's cancerous, what does that mean?"

"There's between a ten percent and forty-nine percent chance it is."

"Nearly fifty percent!" Rachel's knuckles whitened on the chair arms.

"At the upper limit of the range, yes, but at the other end, it's only ten percent." Chatterjee held up her palms. "You have to remember this isn't a diagnosis. Please, I can't stress this enough — the mammogram only suggests the *possibility* that cancer is present, not that it actually *is* present."

Rachel gazed into space. Twenty-four hours ago, she'd been a perfectly healthy young woman. Now? Now her world could be ending.

Chatterjee said, "Think of it like a weather report. If the meteorologist said there was a ten percent chance of rain, you wouldn't build an arc, imagining the end of the world, would you? But you might take an umbrella out to be safe. Yes? The tests I'm recommending are your umbrella in case there's a shower."

"Okay." Right now, she'd prefer to be climbing into an arc and nailing the door shut, but the doctor was the expert.

"So I'm booking you in for a core needle biopsy, which is a small procedure that removes a tiny amount of tissue from the mass for analysis."

Rachel rubbed her brow, struggling to process everything. It was like an out-of-body experience where things were happening, but she could only watch.

Rachel said, "How small is a small procedure?"

"It's done under local anesthetic, so it's nothing to worry about. There might be a little soreness or swelling around your armpit, but nothing a couple of painkillers won't get rid of. Any questions?"

Millions. But such a jumble of thoughts and emotions crashed through her, she couldn't articulate a single one. She blew out a breath and shrugged.

"Great. So we have a cancellation on Wednesday at ten thirty a.m. Would that work for you?"

Dear Lord, this was really happening.

Chatterjee must have sensed her floundering. "I know this is a lot to take in, but the sooner we set things in motion, the sooner we can get you back to living your life."

Chapter 48

Leaning against the island in her kitchen, Rachel rolled her eyes at Izzy, who was stirring a pan on the stove with a wooden spoon. "I'm not an invalid, Iz. There's an eighty percent chance I'm not even sick."

"You've had a stressful day, so go put your feet up."

"Sitting for Wes was more than enough."

Izzy shook a spice into the pan, then turned. "Look, I'm not good around sick people, so if the biopsy is bad news, I'm out of here. How else am I going to get into your will if I don't push the boat out now?"

Rachel smirked. "You're a wonderful human being, Iz. I'm shocked there isn't a national holiday in your honor." She touched Izzy's arm. "I'm fine. Really."

"But what if you're not? You aren't in this alone, Rach. I'm here for you. I need you to know that."

"I do, but..." Rachel exhaled loudly and stared at the floor.

"Is there something you haven't told me? Rach, we're in this together, so if you've got something to say, for Pete's sake, say it."

Rachel drew a weary breath. "It's just..."

"What, Rach? What?"

"Your cooking sucks."

"Seriously? At a time like this?" Izzy jabbed the wooden spoon at her. A glob of muddy brown gloop dropped off and splattered on the tiled floor. They stared at it, then at each other.

Rachel said, "Is it supposed to do that?"

"Yeah, my grandma taught me. It's like seeing if spaghetti is cooked by throwing at the wall."

Rachel looked down again. "So is it ready?"

"If you have to ask, you're not the cook you think you are." Izzy shoved the spoon at her and sauntered away.

Over her shoulder, Izzy said, "If you need me, I'll be lying on the sofa."

Rachel boiled some potatoes and vegetables, and she grilled three salmon steaks. She offered the brown gloop to Harley, but he sniffed it from two feet away and wouldn't get any closer.

Because her appointment had ruined Wes's all-important routine, he'd ensconced himself in his room to rearrange his soup cans, so after they ate, they had Harley fetch a selection of items to lighten the mood. Wes laughed and laughed, and for an hour, it felt like an ordinary day.

After Wes went to bed, Izzy joined Rachel on the sofa. "*Is* there anything you haven't told me?"

"No."

"So what are you going to tell Wes?"

"Until there *is* something to tell him, nothing." She wasn't sure how much he'd grasp, especially pertaining to the worst-case scenario. However, even if he could only grasp a fraction, there was no point in stressing him until she knew the whole story.

"How about your mom?"

Rachel winced. "Yeah. I'm not looking forward to that conversation."

"You don't think she'll be supportive?"

"Oh, she'll want to be on the next flight here."

"And that's bad because...?"

"Because this is *my* problem, and I have to deal with it *my* way. We don't know if it's serious yet, but if it is, the only way I'll get through it is if I'm allowed to do it the way I want to do it, and not have to take other people's feelings into account."

"She'd mean well."

"I know," said Rachel. "But I'd have to make allowances for her and her feelings, and I can't do that. If this is bad, I'll need all my energy to fight it. No distractions."

"She'll be upset."

"Better upset than resented."

Izzy placed her hand on Rachel's leg. "If you explain it to her, I'm sure she'll understand."

"If the biopsy shows I need treatment, I'll involve her then. In the meantime, I have to downplay this and not give her the chance to turn it into some big drama."

"But it *is* a big drama."

204

Folding her arms, Rachel shook her head. "No, it's not. Right now, it only has the potential to be a big drama. If it becomes one, that's going to be life-changing, so the longer I can put that off, the better. For me and Wes."

Izzy nodded. "Do you want me to drive you on Wednesday?"

Rachel shook her head.

"You don't want moral support?"

Rachel patted Izzy's thigh. "I already have it."

Chapter 49

Lying in the cream-colored treatment room, Rachel stared at the ceiling. With wood-effect cupboards, tube lighting, and a plastic rack of pamphlets, it looked more like a dentist's office than an operating room. Thank heavens.

She'd barely slept the night before, partly because of the nightmarish visions of what could happen if the biopsy results were bad, partly because she was formulating the two plans to secure Wes's future.

Strangely, she wasn't tired. With the whirlwind of emotions swirling within her, she could have been on intravenous espresso.

Chatterjee had explained the procedures, but Rachel had barely listened. She'd ached to bundle Wes and Harley into the car and take off, denying this was happening. The only way she'd resisted was by convincing herself it was little more than a trip to her dentist — she'd walk in, lie back, a medical specialist would poke about inside her, then she'd walk out.

Chatterjee said, "This is going to feel cold as I disinfect the area."

A cold wetness stung her skin as Chatterjee swabbed her bare chest. Chatterjee then laid a green cloth over her, positioning a hole to reveal her right breast.

Okay, if Rachel looked down and her dentist had exposed her breast, the police might become involved, but today, this was an uneventful trip to the dentist. Period.

The doctor squirted a dollop of gel onto Rachel's breast, then, watching a monitor, stroked a handheld ultrasound scanner over it to locate the most appropriate site for the procedure.

Chatterjee took a syringe from a metal tray. "You're going to feel a slight pinch. This is the local anesthetic."

Rachel gritted her teeth as a needle was stuck into her. It felt like cold water was being pumped in, but the feeling faded and then she felt nothing. Chatterjee made a tiny incision and picked up a biopsy gun — a plastic device the size of a large candy bar with a needle around six inches long.

"You're going to hear a bang like this." Chatterjee clicked a button, which "fired" the gun and it made a sharp bang. "It's perfectly normal, so don't be worried when you hear it."

Watching the monitor to guide her, Chatterjee pushed the needle into the cut, sticking its tip into the mass. She fired the gun to obtain a sample, then withdrew the needle and deposited a sliver of Rachel's flesh in a white plastic container. As a safeguard to ensure the pathologist had a viable sample to test, Chatterjee repeated the process.

Sticking a Band-Aid on the incision, Chatterjee said, "That wasn't too bad, was it? Once the anesthetic wears off, there could be some soreness, but any over-the-counter painkiller will take care of that."

And that was it. All that dread and anxiety over a procedure that took less time than cooking their evening meal. Just another trip to the dentist.

Chapter 50

Cozy and happy.

In Rachel's darkened bedroom, Harley gazed at her so cozy and happy. She'd been so stressed lately, it wasn't fair to wake her, so he padded toward the door but stopped midstride. He'd incurred her wrath a number of times recently because he'd disappointed her, so was neglecting one of his jobs a good idea? Picturing the dark, lonely garage, he shuddered. No, he couldn't face that again, so he had to do his job. He wandered back to her bedside.

Delicately, Harley nudged her cheek with his nose.

Rachel didn't wake but moaned gently.

Awww. She was so sweet when she slept. He rested his chin on the side of the bed and gazed at his alpha. It was as if all her worries had melted away, leaving the real her. Innocent. Peaceful. Wonderful.

He jerked his head up. This wasn't getting his job done, was it? And that garage was as lonely and as dark as ever it was.

He poked her cheek a little harder.

Exhaling, Rachel rolled onto her back.

Harley whimpered, a morning in the lonely garage drawing closer and closer. No way was he going in there. This called for a drastic solution.

Harley barked a little yap, then immediately bobbed below the level of the bed to hide. Ears pricked, he listened.

Nothing stirred.

He poked his head up. Rachel slept blissfully.

A louder yap, and he bobbed down again.

Rachel groaned and stretched.

A groggy voice said, "Harley?"

Harley dared to peek.

"Hey, boy." Rachel patted him. "Sorry, but no run today. Maybe tomorrow." She rolled away from him.

So what had he done wrong this time? She didn't sound upset, but she obviously was if she wasn't getting up for their run. People were so confusing. It was a wonder the world wasn't in perpetual chaos.

At least when he was hauled into the garage, he knew he'd been bad, but being left in limbo like this was even worse. He whimpered.

"Tomorrow, Harley. Promise." Rachel patted him again.

Right, this was even more confusing — her kind voice, a nice pat, but still no run. Was this some new punishment she'd invented? Boy, he must have been unbelievably bad to warrant such torture. If only he could figure out what he'd done wrong.

He whined. He never meant to be bad; it just happened.

Rachel sighed and clicked on her lamp. "Okay. I get it — you need your run. Good grief, is it too much to expect to sleep in — just once — after all that's been happening?"

She whipped the covers off and clambered out of bed. She grabbed her clothes. "Happy now?"

As if things weren't confusing enough, that was her unhappy voice and yet she was dressing for their run. So when she was happy, she didn't want to run, but when she was unhappy, she did. He was never going to understand people. Well, most people. Thank heavens Wes would be up soon — the one person Harley could rely on to be reasonable, logical, and unemotional.

Once they were running along the roadside, it was like Rachel had been reborn. The fear and anxiety Harley had sensed had vanished, replaced by the serenity that only running could bring.

His paws pounded into the damp ground, his tongue lolling, breath billowing. Though running together, they were no longer a pack but a single animal. In tune. Supremely free. Living only to run.

She felt it too. She obviously loved Wes and Izzy, but she clearly reveled in this time apart from them, coming alive like a beast let out of its cage. He never felt closer to her than at these moments, when they could leave their jobs behind, forget their purposes, and just run for no reason other than the love of running. What could be more animal-like?

Where the road steepened, Rachel pumped her legs, tugging on his leash. "You wanted to run, dog, so come on, run."

Breathing harder, they raced up the hill. Wild. Unthinking. Joyful.

Blasting over the crest, her trailhead parking area in sight, they slowed to a walk. Harley licked Rachel's hand. He'd had some wonderful times with Barney, but not one where they'd connected on such a primal level. Rachel was such a special alpha. He was so grateful she'd accepted him into her pack.

After they ran back home, Rachel showered, they had breakfast with Wes, and then they all sat at the desk.

Wes hid a blue jelly bean under one of five plastic cups and switched them around, watching Harley from the corner of his eye while struggling to stifle a sly smile.

Harley yawned. As usual, Rachel didn't seem to have any idea under which cup the candy was. She was a wonderful alpha, but she certainly hadn't achieved that status thanks to her sense of smell. In fact, today she didn't even seem to be trying as she stared off into space. Thank heavens he was here.

Wes stopped moving the cups. "Harley?"

So Wes had lost track of it again, too? Harley yawned and, without even looking at the cup on the far right, nudged it with his nose. What would they do without him?

Wes peeked under it and hit his forehead with his palm, then laughed. He seemed surprised that Harley had found the candy. Again. There had to be more going on here, but what?

Years ago, so he could fulfill his purpose, Harley had had to perform the same jobs over and over. Barney also had to do jobs. All that work helped them learn how to work as a pack. That had to be what was happening here. This wasn't about finding the jelly bean; this was about strengthening the pack by working together. Of course. The pack was everything, so the stronger it was, the better the life of each member would be.

How stupid he'd been. Rachel must have instructed Wes to run a pack-building exercise, he being expert in cold, hard logic. It was so simple when Harley thought about it. Rachel the alpha and Wes the brains — the game exemplified those roles.

And Harley had thought they were a little dim. He was the dim one for going on first impressions and not digging deeper to uncover their true motivations.

He licked Wes's hand to apologize for doubting him. Harley had learned to trust Barney implicitly; now he'd learned the same of his new pack.

"Harley, TV remote," said Wes.

Harley scampered away to the coffee table. He'd seen the device there earlier, which meant he could complete this job in double-quick time. Fantastic. He scampered back and presented it to Wes.

He loved helping Wes. It was a different kind of help from that which Barney had needed, but no less fulfilling. In fact, even more so. Wes was so smart he obviously thought on a higher level than everyone else, so dealing with everyday things was a problem. Harley loved being Wes's savior, freeing the boy to devote his mental energies to solving life's more important riddles, such as why only flies and dogs found poop so fascinating, what made cats such self-absorbed prima donnas, or how, when people itched, they resisted dragging their butts across the floor.

Wes laughed as he took the TV remote and set it aside, then sat waiting for Rachel to indicate which pack-building exercise was to be next. But Rachel was staring into space again. So Wes stared into space too.

Harley looked from one to the other. This wasn't how the morning sessions went. There was the cup exercise, then the fetching something exercise, and then the spinning the wheel and rolling the cube exercise. Why had it changed?

Since returning from their run, Rachel's sense of wildness cloaked in serenity had disappeared. Back was that anxiety-tinged fear.

The three of them sat in silence for some time. So long, the smell of the day changed.

Rachel's phone rang, and the sense of anxiety-tinged fear shot through the roof.

Rachel grabbed the device and scurried out. Wes frowned as her footsteps clomped away down the hall.

Something was wrong. But what? Harley scrambled out to see her disappearing into the garage of all places.

Harley reached the garage door but jerked back as it slammed in his face. How could he do his job and help if he couldn't get in the room?

He whimpered. He had a bad feeling about this. Very bad.

Chapter 51

Speaking over Rachel's phone in her garage, Chatterjee said, "I'm sorry, Rachel, but it's not good news. I know you were hoping it was a harmless cyst, but I'm afraid it's a malignant mass, a tumor..."

She didn't hear another word. Her back against the concrete wall, she slid down until she was crouched on the floor, a hunched ball.

Izzy would be great, as usual. Her mom would be distraught, then supportive. But Wes? How could she ever explain this to him? As far back as he would remember, she'd always been there, every single day, but now there would be times when she couldn't because she'd need treatment. What was she going to say? And more importantly, how much would he grasp?

"Rachel? ... Would that be okay? ... Hello?"

She dragged a hand over her face. "Sorry, you were saying?"

"The appointment for the surgical oncologist? I've got you in as soon as I can, but I need to know you can make it."

"Sorry, you lost me. What appointment?"

"No apology necessary. I get how the news must have thrown you. I'll text the details, so you have them in front of you, and phone later to confirm. Okay?"

"Yes. Thank you."

She hung up, staring at her pegboard filled with tools she might now never use. This could be just another chapter in her life. Or it could be the end of it. But which?

Chapter 52

A nurse showed Rachel into the doctor's office. In a white coat, a man sat behind the desk, his ginger hair thinning at the temples, his shoulders so broad he probably picked the desk up and moved it rather than walk around it.

"Hello," he said, his voice deep. He gestured to the chair beside his desk, face impassive, as if he reserved a smile for special occasions. Or at least for those with a decent chance of surviving long enough for it to be worth the investment. "Please."

"Hi." Rachel tried to smile and hoped it didn't look like a grimace.

"I'm Dr. Jacobs. I'm part of your oncology team and will be taking you through your treatment options. Firstly, do you have your phone with you? If so, you might like to record this conversation. A lot of patients find it hard to focus after hearing the word *cancer*, so a recording lets them review things."

"Thanks." Rachel flicked through her phone's apps, then hit record and placed it on the desk next to a box of tissues. He'd have to stretch to reach the box, but the tissues weren't meant for him.

"I have the results of your biopsy, and I'm afraid—"

She screwed her eyes shut, thrusting her palms toward him.

"Sorry" — she drew a deep breath, then exhaled, opening her eyes — "sorry. Can I say something before we get into all this, please?"

He waved for her to continue.

"I want you to be blunt. Brutally blunt. So blunt it could be downright rude. No pussyfooting. Okay?"

"Okay." He raised his eyebrows. "Should I continue?"

"Please."

"I'm sorry to have to tell you this, but you have early-stage localized breast cancer, invasive ductal carcinoma to be precise. Luckily, it's the most common form of breast cancer, so we're well equipped to deal with it."

"Sorry, a what? An invasive...?"

"Invasive ductal carcinoma — the lump you found. It's a form of cancer that begins in the milk ducts and then spreads to the surrounding tissue."

Her mouth felt watery and her stomach churned as if she was going to vomit.

He twisted his monitor toward her. "You can see it, if you like."

She thrust a palm out and turned away. "No."

This wasn't the image of a fetus growing inside her to be celebrated, but a monster that had come to destroy her life. She'd acknowledge it only as much as was needed to kill it.

"In cases like this," he said, "the earlier we can identify a problem, the better chance we have of a favorable outcome, so it's fortunate you adhere to a self-examination routine."

She shrugged. "Well, it wasn't exactly adhering to a 'self-examination routine' that found it."

"No?"

"My dog bit me. I was checking the bruise."

He steepled his fingers. "In that case, you owe your dog the biggest, juiciest steak you can find, because it might have saved your life."

She snorted a laugh. "Hmmm."

"I'm not joking. Some dogs are extremely sensitive to disease. They can smell it the way we can smell rotten food."

"Seriously?"

He gave a curt nod. "Studies prove it. Some are even looking into how we can use dogs to aid diagnosis."

Harley was special. But could he really be *that* special?

He said, "Your notes say you have a son. Do you plan on having more children?"

She frowned. "Why? You're not saying it's spread to my ovaries, are you?" Oh dear Lord, as if things could get any worse.

He held up his hand. "No, don't panic. This is in regard to medication — some chemotherapy drugs can impact fertility."

"So if I take them, I might not be able to have kids again?"

He nodded. "Is that an issue?"

"Not if it kills the thing growing inside me." She had to be there for *Wes*, not some potential future kid who might never exist.

"One option is to freeze some of your eggs, but I doubt that will be covered by your insurance. However, I'm not asking you to make any decisions today, just informing you that some treatments could have a significant impact on your lifestyle. Okay?"

"Whatever it takes. As long as you get rid of this thing so I'm there for my son, I don't care what I have to sacrifice."

"Understood. Now, I appreciate there's a lot for you to process, but there are some decisions we *do* have to make regarding how we're going to proceed. Some stage II cancers are better suited to surgery, while for others, the best plan of attack is chemotherapy—"

She balled her fists. "I want it out."

"Excuse me?"

Her jaw set, she stared at him, unblinking. "I want it out. Now." She clenched her fists so tightly, her fingernails dug into her palms. It was all she could do to stop herself from shaking. No one was allowed to see how terrified she was.

Her voice calm, Rachel said, "The longer that thing is inside me, the longer it has to spread. Take the whole breast, if you have to, but it's coming out. One way or another."

She stared coldly.

If he wouldn't arrange it, she'd get a second opinion. Or a third, fourth, fifth… however many it took. She was killing this thing before it killed her, so it was already as good as dead. A bloody lump on a metal tray in an operating theater.

"As it happens, that is the most appropriate treatment in your case. However, I wouldn't be doing my job if I didn't apprise you of all the available options."

Good. This thing was dead. Dead!

"You'll be relieved to hear the size of your tumor doesn't warrant a mastectomy. In fact, it's so small you shouldn't even need breast reconstruction, though you'll have a small scar. At the same time as the main surgery, you'll also have an SLNB — a sentinel lymph node biopsy — to indicate whether the cancer is localized or has spread via the lymph system."

Rachel gulped. "That's…" She cleared her throat. "That's a possibility?"

"Because of your age and how small the tumor is, it's unlikely, but we need to be as sure as we can be."

Rachel nodded.

"With regard to adjuvant therapy, once we get the pathology report—"

"Adu-what?"

"Sorry, post-surgical treatment. You have what is known as estrogen receptor–positive, HER2-positive cancer. The good news is we have a whole range of drugs to combat these cancers."

There was never only "good" news. "And the bad news?"

"I'm afraid these cancers are some of the more aggressive and fast-growing."

She swallowed hard, gripping her purse, her nails digging her nails into the leather. "Aggressive and fast-growing?"

"I'm afraid so. Your cancer is..."

He kept saying the word *cancer. Cancer* in relation to her! Each time he said the word, she cringed, as if someone was stabbing her with a sharp stick.

She stared at the box of tissues while he talked. If she took one, that would be it – she'd collapse into a blubbering wreck. This monster inside her was not going to do that to her. She was going to beat it. Kill it. For that, she had to be the one in control. She gritted her teeth.

"We've caught yours relatively early, which is good," said Jacobs. "Unless the pathology suggests otherwise, I imagine we'll be going with two chemotherapy drugs as adjuvant therapy: Taxotere and Paraplatin. Taxotere stops cancer cells from dividing and replicating, ultimately killing them, while Paraplatin works to actually destroy their genetic material. That regimen will be for between three and six months."

He looked, as if waiting for a reply.

This had suddenly gotten so, so real. They were talking about destroying cancer in *her* body.

Rachel said, "Sounds like a whole lot of drugs. I'm not going to get busted for possession, am I?" She tried to smile, but her face refused to work properly. She pictured herself looking like she'd smelled rotten eggs.

It didn't help – Jacobs didn't laugh. He'd probably heard it so many times, he was groaning inside.

"We'll also be prescribing Herceptin and Perjeta as 'targeted therapy' drugs to help block the cancer cells from receiving growth signals."

"So even more drugs?"

He nodded.

So many drugs. For so long. Apart from the occasional glass of wine with Izzy, she'd always looked after herself with healthy food and exercise. There was little point in being cured of cancer if her body was left too wrecked to function.

She said, "I'm not keen on taking so many drugs."

"Are you keen on staying alive?"

Her jaw dropped. "Excuse me?"

"You asked me to be blunt."

She ran a hand through her hair and clasped the back of her head. "It's that bad?"

"It isn't. But it could be if we don't take the appropriate action."

She stared at the cream wall for a moment. "But I don't like the idea of filling my body with chemicals. How about radiation therapy? Couldn't that work instead?"

"Radiation therapy is something for after the initial chemo regimen. Then we'll look at endocrine therapy — another drug regimen."

"So I get chemo *and* radiation therapy?"

He nodded.

"Then even more drugs?"

He nodded again.

She blew out a heavy breath. "And that's it? That will get rid of it?"

"In the majority of cases. But" — he gave a tiny shrug — "there are never any guarantees where cancer is concerned."

That was a polite way of saying, "No, it could still come back and kill you."

She cupped her face, then dragged her hands down until her fingertips rested on her mouth.

He said, "Ultimately, I can only advise. What treatment you eventually undertake is entirely your decision. However, in my opinion — and I've been specializing in oncology for sixteen years — radiation therapy is something for the future. Our best course right now is the one I've outlined."

"So surgery, drugs, radiation, then more drugs?" She'd be left shriveled, frail, and decrepit.

"Think of it like waging a war — you have forces on the ground, planes in the air, ships on the seas, subs under the ocean. You attack the enemy on every front, using every strategy and technology you have. It's the same with cancer — we attack it every way we can, so we've got the greatest chance of defeating it."

She nodded. That made sense.

"Should I be worried about side effects?"

He rubbed his hands together. "Different people have different side effects. They can be anything from fatigue, nausea, and headaches to heart failure, nerve damage, and chronic diarrhea."

"Chronic diarrhea."

He nodded. "And prolonged."

"So at least there are some perks to having cancer."

"Now, that's important." He pointed a stubby finger at her.

"Huh?"

"A sense of humor. A positive mental attitude can make a huge difference to the eventual outcome and your quality of life in the meantime."

"Great. So know any good jokes?"

"I'll walk you through the possible side effects nearer the time."

What a warm bedside manner this guy had. Still, she didn't need him to be a great humanitarian, only a great oncologist.

Rachel said, "So there's nothing to be gained from a mastectomy — just whipping the whole thing off to make sure we get everything?"

"Don't underestimate the trauma of losing a breast. It can shatter the sense of self, so unless the cancer warrants it, I see no reason to recommend such drastic action. Plus, recent studies suggest there's little difference in survival rates between a lumpectomy — just removing the tumor — and a mastectomy. With the size of your tumor, I don't think a mastectomy would be beneficial, so we'll remove just the mass and a margin — a thin sliver around it — to make sure we've got it all."

That was it. Her future laid bare. The only problem was that now she knew, she had to tell everyone. How was she going to tell Wes?

Chapter 53

Wes lined up the cups on the desk, smirking at Harley dutifully looking on beside him, as if this time, he knew he'd defeat his nemesis by fooling the dog into picking the wrong cup.

"Wes, before we start today," said Rachel, "there's something I need to tell you." She couldn't put off telling him any longer now she knew what she was facing.

He didn't look up but slipped an orange jelly bean under the middle cup.

She put her hand on top of it to stop him from shuffling. "Wesley, I need to talk to you."

He glanced toward her from under his bangs.

Rachel said, "Remember last year when you were sick with the flu, and the doctor came and gave you medicine to make you better?"

He nodded.

"Well, I'm sick now, and I have to see a doctor to make me better."

He nodded again.

"It means we won't always have our lessons, and other things might happen at the wrong times. Some days, I might not even be here, but someone will be. Is that okay?"

Once more, he nodded.

"So it's okay if sometimes I'm not here and Izzy or Grandma is with you instead?"

He nodded a fourth time.

She hadn't expected it to go so smoothly. Almost too smoothly. He didn't process emotions the way she did, but it would've been nice if he showed some form of disappointment that she wouldn't be there. Was she completely dispensable?

He said, "So it will be Tuesday."

"What will be Tuesday?"

"When you're better. You said it was like when I was ill, and I was ill for six days, which means you'll be better by Tuesday."

Oh heavens. That was why he didn't mind. In trying to tell him in terms he'd grasp, she'd misrepresented the severity of the situation.

"It might be longer than Tuesday, Wes."

"Okay."

Bullet dodged.

"So when?"

"I don't know. Even the doctors don't know."

He nodded, more to himself than her.

Wow. And to think how she'd stressed about telling him, imagining screaming, biting, and kicking. What had she gotten? A few nods. He never ceased to surprise her. Never.

Wes reached for the cups again but frowned. "Doctors? I only needed one. Why do you need more?"

"I don't have the flu. I have something else. Something worse. That's why it will take longer than next Tuesday."

"But you will get better."

"I hope so."

"Hope? You mean you might not?" He shook his head, his voice louder. "No. You have to promise you'll get better. Promise."

Harley shrank down, ears flat to his head.

"Wes, I..." She didn't want to lie, but how could she tell the truth? "It's not that easy. It's—"

"Promise."

"Wes, something like this—"

"Promise!" He lurched up, flinging his arm across the desk, knocking everything flying. "Promise. You have to promise!"

Harley darted under her desk and cowered.

If she promised now but had to break the promise, that would cause even more problems later. "Wesley, this isn't a time when a promise will work."

He screamed. His voice not yet broken, the shriek cut through her like a scalpel through flesh.

Wincing, she pulled away.

He screamed again, then shot past her.

"Wes. Wes, please."

He stamped up the staircase, then slammed his bedroom door. Shrieking sliced through the house, accompanied by stomping and clattering.

Usually, there was little reasoning with him once things escalated to this point. But this problem wasn't going to go away — they had to face it. Now. Together.

She slouched upstairs to his room. His soup cans lay scattered across the floor, his underwear drawer had been upturned, and the blue armchair had been pushed over.

Wes stood with his back to her, staring at the wall. He rocked back and forth, slapping both sides of his head.

"I'm sorry, I upset you, Wes. I'm only trying to explain—"

"You're going to leave. Just like Dad left. You don't want to be with me anymore."

She clutched her chest, the words stabbing her in the heart as deeply as any blade ever could. "Wes, of course I want to be with you. I love you." Tears streamed down her cheeks.

"So why are you leaving?"

"Wes, I'm not leaving like Dad. I'm ill. I can't make you a promise that I might not be able to keep."

"So you really might leave?"

"I don't want to."

"But you might?"

"I—"

He shrieked, dove onto his bed, thrust his face into his pillow, and sobbed. Sobbed with all his heart, his body shuddering.

She ached to reach out to him, hug him, reassure him she'd do all she could to never leave him. But he was Wes — he'd never let her.

Sitting at the foot of his bed, she touched his leg. He shrieked and kicked out, hitting her in the ribs so hard she fell off and smacked into the floor.

Crying, Rachel clambered up and limped out. She didn't know what to do. Her son needed her, but she couldn't help him. What kind of a mother couldn't help her own flesh and blood? Usually, Wes never spoke during such incidents and, as quickly as these situations erupted, everything settled down again. Usually. But today was different.

Holding her hip where she'd hit the floor, she hobbled into her bedroom. With sobbing coming from down the hall, she stared into space, tears flowing. If cancer took her, it wouldn't only be taking one life, but two.

She fell onto her bed. And sobbed.

Through the juddering tears, an idea crawled from the darkness engulfing her thoughts. A tiny glimmer of hope flickering in the shadows. Sniffling, she wiped her eyes. That might just work.

Chapter 54

Harley trembled underneath Rachel's desk, hunched in a tight ball. Wes's sobbing seemed to shake the whole house. What could be so bad that his new pack was falling to pieces? He whimpered, praying for the sorrow-filled wailing to stop and for laughter to light up his heart once more.

Footsteps clomped down the stairs. Instead of her usual graceful gait, Rachel dragged herself into the room as if the air was so heavy it was grinding her into the floor.

Her voice frail, she said, "Harley."

He peered out over his tail.

"Come here, boy."

He cowered. Something bad had happened. He didn't think he was responsible, but it was impossible to tell these days.

Her face twisted as if she were in pain, but he couldn't see anyone or anything hurting her.

"Not you too, Harley." She crouched, holding one hand toward him. "Harley, please."

He trembled. His pack was in tatters, and he didn't know how to help.

Rachel collapsed in a heap on the floor, her eyes bloodshot. She wiped her cheeks, then smiled at him. "Harley, TV remote."

He lifted his head.

"Harley, TV remote."

His ears pricked. Really? She needed him to do a job? Maybe that could make everything right again. He scrambled up, claws scratching on the wood floor, and darted into the living room, scanning for the device. There. He lifted it off the sofa and trotted back to Rachel.

The skin around her eyes crinkled as she smiled. "Thank you, Harley."

She hugged him.

The glow of pack loyalty welled inside him. He basked in its warmth. Maybe everything was going to be okay.

"Now I need you to do something else."

She led him upstairs. With each step, the sobbing grew louder. Wes was in such pain — more pain than his tiny body could tolerate. Harley didn't know what was causing it, but if he found it, he'd bite it to bits.

Rachel peeked in through the bedroom door. "Wes."

"Out!" It was more a scream than a word as he beat his fist into his bed. "Out!" He hammered again and again.

"Harley's frightened. He needs you."

The sobbing eased and the flailing stopped.

"Wes, Harley needs you. Help him. Please."

His head turned away from the door, Wes reached backward, fingers clawing to reach his friend.

Rachel whispered, "Work your magic, boy. Please." She patted him.

Harley nuzzled the reaching hand. The moment he touched it, Wes spun, flung his arms around him, and sobbed against his shoulder.

Barney had been a big, powerful man who'd been able to do many things for himself, just not enough. Even though Harley had loved helping his friend, he'd always gotten the impression that almost anybody else could've helped him just as well.

Wes was a small, frail boy, with a special way. So special the world didn't always understand him. But Harley did. There was no deceit with Wes, no pretense, just brutal logic. Doglike logic. That was why Harley had been brought here — anyone could've helped Barney, but only Harley could help Wes. It was his special purpose. The purpose he'd been born to fulfill.

Harley didn't know why his friend's little heart was breaking, but he'd do all he could to repair it. Luckily, in times of deep trauma, every dog knew the secret to putting things right — Harley licked Wes. Licked and licked and licked.

Wes's sobbing stopped and his shuddered breathing became smoother.

Yes, every dog knew the secret. The problem was, people didn't and often couldn't hear it when a dog whispered it to them. It was lucky Wes was wiser than most.

Sniffling, his voice breaking, Wes said, "Don't leave."

He reached out a trembling hand. Not toward Harley, but toward Rachel.

She gasped and tears streamed again.

Tentatively, she reached for him. But when her fingertips brushed his, he yanked his hand back as if hers were red hot.

Rachel's face twisted with pain.

But, like Harley sensing a stranger could be trusted, Wes relented. He grabbed Rachel's outstretched hand. And didn't let go.

She clutched her mouth, gazing at his hand in hers as if it was the greatest moment in the history of the world.

After a few seconds, Rachel crept closer and patted the bed. "Harley."

He jumped up and lay beside Wes. Still holding Wes's hand, Rachel shuffled to the other side of Harley and snuggled against him, their joined hands resting on his side.

There, the three of them lay, Harley the glue bonding the pack together.

Harley sighed. He'd done his job. It was a good day. The best of days. He drifted to sleep, cocooned physically and emotionally in the warmth of his loving pack.

Chapter 55

A floorboard creaked and a faint light bled into Wes's gloomy room through the open door. Rachel woke, snuggled across Wes's bed with him and Harley. Still holding hands.

In the doorway, Izzy said, "Sorry. I didn't mean to wake you."

Harley wagged his tail, knocking Wes and waking him. He released Rachel's hand and rubbed his eyes.

"Hey, Wes," said Izzy. "How are you doing, buddy?"

He rolled off his bed and picked up two soup cans.

Izzy mouthed to Rachel, "What's happening?"

Rachel nodded toward the hall, then glanced at Wes. "Wes, do you want me to help you?"

"You don't know where they go."

"So, we'll leave you to do it properly."

She and Izzy went to the living room, talking with hushed voices so he couldn't accidentally hear.

"You've told him?" asked Izzy.

Rachel nodded.

"And?"

Thinking of the pain she'd caused him, Rachel covered her eyes.

"Come here." Izzy hugged her.

Her voice breaking, Rachel said, "I hurt him so much, Iz. So much."

Izzy stroked her hair. "It's okay, Rach. It's done now."

"Kind of."

Izzy pulled away. "What do you mean *kind of?*"

"He knows there's a problem, but not how bad it could be."

"Listen, while we're on the subject—"

"Not now, Iz." Rachel turned, but Izzy grabbed her arm.

"Listen—"

Rachel raised an eyebrow.

226

"—your immediate reaction is going to be to say no, but hear me out. If the worst does happen, God forbid, what's going to happen to Wes?"

Rachel shook her head and drew a faltering breath. "I thought I'd always be there for him. Always. But..."

"You will be. Whether your time comes in one year, ten years, or fifty years, you'll always be with him, watching over him."

Rachel rolled her eyes. "Yeah, right."

"What? You think this is all there is?"

Rachel shrugged. Religion had never appealed to her — it had always seemed way too divisive. As for sitting on a cloud with a pair of wings...

"I honestly don't know what I believe." The greatest thinkers and greatest scientists throughout history hadn't come up with an answer, so no way did she have one.

"You don't think there's more to you than just this?" Izzy waved at Rachel's body. "You don't believe in a soul?"

Rachel sniggered. "So I'm going to be looking down on Wes while playing my harp, am I?"

Izzy's shoulders slumped. "Rach, come on. Do you really think I'm talking about some goofy dude with wings sitting on a cloud? I'm talking about the essence of a person — that special spark that gives an inanimate lump of chemicals and compounds life. Gives it hope, desire, dreams, love, gives it everything that makes it *it* — everything that makes you *you*, me *me*, Wes *Wes*."

"And that's so different from angels, is it?"

"So what's the alternative? Everything that makes you *you* can be boiled down to nothing but simple chemical processes happening inside this lump of meat we call Rachel, can it?"

"Where's the evidence? With everything we know now and everything we can do, don't you think we'd have discovered one microscopic shred of proof that life doesn't end when you die? Come on."

Izzy counted off on her fingers. "There's the 21 grams theory. There's the fact that every religion on earth — no matter how far apart in distance, time, or culture they were when created — believes in some form of *continuation* after death. Hinduism, Buddhism, Islam, Christianity, Judaism, Shinto, Sikhism... you name it. And of course, there's Houdini. Then there's—"

"Wait. Escape artist Houdini? What's he got to do with it? Or are you going say he escaped from Heaven to tell people about it?"

"More or less."

Rachel rolled her eyes. "You know, just because something's posted online, it doesn't mean it's true, right?"

"Research it. It wasn't all stage tricks. During the First World War, he taught our troops how to break out of German handcuffs."

"Yeah, right."

"Look it up! It's all there. Anyway, because there was nowhere he couldn't escape, he swore to his wife, Bess, that if there was an afterlife, he'd find a way to contact her. They even devised a secret coded message so she'd know it was him and not some scammer conning her. And all this after he'd debunked countless spiritualists and psychics using his magician's skills, mind you. After he died, Bess spent years visiting mediums, praying one would give her the secret phrase to prove Harry was still with her, and eventually, one came through."

"Seriously? A message from the afterlife?"

Izzy smirked. "Still think it's all just a convenient collection of chemical processes?"

Could it be true? Could the greatest escape artist of all time have returned from beyond the grave to assure his wife they'd be together again? It was wonderful to imagine people spent eternity with their loved ones, but it couldn't be real. There'd have been proof by now. Surely. Not just the unverifiable story of some grieving woman from a century ago.

"Look, we're getting off track because that's not what I wanted to talk to you about," said Izzy. "Now, please don't just automatically say no. Hear me out. Okay?"

Rachel frowned. "Okay."

"So *if* the worst does happen, what's going to happen to Wes?"

"I'm still working on that." Between her life insurance payout and the income from Harley's money, she hoped she'd be able to find him a residential home that would give him something approaching a reasonable life rather than just dumping him in a chair to vegetate.

"Look..." Izzy tilted her head, rubbing her hands together. "If Peter's starting a new family, he won't take Wes, will he?"

"Well, duh."

"And your mom's great, bless her, but she's completely clueless when it comes to Wes."

Rachel slouched, her hand on her hip. "Is there a point coming?"

Izzy locked her gaze.

Rachel shrugged. "Well?"

"Me, Rach. Me!"

Rachel's eyes widened. "You?" She snickered.

Izzy turned away. "Gee, thanks for the vote of confidence."

"Sorry." Rachel grabbed her arm. "I didn't mean it like that, Iz. But you work, so you couldn't be there for him. You don't know his routine or anything about his lessons. You can't cook what he likes... It's a wonderful gesture, Iz." She squeezed Izzy's arm. "Really. But it would never work."

"It wouldn't work today, no, but we're not talking about today, are we? We'd be talking one, two, three, who knows how many years from now. Plenty of time for me to learn what I need to know."

"It's amazing that you've offered, but putting your life on permanent hold to look after Wes?" Rachel shook her head. "I can't ask you to do that."

"You're not asking. I'm telling you what we're going to do. Or do you think Wes would have a better life in a residential facility where people are paid to stick him in front of the TV all day, then put him to bed?"

Rachel bit her lip as her eyes filled up again. "Izzy, there's so much to looking after him, so much you don't know about. It's not fair to you. You're young. You have your whole life to live."

"And I'll live it — with Wes. And if someone else comes along, they'll have to fit in with our lifestyle. If the worst does happen, Wes will have the money from your life insurance, plus Harley's money, so I can spend as much time with him as you do and have the cash to pay for high-level professional care from time to time to give me a break."

Rachel rubbed her chin. "You've really thought this through?"

"That's what I'm telling you. You and Wes are like family, so in case something happens to you, why don't we make it official?"

It was the perfect solution. Izzy could be Wes's legal guardian, so if the worst happened, he'd have as good a life as Rachel could give him.

"You aren't working on Tuesday, are you?" asked Rachel.

"No. Why?"

Rachel offered her hand. "Class starts at eight fifteen sharp. Don't be late."

Izzy beamed and shook hands. "I won't. Promise."

"I suggest you buy a good pair of sneakers too, not those fancy fashionable things you like."

"Sneakers? To teach Wes math?"

"You get Wes, you get Harley. And Harley loves to run."

Izzy laughed.

Rachel sauntered to the kitchen.

"You are joking, right, Rach? ... Rach?"

Smirking, Rachel glanced around as she opened a cupboard. "That hill to the trailhead is an absolute killer. You're gonna love it."

"No, no, no. I don't do exercise. You know that, Rach." She pinched a couple of inches of fat around her waist. "This is me. I like me."

Rachel winked. "Buns of steel, Iz. Buns of steel."

Izzy slouched over. "But I don't want buns of steel. I'm happy with belly of jelly."

Rachel had taught Wes how to read, write, and do basic math. But she'd done it using highly unconventional methods. Could she teach scatterbrained Izzy those methods, or was it destined to be a frustrating farce that damaged their relationship?

Not that that was her biggest problem — no, that arrived tomorrow.

Chapter 56

Sunlight beamed through the massive wall of glass into the airport arrivals hall. Rachel waved at a dumpy woman with graying hair waddling through the mass of passengers – Mom.

Every time her mother had flown in, she'd expected to be picked up without even asking. Every time. Except this time. She'd wanted to take a taxi, but Rachel had insisted she wouldn't hear of it. Wouldn't hear of it because if they met in public, hopefully, her mom couldn't immediately turn this "inconvenience" into a drama befitting a badly written daytime soap.

Mom waved back, but her chin quivered.

Under her breath, Rachel said, "Oh geez. Didn't even make it out of the airport."

They flung their arms around each other. Strangely, though part of Rachel was dreading the visit because of the increased stress it would bring, once they were hugging, she didn't want it to end. Mom was childhood and understanding, tenderness and security. Mom was chicken soup when she was sick, a hug when she was broken-hearted, a proud smile when she had even the most trivial of triumphs. Mom was... Mom.

Rachel said, "Thanks for coming."

"Like you could keep me away." Mom dabbed her eyes with a white lace handkerchief.

Rachel reached for Mom's bag.

Mom yanked it away. "We'll have none of that, for a start."

"I can carry a bag, Mom. I'm not an invalid."

"Oh, listen to you being so brave." She cupped Rachel's cheek. "You make me so proud."

"Brave?" They dawdled toward the nearest exit.

"Yes, in how you're facing this."

"Mom, there's nothing 'brave' about struggling not to die. If you try to swat a bug, it's not being freaking brave when it buzzes out of the way, is it?"

"I know what I know, Rachel, and brave is brave."

Rachel pressed the elevator button to go to the multilevel parking garage.

Mom said, "You didn't bring Wes?"

"After what happened last time?"

"Oh, I'm sure he'd have been fine if he'd known he was coming to see his gram-gram. Especially when I've got him a gift."

"Mom, the only time he's been here, he screamed the place down so badly we got kicked off the plane. It's not exactly filled with happy memories for him."

"Well, you know best, dear." That was her stock response whenever she wanted to say exactly the opposite but didn't want to appear argumentative. Rachel bit her tongue. The woman always meant well but sometimes had a weird way of showing it.

"Mom, he can't cope with strange places or strange people."

"You said he was doing better at school, so I thought he might be growing out of it."

Rachel rubbed her brow. "It's not a phase — not like a kid suddenly refusing to eat anything red — it's a condition. For life."

The elevator doors opened.

Mom entered. "Mrs. Appleyard sends her best, by the way, and says she'll pray for everything going well tomorrow."

"That's nice of her." Whoever the devil she was.

Rachel waited for three other people with luggage to amble in, then hit the button and the dull gray doors closed.

Mom said, "If I'm taking you tomorrow, should I drive to get used to the car?"

"Okay." She handed Mom the keys.

"Izzy doesn't mind looking after Wes? Because I can help, if you like?"

"No, she's looking forward to it."

"How is she?"

"Good."

"Is she still seeing that mechanic?"

"Not for a few months now."

232

They exited the elevator. Rachel pointed to a row of cars on the left of the dimly lit concrete structure.

Mom said, "What color's her hair?"

"It was blue until Friday. Now it's pink."

Mom shook her head. "All those chemicals. She'll be bald as a coot by the time she's forty." She clutched her mouth, then touched Rachel's arm. "Oh, I am sorry, Rachel. I didn't mean to upset you."

Rachel frowned. "Why should I be upset?"

"Because, you know..." She looked around, clearly ensuring no one was listening, and then whispered, "Chemo. Your hair. You know."

Rachel stopped. "Mom, listen to me, please, because this is important. I'm going to beat this thing, but I'm going to beat it my way. That means no pussyfooting around or giving me special treatment. I'm going to need help with the things I simply can't do, but in everything else, I want to be treated as if this never happened. Okay?"

Mom smiled. "Of course, sweetheart. If that's what you want." She handed Rachel her bag and sauntered on. "So when was the last time you had a good meal in you? The way you're wasting away, I'm not surprised you're sick."

Rachel traipsed after her. "I'm not wasting away, Mom. I run three miles every morning. It's called being fit."

"It's called being nothing but skin and bone. We'll stop for groceries on the way. I know I'm only visiting for a few days, but that's time enough to get some proper food inside you."

Rachel got a lump in her throat. Chicken soup and understanding. Yep, that was Mom. This might work out after all.

Rachel chuckled, then remembered why Mom was there and the smile faded. Since that moment she'd found the lump, even though she'd had physical examinations, a battery of tests, and even a biopsy, it hadn't felt real. Now? Things were about to get very freaking real very freaking fast.

Chapter 57

Clouds shrouding the dawn sky bathed the world in gloom. Rachel pounded along the roadside, her breath billowing, Harley beside her.

Cold, damp air bit at her cheeks, reminding her she was very much alive. Alive and free. Today, more than any other day, she let her logical mind melt away, to lose herself in the nothingness of the moment. There was no stress, no worries, no illness — there was no "Rachel." Only a woman, a dog, and a path to run.

Lost in the joy of simply doing, of being and yet not *being* anything, Rachel hammered up the incline toward her trailhead. Exhilaration flooding her body with endorphins, she eased to a stroll. After completing her strength exercises, she looked at the route home.

Turning, she gazed along the tree-lined road in the opposite direction. "Shall we just keep running, Harley? Pretend today isn't happening?"

Harley barked. Rachel snickered. She didn't know what he'd said, which was unfortunate, because considering how smart he was, it could have been the answer to her problems.

Her shoulders slumping, she exhaled loudly. She pulled his leash in the direction from which they'd come. "Come on, boy. I can't outrun this one, not even with your help, so let's get it over with."

The run back was a slog. Each step took her closer to a reality she didn't want to be real, a future as stark as the cloud-laden sky. Anxiety clawed at her, like a dark river fighting to burst a dam — one tiny crack and everything she loved would be lost beneath cold, empty blackness.

Her heart and breath racing as if she'd run thirty miles and not three, she trudged past the tree line, and her home came into view. This was it — one way or the other — the beginning of the end.

After showering and forsaking her moisturizing and cosmetic regimen, she had the final sip of water she was allowed, and... she was ready. She hugged Harley, hugged Izzy, got a "Be okay" from Wes, then tramped to the car.

The drive to the hospital was silent. Rachel didn't want to talk and, possibly for the first time in her life, Mom didn't know what to say, so said nothing. The quiet was both comforting, because it left her alone with her thoughts, and scary for the very same reason.

Standing on the city sidewalk, Rachel gazed up at the gigantic concrete-and-glass hospital as it reared over her. Life and death waged a daily war within those walls. Its corridors were scarred by the shadows of the fallen, and its operating rooms were haunted by the ghosts of what might have been.

She'd run three miles with ease that morning, but the three yards to the automatic glass doors guarding the hospital entrance might as well have been three million yards.

Her hand trembling, she rubbed her face. How was she going to do this? She had cancer. That was indisputable. But what if the surgeon cut her open and found her riddled with the stuff? Right now, she felt stronger than she'd ever been. Invincible. But in just a matter of hours, the truth could leave her nothing but a case study on diagnosis blunders for first-year residents.

She was Schrödinger's cat — she both had a future and didn't.

Her legs as steady as a newborn foal's, she tottered forward but faltered.

Mom took Rachel's hand. "I'm here."

Chicken soup and understanding. Rachel gulped away the lump in her throat.

Holding hands, like a loving mother and her toddler daughter on the first day of school, they shuffled inside.

Minutes later, Rachel transformed from being an independent, healthy woman in charge of her own destiny into a cancer patient with a name scrawled on a wristband.

Rachel lay in a pale blue gown on a hospital bed in a room of white and subtle shades of green. A black nurse, who smiled constantly, took her through a checklist: full name, date of birth, when she last ate, if she smoked, any allergies, whether her teeth were crowned...

The nurse disappeared.

Strangely, now that control had been wrestled from her and everything depended on the skill of the medical staff, Rachel felt calm. Maybe it was the eye of the storm, or maybe her logical mind had overruled her emotional one due to the inevitability of the situation. Either way, the anxious dread had succumbed to a sense of *que será, será*. Having no control, and thus no option but to let events run their course, was wonderfully freeing.

Rachel reached out to Mom, who sat in a blue chair. "You don't have to stay."

"Don't be silly." Mom took her hand. "Of course I'm staying."

"There'll be all sorts of tests and doctors and nurses coming and going."

Mom held up her phone. "I brought a book."

"Mom, I'm not dying. This is a small, routine operation, with minimal risk, so I don't want you wasting a whole day sitting there and staring at the wall. Seriously. I'll call you when I wake up after the surgery."

Mom squeezed her hand. "Today is all about you, sweetheart, so if that's really what you want."

"It is."

"Well, okay, then." They hugged, one of the longest hugs they'd ever enjoyed, and Mom left.

When the nurse returned, she drew some of Rachel's blood, then Rachel had a chest X-ray and an electrocardiogram. Following that, other medical staff discussed the upcoming procedure, and she signed a consent form listing Mom as her medical proxy. One of the doctors even scrawled something on her right breast, saying it was so all his team were on the same page. Finally, the nurse fitted an IV line into the back of her left hand.

A bald man in green scrubs arrived with a gurney and wheeled Rachel along the corridors. The serenity she'd found so reassuring earlier dissipated, her heart pounding like she was running up the hill to her trailhead. She tried to swallow, but her mouth was too dry.

This was happening. *Really* happening. She ached to leap off and bolt but pictured Wes. This was for him. Everything was for him.

Her gurney was pushed into an anesthetic room. Along two walls were a variety of parked carts and wheeled tables containing all manner of medical equipment. The anesthesiologist went through a checklist and administered a sedative through her IV.

Her anxiousness slipped away. She was aware of everything, but as though she'd split a bottle of red with Izzy, none of it bothered her.

In the operating theater, she was greeted by a surgical team clad in blue and wearing facemasks, just like something from a TV show. Helped onto the operating table, she lay down, bathed in brightness from overhead lights on movable arms.

She recognized the anesthesiologist's voice. "Okay, Rachel, I'd like you to count backwards from 100 please."

She made it to 93...

Chapter 58

A blurry world greeted Rachel as she fought to open her eyes. Her nose itched. She winced moving her right arm, so lifted her left. She stared at a lump of plastic clipped to one of her fingers, then touched her face. A plastic tube ran across her top lip.

"Don't disturb that, sweetheart. It's oxygen." A hand covered hers.

Rachel croaked, "Mom?"

"I'm here."

A hand gently brushed her hair.

Rachel blinked repeatedly, and the room she'd been in earlier came into focus. As did Mom smiling.

"You were..." Rachel struggled to swallow, her mouth dry and throat sore. She looked around, then reached for a cup on the bedside cabinet.

Mom passed it. "Go easy. The nurse said only a few sips at first."

Rachel sipped. The water lubricated her mouth, while its coldness eased the scratchiness inside her throat.

She said, "You were supposed to go home."

"As if I was going to leave you here alone."

The smiling nurse bustled in. "Have we got a live one?"

"Just about," said Rachel.

The nurse checked her pulse, blood pressure, and oxygen levels. "Everything's looking good. You should be on your way home very soon. How do you feel? Any pain?"

Rachel pointed to her throat. "Here."

Why did her throat hurt more than where they'd cut her?

"Don't worry, that's perfectly normal. It's partly because you're dehydrated after not eating or drinking all day, and partly because you had an endotracheal tube inserted to give you oxygen during the operation. Sipping water should help. But the best remedy is ice cream." She winked. "Who says there aren't perks to having surgery?"

"Thank you."

Soon after, the anesthesiologist popped in with a list of dos and don'ts until the anesthetic had cleared her system in a further twenty-four hours.

Once her vitals returned to a satisfactory level, Rachel was discharged with an information pack on recovering, plus a follow-up appointment in ten days.

Being driven home in the twilight, Rachel cracked the window, closed her eyes, and sucked in cold air. She didn't know if the anesthetic had messed up her senses, but the air had never tasted so fresh.

It was done. The thing was out of her, and the statistics suggested that was the end of it. While she had a brutal chemo regimen looming, the thing that had had the audacity to invade her body would now burn in the hospital incinerator, if it hadn't already. Done.

Mom gestured to the window. "Close that, sweetheart. You can't risk getting an infection."

Rachel didn't want to jeopardize the future she'd secured for a fleeting moment of pleasure, so she raised the window.

As Mom pulled the car into her driveway, Rachel couldn't help but smile. Home. Everything she knew. Everyone she loved. Home. She sighed as the warm glow of love caressed her like slipping into a fur-lined glove. Now for a relaxed evening of doing absolutely nothing.

Mom unfastened the seatbelt for her, though the strap across her chest had barely bothered her.

Taking her time, holding Mom's arm, she shuffled into the house.

A gleaming banner hung across the living room, reading "Welcome Home!", below which stood Izzy and Wes. Dotted about were vases of chrysanthemums — her favorites. Wes set off a giant party popper, and glittery confetti showered like diamond-and-ruby rain. Harley barked and ran around, snapping at the tumbling jewels.

Rachel clutched her mouth. She hadn't even been gone a full day, and they'd done all this?

"Welcome home, Rach," said Izzy.

"We've got cake," said Wes.

"Please tell me there's ice cream too."

Wes ran to the refrigerator.

Izzy sauntered over. Carefully avoiding Rachel's right side, she hugged her. "I'm so pleased it went well. How you doing? Is there much pain?"

Rachel shrugged. "Surprisingly, no. My sports bra is helping with support, but I thought it was going to be agony, yet..." She shook her head. "Mind you, tomorrow could be different. I'm guessing this is the aftereffects of the painkillers from the surgery."

Izzy nodded.

"Thanks for all this, by the way."

Izzy held up her hands. "Don't look at me. This is all Wes."

"Really?"

"He wanted to do something special. I just provided a few suggestions and went to the store yesterday."

Wes shouted, holding up two cartons, "Chocolate chip or cookie dough?"

"Wesley Taylor, how long have I been your mother that you have to ask that?"

He nodded.

The swivel chair from her bedroom was in front of the window overlooking the backyard. "Oh, you brought my chair down."

"We figured if you couldn't exercise Harley, you could at least watch us play fetch with him in the yard," said Izzy.

"Thanks. I'll like that."

As she sat on the sofa, Wes brought her a bowl heaped with chocolate chip ice cream.

"Oh, wonderful. Thank you, Wes."

His head down, he smiled, then fetched bowls for everyone and sat in his spot.

Mom said, "That reminds me, with everything happening last night, I forgot to give him his gift."

Mom disappeared, then returned hiding something behind her back. Smirking, she stood in front of Wes. "Wes, can you guess what I've got?"

"Mom" — Rachel shook her head — "he doesn't get guessing. For him, it could, literally, be anything in the world."

Mom placed an empty soup can on the coffee table.

Wes gasped, cupping his cheeks. He reached to touch it but pulled back, as if unsure whether that was allowed.

Rachel said, "Go ahead, Wes, it's for you. But what do you say?"

"Thank you."

"You're welcome, Wes." Mom sat down.

Instead of picking the can up, Wes twisted to admire it from different angles.

Finally, he said, "Mull... mullig... mull... igata... wny."

"Mulligatawny," said Mom.

"Mulli..."

"Mull-i-ga-taw-ny," said Mom.

"Mull-i-ga-taw-ny," repeated Wes.

"That's it. Well done."

Instead of picking it up, Wes raced upstairs without a word.

Mom huffed. "I thought he'd appreciate it, but..."

Rachel said, "Just wait."

Wes dashed back, a soup can in each hand. He checked the labels, then put one on either side.

"It goes here," he said, pointing at the first can. "Minestrone" — he pointed at the new can — "mull-i..."

"Mull-i-ga-taw-ny," said Mom.

"Mull-i-ga-taw-ny" — he pointed at the last one — "mushroom." He turned toward Mom. "I have forty-two now." He counted them off on his fingers. "Asparagus, bean and bacon, beef broth, chicken broth—"

Rachel said, "Wes, why don't you just show Grandma?"

He raced upstairs again.

"You better go, Mom, because he'll be waiting."

Mom left for a few minutes. When she returned, she said, "I've never heard him say so much."

Rachel said, "He's always talked about his soup cans. The problem is, it gets really old really fast because there's only so much he can say before repeating himself."

An hour later, Rachel leaned to put her empty second bowl of ice cream on the coffee table. Sitting on the floor, Izzy took it and placed it amid similarly dirty bowls and plates speckled with cake crumbs and smeared with chocolate.

"Thank you, everyone," Rachel said. "I can't tell you how much all this means to me."

Izzy patted Rachel's leg. "You're welcome."

"I mean it," said Rachel. "It's been fantastic. And do you know the best part?"

"The cake," said Izzy.

Rachel shook her head.

Wes said, "Ice cream."

Another headshake.

"The chauffeuring," said Mom, sitting in Izzy's chair.

"Nuh-uh." She gestured to the surrounding mess, not least the confetti covering everything. "Doctor's orders — I'm not allowed to do any housecleaning!"

Everybody laughed.

"Don't worry," said Izzy, "all this can wait till you're better."

They laughed all the more.

Rachel yawned. She tried to stretch but winced and grabbed the right side of her chest.

"Everything okay, Rachel?" said Mom.

Izzy said, "What do you need? I can get it."

"I think — though I hate to be a party pooper — I need some painkillers and to lie down."

"I'm not surprised." Izzy stood and offered her hand.

Rachel grasped it and heaved herself up.

"Where are your painkillers, sweetheart?" asked Mom.

"In the hospital bag with the info pack."

"Okay. I'll bring them up with something to drink."

"Thanks, Mom." Resting on Izzy's arm for support, Rachel said, "I'm sorry, Iz, I'm like a doddery old woman. I don't know why my legs are so weak when it was my boobs getting all the action."

"It's probably the anesthetic. That on top of all the psychological stress — I'm surprised you've stayed awake this long."

Izzy helped Rachel to her bedroom. Rachel lay down, pulling the comforter over her.

Mom brought up a glass of orange juice and the painkillers. Rachel took two.

Mom kissed her on the forehead. "You're home now, sweetheart. Everything's going to be just fine."

"Thanks, Mom. For everything."

Mom smiled and left.

"Give me an hour, Iz. We'll have a proper chat once Wes has gone to bed."

"No rush. Take as long as you need." Izzy closed the door, plunging Rachel into darkness.

Rachel closed her eyes for a quick nap.

When Rachel next opened her eyes, sunlight filtered through her drapes. Groggy, she pushed to rest on her elbows. She sucked through her teeth as pain shot through her right side. The painkillers she'd had during the surgery had obviously worn off, and it felt like her breast and arm were on fire.

She rolled left and sat on the edge of the bed, holding her right arm across her chest.

Her pills and juice were there, so she grabbed them, noticing her clock: 9:23 a.m.

Wow. She'd slept for over thirteen hours, yet she still felt completely drained. Maybe if she moved, it would get her body working again.

Still in her jeans and loose shirt that fastened up the front, she held on to the nightstand and pushed up, testing how her legs took her weight. She seemed stable, though she doubted she'd be able to run to the front door, let alone her trailhead.

First job was the bathroom. Just as the info pack said, her urine was bluish-green because of the dye they'd injected for the surgeon to identify the correct lymph nodes to remove.

Good. That meant everything was going as planned.

She plodded down the hallway and, gripping the handrail, took the stairs one at a time like a tiny girl afraid of falling.

"Hey, how are we feeling?" said Mom, getting off the sofa and heading for the kitchen. "Good enough for some breakfast? Pancakes? Cereal? Bacon and eggs?"

"Something not too heavy, maybe."

"Toast?"

"Please. With strawberry jelly."

"You got it."

"Where's Wes?"

Mom pointed to the study. Rachel shuffled over.

Izzy was sitting at the desk with Wes and Harley. She grinned. "So this is what you call eight fifteen sharp, is it?"

Rachel sniggered. "How's it going?" The cups were grouped near Wes as if they'd been used, while Wes was holding one of the dice.

"Wes has shown me the cups game. Now, we're getting to grips with how the wheel and dice work together, aren't we, Wes?"

It was strange seeing someone else conducting Wes's lesson, especially using the unique tools she'd created for him. Part of her wanted to tell Izzy to get out for violating something so intimate that she and Wes shared; another part wanted to hug Izzy for caring enough to want to share it.

Rachel doddered closer. She pointed at the Wheel of Questions. "If Wes spins and lands on, say, 'How,' which is written in green, he throws the green die and you use that score to formulate a question. So if the die landed on '2 & 2,' you could ask how many things in this room have two arms and two legs. If it landed on '3 & 5,' you could ask him to explain how Harley helps us in three sentences of no fewer than five words."

Izzy nodded. "Ah, I get it."

Rachel placed her hand on the desk to steady herself. "Man, I'd never have thought a simple operation could wipe me out like this."

"Go sit down. We're fine, aren't we, Wes?"

Wes nodded.

Swaying, Rachel trudged to the sofa.

Mom brought her a coffee. "Toast is on its way."

After breakfast, Rachel went to the bathroom. Showering was off-limits for the first forty-eight hours, but she could wash, which would make her feel better. She eased off her shirt but kept her sports bra on. Using a washcloth, she washed what she could with her left hand. Supporting her right arm with her left hand, she washed under her left armpit, grimacing as the movement compressed her right breast.

Finally, she peeked under the right side of her bra at the white dressing. That could come off tomorrow. She cringed at what she might find — how she'd been mutilated. Would she ever be able to look at herself, let alone allow anyone else to?

Someone knocked on the door.

She shouted, "Busy!"

Wes said, "It's lesson time."

"I'm busy, Wes. Izzy is doing your lesson today."

"Not my lesson."

What?

Slowly, she eased on her shirt and opened the door a crack. "Wes, please give me some time today. I'm sure you'll have fun with Izzy."

"But it's lesson time."

"Yes, Izzy's here for your lesson."

"Not my lesson, yours." He held up a sheet of paper from her info pack showing diagrams of arm exercises. While the operation on her breast had an impact on her chest, the SLNB had an even greater one on her arm by disrupting her musculature and removing part of her lymphatic system. These exercises were vital for a proper recovery.

Izzy appeared. "He wants to help. He's been practicing the exercises."

"I'm going to make you better," said Wes.

"Just a second." She shut the door and fastened her shirt.

Since Harley's arrival, Wes had come further and further out of the private world he'd created. He'd never emotionally connected with anyone or anything, until Harley. She'd given him the job of feeding the dog as an experiment — to see if he could accept even a small responsibility. He loved it, and it now seemed to be one of the highlights of his day because she never had to nag him about it. Maybe it was the control it gave him over another being, or maybe it was the sense she trusted him with something important. Or maybe — she hoped — it was that he appreciated other living things had needs just like he did, and by providing for those, he created a better world.

As if to prove that, he wanted to help her. She smiled. Breast cancer was turning out to be a gift that kept on giving — first it had brought her and Izzy closer, and now it was giving her the son she'd always dreamed of.

Rachel exited the bathroom. "Okay, teacher, what's the lesson today?"

Wes had her sit on the sofa while he knelt on the floor at the other side of the coffee table. He arranged three cups in a row on the table. Rachel smiled. This was how she started his lessons to get him to focus. He really was trying to teach her.

He held up a red jelly bean for her to see, then hid it under the middle cup. After switching the cups about, he said, "Which cup?"

She pointed to the left one. "That one."

He revealed the jelly bean. "Well done, Mom. So what lesson are we doing today?"

"Arm exercises."

He put four crudely cut out cigarette-pack-sized scraps of paper on the table. Each had a number scrawled on it in a different-colored crayon: zero, one, two, three.

Wes said, "And how many times have you done your exercises today?"

"Zero."

"Well done, Mom." He pushed the scrap with the zero on it toward her.

She was supposed to do these exercises three times per day, so he was keeping track by mimicking her day-of-the-week cards. That was smart.

He placed the roulette wheel on the table, three of its nine sections covered, the others labeled one through six.

"Now spin the Workout Wheel."

"Did you pick the name?" asked Rachel.

He nodded.

"Great name." Rachel spun four.

Wes consulted the exercise chart. "Four is arm saw." He studied the diagram and text. "Okay, hold your arm like this." He held his upper right arm vertical, and he lifted his forearm horizontal.

Rachel copied him.

He pushed his hand forward, straightening his arm. "Do this."

Rachel did as instructed.

He mouthed, "One." His left hand in a fist, he stuck out the thumb, then brought his arm back to the starting position. "Again." They repeated the movement. He mouthed, "Two," putting out the index finger.

When they'd done this five times, Wes covered the corresponding pockets on the wheel and had her spin again and perform another exercise. They repeated the process until she'd completed all six exercises.

"Well done, Mom," said Wes, his bangs hiding his eyes. "You've done really well this morning." He pushed the scrap of paper marked with a one to her, as if awarding her a certificate.

"Thank you, Wes. I did so well because you're such a good teacher."

A smile flickered across his face as he tidied his teaching resources.

Rachel's chin trembled as she watched him. He was achieving things that only months ago had appeared impossible. If this was the difference Harley had made in just a few weeks, where would they be in a year?

Chapter 59

Wes conducted two more lessons that day, ensuring Rachel fulfilled her exercise requirements. The next day, he insisted on a lesson before she and Mom took him to school.

Back at home, Rachel took Harley for a sluggish walk along their running route. Harley didn't pull on the leash yet regularly looked up, as if asking why they were plodding like old people instead of running free and wild.

"I'm sorry, boy. I promise things will get back to normal in a few weeks."

They shuffled as far as the old oak tree and back. She'd read online posts from people who'd had similar operations yet resumed normal life within days, while others complained their lives were turned upside-down for months. She couldn't risk pushing things too soon and causing even more disruption for Wes.

Mom greeted them at the door. "How was it?"

"Lovely to be out of the house again." Breathing heavily, Rachel smiled. "But enough for one day."

"Give me Harley's leash. I'll take him into the backyard and throw a ball so he gets some exercise."

While Mom took Harley, Rachel went to the bathroom. It was almost forty-eight hours since her operation – she could finally shower.

She cringed as she removed her bra. Would she find something befitting an award at a cosmetic surgery convention or something straight out of *Frankenstein*?

Using the mirror, she delicately peeled away the corner of the white dressing, then closed her eyes. She didn't want to look.

Screwing up her face, she squinted from one eye.

Groups of Steri-Strips covered the two incisions: one on her breast, and one nearer her armpit. Each incision was about an inch long, though it was hard to tell. Where the dye had been injected, her skin was stained blue, while in other places, it was bruised or red and swollen. It wasn't pretty, but it could've been much worse, and it should only get better.

Using her fingertips, she brushed the skin around the wound on her breast. She was taking painkillers, yet it was still tender. Her arm, however, was both numb *and* crawling with a tingly, burning sensation. So odd. The doctor had warned removing the lymph nodes would disturb the nerves, which could cause issues, but he said it should only be temporary.

She brushed her underarm and winced as an unpleasant prickly feeling erupted. Okay, she'd be checking online if that was normal.

As content as she could be, she turned from the mirror. She smiled at the shower.

The moment she stepped under the jetting water, she moaned as if having a special treatment at a luxurious spa. She closed her eyes and basked in the gentle massage. So fresh, so invigorating, so... clean.

The rest of the day she spent relaxing. The weekend was littered with painkillers and arm exercises, but other than that, she barely left the sofa. She was content to binge on Wes's favorite TV shows, which kept him happy while giving her the rest she needed.

Monday brought a modicum of normality — Izzy was working and Wes was at home, so in between him running his classes, she ran hers. Though she was still getting odd sensations in her arm, the painkillers kept her comfortable.

Wednesday morning, with Wes at his extra school session, she stood at the window overlooking the backyard and phoned the lawyer, Jordan Stein.

She said, "I've got rather an unusual request."

"Okay."

"Is it be possible to make a non–family member my son's guardian, should anything happen to me?"

"The easiest option is to appoint someone his legal guardian in your will. Would we be talking about nothing more than day-to-day care, or managing the child's assets as well, meaning anything bequeathed from your estate?"

"Both."

"And the potential guardian is agreeable to this and in a position to accept such responsibilities?"

"Uh-huh."

"How about the child's father? Is he refusing parental responsibility, or are there circumstances which prevent him from fulfilling such a role?"

"I have full custody, so..." Why would Peter come into the equation?

"That doesn't matter. If he wanted to, he could contest the will and petition the probate court to have your son removed from the guardian's care."

The worst thing imaginable would be a protracted court battle leading to Wes being taken from Izzy and dumped with Peter *and Claire*.

Wincing, Rachel scratched her head. "So how do I get around that? Even if I talked to my ex now, what's to stop him from changing his mind later?"

"You could appoint a real shark of an attorney as executor to the will. Someone who doesn't mind fighting dirty and bending the rules to get what's best for his client. If you know of anyone like that, of course."

Jordan had destroyed Denzel with just a few words, all while surreptitiously reeling her in to be Harley's owner.

"Could you do it?" Rachel crossed her fingers.

"Seriously? That's the opinion you have of me?"

"Oh... sorry. I—"

"Relax, I'm yanking your chain. Of course I can do it. Are we just spitballing here, or are you wanting me to draw something up?"

Rachel smirked. Thank heavens she had a guy like this on her side. "Draw something up, please."

"Can I ask what's spurred this decision? Is it simple prudence, or is there something more nefarious I should be aware of?"

Rachel drew a deep breath. Other than close friends, family, and medical professionals, she hadn't said this to anyone yet.

"I have" — she gulped, the words catching in her throat, emphasizing the frailty of her situation — "cancer. I had a lumpectomy last Wednesday and start chemo in a few weeks."

It was a horrible thing to have to admit to a relative stranger, yet now it was done, it was somehow freeing.

He was quiet for a moment. "I'm sincerely sorry, Rachel. I lost my mom to breast cancer three years ago, so I know what you're going through. I'll send you some thoughts on how I'd structure this kind of document, taking into account Harley and the trust. Assuming Harley isn't too much now, and you still want to keep him?"

"Oh heavens, yes. If anything happens to me, it'll be Harley that keeps my son going."

"Good. All that can be incorporated. Leave it with me and I'll get back to you very soon. So long for now."

"Thanks, Jordan. Bye."

It would be easier than she'd thought. Great. But when she turned, she discovered her mother standing next to the island, frowning at her.

"Sweetheart, they caught it early. And you're having chemo as a safeguard. Nothing's going to happen to you."

"I hope you're right, Mom, but there's no guarantee, is there?"

Mom scuttled over to sit on the sofa. She rested a hand on Rachel's thigh. "Sweetheart, you can't think like that. All the experts say a positive mental attitude can have a vast impact on the prognosis of someone with a serious illness."

"I know. And I have a positive mental attitude. But just because I'm being positive doesn't mean I'll get a positive outcome. I have to hope for the best, while planning for the worst. It's only logical."

"Don't you think it's being defeatist, sweetheart? If you think you might" — she swallowed hard — "if you think you might die, don't you think your subconscious might make your body fight less than it would if you believed with all your being that you were going to be okay?"

"Mom, last month you bought burial insurance. Is that you welcoming your own death or just being practical?"

"That's different."

"No, it isn't. You don't want to die, but you can't guarantee you won't, so you're covering the worst-case scenario. You're hoping for the best, but planning for the worst. It's the same thing."

"But I'm not facing a life-threatening disease."

"Which makes it all the more important I cover all the bases now. And doing this *is* giving me the healthy mental attitude I need to fight, because I'm not stressed about what *might* happen to Wes if I'm not here. It's about balance. If I were focusing only on the worst-case scenario, then fine, I've got a problem, but I'm addressing the best case — getting cured — *and* the worst case. That's about as healthy as you can get."

"Well, I don't like it."

Rachel took her hand. "You don't have to like it, you just have to understand that if I'm going to beat this thing, I have to beat it my way — and *this* is my way."

Mom nodded. "Okay."

Rachel kissed her on the cheek. "Now, what's an invalid got to do around here to get something to eat?"

"Oh, big mistake." Mom stood up, wagging her finger. "Big, big mistake."

"I'm the one who just got out of the hospital and is having to beg for a scrap of food."

Mom smirked. "And I'm the one who's old. Who's going to refuse to go into a home and will linger on and on and on so her loving daughter can satisfy her every whim."

Rachel laughed. "It's a good thing I'm a staunch supporter of euthanasia. Voluntary and involuntary."

"Involuntary? You mean murder?"

"It's only murder if you don't get away with it. And I've got a beast of a lawyer."

"So your father and I will think fondly of you while we lounge on our cloud and you bake in the fires of damnation." Mom winked. "Cheese and tomato okay?" She ambled away.

"Please." Picturing her parents on a cloud reminded her of the conversation about Houdini. "Mom?"

Mom opened the refrigerator. "Hmmm?"

"Do you really believe you'll see Dad again?"

"Of course, dear." She took out the cheese and tomatoes.

"Really?"

Mom turned. "I thought you weren't being defeatist, and now you're talking about joining your father in heaven?"

"No, it's something Izzy said, about how even if the worst happened, I'd still be watching over Wes."

"And?"

"And... I don't know if I believe that."

"Your dad and I loved each other. And I mean loved, not that feeling a lot of people confuse for love even though they think it's fine to hop into bed with whoever they feel like. When you truly love someone, it isn't just physical — it binds you together forever. That's how I know I'll be with him again."

"But you can't *know* it, can you?"

"Of course I can." She held up a jar. "Pickle?"

"No, thanks."

When she'd previously pondered an afterlife, she'd brushed it aside — it was frightened people clinging to a celestial lifeboat.

Science couldn't prove things either way, while people of faith didn't need proof. But she *needed* proof.

If this life was all there was, if the endless struggle and heartache and love and devotion ultimately led nowhere, what was the point of it all?

Why bother struggling to meet that perfect someone, struggling to build the perfect life, or struggling with advancement and setbacks, discipline and commitment, moderation and self-control...? If it was all ultimately inconsequential and this microscopic span of time people called a "lifetime" was all there was, why struggle? Even for a second?

Hedonism made far more sense. People could binge on ice cream or sex or chocolate-flavored cocaine — whatever gave them another moment of bliss — *right now* because that was all that meant anything.

But if there *was* something else...

That brought a whole other set of problems. It wasn't surprising that the promise of eternal life had enabled some cults to coerce their followers into mass suicides — why would people accept life's struggles if the alternative was a nirvana with their loved ones? If evidence of a "heaven" became available, billions suffering in poverty might end it without a second thought.

Yet if there was proof, wouldn't governments cover it up for that very reason? Like with UFOs?

UFOs! Good grief, what was she thinking? UFOs, suicide cults, angels... this was what happened when she wasn't kept busy — her thoughts ran amok. She needed normality back. Too long like this and she'd transform her bedroom into the local UFO investigation society's headquarters!

As Mom brought over her sandwich, Rachel caught something from the corner of her eye. What the devil...?

Chapter 60

Harley crept through the kitchen, hugging the far wall and slinking close to the ground as if stalking prey. He gripped his bed in his mouth, his eyes darting this way and that in the hope of remaining elusive.

With Mom fussing over food and Rachel sprawled on the sofa, this was the ideal opportunity.

He skulked farther.

The chance of being dumped in the dark garage was high. Unbelievably high. But he had to risk it — his alpha needed him. She might not know it, but she did.

As Mom sauntered to the living room with a plate, Rachel stared at him. He froze. Not the garage, please!

She frowned.

He hunched lower, trying to melt into the wall, and closed his eyes. If he couldn't see her, she couldn't see him. It was only logical. The trick didn't always work, because some people obviously had better eyes than others, but it did sometimes.

"Do you want coffee with it?" asked Mom.

He pricked his ears, listening for clues as to if he'd been spotted.

Mom continued, "Or tea and a cookie?"

"Maybe later, thanks."

That was Rachel's kind voice. He peeped. Mom stood next to Rachel, blocking her view of him. Perfect.

He crept on, clutching his bed.

His side scraping the corner of the wall, he turned into the hallway, heading for the staircase. This was going to work.

Behind him, Rachel said, "What's Harley doing?"

At the sound of his name, he froze.

"Harley? I don't know, why?"

Had they spotted him? Cringing, he dared to glance back.

Leaning over the sofa, Rachel stared at him. Mom did too.

Oh boy, was he in for it now. But though this might be interpreted as being bad, he was only trying to do his job. So not the garage. Please, not the garage.

He shut his eyes again. If he couldn't see them, they couldn't see him...

No footsteps stomped closer. No angry voices screamed. Had he evaded capture?

As slowly as he could, he peeked again.

He gasped. They were still looking at him.

Hunching as small as he could, he screwed his eyes shut. If he couldn't see them...

Still no feet pounded into the floor and no hand dragged him by the collar to the dreaded garage. Had he done it?

He shuffled farther. Then a little more. Farther still. He padded up the stairs, moving so slowly it was almost painful, but he couldn't risk his claws scraping on the wooden treads to give him away.

His gaze fixed on his goal — the top step — he skulked on. It was the slowest he'd moved in his entire life. Torture for a dog who loved to run. But it would be worth it when he could do his job.

Finally, he reached with his right forepaw and his nails lightly tapped on the wood floor upstairs. He'd done it.

He slunk into Rachel's bedroom and dropped his bed beside her nightstand. To check his idea was sound, he curled up in it and gazed around. Yes, this was ideal. He could see the doorway to check people coming and going, he was close enough to hear the tiniest sound should Rachel be in distress, and it was the perfect position from which to fetch anything she needed in the night.

Wes had been his priority, but Rachel was suffering, so she needed him more. He'd warned her about that strange thing inside her because it smelled like it belonged in the garbage, and now the smell was gone, which was wonderful. However, he could smell blood and wounds healing, so she'd been badly hurt — maybe in a fight over territory with another alpha. As a good dog, it was his duty to help his alpha. After all, by letting him help Wes, she'd given him a purpose, which he'd thought he'd lost forever.

It was a pity he hadn't thought of moving here earlier, or she might have fully healed already.

Rachel and Mom waltzed into the bedroom and gawked at him.

He wagged his tail. It was done now. And what was done couldn't be undone.

"You said he looks after Wes," said Mom. "It looks like it's your turn."

Rachel smiled. "My own personal nurse."

That was her kind voice. He wagged his tail harder.

"Harley." Rachel patted her thigh.

He stayed where he was, the best place from which to do his duty.

"Harley... here, boy."

Mom said, "Looks like he's there for the day."

"I know what will get him out. Harley, TV remote."

A job! He scampered past them and down the stairs.

By the time Rachel had tottered halfway down the stairs, Harley was trotting back with the remote.

She held up her hand. "Stay, Harley. Stay."

He sat, ready to present the device.

At the bottom of the stairs, Rachel took the remote and ruffled the top of his head. "Good boy."

The rest of the day he spent sitting beside her, alert in case she needed him. Wes came home, so Harley did a few jobs for him, then he watched Wes and Rachel perform their funny arm dance. They'd been working on it for days and were wonderfully synchronized, as if they weren't two separate people but had somehow joined.

Seeing them dancing together made Harley feel gooey inside. When he'd first arrived, Rachel and Wes had been so separate, it was like someone had shoved a cat and a dog into the same pack for a joke. Today, he could sense their bond. While his arrival and their changing could be a coincidence, he liked to think he'd helped bring them closer.

That night, he stayed in Rachel's room. Sleeping intermittently, he spent long periods with his ears pricked, listening for any hint that she needed him. Luckily, she never did.

The next morning, Rachel's dance with Wes was even smoother, but for some odd reason, she was far from cheerful. Mom put a plate of bacon, eggs, and hash browns on the dining table, but when Rachel sat down, she munched only a few mouthfuls and shoved the plate aside.

Mom said, "You've got to keep your strength up, sweetheart." She slid the plate back. "Have a little more."

Rachel's kind voice had vanished. "Mom, not now, please. Okay?" She sipped coffee.

"Sorry. Are you worried about tomorrow?"

"Mom, just leave it, huh?" She lurched away to the sofa.

Leaving her own breakfast, Mom slunk over and took Rachel's hand. "I'm sure the test results will be good news, sweetheart. You'll see."

"And what if they're not? Look at Wes. Look at how far he's come. We've never been so close. Never. If something happens to me, what's it going to do to him?"

"You can't think like that, Rachel. Second-guessing what *might* happen will drive you nuts. You've got to stay positive."

"I know. But a positive attitude won't do squat if that freaking SLNB says the cancer has already spread."

"How about one of those support groups the info pack mentions?"

"Sharing everything with a bunch of strangers?" Rachel looked away. "Yeah, right."

"It works for a lot of people. Where's the harm in trying it?"

Rachel held up her palm. "Mom, thanks, but I'd rather be alone right now."

"I'm only trying to help."

"I know. But just give me some time, okay? Please."

Mom plodded back to the kitchen and collected the plates from the table, stopping only to wipe away a tear.

Harley padded over to Rachel. This was probably a bad idea considering her tone of voice and closed body language, but she was hurting. If he could help, it was worth the risk of being shut in the garage.

His ears down, fearing the worst, he sat in front of her and rested his chin on her knee. He gazed up at her with his big brown eyes. He prayed he'd feel her gentle touch and not her wrath as she hauled him away.

She reached toward him. He cringed. Please let it be the kind voice.

"Hey, boy." She ruffled the fur on his neck.

Harley wagged his tail. Another job successfully completed.

All day, Rachel was irritable, using her kind voice only with him and with Wes when they did their dance.

When bedtime came, Harley lay awake in the darkness, listening to the rain pelting the window. For the umpteenth time, Rachel rolled over and sighed heavily.

How was he to help if she wouldn't tell him what she needed?

He waited in the darkness. Together with Rachel, yet so alone.

Again, Rachel rolled over. This time, instead of sighing, she hit her pillow. Then hit it again and again, hammering her fist into it with dull thuds.

Lying in his bed, Harley whimpered. Rachel was in pain, but he didn't know how to help her. Yet he had to do something. Anything. But what?

Maybe there was one thing. It was risky when someone was hurting so much, and could easily backfire, but even the garage couldn't be bleaker than it was here.

Holding his breath, he peeked over the edge of the bed. Mired in shadows, Rachel's gaze locked with his. Such sad, sad eyes.

Harley's heart hurt as if he were trapped in the garbage truck again with the walls closing in to crush him. Rachel was so strong. But when the strong fell, they always fell with the hardest of crashes. He had to help her.

He nuzzled her hand.

Nothing.

He licked her bare arm.

Still nothing.

There was only one other trick he knew. But it was the riskiest of all.

He lifted a paw onto the bed, half expecting to be scolded and shoved away, but he wasn't. Pushing onto his hind legs, he eased onto the bed and snuggled up against Rachel. Her heart pounded and her breathing came quickly. It was no surprise she couldn't sleep when her body was acting as if they were running.

He nuzzled her, shuffling his shoulders to get closer, pressing his fur against her bare skin, feeling her warm breath on his snout.

The icy sadness in her eyes melted. Her chin trembled, then she lurched forward and clutched him.

"Why, Harley?" She sobbed against his neck. "Why?"

She dug her fingers into his fur, gripping him as though she were frightened of falling into the darkness, never to be seen again.

"Why him?" She buried her face in his fur.

With her breath faltering and her voice breaking, she said, "He's never had any sort of a life. Never. Now he finally has something, but it might all be ripped away? It's not fair, Harley. It's not fair."

She cried. Cried for so long that the smell of the night changed. When she finally stopped, they lay together, breathing together, hearts beating together. After some time, she drifted to sleep. Harley waited to be sure he wouldn't be needed again before closing his eyes.

Another job well done. Fulfilling his purpose wasn't always easy, but it was always rewarding. He snuggled next to his alpha, basking in the warmth of his loving pack. Tomorrow would be a grand day.

Chapter 61

Rachel woke snuggled against Harley, her arm draped over him. She didn't know if he was awake, but she gently kissed him on the head. "Thank you."

His wagging tail beat against the bed.

A support group? Between Izzy, Mom, Wes, and Harley, she already had one. After years of being alone at night, the idea of having someone else in her room, even if it was a dog, had felt uncomfortable, but she hadn't had the strength to argue about that on top of everything else. However, having another soul to share such a dark night with, especially one who demanded nothing yet gave everything, was a gift she hadn't expected.

With the mornings getting brighter, the sun struggled to clamber over the mountain tops as Rachel walked Harley partway along their route. Again, his big brown eyes peered up, as if asking when they were going to start running. He obviously sensed something was wrong but didn't grasp why their hectic runs had turned into lazy shuffles. After all he'd done for Wes, she wished she could reassure him.

She gazed at the road curving into the trees.

Running away seemed a tempting option again. The first week after her operation, she'd been too consumed with managing her pain and regaining movement to worry about the follow-up appointment, especially as it seemed such a long way off. But the past thirty-six hours...

She heaved a breath. This morning could dictate their entire future.

Reaching the oak, she said, "Sorry, boy. Home time."

After a shower, breakfast, and Wes's arm exercises class, Rachel drove Wes to school. In a nearby coffee shop decorated with vibrant greens and yellows, she sat in a booth, staring at the steam swirling up from her latte and twirling a teaspoon around in her fingers. She checked the time on her phone: 8:37 a.m.

Mom had offered to accompany her, as had Izzy, but Rachel wanted to face the day alone. She'd felt guilty declining both offers, especially Mom's because she was flying home the next day, but Rachel had to do things her way to get through this. Without emotional support, she was less likely to get emotional. Period. And if there was bad news, getting emotional instead of dealing with the issue was the last thing she wanted.

She glanced at her phone: 8:42 a.m.

She realized she was bouncing her left leg up and down under the table. No one could see it, but she knew she was doing it, so she stopped. She had to be in control. Total control. She, Wes, and Harley were the family she'd always wanted. Nothing was going to take that away from her.

8:49 a.m.

Only 8:49? Was her phone broken? She swiped an app to make sure it was functioning. It was, yet the time was crawling by.

And her leg was bouncing again. She cursed under her breath and stopped it.

She gazed around the coffee shop but couldn't focus to take anything in. If a gorilla carrying a surfboard had strolled in, she'd have had no idea later.

8:52 a.m.

Her latte no longer steamed.

8:58 a.m.

She had one quick stop to make to drop off the will Jordan had put together concerning guardianship of Wes and Harley, and then...

Rachel left the coffee shop, latte untouched.

9:47 a.m.

Behind his desk, Jacobs rubbed his hands together and glanced away, as if he was stalling. Uh-oh.

Rachel tensed in her chair and clasped her hands in her lap. They'd already discussed how she'd managed since the operation; now they were to talk about moving forward and, importantly, her test results.

With emotionless eyes, he locked her gaze. "Please don't be alarmed when I tell you this, because while it isn't the news we were hoping for, neither is it as worrying as it may sound."

Oh heavens, no. She gulped. She dug her nails into the back of each hand.

He continued. "Firstly, the good news is your pathology report, which includes the findings of the SLNB reveals that the margins — the extra tissue surrounding the mass we removed — are clear, showing absolutely no sign of cancer."

That was great news, yes. But what was the bad news he'd warned was coming?

"Secondly, two of the three lymph nodes we removed were also completely clear."

Two out of three? That meant one wasn't. Oh dear Lord, help her. She held her breath.

"The third node..." He glanced at the report on his monitor.

The third node what? For heaven's sake, he couldn't keep her hanging over something potentially deadly.

"The third node has a number of what we call micrometastases, which are tiny clusters of cancer cells."

She gasped, burying her face in her hands.

"Please, like I said, this isn't as bad as it may sound. If you imagine the width of three human hairs laid side by side, that's the size of the cells we're talking about."

She raised her head, her brow furrowed. The width of three human hairs? That was tiny, yes, but it didn't matter how tiny it was — cancer was cancer.

Her voice faltered. "So if there are more, can you cut them out?"

He shook his head. "They're too small. But that doesn't matter because the adjuvant therapy we're about to discuss should more than deal with this situation. So what I want you to take away is that while the SLNB results aren't one hundred percent clear, neither do they show any spread significant enough to warrant real concern. Okay?"

She heaved out a breath. "Okay."

"Regarding adjuvant therapy, initially, we'll be putting you on an anticancer drug regimen to stop the cancer cells from replicating and to destroy their genetic material. Essentially, this should kill the remaining cancer cells."

She nodded.

"Added to that, I'm recommending Herceptin and Perjeta — the 'targeted therapy' drugs I mentioned previously. We've had great success against cancers like yours with this two-pronged attack."

"So all this will stop the cancer from coming back?"

He winced. "I'm afraid that's impossible to say. However, after six months of chemotherapy, you'll have a course of radiation therapy."

"And that will be it?" She watched for a smile or a nod.

"Your cancer is what we term 'hormone receptor–positive,' which in a nutshell means the cancer cells feed on the estrogen hormone your body produces."

She rolled her eyes. "Go me!"

"Endocrine therapy may help us there, but that's a way off."

She blew out a big breath. "I'd never have thought there'd be so much involved." Surgery, of course. Chemo, maybe? But so many different treatments all combined?

"Ms. Taylor" — he leaned forward, his face even more stern than usual.

Uh-oh. Surely not more bad news.

— "as I said previously, HER2-positive cancers are some of the more aggressive and fast-growing cancers."

She cringed at that phrase again — "aggressive and fast-growing."

"This is why we're combining a drug regimen with radiation therapy, and following that with endocrine therapy. This gives us the best possible chance of defeating your cancer and you living a long and happy life, like countless other patients who have sat in that chair over the years and felt just the way you do now." He smiled. "We're here to fight with you every step of the way."

He'd smiled! For the first time ever. Maybe the situation wasn't so dire after all. And why would it be? Her oncology team was used to fighting this cancer — and beating it — so all the drugs and therapies were not to be anxious about but embraced.

"What side effects should I expect?" Sickness she could tolerate, but losing her hair? She cringed at the thought of looking in the mirror and not recognizing the person gazing back. And if she felt like that, how would Wes feel?

"Physically, side effects can range from diarrhea to heart failure, nausea to joint pain. I say 'can' because people often respond differently to the same combination of drugs. Psychologically? One of the biggest issues is hair loss and how it affects your self-image. For some, it's just a case of their hair thinning; for others, it's so severe they prefer to shave it all off. How you might respond is, I'm afraid, impossible to say."

262

"My son has special needs. It could be a real problem for him if I lost my hair."

"Would it be a bigger problem if he lost you?"

Her jaw dropped.

"You asked me to be brutally blunt." He shrugged. "That said, you could try a shorter hairstyle now, so any loss won't be so dramatic. A headscarf or a wig is another option. Or you might find that you're one of the lucky ones who keeps most of their hair. You'd find out three to six weeks into your treatment."

She rubbed her brow. If her appearance totally changed, Wes could be so freaked out, he could shut her out all over again. Losing her hair could mean losing her son!

Rachel said, "Is there anything I can do to prevent it? My son can't handle change — he needs routine. If my appearance alters drastically, it could seriously hurt our relationship."

"How old is he?"

"Eleven."

"He's on the spectrum?"

"Autism, yes."

He typed on his computer. "There is one option we could look at — scalp cryotherapy. It's not without side effects, so we'd discuss those, but essentially, you'd wear a special cap that cools your head before, during, and after chemotherapy. The cold constricts the blood vessels in your scalp to minimize the damaging effect of the drugs on your hair follicles."

"Oh, fantastic. Thank you."

"You'll have to check whether your insurance will cover it or if you'd have to pay for it yourself, but if you want to go ahead with it, I'll need to know to inform the team because it will impact the duration of your chemotherapy sessions." He wrote something on a Post-it note. "I also suggest minoxidil. It's a foam you massage into your scalp to promote hair growth. It's available over the counter at most pharmacies."

He handed her the paper with the product name in capitals.

"Thanks."

"You're welcome. Is there anything else?"

Many people had a blind, irrational belief that "it wouldn't happen to them" and that everything would be fine if they put their faith in God, or medicine, or their own indestructibility. She didn't have that luxury. She had to fight the battles she could, while planning to lose the war, so that whatever happened, she secured Wes's future. But that didn't mean if she was going down, she was going down quietly.

"How soon can I start chemo?"

***

Wisps of steam from another latte curled up in front of Rachel, but she ignored them, sitting in a booth back at the coffee shop. Jacobs seemed extremely positive, and his treatment regimen, by virtue of how frightening it was in its scope, probably couldn't be better. But...

She raked her fingers through her hair until a strand came away. Looping it back on itself three times, she twisted it around and stared at its tiny, tiny thickness. Something that width could be growing inside her with the potential to kill her. Something so ridiculously tiny. How was that possible?

Jacobs didn't seem concerned, and the chemo was supposed to kill everything, so should she be worried?

She glared at the strand, then let it drop to the floor.

There was nothing to be gained from telling anyone because they'd only worry, and their worry would impact her mental state. And she'd have enough to cope with. Her other lymph nodes had been clear, so it was highly likely the micrometastases were isolated in the one they'd removed. And that was gone. Like a tooth she'd had pulled — she could forget it ever existed.

Still, thank heavens she'd covered all the bases by organizing those guardianship papers with Jordan.

She sipped her coffee. She was doing the right thing, wasn't she?

Mom would be heartbroken if she discovered Rachel had lied. Izzy would be livid. Wes devastated. But how could they ever find out?

Well, there was one way...

Chapter 62

Wednesday

Sitting at his desk, Wes shuffled five cups in front of Harley.

Rachel spoke to Izzy, who sat on a stool behind her, watching over her shoulder as she conducted a class. Because Wes took everything literally, Rachel could give Izzy valuable information by talking openly about him as long as she changed any names.

"The cups game was originally designed to help Tom focus so he'd know it was time to start his lessons. These days, he does that himself by playing the game with Jerry."

Izzy scrawled notes on a pad. Having taken two weeks of vacation for a crash course on everything she might need to know, Izzy was enjoying her first day at "Wes school."

Rachel continued, "That's also let the game evolve. Tom loves trying to fool Jerry, even though he never has, which makes switching the cups around a great hand-eye coordination exercise."

"How many times do Tom and Jerry play?" said Izzy.

"Two or three. Tom is getting noticeably better. When we first started, he'd usually forget which cup he'd put the candy under, but now it's about fifty-fifty, so the game isn't just telling him it's time to focus, it's improving his focus."

"Is it always five cups?"

"It was originally three. We started using five to make it trickier for Jerry, but that obviously made it more of a challenge for Tom too."

Wes pointed at the cups. "Harley, which cup?"

Harley nudged the fourth from the left. Wes laughed.

Rachel said, "Is he right?"

Wes nodded and revealed a green jelly bean.

"See? Tom really mixed up the cups that time but still managed to remember where the candy was."

Izzy nodded. "What happens if you use, say, a red jelly bean and a white one? Their ingredients are different, so they must smell different too. Can Jerry detect that difference to find the white one?"

That was an excellent idea. As Wes's skill improved, he'd probably get bored with the game. Using more candy would make it more interesting.

Rachel said, "Look who's angling to be teacher's pet on her first day."

***

Tuesday

In the kitchen, Izzy leaned on her elbows on the island. Rachel tossed a bag of white long grain rice in front of her.

Rachel said, "What would you do with that?"

"Errr..." She winced. "Boil it?"

Rachel gestured for more information.

Izzy turned the bag over and read aloud, "Bring to a boil two cups of water in a saucepan with a lid. Add one cup of rice and add salt — optional. Reduce heat and simmer for fifteen minutes. Fluff with a fork and serve while hot." She looked up. "Easy. Even I could do that. Or are you going to tell me that's not how you do it?"

"That's not how you do it."

Izzy rolled her eyes, then reached for her pad.

Rachel opened a cupboard and gestured for Izzy to remove what was inside. Izzy lifted out something swathed in a blue blanket, making it about two feet square, and put it on the island.

Rachel said, "I made this before you arrived and it's been cooking ever since."

"Cooking?" Izzy scrunched up her nose. "In a cupboard? Is it a magic cupboard?"

Rachel handed her a fork. "You tell me."

Izzy unfolded the blanket to reveal newspaper wrapped around a brown saucepan with a lid. She lifted the lid. Inside, rice steamed. She squinted at Rachel, then dug her fork in and tasted a few grains.

"Mmm." Izzy nodded. "This is good. But how the devil...?" She pointed at the cupboard.

"Once it's boiling, don't waste time simmering it — take it off the stove, and wrap it in newspaper and a blanket. The residual heat will cook it, and it'll stay hot for hours."

266

"Can't I just microwave it?"

"If you want boring, bland rice, yes. But that's been toasted in coconut oil first. That's how you get that amazing taste."

Izzy held her arms wide. "And I'm supposed to do that how?"

Rachel pointed to the stove. "Bring your pad."

Slumping over the island, Izzy said, "But why? Why part-cook it and stick it in a cupboard for hours instead of cooking it when you want it and eating it right away?"

"Doing things like this lets me prepare food while Wes has his afternoon nap."

"And I guess it saves gas, so it's green."

Rachel nodded. "It won't save a lot, but yeah, it'll save some."

"Can you still do the ice cube thing when it's cooked this way?"

Rachel shrugged. "Ice cube thing?"

"If you want to reheat yesterday's rice, you put an ice cube on it and blast it in the microwave."

Rachel arched an eyebrow. "An ice cube?"

Izzy put her hands on her hips. "Oh, so you can cook with a cupboard, but I can't reheat with ice?"

Rachel would try that later. Izzy was proving to be not just a good student but a good teacher, with a unique take on things that built on what Rachel already had. What was Izzy going to think of next?

***

Friday

Light filtered through the trees to dapple her trailhead parking area with sunshine as Rachel did another deep lunge with her left leg in front. Nearly four weeks since her operation, she was far from her old fitness level, but was now at least allowed to jog and do light aerobics.

Mentally, it was a huge leap forward. Not only was she getting back into her old routine, she was getting back in control of her life.

Harley barked, such a joyous bark. He was obviously delighted to be running again, possibly even more so than Rachel.

A heavy wheezing came from behind her. Izzy's sweaty red face appeared over the crest of the incline, the rest of her slowly lurching into view. The moment she was on level ground, she crumpled forward with her hands on her knees, gasping for breath like a three-pack-a-day smoker with only one lung.

Izzy didn't have a smart watch, so Rachel was using her phone's stopwatch to time Izzy's runs. She paused the timer and set the phone on the ground, ready to restart it for the return leg.

Izzy pointed backward and tried to speak, the sound coming more as hoarse gasps than words. "You do" — *wheeze* — "do this" — *wheeze* — "every" — *wheeze* — "day?"

"I sometimes take Sundays off."

Izzy shook her head, clutching her chest. "I can't... I can't..."

They could only run together the two days per week Wes was in school. How running would work if it was only Izzy and Wes would have to be addressed later, but for now, the biggest problem was Izzy's fitness.

"It's like everything, Iz, it takes practice. Believe me, once you start feeling the benefits, you'll love it."

"Benefits? You mean" — *gasp* — "a daily" — *gasp* — "coronary?"

"I mean the increased energy you'll have, all day, every day."

Head down, Izzy reached toward Rachel without looking.

"What do you want?" asked Rachel.

"Phone."

"I'll tell you your time, just a sec." Rachel reached for her phone. It was encouraging that Izzy wanted to know how she'd done. Seeing her times improve over the coming weeks would be a real confidence booster.

"Not time" — gasp — "Uber."

Rachel laughed. "You are not getting an Uber."

"Either Uber" — *gasp* — "or ambulance."

***

Tuesday

At their lessons desk, Izzy handed Wes the new die, which had a different color on each face but no words or numbers. After two weeks of intensive training, Izzy was proving to be not just an exceptional teacher but wonderfully innovative, using an outsider's viewpoint to study Rachel's techniques and expand upon them.

Wearing a white T-shirt, Wes rolled the die. It landed on purple. Without being told, he pulled a purple sweatshirt from a stack of different-colored ones on a nearby stool and put it on. Meanwhile, Izzy covered the purple side of the die with a removable white sticker reading "Roll again" so that color couldn't be landed on next time.

Rachel looked on from her desk — far enough away to give them space to work alone, but close enough should they need her.

Izzy slid the color-coordinated chart to Wes. "And purple means...?"

He checked the subject represented by purple. "Geography."

"Well done, Wes. So, this morning we're studying geography."

With Wes flourishing, Izzy had suggested the more autonomy he had, the better his self-image would become. And the better his self-image, the more interaction he'd want and the more responsibility he'd handle. It was a positive feedback loop.

One easy way to introduce this was not to force Wes to study a particular subject but to let him choose one through a roll of Izzy's new die, giving him a sense that he was master of his own destiny. So far, he was relishing his new freedom.

Spinning the Wheel of Questions, he landed on "Describe" printed in green. Without being instructed, he rolled the green die, scoring "5 & 2."

Izzy said, "Wes, I'm going to name five countries, and for each one, you have to tell me two things, without duplicating anything. Okay?"

He nodded.

"United States of America."

"It has a flag with stars and stripes, and people speak English."

"Very good. Canada."

"It has maple syrup and polar bears."

"Excellent work, Wes. Australia."

"It has kangaroos and..." He stared into space. "And people speak Australian."

Izzy said, "Now, do they speak Australian or do they really speak English, which we've already had?"

Frowning, he said, "It has kangaroos and..." He scratched his head. "Oh, it has kangaroos and reefs. No, reeves. No..." He scratched his head again. "It has kangaroos and ree... ree..." He blew out a heavy breath.

"Reefs, Wes. When there's more than one reef, it's reefs."

He glanced sideways toward her. "So why's it leaf and leaves?"

"Er... that's an excellent question." Her eyebrows raised, Izzy looked to Rachel.

Rachel said, "In English, Wes, we have lots of rules about how words work, but every so often, there's a tricky one that likes to break those rules. Some words that end in f are tricky. For example, *hoof* becomes *hooves* when there's more than one, ending in *v-e-s*, while other words change to end with *f-s*, like *cliff* and *cliffs*. It's very confusing, isn't it?"

Wes nodded.

Izzy tipped her head in thanks to Rachel. "Okay, Wes, a quick side lesson. See if you can figure out which ending these words have. *Wolf* — is it *wolfs* or *wolves?*"

"Wolves."

"Well done, Wes. Next one is *shelf* — is it *shelfs* or *shelves?*"

"Shelves."

"Excellent, Wes." She smiled. "You're really good at these, aren't you?"

Even with his head down, he couldn't hide his smile.

Rachel smiled too. If anything did happen to her, Wes was going to be in the safest hands she'd ever find and have the life she'd always wanted for him. And the coming week would prove crucial in deciding if she accompanied him on that wondrous life journey or not.

Chapter 63

A deathly quiet enveloped the chemotherapy room. Rachel had hoped there wouldn't be interminable piped music, but she hadn't expected silence. She sat in a cream faux leather recliner against a cream wall; each of the room's eight treatment areas were differentiated from the next by a section of the wall being blue floor-to-ceiling.

A rosy-cheeked nurse named Chrissie swept up sections of Rachel's hair and sprayed water down to the roots from a handheld bottle.

A man with a bald head — maybe natural or maybe the obvious — sat with a book on the far right, and a wrinkly woman in the next seat was sewing, maybe starting a quilt. Two seats away on her left, a woman about Rachel's age stared at a tablet, her head covered with a bright orange-and-blue scarf, her cheeks sunken, and her skin a healthy shade of gray. That woman's story was one Rachel was certainly not going to listen to. Even if she had to be rude about it. She might miss the most inspirational story of courage ever to grace mankind, but who cared? This was her illness; she was dealing with it her way — alone. Just another trip to the dentist.

Chrissie parted Rachel's hair down the middle, then held up a white cloth, which kind of looked like a large T about two feet wide, with smaller rounded projections sticking out — like someone had steamrolled a giant deformed mushroom. "This is your cooling wrap. Can you hold these two ends behind your head, please?"

Rachel took an end in each hand and did as requested. From either side, Chrissie draped the horizontal length around Rachel's head and folded the longer part that had been the vertical spine of the T over, so all three ends met on her forehead. She velcroed them in place and pressed down each of the smaller parts, velcroing those over Rachel's head too.

While Rachel held the wrap in place, Chrissie eased a blue neoprene thermal cap over it to press the wrap to Rachel's scalp. Finally, Chrissie fastened a chin strap to stop anything moving.

"How's that feel? Snug?"

"Uh-huh."

"Not too tight?"

"No."

A black hose dangled out of the back of the wrap and disappeared into a wheeled gray machine about three feet tall and eighteen inches square. Chrissie touched the LCD housed in a blue section on the top.

Chrissie said, "It will start to feel cold pretty fast as the coolant is pumped through, so if there's any discomfort, let me know. I can either give you painkillers or, if it hurts too much, we can abort the treatment."

A little brain freeze was a small price to pay for keeping her hair. "I'll be fine, thanks."

"Okay, if you need to detach yourself, like for a bathroom break, just..." She unclipped a section of the hose, freeing Rachel, then clipped it back. "Easy, yes?"

"Uh-huh."

"Finally, I need you to take these, please." Chrissie handed her a plastic cup of water and a paper medicine cup containing small white pills and bigger yellow ones.

"Is this the steroid?" One of the doctors had mentioned medication to prevent a reaction to one of the chemo drugs.

"Yes. Antinausea and anti-inflammatory, too."

Rachel took them one at a time with a sip of water.

Chrissie said, "Excellent, so I'll see you in around thirty minutes to start your chemo."

"Thank you."

Rachel put in her earbuds and clicked play on her phone. She tapped her foot to Katy Perry singing "Firework."

Soon after, she felt a brain freeze like she'd downed a gallon of chocolate chip ice cream. She gritted her teeth. So much medication would be pumped into her today it was horrifying; if she could avoid taking even more, she'd brave this out.

Luckily, the pain subsided after a few minutes. That was a relief. Her insurance hadn't covered the scalp cryotherapy, so she'd sprung for the treatment out of her own pocket, thanks to Harley's contribution to her monthly income. Wes would be suffering enough disruption without the trauma of his mother radically changing. Although, there was no guarantee she'd keep her hair even using this contraption.

Her eyes closed, nodding her head in time to "Empire State of Mind" by Alicia Keys, Rachel felt a tap on her shoulder. She stopped her music as Chrissie smiled at her, another nurse beside her. "Sorry."

"No worries. You're doing the right thing — the day will go much smoother if you stay occupied." Chrissie held out a transparent bag of clear fluid. "It's time to do a two-nurse check of your chemo."

"Okay."

The two nurses completed the check of her chemo, then Chrissie showed her the bag. "I need you to verify this is your full name and date of birth, so we've confirmed this is your treatment."

The details on the label were correct. Chemotherapy drugs were precisely created for each particular patient, so the wrong drugs going to the wrong person could have dire consequences. Not surprising when some were based on poisons such as mustard gas, which had killed tens of thousands in World War I.

"Is that all of it?" asked Rachel.

"No," said Chrissie. "To start with, you get each drug separately, so we can make sure you're not having any sort of reaction. This is the Perjeta. The infusion time is around sixty minutes. You'll then have a thirty-minute break so we can ensure it's safe to proceed. If it is, we'll move on to the Herceptin, which will take about ninety minutes. Then another break, and so on. But don't worry, that's only today. Once we know you aren't likely to have a reaction, we can speed things up in future sessions."

With the number of different drugs lined up for her, receiving them one at a time would consume more or less the entire day.

"And it won't hurt?" said Rachel. The nurses had explained the process, but now it was happening, she couldn't help worrying.

Chrissie hooked the bag to an IV stand.

"You shouldn't feel a thing. If you have any side effects, they probably won't manifest until this evening or tomorrow." She fitted a tube to the cannula they'd stuck into the back of Rachel's hand earlier.

"Any problems — anything — tell me or one of my colleagues immediately. Okay?"

"Okay. Thanks."

Chrissie smiled and toddled away.

And with that, chemo started to *drip-drip-drip* into Rachel's vein. She stared at the tube leading from the bag, then at the cannula. Stared at the poison being fed into her body. Chrissie was right — Rachel felt nothing. Which seemed so wrong. Either these drugs would kill whatever microscopic cancer remained inside her or the cancer would grow and kill her. It was, literally, a life-or-death situation. And yet, the moment felt as inconsequential as when she added milk to her coffee. Such a moment should feel... bigger.

Over the next few hours, lounging in the recliner, Rachel listened to music, set aside *The Grapes of Wrath* and its story of broken dreams in favor of a lighter read about a zombie apocalypse, and laughed at a bunch of cat videos on YouTube. In between, she munched the tuna sandwiches she'd packed and drank the water into which she'd squeezed fresh lemon.

And all the while, poison *drip-drip-dripped* into her.

Finally, the last bag dripped its last droplet.

Chrissie removed the IV and cannula. "Just another hour or so with your cooling cap and you'll be good to go."

Rachel nodded but sighed, the day dragging like no day she'd ever known. Unable to face another cute kitty or another victim being devoured by the living dead, she gazed around. Trapped for another hour. A prisoner to this medication. Oh, the cell was luxurious and the guards amenable, but this was no less a prison because there was absolutely no escape. Not if she wanted to live.

Nope. Not even Houdini could break out of this one!

Houdini?

The conversation with Izzy resurfaced. She'd always intended to investigate Izzy's tall tale but never had time for idle web browsing. Well, she wasn't exactly rushed off her feet now.

She fired up her tablet. The first few sites in the search results told her all she needed. After Houdini's death in 1926, his wife, Bess, had indeed offered a $10,000 reward — the equivalent of $150,000 today — to anyone who could communicate with him and give her the secret coded message. Like $150,000 wouldn't have sleazeballs crawling out of the woodwork.

Bess spent years trying to contact her husband. Then came January 6, 1929...

Pastor Arthur Ford contacted Houdini and delivered the secret message: "Rosabelle, answer, tell, pray-answer, look, tell, answer-answer, tell." When decoded, it read: "Rosabelle, believe."

Wow! So who wouldn't believe?

Except the "secret" code was one Houdini had used during his mind-reading act and had been published in a book a year earlier, so was hardly secret, being available to anyone who could read.

"Oh, Izzy, when you gonna learn, girl?"

Rachel shook her head, happy she'd debunked the afterlife but disappointed it was so easy.

She clicked a video on the website. A grainy black-and-white film showed Houdini being shackled outdoors while thousands of New Yorkers watched.

As if by magic, Izzy called.

"Hey," said Izzy. "Shall I get a taxi in to drive you home?"

"Thanks, but I'll manage."

"You're feeling okay?"

"Exhausted. It's been such a long day."

"I can believe it. Have you long to go?"

"No, it's nearly done." A man locked Houdini inside a wooden packing crate. "Funnily enough, I'm killing time by reading about Houdini."

"Yeah? Man, fascinating, isn't it? Really makes you wonder."

"About...?"

"About the possi... Oh, please don't tell me you read the first thing to pop up in Google and quit."

"There didn't seem much point in reading any more."

"Rach!"

"What?" A crane lowered Houdini, imprisoned in the crate, into the East River. He sank. "The pastor got the code from a book and scammed poor Bess out of ten grand. What more is there?"

"The code wasn't in the book."

"So how did the pastor get it?"

"Well, duh. He didn't get the reward either because Bess had withdrawn it."

So no one knew the code or the secret phrase. And there was no reward. Yet the correct message had been delivered.

Rachel frowned. "So Ford somehow gave her the right message but didn't get one red cent for doing it?"

"Exactly."

It had seemed cut and dried, but there were more smoke and mirrors around this than Houdini's stage show.

Rachel said, "What kind of scam is that?"

"You tell me. Then it gets even weirder — a few years later, Bess publicly denounced Ford, claiming it was all a hoax, yet in private letters, she suggested something very different."

Houdini broke the surface and swam for shore.

Rachel scratched her head. "So was it real or not?"

Chrissie said, "I bet you're dying to escape, aren't you?"

Rachel glanced around, eyebrows raised. "Hmmm?"

"Time's up." Chrissie smiled.

"Sorry, Iz, I've got to go. See you soon." She hung up.

"How you feeling?" asked Chrissie.

"Shattered." Rachel stretched. "Even though I've done nothing, it feels like the longest day ever."

"That's perfectly normal, so go home and put your feet up." Chrissie removed the two caps, taking care not to disassemble any part of the velcroed wrap. "Don't do too much until you see how you're handling the chemo. Remember, listen to your body and do what it tells you."

She handed Rachel the neoprene cap and wrap. "These are yours for your coming sessions."

"Thank you. And thanks for all your help today."

Chrissie smiled. "You're welcome."

By the time Rachel pulled into her drive, evening gloom was enveloping the house. A yellowy light flooded out from the living room windows to beckon her in.

When she tramped through the front door, Wes glanced from the sofa and Harley wiggled his way over, tail wagging frantically.

"Hey, boy." She crouched, ruffling his fur.

Dropping a wooden spoon into a pan in the kitchen, Izzy darted over. Rachel groaned as she stood up.

Izzy hugged her. "How was it? As bad as you imagined?"

"No. Just long. Unbelievably long." They separated.

"You should've let me come for company."

"No, I want to do this my way. Besides, who'd look after Wes?"

"Well, you're home now." Izzy headed back for the kitchen. "I hope you're hungry. It's chili."

"*My* chili, or *your* chili?"

"*Your* chili."

"In that case, I'm starving." Rachel melted into the sofa. "You better put mine on a tray, Iz, because I'm not getting up anytime soon."

"No problem."

"School okay, Wes?"

He nodded, then toddled away, returning with his resources for the arm exercise class. Rachel had a full range of motion now but had continued the classes because she enjoyed the interaction. But tonight?

She waved a hand at him. "Thanks, Wes, but not tonight, please, kiddo. Remember we talked about how I might need a few days' rest?"

He nodded and returned to the sofa.

They ate in the living room on trays. Rachel wolfed down the first half, but lifting her fork became such an effort that the second half was cold by the time she finished it. After chewing the last mouthful, she closed her eyes to rest for a moment.

At 9:45 p.m. Rachel woke. She winced and clutched the left side of her head, a throbbing pain stabbing all the way from her eyebrow over to the base of her skull. As if that wasn't bad enough, she felt queasy, like she'd spent hours hurtling around on an out-of-control roller coaster.

Wes had disappeared, and Izzy now sat in his place. "You okay?"

"I've got a blinding headache, so I'm hitting the sack." Gritting her teeth, she heaved off the sofa. She swayed but caught herself.

"Do you need me to steady you?"

Rachel shot her a sideways glance. "Yeah, in about fifty years." She shook her head, trudging to the stairs. "The day I can't make it around my own house is the day I want someone to put me in the ground."

Tomorrow would be a better day. The first day was bound to be rough, but as young and fit as she was, she'd be back to normal come morning. She'd bet on it.

***

Rachel's alarm blared: 5:45 a.m. She slapped her nightstand until she hit the device and shut it off.

She winced, her headache pounding away as if it had never gone.

A whimper dragged her attention to the side of her bed. Resting his chin on the comforter, Harley looked as concerned as a dog ever could.

She rubbed his shoulders. "Sorry, boy, no run today. Maybe tomorrow."

Swallowing hard, she rested a hand on her stomach, queasiness still churning inside her.

She'd figured a good night's sleep was all she'd need to recover, but obviously the supplementary meds she'd brought from the hospital were going to be far from optional.

Grimacing, she heaved around to sit on the side of the bed. If she'd known she was going to feel so rough, she wouldn't have left the meds downstairs.

The hallway light clicked on. Had her alarm woken Izzy in the next room?

Izzy appeared in the doorway in her pajamas. "Tell me you're not thinking of going running."

Rachel sniggered. "Yeah, right. The way I feel, I wouldn't make it to the end of the yard."

"So why are you up?"

Rachel shrugged. "I forgot to turn off my alarm."

"I heard, but that doesn't mean you have to get up."

"I need my meds." She rubbed her stomach.

"Get back into bed. There's no point in me sleeping here if you're going to try and carry on as normal." Izzy headed downstairs.

Rachel snuggled up in bed. Izzy returned with the medication and a glass of water.

Rachel took the pills, but after swallowing, smacked her lips, staring at the glass. "Where's this from?"

"The tap. Where else?"

"Really?" She sniffed it, then again smacked her lips. "It tastes metallic."

Izzy shrugged. "I just poured it. Do you want OJ instead?"

Rachel shook her head. "Thanks, but I feel like I could hurl, so I'm going to rest until the meds kick in." She shuffled back down into bed.

"Anything else before I go?"

"You could take Harley for a pee, but use the word *leak* as well, as in 'Harley, do you want a...?'"

"Okay." Izzy patted her thigh. "Harley."

Still with his head resting on the bed, he looked from Rachel to Izzy, then back to Rachel.

Rachel scratched behind his ear. "Go on, Harley. I'll be here when you get back."

"Harley." Izzy sauntered for the door. "Here, boy."

He trotted after her. Rachel closed her eyes. Now she'd had her meds, another few hours' sleep would see her raring to go again. It was handy having Izzy in the guest bedroom, but it was overkill, especially as she'd had to swap her hours about to get a long weekend off. Still, now that Rachel knew what to expect from the chemo sessions, and how important the supplementary meds were, they could organize a routine as close to normal life as possible.

Because of the discomfort, Rachel only dozed intermittently, so when she struggled up at 10:30 a.m., she felt no better. After using the bathroom, she pulled on a sweater and sweatpants and split her meds in half to have some upstairs and some downstairs. Finally, she doddered down the stairs like an octogenarian with a bad hip.

Izzy was sitting in her swivel chair reading a magazine. She twisted around. "How you feeling?"

Slouching over, Rachel curled her lip.

"That good, huh?" Izzy moved from Rachel's seat. "Ready for something to eat?"

Rachel shook her head. "Where's Wes?"

Izzy pointed to the backyard. "I'm keeping an eye on them."

Rachel plonked down. Wes was in the backyard with Harley, but she barely had the strength to look.

Izzy said, "Still got a headache?"

"Like you wouldn't believe."

"Give me a sec." After fishing in the refrigerator, Izzy wrapped a towel around something flat, floppy, and the size of a small tablet. "I found this at home."

Taking it, Rachel grinned and placed it on her head, closing her eyes and moaning with delight as coldness cocooned her skull.

"Good?" asked Izzy.

Rachel said, "Like you wouldn't believe."

"How about a sandwich or some soup? Something light?"

"Thanks, but my stomach's too iffy."

"Okay. Just let me know when you're ready for something." A chair scraped on the floor as Izzy pulled it out to sit at the dining table.

Rachel said, "I never thought it would wipe me out like this. I mean, they warned me it might, but I just didn't think it would."

"Yeah, it's rough."

"I figured being young and fit, I'd shrug it off, you know. Be back to normal the next day, no matter what they pumped into me."

"Lucinda had chemo three years ago and had good weeks and bad weeks. She said the secret was listening to what her body told her, especially about resting, because when she pushed herself to do things, she usually suffered twice as much."

"That's what the nurse said." Rachel removed the cold pack and looked at Izzy. "But I haven't done anything to have done too much of it."

Izzy shrugged. "So the human body doesn't like chemo. What else is new?"

Rachel replaced the cold pack. If she could get rid of the fatigue, *or* the headache, *or* the queasiness, she could probably function at a basic level. But with all three? It was like having the worst hangover in history — totally debilitating.

After the cold pack soothed her for a few minutes, Rachel peered out of the window. Wes threw a stick underhand, just as she'd taught him, and Harley tore after it, then returned to drop it at Wes's feet. Wes picked it up and teased Harley with it, holding it in the air. Harley jumped, but Wes whipped it away.

Grinning, Wes twirled around, holding the stick high while Harley jumped and jumped, snapping at it. Eventually, to put Harley out of his misery, Wes hurled the stick again. Harley tore after it faster than ever.

To anyone passing by, it would be an ordinary scene of an ordinary kid playing with his ordinary dog. She smiled. *Her ordinary kid.* Harley was giving Wes such a life. Such a wonderful life.

She basked in the ordinary life outside.

When they were due, she took more meds, hoping they'd build up in her body to counteract the side effects. They didn't. She spent the day lounging on the sofa with the cold pack, occasionally nibbling toast in the hope it would line her stomach. It didn't.

The next day started as the previous one had ended — fatigue, headache, and nausea. The day after was the same, revealing a frightening trend. This couldn't be her life now — six months of feeling like death. Desperate, Rachel phoned the hospital. Her oncologist assured her it was nothing unusual and prescribed alternative medications to combat all three issues, which Izzy fetched from the pharmacy.

After staying up late enough to squeeze in two doses of the new medicines, Rachel trudged to bed, praying things would be different come morning. They had to be.

Chapter 64

Harley padded upstairs after Rachel. Something was wrong with his alpha. Very wrong. For a person, she moved gracefully and quickly. Usually. Now? She was moving the way Barney had in those last months. That wasn't good. But that wasn't the worst part... That stench!

Harley had never smelled anything like it. While the scent itself was different, the structure was similar to the smell from Barney's backyard when he'd spray chemicals onto plants, which later turned brown and shriveled.

Barney had moved like Rachel and he'd stopped.

The plants had smelled like Rachel and they'd stopped.

Was he losing another alpha?

Harley whimpered. He hadn't been able to save Barney from stopping, but he was going to save Rachel.

While she was in the bathroom, he trotted to his blue bed on the floor beside hers.

A few minutes later, Rachel tramped to her bed, pulled the comforter back, and slumped in.

Harley whimpered, resting his head on the edge of the bed. Gazing at her with his big brown eyes, he willed her not to stop. He'd do everything *he* could, but as he'd seen with Barney, that wasn't enough — Rachel would have to fight like crazy, too.

Her hand wavering, she patted him. "Good boy, Harley."

Soon after, her breathing changed, suggesting she was asleep.

Good. Whenever he felt unwell, a long rest worked wonders, so maybe that was all she needed. However, to be safe, he'd have everything ready for when she woke in the morning, and in the meantime, he'd stand watch in case there was an emergency and she needed him.

In the early hours, Harley woke, half in, half out of his bed. His eyes flickering open, he realized where he was and jerked upright. He was supposed to be watching over Rachel, yet instead, he'd gone to sleep? Stupid. Stupid. Stupid dog!

Peeking over the edge of the bed, he gazed through the gloom. Rachel had barely moved, but her breathing was steady and strong. That was good.

Though he fought to stay awake, his eyes closed and blackness once more cocooned him.

The next time he woke, the room was still swathed in darkness. He sniffed the air: almost time for their run. Fresh air and running always made him feel wonderful, but maybe that wasn't a good idea today, considering how Rachel had struggled to move the previous evening. A pity.

When they ran together, they moved like one animal: in sync outwardly, in tune inwardly. He'd never known anything like it. He ached to feel that again.

After stretching, he crept across the bedroom and down to the kitchen. His plan was simple yet infallible.

Of all the jobs he'd been asked to do since he'd arrived, finding the TV remote had been the most requested. For his first job, he took it upstairs and laid it on the floor beside Rachel's bed.

Next he fetched Rachel's phone. She handled that a lot, too, so it was obviously important. That went on the floor next to the TV remote.

Over the next thirty minutes or so, he padded back and forth, scouring the house for whatever resources Rachel might need to get better.

Finally, he sat back on his haunches and studied his pile of treasures: TV remote, phone, tablet, can of beer, can of soda, bottled water, pack of cookies, sliced ham that had made his mouth water while carrying it, block of cheese that made his butt quake just smelling it, paperback book, slippers, green die, five cups, and a bag of jelly beans. Every treasure he could think of.

Yes, that was a good job well done. The pile covered just about everything, so if this didn't make Rachel better, nothing would.

He sniffed the air again — not long now till Rachel's usual waking time. He lay down beside his treasures and waited. And waited. And waited.

But Rachel didn't wake. Odd. And the device on the nightstand that made the horrible blaring noise didn't make the horrible blaring noise. That was odd, too.

Sitting up as feeble sunlight struggled through the drapes, he rested his chin on the bed and stared at Rachel's face. Rachel looked so peaceful in the half-light. Like a puppy nestling against its mother's chest. Safe. Content. Happy.

He sighed, aching to prod her cheek with his nose, see her eyes flicker open, see her smile just for him, and then hear her whisper that one magical sound — "Harley." He'd loved hearing Barney saying his name, but because of the special closeness he shared with Rachel, the way she said it was like someone stroking him on the inside.

Movement in the next room suggested Izzy was up — it was nice she'd moved in with the rest of the pack. Her bedroom door opened and she shuffled along the hall. Wes's bedroom door opened, Izzy entered, and she and Wes mumbled together.

A few moments later, Izzy appeared in Rachel's doorway. She whispered, "Pee, Harley, pee."

Pee? If he wasn't standing guard over Rachel, a pee would have been an excellent idea.

But how did people always know when he wanted to take a pee? It was one of the great unsolved mysteries of all time. He was as close to Wes and Rachel as any dog could be to a person, but he had no idea when they wanted to pee, so how could they tell when he did? And now Izzy could tell as well? Their stubby excuses for noses couldn't possibly smell the pee pooled inside him, so what was it?

Did the pee squeak inside him like a tiny mouse? Surely not. His hearing was excellent, and he'd never heard pee squeak.

So did it move and they felt it when they stroked him? Surely not. He licked his bits ten or twelve times per day; if something was moving down there, he'd have spotted it.

Well, they couldn't possibly see inside him... or could they?

They often looked at their phones as if they contained something vital, yet he never saw anything but squiggles or colored shapes. Likewise, they sat glued to the large rectangle in the living room, but that was just bigger squiggles and bigger colored shapes. That could mean only one thing — they could see things he couldn't. It sounded preposterous, yet it was the only logical explanation. They could see inside him, see the pee pooling.

"Harley, do you want to take a leak?" Izzy beckoned him.

He'd pee later. Now, the most important thing was watching over Rachel.

Instead of leaving him to do his job, Izzy tiptoed over, brow wrinkled.

Whispering, she pointed at his pile of treasures. "Harley, what have you got?"

Why was she interested in his pile? This was nothing to do with her. He stood guard over it.

She peered around him. "Is that the TV remote? Harley, you can't have that up here."

Closing in, she reached for his pile.

No! She couldn't take his treasures! He needed them to make Rachel better. But what was he supposed to do? How could he stop her?

He shuffled around to block her access to the pile. She sidestepped, so he did too.

She snickered. "Harley, be good. Wes will need the TV remote."

Shoving him aside, she grabbed the remote.

He gasped. Short of biting her, there was little he could do. But he had to do something because he had to save Rachel.

Harley did the only thing he could do — he barked.

"Shhh!" Izzy leaned down to him.

Groggy, Rachel said, "What's going on?"

"I'm sorry, Rach. Harley's acting up, and I was trying to get him to behave."

Rachel cupped the side of her head, wincing. "What's he doing?"

Izzy sat on the bed. "He's brought a load of junk up here — heaven only knows why — and now he's guarding it like it's some sort of treasure he doesn't want me to take."

Without looking, Rachel reached toward him. He nuzzled her hand and her fingers reassuringly dug into his fur.

"Be good for Izzy, Harley."

Rachel grimaced and clutched her stomach.

Izzy grimaced too. "Oh, babe, is it no better?"

"I think it's worse." She twisted to her nightstand.

"What do you need?"

"My water. My mouth's horribly dry."

Izzy took the glass. "It's empty. Give me a sec and I'll—oh..."

"What?"

Izzy crouched and poked Harley's pile. "You're not going to believe this, but Harley's brought you quite a selection."

"Is there water?"

"Yep" — Izzy picked up the plastic bottle — "and a can of beer and a can of soda."

"What kind of soda?"

"Er" — Izzy snatched the can — "ginger ale."

"Oh, that sounds so good right now."

Izzy opened the can with a *pshhh*, then poured some into the glass.

Harley's eyes popped wider. That was for Rachel, not Izzy! Izzy had already commandeered the TV remote and now she was taking a can too! How could he heal Rachel if people stole all his treasures?

But Izzy handed the glass to Rachel and she drank.

Harley sighed. Thank heavens for that. Now maybe they could get back to normal around here.

"Ahhh." Rachel took another swig. "I don't care if it makes me hurl, it's so good to have something with some flavor for a change."

"If you're in kill-or-cure mode, how about a proper breakfast today, instead of toast or crackers?"

"If I can keep this down for the next half hour, you're on."

"It's going to take me that long to take care of Harley and sort Wes out, so we'll see how you feel then, okay?"

Rachel nodded, sipping ginger ale.

"You'll be okay with Wes if I take Harley out for fifteen minutes?"

"Uh-huh."

"You're sure?"

"Iz, I'm not dying. I just feel like garbage."

"Okay then." She headed for the door, patting her thigh. "Harley, pee, pee, pee. Leak, leak, leak."

If Izzy was going to make those sounds so much, no way could he resist his need. He looked at Rachel. She wasn't her usual self yet, but she was using the treasures he'd brought to heal her. He wagged his tail — his plan was working.

At the back of the house, he took care of business in his usual spot, then walked with Izzy on the grass beside the road.

286

Checking for fresh scents since his last outing, he sniffed the air. The coldness bit his nose, like he was shoving his snout into a puddle through a thin covering of ice. Glorious. There was nothing like the biting freshness of the early morning to make him feel alive.

The old oak came into view — the sign at which point their warm-up walk turned into a full-fledged run. Oh boy, oh boy, oh boy... was Izzy going to run with him? She couldn't run wild and free like Rachel — Izzy favored more of a plod and gasp style — but a run was a run.

He didn't pull on the leash because he was far too polite for that, but he took up the slack, ready to break into a trot the moment he was given the word.

But at the oak, Izzy turned back. Harley slumped, dragging his feet. No run again. If he didn't run soon, he'd be the one needing special care. However, thanks to his help, Rachel was already getting better, so maybe tomorrow they'd be running once more.

With future runs so close, Harley renewed his sniffing, scouring the air for interesting aromas. Even though this was a leisurely stroll, barely more "wild and free" than lying on the sofa, it still felt good to be out among the trees.

A brown bird flew overhead, chirping. Away in the trees, another chirped in reply. Under his paws, the ground was no longer solid with the cold but had a slight bounce. And amid the trunks and shadows, the smell of new life was breaking through the earth as plants woke from their winter slumber.

He bounced along the grass shoulder, savoring the sights, scents, and sounds.

Using treasures to heal Rachel was working nicely, so his next job was to formulate the second stage of his plan. He stopped. Or had he done that already?

"Come on, Harley." Izzy tugged on the leash. "We can't leave Wes and Rachel too long."

He set off again. Maybe he already had his plan — if such a short walk was such a joy for him, surely it would be a joy for Rachel. The next stage was obvious. But how could he put it into action? Maybe...

Chapter 65

Opening the front door, Izzy led Harley in. A scent hit him immediately. A scent that was the best news he could get. An exciting human scent. He wagged his tail.

As Izzy unclipped his leash, banging came from the kitchen. "Oh no, what's Wes doing now?"

Free, Harley bound to the kitchen.

Izzy dashed after him, but stopped. "Oh, you're up."

In her red robe, Rachel rooted through a cupboard. "Have you seen the ginger?"

"So you're feeling better?" Izzy strolled over, removing her coat.

"Yes, but I need the ginger. Have you seen it?"

Harley nuzzled Rachel. She patted him. "Hey, boy."

Izzy frowned. "Why do you need ginger? What kind of breakfast are you cooking?"

"Not to cook." She dumped a collection of packets and jars on the island. "To drink."

"To drink?" Izzy touched her arm. "Rach, are you feeling okay? Maybe that new medication is causing some sort of reaction."

Harley sat beside the island, tale swishing over the floor. She was moving better. Not gracefully like normal, but more fluidly than the past few days.

Rachel handed Izzy the empty soda can from upstairs. "Ginger. That's the secret."

Izzy shook her head, then pulled Rachel's arm. "Sit down. I think we need to call the doctor."

Rachel sniggered. "I'm not having a psychotic break, Iz." She prodded the can. "*Organic ginger.* I've checked online — you won't believe how many chemo patients rave about it fixing their stomach problems."

"Really?" She squinted at the can, then Harley. "So by accident, Harley has done what all your doctors and medications couldn't?"

Rachel laughed again. "Harley to the rescue once more."

Izzy scratched her head. "He found the lump, now he's curing your chemo. Dear Lord, he really is your guardian angel."

Rachel continued searching. "It's here somewhere, I know it is."

Izzy said, "Maybe he's the reincarnation of your dad or a grandparent or something."

"Yeah, right."

"You think it's all just a fluke?"

"Well, if he's been" — she made air quotes — "'*sent to help*,' he can fix my head, because it's absolutely killing me."

"Seriously, Rach. Look at what he's done for Wes, and now what he's doing for you. You can't ignore something like this."

"You're right. We should book a stadium tour. Travel the world with Harley the Healer." She grabbed something from the back of a cupboard and held up a jar. "Got it."

Izzy grabbed Rachel's wrist. "Don't you believe in anything, Rach?"

"I believe Harley is a remarkable animal. But at the end of the day, that's all he is — an animal. I love him, and I'll be thankful to him forever for what he's done for Wes, and me, but I'm not going to turn him into something he isn't just because of a series of fortunate coincidences. Or do you think we need to call the Vatican to have this *miracle* ratified?"

Izzy hung her head and sighed.

"I'm sorry, Iz, but you know I'm not into all that mumbo-jumbo."

"Mumbo-jumbo?" Izzy looked up. "Across 200 countries, speaking 6,000 languages, and following 4,000 religions, seven billion people believe there's more than this." She held her arms wide. "Seven *billion*, Rach. Are they all wrong? All deluded because this is all there is?"

Rachel brushed Izzy's arm. "I'm sorry. I don't mean to belittle the things you care about."

"It's not that you're belittling things, it's that you've closed your mind to so many possibilities. Biologically, Harley might be *just a dog*. God and the afterlife might be nothing but constructs designed by the church to control us. And each of us might be so utterly alone in the vastness of the universe that when we're gone" — she snapped her fingers — "we really are *gone*. Those are all possibilities, yes, but they don't show the whole picture because we haven't yet evolved the consciousness to even grasp there's a picture to look at. Our thinking is so limited, it's like we're still using stone tablets while the rest of the universe has iPads."

Rachel bit her lip. "I really am sorry."

"I know. Now sit your butt down before you overdo it, and let me make breakfast."

"Thank you." Rachel handed her the ginger. "Half a teaspoon in boiling water with some lemon juice, please?"

"Will do."

Though far from graceful, but no longer hunched over clutching her stomach, Rachel shuffled to the sofa. Harley sat beside her.

She scratched behind his ear. "I don't know how you do it, Harley, but thank you."

To be moving and chatting as she was, Rachel had to be feeling better. She still stank like shriveled plants, but things were definitely improving. Now all he had to do was implement stage two of his plan, and she'd be running wild and free in no time.

Izzy called, "Where's Wes? Is he okay?"

"Reorganizing his soup cans."

Harley nuzzled Rachel and, having gotten her attention, strolled to the other end of the sofa. If he could only keep her attention and get her to follow him.

Izzy said, "Anything in particular you'd like to eat?"

Rachel looked away from Harley. "Nothing too heavy or spicy, but something decent while my stomach's settled."

"Pancakes? Egg and bacon?"

"Maybe pancakes. The advice is to eat smaller meals more often."

"You got it."

Rachel picked up one of the magazines Izzy had been reading.

Harley yipped.

"What's wrong, Harley?" said Rachel. "You going stir-crazy too without our runs?"

She was looking at him again, so he held her gaze and took a few more steps toward the front door.

"Maple syrup, chocolate, honey, fruit...?" asked Izzy.

"Chocolate. I don't know how long my stomach will be good, so I might as well splurge."

Harley dropped his tail. She'd turned around again. She was never going to get better if she was going to ignore him. He yipped again.

Rachel frowned. "Are you okay, Harley?"

Izzy sauntered over and placed a steaming cup on the coffee table.

Rachel said, "Has he been eating all right?"

"Yes."

"So what's wrong with him?"

"Well, it can't possibly be to tell you Timmy has fallen down a well because Harley's *just a dog*." She smirked, arching an eyebrow.

"I didn't say I don't believe in *anything*, just not angel dogs."

Izzy said, "Yeah, well, take solace in that when they finally pull up Timmy's skeleton covered in cobwebs."

Rachel swatted Izzy on the thigh. "Shut up and make my breakfast."

Izzy saluted. "Yes, sir. Immediately, sir. Sorry for the delay, sir." She scurried back to the kitchen.

Harley's plan wasn't working. He could only hold Rachel's attention for a few seconds. He needed another tactic.

He wandered over, sat next to the front door, and whimpered quietly — he wanted Rachel to hear, but not Izzy.

Rachel didn't react.

He tried louder.

Rachel turned, her brow knitted. "Harley? What's wrong?"

He pawed the air.

Izzy put a pan down. "I'll see if he needs another pee."

"No, I'll go. There's obviously something wrong, and I want to know what?"

"Maybe he's heard something outside?"

"Maybe." Rachel dawdled over. "What is it, boy?"

This was his chance.

He bit into one end of her robe's dangling belt and shoved his snout against the door where it opened, pulling Rachel toward it. This was it. He was going to make her better.

"Harley, I'm not going outside." She tugged her belt, but he gripped it harder.

He pawed the door. If he could just get her outside. If she felt the sun on her cheeks, the wind through her hair, the call of the hills, the trees, the sky... how could she not be rejuvenated by the glorious wildness of it all?

She laughed. "Harley, be good."

Izzy ambled over. "Is he okay?"

"He's desperate for me to go outside, for some reason."

Izzy took his leash from the drawer in the unit beside the door. "I'll let him have a sniff about. See if that settles him."

Rachel grasped the leash. "You know what, I'll do it. I haven't had any fresh air for days, so it might actually clear this headache."

"Is that a good idea? You could see your breath this morning. The last thing you want is to catch a chill."

"I'm not going like this, am I?" She nodded to the closet. "Pass my parka, please."

Izzy handed Rachel a dark green coat with fake fur around the hood.

Harley wagged his tail. He'd done it — they were going out. They were going out. They were going out!

Chapter 66

Stepping outside, Rachel yanked her hood up, even though she was wearing a red woolen cap and matching gloves. She tottered a few steps along the stone flag path, holding Harley's leash, then stopped. Closing her eyes, she tilted her face upward. A breeze brushed her cheeks, and sunlight made the insides of her eyelids glow a fiery red.

She drew in a deep breath through her nose, then exhaled through her mouth with an *ahhh*.

The chilly air prickled her cheeks, while its freshness smelled of a world erupting with lush greenery.

She opened her eyes. The light was crisp and the colors surreal, like the world had been Photoshopped while she'd been cooped up. How had she stayed indoors so long? It didn't matter how sick she was, she needed this connection. It nourished her soul.

She chuckled. Nourished her *soul*? Maybe Izzy had a point. Because of Wes's love for animal shows, Rachel had discovered some astounding facts — bees could count up to five, peregrine falcons dive-bombed prey at 200 mph, and dolphins gave themselves a unique name which their friends used. 100 years ago, any researcher claiming anything so outlandish would've been laughed out of the scientific community. Thanks to technology, today, such facts were irrefutable. Who could say what marvels science would reveal in the next 100 years as people opened their minds to the infinite possibilities of an infinite universe?

She looked down at Harley. "So what was the big emergency?"

Brown eyes gazed up and a tail swished through the muck.

She smiled. There was no big emergency — he'd gotten exactly what he wanted. She didn't like to admit it, but maybe he was an angel dog.

Rachel dawdled along the path toward the road, Harley keeping pace with her, constantly looking up, as if checking she was okay. Not once did he whine, wanting to run. Not once did he pull, wanting to sniff something. He walked as slowly as she did, simply happy to be with her, watching over her.

She rested on the gate in the middle of the white picket fence she'd always dreamed of having as a little girl and which Peter had created for her, partly as a joke, partly out of love.

She gazed along the road and their running route. Sunlight through the trees dappled the asphalt with dancing golden coins. She ached — truly ached — to cut loose and run and run and run, a hollow in her gut gnawing at her as if something was missing. She didn't just like to run, she *needed* to run.

Patting Harley, she said, "Not long now, boy. I promise."

She sucked in another refreshing breath, and the pounding in her head eased.

Maybe a short walk wouldn't do that much harm. Maybe just to the oak tree and back. She eased the gate open. But in midstep, she pulled back.

With her newfound remedies for nausea and headaches, chemo no longer appeared the monster it had. But it was best not to push her luck. She closed the gate and ambled back toward the house.

Cancer didn't stand a chance. She smiled down at her secret weapon, and he gazed up at her.

Chapter 67

The next day, Rachel felt marginally better, and the day after, better still. It seemed the first few days after chemo got progressively worse, with the fourth being horrendous, then her body fought off the side effects and returned to some semblance of normality. Regular bursts of fresh air, endless ginger-based drinks, and her meds meant that by day eight, apart from constant weariness, she felt pretty much herself. So much so that the next day, a Sunday, she stepped outside in her running gear, Harley bouncing up and down with glee.

If she crashed and burned, Izzy was home to help, so this was an ideal chance for Rachel to test how "herself" she really was.

As they walked along the grass toward the oak tree, Harley leaped and yipped. Like a kid on Christmas morning desperate to get to their presents, he just couldn't contain his excitement. His training was so ingrained, he always behaved impeccably, so for him to go against that showed how important their runs were.

Harley yipped again and looked up at her, as if he couldn't believe they were preparing to run.

"If we don't run after all this, you're going to implode, aren't you?" She laughed. It was wonderful to see such joy.

But as she neared the gnarled oak, she wiped her palms on her thighs. What if she ran too far and couldn't get back? What if she was unsteady, so fell and broke something? What if she collapsed on the road and was squashed by a truck?

"Oh boy, get a grip, Rach."

At the tree, she stopped and set her feet to push away. Now or never. She drew a deep breath.

"You ready, Harley?" She winked. "Let's go."

She ran.

The wind blew into her face, burning her cheeks, making her hair flail behind her. And Harley ran beside her. Never pulling, never falling back, perfectly in sync.

Free.

She felt so free. Free of worries, free of stress, free of illness. It was as if she was made to run, like a fish was made to swim and a bird made to fly. While she was a mother, an artist, a woman, a homeowner, a businessperson... it wasn't until she was running that she felt truly "her." It wasn't what she did, it was what she was. It was the freedom of the empty path. The rhythmic exertion. The focusing on a goal and driving toward it, knowing her will and her will alone would see her attain it. But above all, it was the wildness — losing herself to be one with the trees, the mountains, the sky.

She'd never talked about it with anyone, because she'd never thought anyone would understand. But someone did. She smiled at Harley.

At a modest pace, they ran to the foot of the steep incline, then ran back home.

No sooner was Rachel home than she nodded off on the sofa. When she woke, she was relieved to find no ill effects.

For almost two weeks, life went back to a kind of normal — runs in the morning, followed by classes with Wes, then work in the afternoon. All at a delicate pace, but normality nonetheless. And then the second round of chemo knocked her sideways. Medication, ginger supplements, as much water as she could drink, and gentle outdoor walks combated the headaches and nausea, but the fatigue was invincible.

The investment in the scalp cryotherapy proved sound, however. Her hair thinned, but thankfully, Wes didn't seem to notice.

After another week or so, life resumed once more. And the whole sickly cycle started over, week after week, month after month. Every so often, just when she thought she was getting a handle on how to manage her condition, chemo introduced new side effects, as if it thought she was getting cocky — aching joints, fuzzy thinking, burning hands and feet. On one occasion, she had diarrhea *and* constipation at the same time — a feat she would've thought impossible and yet there it was. Izzy suggested she contact the local news.

Finally, her last round of Taxotere and Paraplatin came and went, leaving her with only the targeted therapy drugs Herceptin and Perjeta to contend with. That meant her hospital sessions would be shorter and hopefully the side effects milder. Life was slowly but undeniably returning to normal. What better way to celebrate than with a family day out? And if that went well, later, a full-fledged road trip to visit Grandma.

Rachel spoke on her phone in the car in her drive. "A service dog, yes. I have documentation if you need it."

A woman with a southern lilt said, "Is your son visually impaired?"

"He's autistic."

"Then, yes, the information you've been given is correct — we welcome service dogs."

"Great. Thanks for your help." She'd already phoned last week but wanted to double-check to avoid any nasty surprises.

Hanging up, Rachel turned to Wes and Harley strapped into the back seat. "We're good to go, guys!"

An hour later, Wes laughed as, for the umpteenth time, a penguin clambered partway out of its indoor pool onto a slippery rock, only to fall on its belly and splash back into the water.

Rachel leaned on the transparent Perspex wall of the pool. "It's so funny that penguin, isn't it, Wes?"

"It's the funniest penguin ever." Crouching, he pressed his hand against the Perspex as the penguin glided by underwater. His eyes sparkled.

"That's a lovely dog you've got," said a gray-haired woman with thick glasses and who held a small boy's hand. "He's a service dog, isn't he?"

"Thank you. Yes, he is," said Rachel.

"You can always tell — they're always so calm wherever they go." She smiled. "My daughter keeps promising Petey here a dog, but they're such a commitment, aren't they? Anyway, have a lovely day." The pair toddled away.

"And you." Rachel turned. "Shall we see the otters, Wes?"

He nodded.

Rachel wandered away, Harley's leash in one hand and Wes's harness strap in the other. The path curved between blue walls painted with cute images of sea creatures — octopuses, dolphins, butterflyfish...

As a horde of youngsters passed, a couple ran to get ahead. A bearded man said loudly, "No running, please. The cafeteria won't run out of food."

Rachel gripped the leash and the harness tighter, not wanting any accidents to mar what was turning into a perfect day.

Wes hadn't stopped smiling since they'd arrived at Marineland — his favorite place in the world — but she'd been a little anxious about Harley. How stupid. His behavior was impeccable, as usual.

Wes's condition meant field trips could be a nightmare just as easily as a joy, even oscillating between the two on the same day. If today went well, as indications were suggesting, Harley would open up a whole new world for Wes outside the house, just as he had inside it.

At the otter enclosure, one of the cutest creatures Rachel had ever seen lay on its back in the water, looking as cozy and relaxed as she would in a hammock on a Caribbean beach. Wes waved at it, and it locked its gaze on him.

"He's looking at you," said Rachel.

Wes waved harder.

Another otter headbutted a football, which landed on the cozy one. The cozy one bolted after the offender. They tore through the water, scooted up a slanted tree trunk and across a concrete platform, then dove back into the water.

Wes giggled so much, he held his sides, wincing.

The action having died down, Rachel said, "Do you feel like some lunch?"

Wes nodded.

"I wasn't talking to you. I was talking to Harley."

Wes laughed again, then put his ear down to Harley's snout. "He says he's not hungry, so I can have it."

"If you eat your lunch and Harley's, you'll end up with a big belly like that penguin. Is that what you want?"

He shook his head, beaming.

They meandered to the cafeteria in the center of the building, where they bought cheeseburgers, Wes having fries with his. They sat at one of the few free tables, most occupied by the youngsters who'd passed earlier and a group of young teens, all appearing to be on school field trips.

Rachel's mouth watered as she smelled the succulent beef and melted cheese. She chomped into it, reveling in the joy of junk food instead of her usual healthy choices.

"Good, yeah?" she asked.

A smudge of ketchup on his mouth, Wes nodded, chewing.

Rachel took a bowl and a bottle of water from her bag and gave Harley a drink.

She ripped another piece of her burger away. She'd forgotten how good bad food tasted. And that was when the nightmare started...

Chapter 68

The fire alarm blasted.

As most other people did, Rachel glanced around, expecting either the noise to stop or someone official to appear and declare it a false alarm. No one rushed for an exit.

Wes rocked back and forth, moaning, ears covered, eyes screwed shut.

Rachel said, "Wesley, don't panic. I'm sure it will stop soon."

But it didn't stop.

A skinny woman in a green polo shirt bearing the Marineland logo pointed to the hallway along which Rachel had come. "Can everybody leave through the fire exits, please? Nice and orderly, thank you."

The bearded man shooed his youngsters toward the hallway, helped by two young women. Likewise, the teens were directed to leave by the adults accompanying them, though some ignored the requests, slouching in their seats and staring at their phones.

Rachel stood. "Wesley..."

He continued rocking, eyes closed, despite her using his full name.

"Wesley! We have to leave. Now."

Rocking, rocking, rocking.

She scanned the room. No smoke. No smell of burning. But some of the younger kids were complaining or squabbling among themselves. Near the back, a fat woman with cropped hair stabbed at the exit and snarled at a bunch of teens still fixated on their phones.

It was probably a drill. But whether it was or not, they still had to leave.

Rachel yanked on the harness strap. "Wesley, stand up."

Harley whimpered. He probably couldn't understand why so many people were so agitated.

"Wesley, Harley's frightened. You have to leave to help him."

His chair scraping on the floor as he shoved it with his legs, Wes stood, still cupping his ears, and they joined the throng politely shuffling out.

"You're doing well, Wesley. Nice and steady."

In a circular room, with fish tanks lining the walls, people merged from another hallway, all heading toward a right-hand pathway above which hung numerous signs to exhibits, plus one to a fire exit.

Someone behind her shouted, "Smoke!"

The hairs bristled on the back of Rachel's neck. She twisted around, eyes wide, as screams erupted.

She couldn't see smoke, but that didn't mean there was none.

People barged into her, barged into Wes. Someone stood on Harley's paw and he yelped. Wes screamed. She pulled them both close as they were buffeted from all directions.

Oh, God help them. She had to get Wes and Harley out. Had to keep them safe. But a smell made her gasp in horror. She spun.

Smoke billowed across the ceiling behind them.

The rough jostling became a stampede. A stocky teenage boy shoved her aside, knocking her into a freestanding display. The unit collapsed. Leaflets on sea creatures and maps of the facility scattered everywhere.

A little girl tripped and sprawled over the concrete floor. Rachel stooped to help her, but with Wes's harness in one hand and Harley's leash in the other, she floundered.

Two teenage girls scrambled by, one panning her phone to film the chaos. She stumbled into Rachel, knocking her flying. Rachel crunched into the concrete beside the little girl, crying out as her shoulder slammed into the unforgiving floor.

Rachel struggled onto all fours. Someone dashed by and their knee smashed her in the temple. She crumpled.

Rachel's vision darkened and lights pulsed before her eyes. Instinctively, she pulled her arms and knees up to protect herself as people thundered past.

The rampaging crowd blurred and the shrieks dulled.

And a dog barked. Barked and barked and barked.

A hand grabbed hers. She screamed and pulled to rip free, but she was caught fast.

Someone heaved her up.

Rachel held her head as her sight cleared, and she recognized the gray-haired woman with the glasses.

Barking and snapping, Harley stood between Rachel and the stampeding horde, obviously trying to scare people from trampling her.

"Thank you." Rachel rubbed her temple.

"Didn't you have a boy with you?"

Rachel gasped. Wes? Where was Wes?

She spun, around and around, frantically scanning the area and the hallways leading off. Where was he?

The woman said, "He's probably been swept out in the crush." She pushed Rachel in the direction of the exit, yanking Harley along with her.

"No. I have to check."

The skinny woman in the Marineland polo shirt dashed over, arms out wide, herding stragglers. "To the exit, please. As quickly as you can."

"My son. I've lost my son."

"There's no one else back there," said Polo Shirt.

"I have to check. I can't leave until I've checked."

Rachel pushed to get by her but staggered and almost fell over Harley, her head spinning.

Polo Shirt caught her around the waist and supported her.

The old lady said, "She was trampled. I think she got kicked in the head."

Polo Shirt eased her toward the exit. "He's probably outside already. Don't worry, I'll help you find him."

The woman was probably right, and Rachel could barely stand to search anyway. Supported, she stumbled away and through a fire exit.

In the parking lot, adrenaline and fresh air kick-started Rachel. She scrambled toward the mass of people standing at a safe distance.

She shouted, "Wesley? ... Wesley?"

Polo Shirt asked, "What does he look like?"

"He's eleven, skinny, with shaggy brown hair. He's wearing blue jeans and a gray sweater. He's autistic, so he'll be terrified. He might even be hiding somewhere."

Rachel scoured the straggly crowd staring at the building. Polo Shirt and the old lady clutching her grandson's hand did likewise.

"Wesley?" Rachel shouted, marching through the crowd and hauling Harley behind her. He seemed determined to go in any direction except the right one. As if he couldn't have chosen a worse time to be obstinate.

Peering around people, checking behind parked cars, she shouted and shouted, "Wesley? ... Wesley?"

Sirens wailed in the distance. Getting closer. Quickly. Rachel glanced back. A pall of dirty brown smoke curled from the building's roof.

She clutched her mouth, as tears streamed down her cheeks. Oh, God help her. What if he was still in there?

Two fire engines pulled into the parking lot, stopping outside the main entrance.

Rachel ran. Ran faster than she'd ever run in her entire life, as if all those years of driving herself to run faster and faster had been building to this one moment. And Harley ran with her. Barking and barking.

Donning breathing equipment, firefighters made preparations to enter the building.

One saw her racing toward them and strode forward, arms out blocking her way.

"Back up, please, ma'am." He pointed to the crowd. "Join the others, please."

She swerved to get around him, but he lunged, smothering her with his big arms. "Ma'am, please don't make me involve the police."

Flailing to break free, Rachel shouted through the tears, "My son's in there! My son's in there!"

A second firefighter marched over. He nodded to the first who released her. "Are you sure, ma'am?"

Trembling, Rachel said, "We got separated and he's not out here. He's got autism. He could be hiding in there."

The first firefighter heaved a breath. "Hiding? That's all we need."

The second firefighter said, "What's his name?"

"Wesley. He's only eleven. He'll be terrified. Please. You've got to let me find him."

"Rest assured, ma'am, we'll do everything possible. Now, if you'll join the people over there, please." Taking her arm, he pulled her away from the building.

"You won't find him without me. He'll be hiding where he thinks it's safe and won't come out if I'm not there."

Rachel twisted to break free and dash to find Wes, but in the struggle, she dropped Harley's leash.

Harley bolted. Straight into the smoking building.

Rachel shrieked, "No!"

She curled her arms over her head and rocked the way Wes did. But then something clicked. Was it possible Harley knew where Wes was? Was that why he'd been pulling?

She stabbed at the building. "Follow Harley! Follow my dog!"

Chapter 69

Harley shot through the double doors they'd scurried out of. Smoke hugged the ceiling, and the stench of burning stung his nostrils.

Tilting his snout upward and turning in an arc, he sniffed long and hard, filtering all the scents for that special one. But it wasn't there.

He panned his gaze over the area: an archway formed from the jaws of some gigantic beast with a tunnel disappearing down its throat; glass cylinders taller than Rachel containing creatures seemingly made of jelly; the hallway down which they'd raced and down which smoke now loomed.

Where was Wes? Harley sniffed again.

Not a trace of the boy.

He stared at the smoke creeping across the ceiling, aching to suffocate him in its clutches. The last thing he wanted was to run into that billowing brown monster, but that was the last place he'd been with Wes...

Harley raced into the hallway, smoke thick above him. He hurtled by window after window behind which fish floated in water. With every step, the air tasted thicker and burned his throat, as though it refused to be swallowed and was clawing its way back out.

He burst into the wide room where Rachel had fallen. In the middle, he stopped. This was the last place he'd seen Wes, so if he could find his scent, he could track him. He drew a huge breath, but it was so tainted, he spluttered and couldn't stop coughing.

Staggering as he struggled to control his breathing, he wandered onto the spilled leaflets. He stopped dead – Rachel. He smelled Rachel on the floor. He pressed his snout to the blue concrete and took a few steps. His nose and throat burning, he filtered all the smells to home in on that one special person and... Wes!

Harley followed the trail. Instead of going down the right-hand pathway and outside like everybody else, Wes's scent disappeared down the left hallway, as if he were trying to avoid everyone.

Harley barked, hoping Wes might hear and follow his voice so they could run to safety.

Nothing.

He barked louder.

Nothing.

Sniffing the floor, he headed down the hallway.

His eyes watering and the air darkening, objects blurred until he was almost upon them. But that didn't matter — as long as he had his nose, he could find Wes.

Stumbling blindly down the hall, he followed the scent, farther and farther from Rachel and safety.

The bad air raking his insides, he coughed and coughed. Coughed so hard he lost his balance, slipped, and crashed to the floor, his teeth jarring as he smashed into the concrete. A wet taste of metal filled his mouth.

Spluttering, he pushed up and trudged farther. He had to find Wes. It was his purpose. And his purpose was the thing he was born to do.

Smoky, blurry objects loomed in the haze, but he ignored them all; the only thing that mattered was the scent. A huge shiny box with a glass front and rows of objects stacked inside reared out of the gloom, its back against the side of a staircase that disappeared into the smoke.

Harley drew another big breath to check the direction of the scent, but once more, a fit of coughing consumed him. And then he heard it — he wasn't the only one coughing.

Between the concrete steps climbing upward and the back edge of the shiny box was a hole. Harley prowled closer. And the closer he got, the stronger Wes's scent got. He barked.

A voice croaked, "Harley."

He barked again, encouraging Wes to crawl from under the stairs, but the boy didn't. Harley had no choice — he crawled under.

In the gloom, Wes lay curled in a ball on the floor. On seeing Harley, he flung his arms around him, clawing his fingers into his fur.

The boy might have been the brains of their pack, but he'd made a deadly mistake if he thought they were safe here. They had to get out and get away from the smoke.

Setting his claws against the floor, Harley bit into Wes's sweater and pulled to drag Wes into the hallway.

But the boy didn't move.

Harley braced himself, then hauled with all his might...

Wes leaned forward onto all fours and, with Harley pulling, crawled for the hole.

Yes, they were going to make it!

Harley tugged harder, willing Wes to move faster. Finally, they emerged from under the staircase.

They'd done it. Now just to run outside, to safety, to Rachel.

Wes must have sensed the urgency, because he stood up. His head now higher, the smoke swirled around him and he coughed violently. He staggered and banged into the shiny box. Wes crashed to the floor, his head smashing into the concrete.

He lay unmoving.

Harley nuzzled him. Whined. But Wes ignored him.

Harley whimpered. He pawed Wes, but still the boy didn't move.

Wes, don't stop. Please, don't stop!

Harley had been trained to handle all kinds of situations and emergencies, but he'd never experienced anything like this. What was he supposed to do? If he didn't save Wes soon, it would be too late — they'd both stop.

He needed help. Needed Rachel. And when a desperate dog needed its pack, only one thing could save it...

Harley raised his snout to the heavens and howled. Howled and howled and howled.

Chapter 70

Rachel paced in the parking lot, breath juddering, cheeks wet. She glared at the exit through which Harley had run. Even more smoke billowed out now.

She shook her head. "No, no, no, no, no."

Polo Shirt said, "They're doing everything they can, Rachel. I'm sure they'll find him."

Two firefighters had been dispatched solely to search for Wes. It felt like hours ago, even though it was only minutes.

Rachel held her head and tugged her hair. "I can't do this. I have to help."

She marched toward the doorway, but Polo Shirt yanked her back. "Rachel, don't."

Rachel shouted, "I can't do nothing while my son might be in there..." Dying. She couldn't bring herself to say the word.

"And if they find him and he needs you, but you're in there somewhere?"

"So what am I supposed to do?"

"Let them do their job — rescue your son."

She buried her face in her hands. "What if I lose him?"

Polo Shirt hugged her. "Don't even think that. I'm sure they'll find him."

A firefighter emerged from the smoky doorway, carrying a limp body.

Rachel shrieked. She knocked Polo Shirt aside and tore toward the firefighter.

She couldn't have gone through all she had for it to end like this. Dear Lord, no. Please no!

The firefighter shouted, "I need a paramedic!"

From beside a parked ambulance, two paramedics darted over with a gurney.

"Wesley!" Rachel stroked his hair as he hung motionless in the firefighter's arms, soot around his nose and mouth. "Wesley, no."

"He's alive, ma'am," said the firefighter, "but he's inhaled a lot of smoke."

He laid Wes on the gurney. A Latina paramedic immediately placed an oxygen mask on Wes, while her big-nosed male colleague checked vital signs.

The firefighter said, "We wouldn't have found him without your dog, ma'am." He turned as his colleague carried a dog outside, its head lolling, tongue hanging out. "That there dog's a hero."

She clutched her mouth, her words catching in her throat. "Is he...?"

The other firefighter winced, rushing over. "He's hanging on, but..."

Rachel grabbed the big-nosed paramedic examining Wes. "You have to save my dog."

Big Nose pulled free. "Ma'am, I'm busy with your son."

Rachel clutched his hand. When he tried to rip it free, she gripped harder.

"Ma'am, you need to let me do my job."

"Please. He saved my son. You need to save him."

He looked at Harley, then at the firefighter carrying him.

The firefighter said, "Hey, you've gotta save the dog, man!"

Big Nose nodded to the ambulance. "Bring him over."

The paramedics loaded Wes into the ambulance, Big Nose helping Rachel inside while his partner fired up the engine. Rachel crouched beside Wes and clutched his hand. Meanwhile, Big Nose laid Harley on the bench seat.

The ambulance raced away, siren screeching.

The paramedic listened to Harley's chest with a stethoscope and nodded. "His heartbeat is strong."

Sticking an oxygen mask over Harley's snout, he said, "Hold this, please."

Sitting beside Harley, Rachel cupped her hands around the mask to try to form a seal.

Big Nose moved over to Wes and listened to his chest. "Any respiratory conditions? Asthma, COPD, bronchitis...?"

"No."

"Any medical conditions that could affect lung or heart function?"

"He's autistic, but healthy."

"Allergies? Medications?"

"No."

Big Nose took more of Wes's vitals and hooked him up to a monitor. Harley coughed.

"Harley?" Rachel stroked his side.

His eyes flickered open.

"Harley!" She hugged him.

The paramedic touched her back. "Please, ma'am, give him space to breathe."

"Sorry."

Harley twisted away from the mask.

Rachel leaned on his shoulder to hold him there, stroking his head with her free hand. "It's okay, Harley. Stay there."

He pawed at the mask.

Rachel said, "He'll get distressed if I pin him down with this on his face. Can I take it off?"

"Okay."

She removed the mask. Harley shook his head and snorted, then his big brown eyes looked at her. And his tail wagged.

Smiling, she stroked him. He was going to be fine. Did that mean...?

"Does this mean Wes will be waking up soon?"

"I can't say. I don't know anything about canine anatomy or the incident itself." He shrugged.

The ambulance arrived outside the double doors to the emergency room. Wes was rushed in on his gurney, Rachel dashing behind, grasping Harley's leash.

In green scrubs, a chubby woman blocked Rachel's way. "Sorry, but you'll have to wait outside with your dog."

"He's a service dog."

The woman stepped aside, gesturing for Rachel to enter. She darted in.

Big nose said, "Wesley Taylor. Eleven-year-old male. Smoke inhalation at the Marineland fire. Unresponsive. Respiration 12 and regular. Pulse 120. BP..." He continued listing Wes's stats to a black female doctor with hair cropped so short she looked almost bald.

The doctor said, "Get me a chest X-ray, CBC, ABG, carboxyhemoglobin and methemoglobin." She turned to Rachel. "Are you with him?"

"He's my son."

The doctor frowned. "And the dog?"

"It's a service dog. Wes has autism."

"So he could panic if he comes to surrounded by strangers?"

"Yes."

"Then stay close. But please keep your dog from under people's feet."

They transferred Wes to a bed separated from those on either side by a gray curtain, then performed a series of tests, including drawing blood, using a portable X-ray machine, and sticking some implement down his throat.

While the staff were busy, Rachel took out the bowl and water to give Harley a drink. He seemed fine, but his throat had to be raw after inhaling so much smoke.

With Wes stable, everybody left, so Rachel held his hand. He looked so small. So fragile.

She bit her lip. Why hadn't Wes woken up like Harley? Okay, he'd been inside breathing smoke for longer, but it wasn't that much longer.

She couldn't lose him. He was her life. Seeing him grow over the last few months had been the greatest pleasure she'd ever known. He couldn't have come this far — further than any doctor had believed possible — only for it to end like this.

She wiped her eyes with her fingers.

"Ms. Taylor?"

She turned.

The black doctor said, "Wesley's blood pressure and blood oxygen levels have risen, while his heart rate has lowered, which are all good signs, and none of the tests or the bronchoscopy show anything we should be concerned about, which suggests he should make a full recovery. However, I'd like to keep him overnight for observation."

"Why hasn't he woken up yet?"

"That's why I want to keep him in. We found a contusion near his left temple, suggesting he may have fallen and hit his head, which rendered him unconscious."

Rachel's chin trembled. She'd let go of him. This was all her fault.

"Don't worry," said the doctor, "that was probably the best thing that could've happened — the closer he was to the floor, the cleaner the air he was breathing. Anyway, I'm ordering a CT scan to rule out any intracranial injury and then he'll be transferred to pediatrics. I can have them call you the moment he wakes or—"

"No. We're staying with him."

"I thought you'd say that. I've already informed my colleagues that he's on the spectrum, so it might be prudent to have you with him. Luckily, they have a private room available."

"Oh, thank you."

The doctor pointed at Harley. "Is it true your dog ran back into the burning building to find your son?"

"Yes."

She smiled. "In that case, you owe him the biggest bone you can find, because without a doubt, he saved Wesley's life."

Rachel clutched her mouth. She'd come so close to losing him. So close.

The doctor said, "I'd have your vet give him the once-over. He might look like he's shrugged it off, but left untreated, carbon monoxide poisoning and hypoxia can have serious repercussions down the line."

She couldn't risk losing Harley, so she'd make an appointment as soon as possible.

The doctor left, and within the hour, Wes had a scan and was transferred to a private room. There, she sat in a green chair with wooden arms, staring at him, willing him to wake.

Her forearms resting on the bed, she clutched Wes's hand in both of hers. Wes now had a cannula under his nose delivering oxygen instead of a mask, which made him look less sick, but no less fragile.

On the other side of the bed, Harley lay beside Wes. If people in comas could hear their loved ones talking to them, maybe Wes could sense Harley beside him.

"Hey."

Rachel turned. Izzy stood in the doorway.

Rachel rushed to her and buried her head against her shoulder.

"It's okay, babe." Izzy enveloped her and stroked her hair. "It's going to be okay."

Crying, Rachel said, "It's all my fault." Her breathing shuddered. "I let go of him."

"Don't be silly, Rach. You were pushed over and trampled. Anyone would've let go. So don't even think that."

"It was a nightmare, Iz. I couldn't get to him. He needed me, but I just couldn't get to him."

"Thank God Harley was there."

Rachel nodded. "You were right."

"Yeah?"

"He's" — she sniffled — "he's an angel. If it wasn't for him..." She sobbed.

"Hey, easy. He was there, so everything's fine. Now, what can I do?"

Rachel wiped her eyes. "You could see if Harley needs a pee. The poor thing must be fit to burst."

Izzy nodded. "I'll ask the nurses for a bag and find some grass outside."

Taking Harley's leash, Izzy rested an overnight bag on the end of the bed. "I didn't know what to bring, so I just grabbed whatever. Oh, and I moved your car to that parking garage one block over. Level two."

"Thanks." Izzy was a godsend.

Izzy left with Harley.

Rachel cradled Wes's hand. When he woke, how could she explain what was happening in a way that wouldn't freak him?

And if he didn't wake up?

No! That wasn't an option. He was going to wake up. Soon. Very, very soon.

A few minutes later, Izzy and Harley waltzed in. Izzy said, "Man, talk about a geyser. I thought he was never going to stop."

"Awww. I wish I'd thought sooner."

A hoarse voice said, "Mom."

Rachel gasped. "Wes!" Tears streaming, she squeezed his hand. He didn't pull it away.

His gaze scanned the room, then fear filled his eyes. He hunched up and clutched his hands to his chest, making himself as small as possible. He rocked, moaning.

"Wesley, don't panic, kiddo. You're here to help Harley, don't you remember?" Rachel beckoned for Izzy and Harley to come closer.

He shook his head, moaning.

Izzy said, "Hey, Wes."

Rachel patted the bed. "Harley."

Harley leaped up.

"Wesley, you were both lost in the smoke, remember? Harley had to come to the hospital for some tests to make sure he's okay, but he was so frightened the nice doctor said you could stay to show him there's nothing to be afraid of. Do you think you can help him, Wesley? Help Harley?"

Harley whimpered, obviously sensing Wes was in distress, but he couldn't have timed it better.

Still hunched, but no longer rocking, Wes reached a trembling hand and patted Harley. "It's okay, Harley. I'm here."

Harley nuzzled Wes.

"Oh, good job, Wes. Harley's feeling better already, see?"

Wes nodded.

"So when the nice doctor comes, can he pretend to do the tests on you first, so Harley can see there's nothing to be frightened of?"

Wes nodded again.

Rachel wiped her eyes. She didn't like to trick her son, but she couldn't be prouder of how he was stepping up to help his friend.

She visited the nurses' station and explained the situation regarding Wes's autism, his affinity for Harley, and the deal she'd struck with him. It being a pediatric ward, the nurses said they'd do their best to accommodate the odd request.

Minutes later, a bald doctor with a paunch came to check on him. Remarkably, Wes didn't scream, hit, or bite at being touched. Instead, he remained calm, doing whatever the doctor requested. He then held Harley's paw while the doctor shined a light in Harley's eyes and pretended to take his pulse and listen to his heart.

The doctor said, "Wesley, you've done such a great job of helping Harley that I'm pleased to say you'll be able to take him home in the morning. Isn't that good news?"

Smiling, Wes nodded. He rolled over and hugged Harley.

Rachel mouthed to the doctor, "Thank you."

The doctor winked. "I'll pencil him in as being discharged tomorrow, pending an examination by one of my colleagues. Keep an eye on him for the next few days, and any problems, you know where we are."

After the doctor left, Izzy slid the other chair closer to Rachel's, but Rachel stopped her.

"Iz, thanks for rushing here, but it's getting late, so you get off home."

"Don't be silly!" She plonked down in the chair. "Ironic, huh? A place with so much water having a fire? At least the news report said none of the animals were seriously hurt."

"That's great, but why are you sitting here?" Rachel gestured with open palms. "You've got work tomorrow."

Izzy shrugged. "So?"

"Okay, I'll put it this way — Izzy, go home, please."

"Yeah, right." Izzy sniggered.

"Seriously. Look, if it had been bad news, I'd have loved you being here with us, but it wasn't, so there's no point in you killing time here."

"It's called support, Rach. It's what friends do."

"I know. And I appreciate all the support you've given over the months, which is why I want you to go home. I feel bad putting you out like this, when I don't need it."

"Putting me out? Rach, if I didn't want to be here, *I wouldn't be here*."

Rachel grasped Izzy's arm. "There might come a time when I need you — really need you — and I want you to be there because you want to be, not because of some misplaced sense of duty, when really you're thinking 'Oh boy, not again!' Do you get what I mean?"

Izzy exhaled loudly, then stood. "You'll call me if anything changes?"

"Of course."

"Then I'll see you tomorrow." She waved. "So long, Wes."

Izzy left.

Rachel had always believed English had an incredibly rich vocabulary, with a word for every object, emotion, action, and scenario imaginable. But it wasn't. Izzy wasn't Rachel's sister, nor her mother, spouse, or partner... just a "friend." How could that meager word do justice to Izzy and all she'd done since Rachel's diagnosis?

If only there was some way Rachel could repay her. She'd have to find something. Nothing grand that would embarrass Izzy, yet big enough to portray her gratitude.

Her next job, however, was to have Harley examined. She didn't want any nasty surprises down the line.

Harley and Wes had fallen asleep cuddling. Looking at them, it was hard to imagine they'd both almost died only hours ago.

She pictured the firefighters dashing out of Marineland carrying their two limp bodies. Tears welled again. An aching hollow in her stomach like she hadn't eaten for a week slowly spread through her entire body. The ache of a woman wanting to feel a mother.

As delicately as she could, she eased onto the side of the bed beside Harley and snuggled against him. Again, he was the buffer between her and Wes, a suture drawing together their wound of a life.

Chapter 71

Cold and clammy.

Her sleep disturbed, Rachel pried her eyelids apart. Harley's big brown eyes gazed at her and his tail swished rhythmically over the hospital bedding. Still perched on the edge of the bed, Rachel swung around to sit and stretched. She checked her phone: 5:37 a.m.

She chuckled, then scratched Harley behind the ears. "Yes, we're going running today, don't worry. After what you did yesterday, you're going to be so spoiled, you'll get sick of it." She kissed him on the forehead.

For a few hours, Rachel lounged in the chair, figuring what she could give Izzy to show her appreciation and what changes she could make to give herself, Wes, and Harley a richer life. Coming so close to losing everything was a wake-up call; now, she would live every moment to the fullest with those she loved.

Wes was discharged midmorning. Instead of having classes, they played with Harley, watched animal TV shows, and ate ice cream on the sofa. Apart from phoning the vet when Wes napped, they spent the day having fun. The next day was pretty much the same.

Friday, with Wes appearing fine, Rachel took him to school to establish some normality. She informed Consuela of the Marineland incident and stayed to monitor Wes until 11:20 a.m., when she popped out to take Harley to the vet a few minutes' walk away.

In the examination room, she patted the stainless steel table. "Harley."

Harley leaped up. His tongue out, eyes sparkling, he looked at her as if expecting another command.

"Good boy." She stroked him. "You see, he seems fine. If he was suffering from smoke inhalation, wouldn't it show?"

Wearing chrome-rimmed glasses and her hair tied back in a bun, Claudia, the vet, checked Harley's eyes and gums. "You say he received oxygen in the ambulance?"

"Yes."

"He's eating and drinking regularly?" She felt up and down his throat.

"Yes. Everything's been fine."

She peered in his mouth. "There's no swelling of the trachea, which is good. Because he's so much closer to the ground than we are, unless the room was floor-to-ceiling smoke, he would've passed under the thick of it, so hopefully, he avoided inhaling that much."

Rachel nodded.

Claudia placed her stethoscope on various spots on his abdomen. Listening, she nodded. "Heartbeat is strong. Lungs clear, breathing smooth."

Rachel smiled. "So he's okay?"

Claudia kneaded Harley's stomach and felt her way up under his ribs. She furrowed her brow and continued probing the area with her fingertips.

Rachel's smile vanished. "He is okay, isn't he?" *He'd* saved Wes, so she'd made the paramedic save *him*. She couldn't lose him now.

The vet said, "I can feel something. It's too far under his rib cage to feel properly, but there's definitely something there."

Rachel swallowed hard, dread gripping her like a cold wind at midnight. "You mean something caused by smoke inhalation?" *Please say yes. Please say yes. Please say yes.*

The vet shook her head, still massaging Harley.

Rachel's legs wobbled. She gripped the table, worried she'd fall. She didn't want to ask, but she had no choice. "What is it?"

Claudia said the worst words Rachel could have heard, "A mass."

Her hand on the wall to steady herself, Rachel sank into the gray plastic chair.

Claudia checked the clock on the wall. "Are you on a tight schedule, or do you have some time free?"

"If it's going to help, I can make time. Why?"

"You're my last appointment this morning, so if I work into my lunch hour, I could get an ultrasound of the mass, and if need be, do a biopsy to get a sample to the lab today."

Rachel cupped her face. Biopsy!

Claudia continued. "If he's even half the hero you've described, it's the least I can do to give him every chance possible."

This couldn't be happening to Harley as well. No, no, no.

"Ms. Taylor?"

Rachel stared at the woman. Hating everything about her because of what she'd just done to her family.

"If it's a serious condition," said the vet, "the sooner we treat it, the better chance Harley has of surviving it."

Rachel nodded.

"You'd like me to go ahead?"

Rachel nodded again.

"Okay. Take a seat in the waiting room and I'll have my staff prepare the paperwork."

Chapter 72

Sitting on the living room sofa, Wes said, "Harley, light switch." Harley trotted to the wall, pushed up, and swatted the white plastic square. The room brightened to Wes's giggling.

Whenever Wes giggled, Harley felt gooey inside. It was as if he was lying down and someone was scratching his belly, yet fingers could never reach as deep as Wes's giggle.

"Harley, can of soda."

Standing in the kitchen with Rachel, Izzy stared at him as he meandered to the refrigerator. He yanked on the strap hanging from the handle to open it, grasped a cold can in his jaws, and ambled back to Wes. Again, the gooey giggle tickled him in ways fingers never could. It was his superpower.

Izzy said in a hushed tone, "But he looks absolutely fine."

"Yeah, and so did I." Rachel rubbed her puffy red eyes.

Izzy stroked Rachel's arm. "It's probably nothing. I mean, both of you getting a life-threatening illness at the same time? Come on! I bet you've a more chance of winning the lottery."

Rachel shrugged. Her chin trembled, and she turned so Wes couldn't see her face.

Izzy put her arm around Rachel. "Even if it is something bad, he can beat it, just like you are."

"But am I beating it? It's not like I get monthly scans. Anything could be happening. And now Harley? What will happen to Wes if" — her voice broke — "if he loses both of us?"

"Rachel, he's not going to lose you *or* Harley. When do you get the results?"

"Monday or Tuesday. That's why we need to go this weekend. Before anything bad happens to ruin everything. While we're still a family."

"Well, I can ask Lucinda, but it's short notice, so..." Izzy winced.

320

Rachel grabbed Izzy's forearm. "You have to come, Iz. Promise me you will. Tell one of your colleagues I'll double their pay if they cover your hours."

"It means so much?"

Rachel nodded. "We have to do it now, Iz. While everything's still okay. While Harley's still Harley, and not just another cancer victim... like me."

"Okay. I don't know how, but I'll swing it. Promise."

Rachel flung her arms around Izzy. They hugged.

Harley didn't know what was happening tonight — one side of the room couldn't stop laughing, yet the other couldn't stop crying. Confusing. But that was easily solved — after all, it was his purpose to look after everybody.

He trotted over to Rachel and sat on the floor, the TV remote in his mouth. As his jobs went, it was one of the simpler ones, but it never failed to entertain his pack. He gave a little yip.

Rachel and Izzy looked down. Though they each had tears on their cheeks, they both smiled.

Harley wagged his tail. Another job well done.

Choose Your Ending

A. Dark and Powerful — simply turn to the next page.

B. Warm and Fuzzy — turn to page number 346.

Chapter 73A

Rachel smiled, driving past her trailhead. She eased down on the gas as the road curved upward to the left, trees lining either side, with conifers becoming more predominant the higher they climbed.

In the passenger seat, Izzy said, "I spy with my little eye something beginning with" — she paused for dramatic effect — "t."

Immediately, Wes shouted, "Tree!"

"Yes!" Izzy clapped while Wes laughed. "Your turn."

Wes said, "I spy with my little eye something beginning with" — he paused for dramatic effect too — "t."

Izzy said, "Tree!"

Wes clapped. "Yes. Your turn."

"I spy with my little eye something beginning with" — Izzy paused — "t."

Wes shouted, "Tree!" He held his stomach, laughing so much his eyes watered.

Smiling, Rachel said, "Okay, okay, okay. Unless you want me to drive off the side of this mountain, someone's little eye better spy something other than a tree pretty darn fast."

Izzy saluted, adopting a stern, deep voice. "Aye-aye, Captain. Should I flog the child for mutiny, sir?"

Rachel shook her head. "It's a five-hour drive to my mom's. Remind me why I insisted you come."

"Oh dear, Wes," said Izzy, "it looks like we've got a grumpy chauffeur today. How about another game? Do you know the 'I'm going on an adventure' game?"

He shook his head.

"Oh, you'll love it. You have to imagine you're going on a great adventure — which should be easy because we are — and you say what you're going to see. For example, 'I'm going on a great adventure and I'm going to see a tiger.' Then the next person has to repeat that and add one thing on the end, so something like, 'I'm going on a great adventure and I'm going to see a tiger and a mountain.' Then the next person has to remember those two things and add another one. Do you want to try?"

He nodded.

Rachel nodded too. "That's good. He loves lists."

"Do you want to go first, Wes?" asked Izzy.

He nodded again.

Izzy said, "So you say 'I'm going on a great adventure and I'm going to see...' and then say whatever you like."

Wes said, "I'm going on a great adventure and I'm going to see... a tree."

Izzy laughed.

Rachel shot her a sideways glance. "Don't you dare."

Izzy smirked. "I'm going on a great adventure and..."

Rachel said, "You'll be walking. I'm warning you."

"... I'm going to see a tree and..."

"I can pull over, right here, right now."

"... another tree."

Wes belly laughed so loud, it startled Harley who'd been dozing. He barked.

Rachel couldn't resist smiling. With the pleasure Wes was getting, it was impossible not to. "You know you're flying home, don't you?"

Izzy playfully slapped her arm. "But it's your turn, Rach."

Rachel heaved a sigh. "I'm going on a great adventure and I'm going to see a tree and" — she arched an eyebrow at Izzy — "another tree and..." — a cheeky grin spread across her face — "another tree."

"Yay!" Izzy clapped, so Wes joined in.

Climbing higher, they continued playing games as they left the woodland behind and wound their way through the mountain range, the road clinging to the mountainside.

"I love it up here." Rachel snatched a glance at the wooded valley below, stretching away to a glistening lake against a backdrop of snowcapped mountains.

Izzy nodded. "It's like from Nat Geo."

Rachel's phone rang. The caller ID said "Vet."

"Why's your vet calling? I thought the results weren't due till Monday."

Rachel shrugged. "That's what she said." She took the call. "Hello?"

"Hi , it's Claudia from The Pet People. Harley's results have come in early, so I wanted to—"

Rachel's heart pounded. The incredible life they'd developed over the last few months might be about to be ripped apart.

Her knuckles whitened on the steering wheel. "I'm sorry, Claudia, but we're having a family weekend away, so the last thing we want is bad news. Can this wait till Monday, please?"

"That's why I'm calling — it's not bad news. I won't go into detail if you're away, but the condition is completely manageable. If you book an appointment later, I'll take you through the treatment options."

"That's fantastic."

"It is, isn't it? Anyway, I know how precious Harley is to you, so wanted to let you know as soon as possible."

"Thank you, I really appreciate that."

"You're welcome. Enjoy the rest of your weekend." She hung up.

Rachel beamed as tears ran down her face. Everything was going to be okay. Deep down, she'd expected the worst after the string of bad luck they'd had. But this? This was everything she'd prayed for.

Izzy gripped Rachel's shoulder. "I told you it would work out."

"Uh-huh." Rachel sniffled. "Can you pass me a tissue, please?" She gestured to the glove box.

Izzy poked through the contents. "Are you sure you have some?"

"I bought some recently." Rachel craned to look as much as she felt safe doing while driving, snatching a look in the compartment, then back at the road, then again to the compartment as Izzy shoved things about.

A horn blared.

Rachel snapped fully back into driving mode. She'd drifted out of her lane. An oncoming truck honked its horn again.

She yanked the wheel and swerved out of danger.

Rachel exhaled loudly. "I think we'll forget the tissues."

Izzy nodded, gripping the seat belt across her chest with both hands.

Rachel looked in the rearview mirror. "Okay back there?"

Wes nodded, seemingly oblivious to the close call.

One at a time, she wiped her palms on her jeans and eased off the gas. There was no rush to get to Mom's, and the last thing they wanted was some silly distraction sending them hurtling over the precipice.

Rachel's gaze glued to the road, she focused on negotiating the hairpin bends, Izzy sitting silently. As the road hugged the mountain's contours, they snaked around a bend to the left, then one to the right, a flimsy-looking metal barrier the only thing between them and a drop that seemed to fall away forever.

A length of straight road ahead, and the precipice a couple of car widths away across rough ground, Rachel relaxed and accelerated away.

Behind them, a red pickup truck pulled out and gunned the engine. As he drew alongside, an almighty bang made Rachel jump. A hunk of tattered black rubber crashed into her door window, shattering it.

Izzy shrieked.

Instinctively, Rachel yanked the steering wheel and swerved away from the pickup. But with a blown-out tire, the truck driver lost control. His vehicle veered toward them. It slammed them in the side.

Rachel's car careened right. She hammered the brakes, but the edge of the mountain hurtled toward them. Closer and closer. She flung the wheel around, desperate to swerve clear of the edge. But they were too close. Going too fast...

Rachel screamed. The car flew over the edge and soared through the air.

For a moment, the world froze. The scene through the windshield was a picturesque landscape of the lake and mountain range that could grace any calendar.

Time resumed, and the car pitched downward, the beautiful view replaced by crushing rocks and rushing trees. Cries erupted inside, as if someone had bottled the essence of a lunatic asylum.

The wheels hammered into the hillside. Like a roller coaster in a nightmare, the car thundered down the incline, Rachel instinctively gripping the wheel as if she had some control.

Bouncing and thumping, jerking and jolting, the vehicle tore ever downward. Bushes, trees, and rocks blurred past.

Rachel stretched between the seats to reach Wes, but the car shot over a flat rocky outcropping and once more plummeted through the air.

Massive gnarled tree trunks raced toward them. Rachel flung her arms up to shield her head.

With a devastating crunch, the front driver's side hit a trunk, spinning the car around. The passenger side slammed into another tree full-on. The car dropped, the driver's side smashing into the ground like a bird shot out of the sky by a shotgun blast.

Stillness descended.

Chapter 74A

Cold and clammy.
    "Just another minute, Harley, then we'll go for a run. Promise." Rachel frowned. Had she said that or imagined it?

Chapter 75A

Rachel heaved a breath.

Crunched over on her left side, her face warm and wet, as if a soggy piece of muslin had been draped over it, she strained to open her eyes. Her right eye refused to respond, but her left eyelid flickered up and a sliver of light bled in.

The world was a blurry smudge of colors lying on its side.

Where was she?

Horrific images flashed through her mind: the truck blowout, the hillside plummet, the car crash-landing on its side.

She gasped again. Wes!

She twisted to check on everyone but screeched as pain stabbed her right shoulder and both legs.

Blackness.

Chapter 76A

One eye opened again.

Her voice thin, Rachel said, "W-W-Wesley...?"

No answer.

She panted, as if she'd run up the mountainside, not careered down it. "Izzy...?"

Nothing.

The only sound, branches above her creaking in the breeze.

Shrieking as knives sliced through her side, she turned a few degrees to her right to look upward through her only working eye. Above her, a blurred shape that looked like Izzy dangled limply, held in the seat by the seat belt. The shape gurgled as it breathed.

Alive!

Thank heavens. And if the two of them were, the rear passengers should be as well.

"Har-Harley?" Harley was smart. So unbelievably smart. If he could reach the road, he'd make someone understand they needed help.

Or maybe she could. The steering column had dropped to pin her legs, but if she could pry the unit up a couple of inches, maybe she could wiggle out.

She gripped the wheel with both hands and heaved.

She cried out as if red-hot spears were thrust into her thighs.

Blackness.

Chapter 77A

A noise jolted her conscious. The most beautiful sound she'd ever heard — Wes laughing. But it was coming from outside the car. He'd gotten out!

Her lips moved, barely, but she didn't have the breath to make even the tiniest of sounds. This was the end. Yet with one blurry eye, she could still see two shapes moving near the vehicle.

She'd believed it would be the cancer that ended her, but boy, was she wrong. The cancer was a gift — if she hadn't had it, she'd never have put everything in place to give Wes the life he deserved with Harley and Izzy. She imagined she was smiling, though she didn't know if she was. Who would've thought it — cancer was one of the best things to ever happen to her.

Harley barked and Wes laughed again.

The last of her strength ebbing away, Rachel fought to keep her eye open. Just one more second with her son. Just one! It closed.

She didn't want to leave Wes — didn't want to miss him growing into a man and achieving things all the experts had said were impossible — but instead of loss, she felt peace. Surprising. Izzy was right. For Rachel's life to have played out like this, there had to be more. More than just a random sequence of events and unrelated coincidences. Much more.

She'd be with Wes. Always. Watching over him and Harley — without whom none of this would have been possible — until the day they were reunited.

The light bleeding through her eyelids faded.

The rustling of the wind through the trees came from farther and farther away.

The world slowed as if time was caught in thick mud, as all around her became silent and still and very, very dark, until everything...

Stopped.

Chapter 78A

blackness

emptiness

silence

Chapter 79A

In silent darkness, Rachel sensed Harley nestled beside her. She basked in the safe cocoon of his breathing, his warmth, his love. So peaceful. Like slowly, ever so slowly, waking from the most rejuvenating sleep imaginable.

Without a sound, Harley eased up to leave. She didn't want him to go, but she somehow knew the time had come.

The silence faded. As if someone were turning up the volume of the world, sounds swirled around her — a breeze gusting through trees heavy with leaves, birdsong like a glorious dawn chorus, a stream babbling around stones as insects skated across its surface.

A smell tantalized her — freshly opened flowers reaching for the sun. Chrysanthemums. Her favorite.

The darkness transformed into light, the inside of her eyelids bright red, aglow with life. Her eyes flickered open and blinding light flooded in. Too bright.

And a voice.

Distant. But getting closer. As if the person was moving at tremendous speed from a long way away to right beside her.

A voice she knew. A voice she loved.

"Hey, sweetheart."

Mom.

Rachel moved her mouth to speak but only croaked.

Mom held a glass of water to Rachel's lips. "Just a drop."

Rachel sipped as shapes appeared in the brightness. She tried to take the glass, but her right arm wouldn't move.

Her voice croaked. "Where...?"

Mom caressed her brow. "Hospital, sweetheart. Two days now."

"I thou..." Rachel swallowed and licked her lips. "I thought I'd... died and..." She shook her head. That didn't matter now.

"You were so lucky, sweetheart. The paramedics brought you back. They said if they'd arrived just one minute later..." She sniffled. "But they didn't." She smiled. "And you're here."

The dazzling brightness faded to reveal a hospital room, all whites and pastel blues. Her left leg was suspended above the bed in a cast and her right arm was in a cast too, with a cannula in the back of that hand hooked up to an IV. She couldn't feel a thing, so she was obviously on powerful painkillers.

A vase of chrysanthemums stood on a table at the foot of the bed, another on the bedside cabinet beside a portable CD player.

Mom clicked the stop button and the woodland sounds disappeared. "I brought it from home. I hoped it might bring you back to me."

"Wes?"

Mom held Rachel's hand. "You have to concentrate on getting yourself better, Rachel. You can think about everyone else later."

"He-he'll worry. I-I need to see him."

Mom pursed her lips, tears welling in her eyes. She looked away.

Rachel glowered. "Mom, where's Wes?"

Looking at the floor, Mom squeezed her hand but didn't answer.

"Mom?" Something was wrong, but what?

Her voice breaking, Mom said, "I'm so sorry, Rachel."

"Sorry? About what? Wes was okay. He got out. He and Harley."

Mom clutched her mouth and shook her head.

"They did. I heard them outside the car."

Mom wiped tears away. "No, sweetheart. Only you came back to me." She squeezed Rachel's hand harder. "Only you."

"No, that's not right. Wes was okay. And Izzy was hurt, but she was okay, too."

Mom shook her head again. "Izzy's in a coma. They're worried she won't make it through the night."

"Iz..." Rachel's jaw dropped. She stared into space. "But Wes got out. I know he did."

"I'm so sorry, sweetheart."

Her chest tightened. She couldn't breathe. "No... No... Nooo!"

Rachel screamed. Wes, Harley, Izzy... her life had been wiped out.

Pain sliced through her. Unbelievable pain. Like a surgeon had slashed her open without anesthetic. Like he was grabbing her insides and crushing them in his fists.

"Nooo!" She sobbed. "Mom, no. No. Tell me he's not."

And her mom sobbed too.

A nurse with a ponytail and a doctor with a graying goatee dashed in.

The doctor said, "How can we help? Do we need to increase your pain medication?"

"My son. Where's my son?"

"Ahhh." He rubbed his chin. "I'm sincerely sorry for your loss, Ms. Taylor. If there's any—"

"I want to see him."

The doctor looked to Mom. "Have you explained everything?"

Mom buried her face in her hands and shook her head.

"Everything?" What could possibly be worse than what she'd just learned? "Mom, what haven't you told me?"

The doctor approached. "I'm sorry to have to tell you this on top of everything else, Ms. Taylor, but as a matter routine in cases such as yours, we did a chest X-ray." He drew a breath. "We found a shadow on your lung, so conducted a biopsy and—"

"You found another tumor?"

"I'm sorry, but HER2 cancers are notoriously aggressive and fast-spreading."

That phrase again!

Rachel drilled her gaze into him. "So when I could've been spending quality time with my son but was too sick to function from being poisoned by chemo, it wasn't even freaking working?"

"Again, I am so sorry, but these things do happen. Rest assured, your current regimen will be strictly monitored to ensure—"

She glared at the cannula in the back of her hand. "Excuse me? *Current* regimen?"

"Your admission paperwork gives your mother as your medical proxy. As you were unable to give your permission, we—"

Rachel held her hand toward him. "Take it out."

Mom touched Rachel's shoulder. "Sweetheart, you need this to fight the cancer."

Rachel screamed, "Get it out!"

The doctor sighed, then nodded to the nurse. She strode over and took Rachel's hand.

Mom grabbed the nurse's arm. "No! You said the cancer would kill her if she didn't have it!"

The doctor addressed Mom. "Your daughter is the patient. Now she's conscious, we have to abide by her decision." He pursed his lips.

Mom said, "Rachel, please, sweetheart. I can't lose you, too. Please, Rachel. Please."

Chapter 80A

Sitting in her bathroom at home, Rachel shouted, "Mom!" She waited.

No answer.

Her hands either side of her butt on the wooden toilet seat, she heaved. She raised a couple of inches, her legs trembling with the effort. She gritted her teeth. Groaning, she strained with all her might but collapsed on the toilet again.

Gasping, she clenched her fists. Stared at her bare thighs, her panties around her knees. "Freaking useless, freaking—" She grunted in frustration.

She massaged her quadriceps. Three months in a leg cast would have weakened anyone's muscles. She'd figured within a few weeks of the cast coming off, she'd get her strength back, but it hadn't worked out like that. She was getting weaker if anything. Not surprising considering all the punishing medication she'd had pumped into her — her body was wrecked.

She shouted louder, "Mom!"

Getting around was easier since losing the cast, but today, her quads were beat. Maybe she should be thankful for small mercies — at least she had the strength in her arms to clean herself. Thank the Lord she'd been spared that indignity. Thus far.

"Rachel?" Mom's voice came through the door. "Is everything okay?"

"It's open. I..." She dropped her face into her hands.

Mom peeked in. "What's wrong?"

"Mom, I..." Her arms wide, she shrugged. "I can't get up. It's too low."

Mom rushed over.

"I'm sorry, Mom."

"Don't be ridiculous, Rachel. It's not your fault. And it's not like I've never had to wipe your butt before."

"I can wipe my own butt, thanks. I just can't pry it off this freaking seat!"

Mom gripped her under the arms, and Rachel grabbed her panties and jogging pants to hitch them up at the same time.

"On three," said Mom. "One, two, three."

Together, they hauled her to her feet.

They shuffled out and down the hall, Rachel gripping Mom's arm for support. Halfway down the stairs, Rachel held a hand up, panting for air. "Just... just a minute."

"You okay?" Mom's face lined with concern.

She nodded, slumped against the wall. "Just..." She gasped. "Just give me a minute."

No matter how much air she sucked in, it never seemed to give her the energy to move like a normal person.

A modicum of strength returning, she gripped Mom's arm again. "Okay."

Resuming their shuffle, they descended the stairs and inched closer and closer to her swivel chair that looked onto the backyard.

Once close enough, she grabbed the seat back for support, shuffled around, and flopped into it like a dropped sack of potatoes.

Mom gazed down, worry aging her face more than her sixty-odd years ever could.

Rachel waved her away. "I'm okay." She gasped. "Really."

"I've prepared a salad with some salmon. Can you manage a small plate?"

"Maybe."

Mom scurried to the kitchen. A few moments later, she returned with a plate on a tray, a fishy aroma beating her over.

Rachel nodded a thank-you and picked up the knife and fork. But when she looked down at the food, her stomach clenched into a tight fist. She popped a piece of fish in her mouth. The flavor was there, the seasoning just right, but... as she chewed, she cringed at the thought of having to swallow it, so she chewed and chewed and chewed.

"Is it okay?" asked Mom.

"Great, thanks."

Mom smiled and continued to hover. Watching.

Rachel grimaced, forced the chewed glob to the back of her mouth, and gulped hard to force it down.

"I might leave the rest for later." Rachel placed her silverware down and returned to the wooded mountain landscape beyond her garden.

"The rest? You've had one tiny nibble. You've got to eat, sweetheart."

Rachel stared out, scouring the treeline for the faintest sign of movement — the mountain on which she'd crashed a dark monster far in the background.

She knew what she'd heard. They might still be out there somewhere, and if they were and they came, they'd come this way.

"Rachel."

No reply.

"Rachel."

"Huh?"

Mom nudged Rachel's plate closer. "Eat something. Please."

"I can't. And if I do, I can't keep it down."

"Aren't those pills helping?"

"Huh?"

"The pills the doctor prescribed. The, er, whatchamacallit..."

"Antiemetics." She didn't look at Mom but focused on the wood.

"That's it. You are taking them, right?"

"Of course."

"So they're not helping?"

"No."

Mom stood in front of the window. "Rachel, look at me. Rachel."

Rachel stared at the yard. If she relaxed her eyes so the focus blurred, she could almost see Wes twirling around with a stick and Harley jumping and jumping to get it. She smiled.

Mom crouched with a groan. "Rachel" — she cupped Rachel's face and turned it so they looked into each other's eyes — "it's killing me to see you like this. We both know what's around the corner." She drew a faltering breath. "And that it's not far off. Isn't there anything you want to do? Visit somewhere you love? See someone special? Even just binge on some TV show? This isn't..."

"Isn't what? Healthy?" She sniggered.

"How about visiting Izzy again? There's always a chance she'll wake up. Imagine how wonderful that would be."

Guilt gnawed at Rachel over giving up on Izzy, but when she had so little time left, it felt like she had to pick — give up on Izzy or give up on Wes.

340

Mom said, "There must be something, sweetheart. When time is so precious, I don't want you to waste a single second of it."

"I love you, Mom."

Mom's eyes teared up. "Try for me. Please. I lost Wesley, I can't lose you, too."

"But you're going to. I'm sorry. You know there's nothing anyone can do."

"But we could delay it and spend more time together."

"It's been nearly five months. The doctor gave me six max."

"But it could be longer if you'd take all the medication they recommend and if you'd get some proper nourishment inside you. How about one of the clinical trials the doctor suggested?"

Rachel pinched the bridge of her nose. "Mom, it took almost four minutes to walk from the bathroom just now. Four minutes to make it maybe fifty steps. And that was with you helping."

"I don't mind helping, sweetheart. That's why I'm here."

"You're missing the point. What I'm saying is, no matter what we do, it's only going to get worse. Is that living?" She paused and drew a breath. Not for dramatic effect but because talking was such an effort. "No decent human being would dream of making an animal suffer like this, so why must a person? At some point, you just have to say enough is enough."

Mom turned away, her shoulders trembling.

Rachel held Mom's arm. "I'm sorry, Mom. But we're lucky in a way."

Mom turned back, her cheeks glistening. "Lucky? In what way is any of this lucky?"

"Some people never get to tell their loved ones how much they mean to them."

Izzy hadn't. That first month, Rachel had all but lived at Izzy's bedside, talking and talking and talking, trying to reach her friend, trying to bring her back. But Izzy wasn't there. The doctors didn't hold out much hope she ever would be.

Mom flung her arms around Rachel. She sobbed.

"It's okay," said Rachel. "Everything's going to be okay."

She gazed over her mother's shoulder, through the window, away into the trees. Waiting. Waiting for the slightest sign of movement.

But as was always the case, the only thing that moved was the trees as the lonely wind howled through their bare branches.

***

As the weeks passed, snow fell from gray skies, once more topping the mountains in the distance, then slowly enveloping the mountainside, like the sky was melting over the landscape.

Rachel's breathing wheezed as she stared. She'd marveled at this winter spectacle every year but had never taken the time to simply sit and watch it literally blossoming before her eyes. It was stunning.

Mom drew the brush through Rachel's hair, standing behind her chair, then smoothed her hand over it.

"I used to do this for you when you were tiny." Mom combed again. "Do you remember? One hundred strokes because you'd read it in a fairy tale. One hundred exactly or you'd refuse to go to sleep."

Rachel's lips curled into the tiniest of smiles. "I remember." Another wheezing breath.

"I could read to you. Like I did then."

Rachel stared at the treeline. The unmoving treeline. The treeline that stood so, so still, as if determined to taunt her until her dying breath.

"Rachel?"

Rachel ran her gaze over the trees. Squinted. There had to be something. Something sometime.

"Rachel?"

"Yeah, I'll eat something later."

Mom sighed and stopped brushing. Moving around, she crouched at the side of the chair and held Rachel's arm.

Rachel turned from the window and smiled at her, then turned back.

Mom squeezed her arm, so again Rachel turned.

"Listen to me, sweetheart. I know what you think you saw that day, but there's no guarantee you really did. With the pain you must've been in – goodness, you even died, for crying out loud – who's to say what was real and what was your mind playing tricks on you to help you cope?"

"I saw them, Mom."

"And I believe you believe that, sweetheart. But can't you hear how it sounds?"

"I know just how it sounds. And not long ago, I'd have thought just what you're thinking – that it's utter bull poop. But I saw what I saw."

Mom cupped Rachel's hand in both of hers. "I just worry you're going to be so hurt if all this precious time is wasted because what you want to happen never happens."

"I won't. Don't worry."

"Isn't there anything you want to do? Anything at all before it's too late? You know I'll help any way I can."

Rachel arched her eyebrows. "You want to help?"

"Of course, I do. Why would you ever think I don't?"

"Then be with me, Mom. Just be with me. Pull that chair over and sit. That's all I want. Just be with me. Nothing else."

Mom hauled another chair over, its casters rumbling over the hardwood floor. She sat, reached over, and took Rachel's hand.

Mom wiped a tear away. Rachel waited for her to say something else, to try to convince her to change her mind. But she didn't. She just held Rachel's hand and stared out of the window with her.

With a hushed voice, Rachel said, "Thank you."

Mom gently squeezed Rachel's hand in reply.

***

Week by week, the snows swept across the valley, burying everything under an icy shroud. Before long, nothing was left but whiteness and the wind howling through the trees, their branches like dark, crooked fingers clawing at the sky.

Still Rachel stared. Waiting. Her breath shallow, raspy pants.

Dark against the gray sky, a bird fluttered into the trees and disappeared, but nobody and nothing else moved. It never did. It was as if she and Mom were the only beings left in the entire world.

Mom shuffled back from the kitchen and put a tray in Rachel's lap. A gigantic expanse of white porcelain surrounded a minuscule morsel of chicken breast, like a vast desert imprisoning a tiny oasis. Mom had already cut the meat into pieces that would be called bite-sized for a small child. She placed a spork in Rachel's hand.

"Thank you." The words came out so quietly, Rachel might as well have mouthed them.

Mom lifted a book off the seat alongside, then sat. "Now, where were we?"

She opened *Wuthering Heights* and slipped out the leather bookmark. She read aloud, "'My great miseries in this world have been Heathcliff's miseries, and I watched and felt each from the beginning: my great thought in living is himself. If all else perished, and he remained, I should still continue to be; and if all else remained, and he were annihilated, the universe would turn to a mighty stranger: I should not seem a part of it.'"

Rachel stabbed a piece of chicken with the spork and lifted, but it fell off. She tried again, managing to push that little harder. The spork's fat tines held the meat, so she popped it in her mouth, chewing with all the ferocity of a cow chewing cud.

All the while, she gazed away into the trees and snatched another stolen breath.

It was taking so long. So very long. But they'd come. One day. She just had to be patient. And wait.

Then they'd all walk and laugh and play. And Wes wouldn't have the troubles he'd had. He'd still be her Wes — still be funny and awkward and loving and infuriating, still be "him" — but he'd be more. So much more than he could ever have been here.

Yes, one day they'd come.

One day.

She just had to be patient and watch for them. Always watch. She didn't want to miss the moment they finally came for her.

But she was just so tired. So unbelievably tired. Keeping her eyes open felt like holding up the whole world.

She fought and fought to watch, but...

Her eyelids drooped.

And drooped.

And drooped.

Closed.

The world ebbed away.

Mom called her name, her tone urgent, desperate. But getting more and more distant. As if she were speaking from the far end of a long tunnel. How odd.

The light bleeding through Rachel's eyelids became darker, while the wind rustling through the trees became fainter.

Her world became silent and still and black, until everything...

Stopped.

...

...

...

Cold and clammy.
Rachel smiled. *Finally.*

The End.

(The Warm and Fuzzy ending follows.)

Chapter 73B

Rachel smiled, driving past her trailhead. She eased down on the gas as the road curved upward to the left, trees lining either side, with conifers becoming more predominant the higher they climbed.

In the passenger seat, Izzy said, "I spy with my little eye something beginning with" — she paused for dramatic effect — "t."

Immediately, Wes shouted, "Tree!"

"Yes!" Izzy clapped while Wes laughed. "Your turn."

Wes said, "I spy with my little eye something beginning with" — he paused for dramatic effect too — "t."

Izzy said, "Tree!"

Wes clapped. "Yes. Your turn."

"I spy with my little eye something beginning with" — Izzy paused — "t."

Wes shouted, "Tree!" He held his stomach, laughing so much his eyes watered.

Smiling, Rachel said, "Okay, okay, okay. Unless you want me to drive off the side of this mountain, someone's little eye better spy something other than a tree pretty darn fast."

Izzy saluted, adopting a stern, deep voice. "Aye-aye, Captain. Should I flog the child for mutiny, sir?"

Rachel shook her head. "It's a five-hour drive to my mom's. Remind me why I insisted you come."

"Oh dear, Wes," said Izzy, "it looks like we've got a grumpy chauffeur today. How about another game? Do you know the 'I'm going on an adventure' game?"

He shook his head.

"Oh, you'll love it. You have to imagine you're going on a great adventure — which should be easy because we are — and you say what you're going to see. For example, 'I'm going on a great adventure and I'm going to see a tiger.' Then the next person has to repeat that and add one thing on the end, so something like, 'I'm going on a great adventure and I'm going to see a tiger and a mountain.' Then the next person has to remember those two things and add another one. Do you want to try?"

He nodded.

Rachel nodded too. "That's good. He loves lists."

"Do you want to go first, Wes?" asked Izzy.

He nodded again.

Izzy said, "So you say 'I'm going on a great adventure and I'm going to see...' and then say whatever you like."

Wes said, "I'm going on a great adventure and I'm going to see... a tree."

Izzy laughed.

Rachel shot her a sideways glance. "Don't you dare."

Izzy smirked. "I'm going on a great adventure and..."

Rachel said, "You'll be walking. I'm warning you."

"... I'm going to see a tree and..."

"I can pull over, right here, right now."

"... another tree."

Wes belly laughed so loud, it startled Harley who'd been dozing. He barked.

Rachel couldn't resist smiling. With the pleasure Wes was getting out of such silly games, it was impossible not to. "You know you're flying home, don't you?"

Izzy playfully slapped her arm. "But it's your turn, Rach."

Rachel heaved a sigh. "I'm going on a great adventure and I'm going to see a tree and" — she arched an eyebrow at Izzy — "another tree and..." — a cheeky grin spread across her face — "another tree."

"Yay!" Izzy clapped, so Wes joined in.

Climbing higher, they continued playing games as they left the woodland behind and wound their way through the mountain range, the road clinging to the mountainside.

"I love it up here." Rachel snatched a glance at the wooded valley below, stretching away to a glistening lake against a backdrop of snowcapped mountains.

Izzy nodded. "It's like from Nat Geo."

Rachel's phone rang. The caller ID said "Vet."

"Why's your vet calling? I thought the results weren't due till Monday."

Rachel shrugged. "That's what she said." She took the call. "Hello?"

"Hi , it's Claudia from The Pet People. Harley's results have come in early, so I wanted to—"

Rachel's heart pounded. The incredible life they'd developed over the last few months might be about to be ripped apart.

Her knuckles whitened on the steering wheel. "I'm sorry, Claudia, but we're having a family weekend away, so the last thing we want is bad news. Can this wait till Monday, please?"

"That's why I'm calling — it's not bad news. I won't go into detail if you're away, but the condition is completely manageable. If you'd like to book an appointment when you get back, I'll take you through the treatment options."

"That's fantastic."

"It is, isn't it? Anyway, I know how precious Harley is to you, so wanted to let you know as soon as possible."

"Thank you, I really appreciate that."

"You're welcome. Enjoy the rest of your weekend." She hung up.

Rachel beamed as tears ran down her face. Everything was going to be okay. Deep down, she'd expected the worst after the string of bad luck they'd had. But this? This was everything she'd prayed for.

Izzy gripped Rachel's shoulder. "I told you it would work out."

"Uh-huh." Rachel sniffled. "Can you pass me a tissue, please?" She gestured to the glove box.

Izzy poked through the contents. "Are you sure you have some?"

"I bought some recently." Rachel craned to look as much as she felt safe doing while driving, snatching a look in the compartment, then back at the road, then again to the compartment as Izzy shoved things about.

A horn blared.

Rachel snapped fully back into driving mode. She'd drifted out of her lane. An oncoming truck honked its horn again.

She yanked the wheel and swerved out of danger.

Rachel exhaled loudly. "I think we'll forget the tissues."

Izzy nodded, gripping the seat belt across her chest with both hands.

Rachel looked in the rearview mirror. "Okay back there?"

Wes nodded, seemingly oblivious to the close call.

One at a time, she wiped her palms on her jeans and eased off the gas. There was no rush to get to Mom's, and the last thing they wanted was some silly distraction sending them hurtling over the precipice.

Rachel's gaze glued to the road, she focused on negotiating the hairpin bends, Izzy sitting silently. As the road hugged the mountain's contours, they snaked around a bend to the left, then one to the right, a flimsy-looking metal barrier the only thing between them and a drop that seemed to fall away forever.

A length of straight road ahead, and the precipice a couple of car widths away across rough ground, Rachel relaxed and accelerated away.

Izzy said, "I spy..."

Rachel rolled her eyes, but smiled, Izzy's gesture evaporating the tense atmosphere in the car instantly.

"... with my little eye..."

Rachel shot Izzy a sideways glance and sniggered. "Don't you dare." The nearest trees were over the edge and way, way down the mountainside, so surely Izzy wouldn't. Would she?

Izzy smirked. "... something beginning with..."

Rachel winced. Please not t, please not t, please not t.

"... t."

"God give me strength." Rachel glanced to the heavens as Wes burst into hysterics.

Behind them, a red pickup truck pulled out and gunned the engine. As he drew alongside, an almighty bang made Rachel jump. A hunk of tattered black rubber crashed into her door window, shattering it.

Izzy shrieked.

Instinctively, Rachel yanked the steering wheel and swerved away from the pickup. But with a blown-out tire, the truck driver lost control. His vehicle veered toward them. It slammed them in the side.

Rachel's car careened right. She hammered the brakes, but the edge of the mountain hurtled toward them. Closer and closer. She flung the wheel around, desperate to swerve clear of the edge. But they were too close. Going too fast...

Rachel screamed. The car flew over the edge and soared through the air.

For a moment, the world froze. The scene through the windshield was a picturesque landscape of the lake and mountain range that could grace any calendar.

Time resumed, and the car pitched downward, the beautiful view replaced by crushing rocks and rushing trees. Cries erupted inside, as if someone had bottled the essence of a lunatic asylum.

The wheels hammered into the hillside. Like a roller coaster in a nightmare, the car thundered down the incline, Rachel instinctively gripping the wheel as if she had some control.

Bouncing and thumping, jerking and jolting, the vehicle tore ever downward. Bushes, trees, and rocks blurred past.

Rachel stretched back between the seats, trying to reach Wes, but the car shot over a flat rocky outcropping and once more plummeted through the air.

Massive gnarled tree trunks raced toward them. Rachel flung her arms up to shield her head.

With a devastating crunch, the front driver's side hit a trunk, spinning the car around. The passenger side slammed into another tree full-on. The car dropped, the driver's side smashing into the ground like a bird shot out of the sky by a shotgun blast.

Stillness descended.

Chapter 74B

Rachel heaved a breath.

Crunched over on her left side, her face warm and wet, as if a soggy piece of muslin had been draped over it, she strained to open her eyes. Her right eye refused to respond, but her left eyelid flickered up and a sliver of light bled in.

The world was a blurry smudge of colors lying on its side.

Where was she?

Horrific images flashed through her mind: the truck blowout, the hillside plummet, the car crash-landing on its side.

She gasped again. Wes!

She twisted to check on everyone but screeched as pain stabbed her right shoulder and both legs.

Blackness.

Chapter 75B

One eye opened again.

Her voice thin, Rachel said, "W-W-Wesley...?"

No answer.

She panted, as if she'd run up the mountainside, not careered down it. Her voice barely a whisper, she said, "Izzy...?"

Nothing.

The only sound, branches above her creaking in the breeze.

Shrieking as knives sliced through her side, she turned a few degrees to her right to look upward through her only working eye. Above her, a blurred shape that looked like Izzy dangled limply, held in the seat by the seat belt. The shape gurgled as it breathed.

Alive!

Thank heavens. And if the two of them were, the rear passengers should be as well.

"Har-Harley?" Harley was smart. So unbelievably smart. If he could reach the road, he'd make someone understand they needed help.

Or maybe she could. The steering column had dropped to pin her legs, but if she could pry the unit up a couple of inches, maybe she could wiggle out.

She gripped the wheel with both hands and heaved.

She cried out as if red-hot spears were thrust into her thighs.

Slumping forward, she collapsed over the wheel. Gasping.

She couldn't give up. She *wouldn't* give up. She had to save them all. Had to. If she could only...

Gathering her strength, she heaved to push up and try again. She strained and strained against the steering wheel, but couldn't even raise off it, let alone then lift it. She slumped over it, breath wheezing.

Her lips moved, barely, but she didn't have the energy to make even the tiniest of sounds.

This was the end.

She'd believed it would be the cancer that ended her, but boy, was she wrong. The cancer was a gift — if she hadn't had it, she'd never have put everything in place to give Wes the life he deserved with Harley and Izzy. She imagined she was smiling, though she didn't know if she was. Who would've thought it — cancer was one of the best things to ever happen to her.

The last of her strength ebbing away, Rachel fought to stay present, to stay with Wesley, even though she couldn't see or hear him. She fought to keep her one eye open.

Just one more second with her son. Just one!

But she was so tired. So unbelievably tired. Keeping her eye open felt like holding up the whole world.

She fought and fought, but...

Her eyelid drooped.

And drooped.

And drooped.

Closed.

She didn't want to leave Wes — didn't want to miss him growing into a man and achieving things all the experts had said were impossible — but instead of loss, she felt peace. Surprising. Izzy was right. For Rachel's life to have played out like this, there had to be more. More than just a random sequence of events and unrelated coincidences.

Much more.

She'd be with Wes. Always. Watching over him — and Harley, without whom none of this would have been possible — until the day they were reunited.

The light bleeding through her eyelids faded.

The rustling of the wind through the trees came from farther and farther away.

The world slowed as if time was caught in thick mud, as all around her became silent and still and very, very dark, until everything...

Stopped.

Chapter 76B

blackness

emptiness

silence

Chapter 77B

The dark quiet faded. As if someone were turning up the volume of the world, sounds swirled around Rachel – a breeze gusting through trees heavy with leaves, birdsong like a glorious dawn chorus, a stream babbling around stones as insects skated across its surface.

A smell tantalized her – freshly opened flowers reaching for the sun. Chrysanthemums. Her favorite.

The darkness transformed into light, the inside of her eyelids bright red, aglow with life. Her eyes flickered open and blinding light flooded in. Too bright.

And a voice.

Distant. But getting closer. As if the person was moving at tremendous speed from a long way away to right beside her.

A voice she knew. A voice she loved.

"Hey, sweetheart."

Mom.

Rachel moved her mouth to speak but only croaked.

Mom held a glass of water to Rachel's lips. "Just a drop."

Rachel sipped as shapes appeared in the brightness. She tried to take the glass, but her right arm wouldn't move.

Her voice wheezed. "Where...?"

Mom caressed her brow. "Hospital, sweetheart. Nearly a week now."

"I thou..." Rachel swallowed and licked her lips. "I thought I'd... died and..." She shook her head. That didn't matter now.

"You were so lucky, sweetheart. The paramedics brought you back. They said if they'd arrived just one minute later..." She sniffled. "But they didn't." She smiled. "And you're here."

The dazzling brightness faded to reveal a hospital room, all whites and pastel blues. Her left leg was suspended above the bed in a cast and her right arm was in a cast too, with a cannula in the back of that hand hooked up to an IV. She couldn't feel a thing, so she was obviously on powerful painkillers.

A vase of chrysanthemums stood on a table at the foot of the bed, another on the bedside cabinet beside a portable CD player.

Mom clicked the stop button and the sounds of the woodland disappeared. "I brought it from home. I hoped it might bring you back to me." She smiled at Rachel, her eyes teary.

"Wes...?"

Mom held Rachel's hand. "He's fine. But you have to concentrate on getting yourself better, Rachel. You can think about everyone else later."

Fine? *Fine?* How could he possibly be *fine* with the mess she was in? "He-he'll worry. I-I need to see him."

Mom looked away while she dabbed her eyes with a tissue.

Was something wrong? Dread sliced through Rachel like a surgeon had slashed her open without anesthetic.

Rachel's chin quivered. She hadn't been able to turn to look at Wes or Harley in the car and she hadn't heard a sound from either of them. But if she and Izzy had survived, he must have too.

Oh God, what if he hadn't?

Her voice cracked as she said, "Mom, wh-where's Wes?"

"Rach?" Izzy stood in the doorway, head bandaged and right arm across her chest in a sling, a can of soda in each hand. She covered her mouth. "Oh, Rach, thank heavens." Her bruised face twisted as if she were in pain but then she broke into a beaming smile.

"Iz." Thank the Lord, Izzy *was* okay. So where was her Wesley?

Limping, Izzy shuffled toward her.

"Where's Wes, Iz?"

"Wes?"

"For God's sake, where's my son?"

Izzy pointed to the doorway. "Here."

Rachel gasped as Wes ambled in as casually as if he'd just come from watching TV on their sofa, a bag of potato chips in one hand, a dog leash in the other. Harley hobbled alongside, his right front leg in a cast. Wes held an open palm out to Harley to offer a chip. Harley gently gobbled it up.

Tears streamed Rachel's cheeks. Streamed so much the world blurred once more. She dragged her left hand over her eyes.

Izzy said, "Wes...?" When he glanced toward her, she pointed at Rachel. "You're missing something."

Wes looked sideways from under his bangs toward the bed. His jaw dropped. He turned and gawked at Rachel. His voice soft as if he was unsure of what he was seeing, he said, "Mom?"

Rachel reached for him, so choked she couldn't speak.

He shouted, "Mom!" He scurried to her bedside, Harley bounding with him, and clasped her free hand.

Harley whimpered.

"Hey, kiddo." She squeezed his hand. And he let her. For a few seconds at least, then he pulled away. Her cheeks glistening, Rachel beamed at him, her incredible son who didn't appear to have a scratch on him.

After resting the sodas on the table as she passed, Izzy leaned down and hugged Rachel, sobbing into her shoulder. Her voice shuddering, she said, "I thought we'd lost you."

"Me too," said Rachel, clinging onto her friend.

Izzy broke away. Shaking her head, she smiled down at Rachel while she dragged her fingers over her wet face. "You know, next time someone says 'I spy with my little eye something beginning with *t*', you can just *say* tree, you don't have to crash into one."

Rachel chuckled. "Okay. I'll try to remember."

Beside her, Harley whimpered again.

Turning, Rachel found the saddest, biggest brown eyes she'd ever seen peering up at her. Obviously, he ached to celebrate their reunion but sensing her condition, feared he wasn't allowed.

Rachel smiled at him. "Awww, sorry, Harley. Did you think I'd forgotten you?" She patted the bed.

Tail swishing so much his whole body wiggled, he eased his front paws onto the bed and gently raised up, his cautious gaze watching for any objection.

Rachel stroked his neck. "Sorry boy, but it looks like we won't be running for a while. But not too long. Promise." She kissed his forehead.

Harley nuzzled her cheek. Cold and clammy.

She chuckled again and hugged him.

Over the last year, she'd battled cancer, Wes had almost died in a fire, and Harley had lost his best friend and his home. They'd survived the worst the world had to throw at them. In fact, not just survived it, but flourished in spite of it. Whatever came next didn't matter because they were a family — a proper family — so they'd face it together and beat it together. No matter what nightmare threatened, it didn't stand a chance against them.

She beamed at her family. *Her* amazing family.

The End.

Turn the page...

Where the Echo Calls

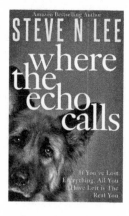

Sometimes a dog isn't just a dog — it's your whole world.

Left for dead in the gutter, Rio struggles to his feet and lurches into the shadows for a place to hide. Life has always been brutal, thanks to a monster of an owner, but at least he'd had food, a bed, a place to call home. Now...?

Ben's life ended when he lost his family. Drink no longer dulls the pain; therapy is a joke; friends have moved on. He'd had everything, yet now...?

But when the broken man meets the broken dog, they discover something neither had ever dreamed could exist... a reason to go on.

In a story as heartwarming as it is heartbreaking, *When the Echo Calls* explores how hope can be found in the most unexpected of places if only we have the courage to look for it.

Get *Where the Echo Calls*. Use this link:
www.stevenleebooks.com/echo

Free Book

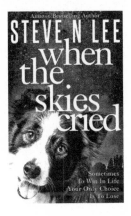

An exclusive ebook for *When the Skies Cry* readers only.

If you enjoyed *When the Skies Cry*, you need the accompanying ebook written by Steve especially for you. In this book, you will:

> discover how the story came about after Steve had said he'd never write another dog book

> unravel how the characters were created and what makes them tick

> uncover a huge secret Steve has lined up for his next dog story

> learn how researching the issues the story explores was undertaken

> read what story developments Steve wanted to put in the story, but decided not to

> enjoy a revealing interview with Steve

> have an extensive selection of Book Club Questions

> find out which parts of the story were unplanned and came about "magically" during the writing

> and learn much, much more.

You'll also join Steve's VIP Readers Group to get news about his books, discounts, behind-the-scenes gossip on the writing process, personal adventures he goes on...

Get When the Skies Cried. Use this link now:
www.stevenleebooks.com/cried

Made in the USA
Coppell, TX
15 July 2023

19188068R00215

Running Home

35 Moving Meditations for Runners

by
Toby Estler

Robert D. Reed Publishers • Bandon, OR

Copyright © 2007 by Toby Estler

All rights reserved.

Robert D. Reed Publishers
P.O. Box 1992
Bandon, OR 97411
Phone: 541-347-9882 • Fax: -9883
E-mail: 4bobreed@msn.com
web site: www.rdrpublishers.com

Editor: Cleone Lyvonne
Cover: Cleone Lyvonne
Author Photos: Angus Ross
Illustrations: Kim Garrison
Typesetter: Barbara Kruger

ISBN 978-1-931741-81-1

Library of Congress Control Number 2006907514

Manufactured, typeset and printed in the United States of America

Dedication

For Teresa and Hayden.
Home is where the heart is.

Acknowledgments

Thank you Jacques and Dawn for the very first home; Teresa and Hayden for the unconditional loving, support, encouragement, and patience; the Renner clan for "adopting" me; Steve Chandler for bringing the game alive; Heidi Buckland for assisting so lovingly with the birth; my band of additional, cherished proof readers: Karen Romine, Angela Phipps Towle (my prayer is that you are at home now), DJ King, Elyssa Nelson, James Price, and Tara Carson; John-Roger for the inner space; Rev. Dr. Michael Beckwith for the introduction to God; Drs. Ron and Mary Hulnick for holding the vision; all the staff, faculty, volunteers, students, and grads at the University of Santa Monica for daring to leap; USM classes of 2002 and 2006: you saw all of me and loved me all the more; James, Lynn, and Tara, for the unconditional love, the irreverence, and the head caught in deerlights; Johnny Seitz for the outstretched hand; Tim Brady for showing me what fatherhood could offer; Elana Golden for honoring my first writings; Jack Grapes for all the new voices; Robert Carroll for the invitation; Judi Kaufman for that first big stage; Brad Silver, Richard Jones, and all the Art of the Brain family for the courage and inspiration; Robert Reed for the opportunity; Cleone Lyvonne for the enthusiasm and caring attention; Lucy ("Looch") for the gifts of education, transportation, and freedom; Carolyn Freyer-Jones for keeping the days Light-filled; John Hruby for the humor; Connor Hruby for the hellos; Amy Hruby for encouraging me to ask for what I want; Angus Ross for the photos, the rumble, and the lunches; Kim Garrison for the cabin and the gorgeous illustrations; the millions of runners who get it done, day after day; Natalia for being you—it's all good baby; all the Brighton Anarchists for a magical awakening; Jez McDonald for Poland and so much more; all those early friends who helped to awaken my heart: Tim, Julian, Jerry, Sarah, Louisa, Meredith, Rachael, Jessica, and the other Toby; Ray for the second home; myself for the courageous way I live my life; Spirit for the amazing dance of bringing all these angels into my life; and God for keeping me safe all along the way . . . and for the welcome home.

Contents

Introduction

"The earth seemed almost to move with me. I was running now, and a fresh rhythm entered my body. No longer conscious of my movement I discovered a new unity with nature. I had found a source of power and beauty, a source I never dreamt existed."
Roger Bannister, *The Four-Minute Mile*

On May 6, 1954, Roger Bannister became the first human to run a mile in under four minutes—an accomplishment as groundbreaking as the first landing on the moon. Yet the quotation above is not, as one might think, from the height of Roger Bannister's record-breaking career. It does not describe that first, illustrious sub-four-minute mile. It is not the peak experience of a highly trained athlete. It is a memory from his childhood: the experience of a young boy so filled with the beauty of the beach surrounding him that he ran for joy—and discovered the majesty of running.

This experience is available to all of us, and certainly to those who give themselves to running. For when we give ourselves to running, we give ourselves to the very best that life has to offer.

As I have run over the last 15 years, I have discovered deepening layers of tranquility: a new stillness, an expanded sense of freedom, and a peace and joy previously unknown to me. In these moments, I feel "on," in the zone. I am connected with the environment around me. Not just to it, but as a part of it. I cease to be a spectator of my surroundings and become immersed in them. I am able to think more clearly and creatively, and problem solve faster. I find myself more open to the miracle of inspiration than ever before. In this way, running has become a moving meditation for me, and the doorway to a new, more spiritual approach to life.

For many years, this wonderful experience during running was a refuge that I could turn to at any time. When things weren't going well in other areas of my life, I could always find shelter in running. I ran my way out of both drug and alcohol addiction.

Yet, while running was an incredible sanctuary, it remained just that: somewhere outside of the rest of my life that I would retreat to—a beautiful, peaceful, and private island that I visited as many times as I could each week. There was running, and then there was the rest of my life.

As the miles rolled by, I would think, "If only I could feel like this for a larger part of each day. If only I could take this feeling into the rest of my life, into my job, and into my relationships with my family and friends." While the calming and uplifting effects of my run might last into the late morning, by the afternoon they would be crowded out by the business of living. Then, for the rest of the day, I would either be daydreaming about that morning's run, or about where I would be running the following morning.

I knew one way that I could extend my experience—by running longer. This certainly supported my marathon training! I began to run further and further in preparation, but I eventually had to concede that there was a limit to how far I would be able to run each day and have any other life! For the majority of runners, even competing professional athletes, the fact is we are *not* running for 22 or 23 hours out of each 24. For most of us, most of the time, we run between one and two hours a day. The answer, it seemed, was to somehow remove the protective barrier I had placed between my running and the other areas of my life.

So I began taking my life into my running and bringing my running more fully into my life. My goal was to initiate a conversation between my running and the other areas of my life, so that running no longer insulated me *from* life, but rather propelled me *toward* the very best in life. I began to bring a more conscious, meditational focus to a number of my workouts each week.

This book is the result of this shift in approach. It contains 35 ways to bring this focus to your running, which can help create a seamless flow between your exercise, your passion, and your wider life. Through using the guided meditations in this book, the great majority of which have been written to be used *while you run*, you can focus upon and actively prepare yourself for a deepening of the energizing and uplifting experiences that running has to offer.

You may also discover that your running improves. As your present-moment awareness increases, the level of your performance and personal satisfaction will also increase. Physically, you'll get more miles to the gallon. In other words, you'll find that you can use less energy to cover the same distance and recover quicker from your runs. On a mental level, with increasing frequency you'll find solutions to work and other challenges without actively thinking about them. With the help of this book, you can learn to focus not so much on looking for a solution, but on *preparing a place for the solution to appear*.

Running is certainly a wonderful experience in and of itself. It can be a vehicle through which to establish, nurture, and deepen our relationship with the divine inside of us. As a result of your focused and intentional running, you will feel more balanced, and for longer periods of time. Simply, and through conscious intention, you can enjoy the peace and calm of your workouts throughout your day. Beyond that, even, can be the experience not just of running, but the sensation of *being run*.

The aim of this book is threefold. First, to support those of you who are existing runners in building upon the levels of freedom, peace, and expansiveness that you enjoy in your running. To assist you in carrying those qualities deeper into your lives—into your relationship with yourself and others, into your workplace, and into your wider world so that it is infused with the joy and possibility you experience when running.

Second, to support both existing and new runners in bringing more *into* their running, by consciously preparing not just physically, but also mentally, emotionally, and spiritually. By bringing a focused awareness to your runs, you can connect with the experience of who you truly are: not a human being with a soul, but rather a soul—a spiritual being—having a human experience.

Third, this book is here to *welcome* those new to running, encouraging them to embrace running as so much more than mere physical exercise. Running is not only a tool for relaxing and strengthening the body. It can also ease the mind and free the soul.

Each chapter can certainly be used more than once. The wonder of this approach to running is that the meditations will meet you wherever you are in your life. You can return to a particular meditation when it seems appropriate and experience it in a new way—because you will be coming from a new place.

Why *Running Home*? This book is here to support you in running home to your heart, to your dreams, and deeper into your spiritual life.

Each day as I set out on my run, I remember that the place I am headed for is the place that I am about to leave—that I am running home. It may be a 20-minute loosener or a 20-mile training run; either way my destination is home. I like to think of the soul's journey as the same. We are all journeying home to the place we started from, the very heart of God (whatever that means for you). For some of us, the journey may be longer than others; in the end, we will all make it home.

How to Use This Book

Each chapter of this book contains certain significant elements to support each reader in gaining the most value from their experience. The major elements are outlined below, along with a handful of suggestions in approach.

Qualities
Each meditation is anchored with a quality, such as courage, independence, or forgiveness. Each chapter's quality provides an over-arching theme, which offers a context for the material that follows. In running terms, this part of the chapter lays out the course.

Quotations
Quotations will illuminate the chapter's quality. They have been chosen to lead readers into the energy of the day's meditation theme. The first quotation is drawn from someone who is regarded highly in the world of running: a runner, a coach, or an author who writes with runners specifically in mind. The second is drawn from a wider circle of inspirational figures. In running terms, these uplifting snapshots will bring you to the starting line, poised and prepared.

Meditations
Next comes the heart of the chapter, often illustrated with details from my own running and wider life, which will elaborate upon the theme for the meditation and give clear directions on how to

approach it to gain the maximum value available. In running terms, this is the run itself.

Affirmations
Introduced in Chapter 2, and included in each subsequent chapter, is a suggested affirmation to help you keep your focus on the particular meditation that you are using on that given day. In running terms, these are the fuel stations along the way, keeping you fresh and strong.

Other Suggestions

The book has been written so that each chapter builds upon the previous one. When approaching the book for the first time, I would suggest that, for the most part, you follow the chapters in order.

The chapters have been written so that they are able to adapt to a timeline that works best for each individual. You can use a different chapter each day, or you can work with one chapter for a week, a month, even a year! In my own practice, I tend to choose a chapter to focus on for the week, while occasionally interspersing that with other daily meditations, as my life requires them.

I have found that if I read the meditation for the following day before I go to bed the previous night, in addition to reading it just before I set out for my run, I journey deeper into the material during my workout. You may want to try the same approach.

Keeping a journal to record my thoughts and inspirations after I return from my runs helps me to anchor the insights that I gain. You may want to create such a journal for yourself, too.

The meditations do not have to be used by runners alone. I have friends that have used many of the meditations whilst walking, cycling, swimming, and even as part of their sitting meditation practice. Feel free to adapt this book to fit your life!

After completing the book for the first time, you can return to any of the meditations, as you feel called. You may find that you revisit certain chapters many times. The wonder of this is that each chapter will meet your current situation, offering new insights, fresh learnings, and greater clarity.

Above all, have fun!

"Movement is what creates life. Stillness is what creates love. To be still and still moving . . . that is everything."

Do Hyun Choe, Sugi master

1

Setting Out

Quality: Clear Intention

*"For all of us, the miracle isn't that we finish, the miracle is
that we have the courage to start."*
John Bingham
The Courage To Start: A Guide To Running Your Life

*"Your own resolution to success
is more important than any other one thing."*
Abraham Lincoln

I am sure that I am not alone among runners in the
precision of my preparation before each run. I have my
favorite shirt, my most comfortable socks (that need to be
pulled up just-so on my ankles), and my shoes need to be
laced just right—then I feel fully prepared to step out of the
house. I know that I am going to get the most out of my run.

As runners, we feel comfortable spending time preparing
our physical bodies for exercise: clothes, water bottles,
snacks, warming up, and stretching. This is often the full
extent of our preparation, and there is an opportunity to
prepare ourselves on still other levels, too. Through a
holistic, multilayered approach, which you will learn more of

in this and following chapters, you can open yourself up to a broader and deeper experience during your workouts. This enables your running to be even more uplifting, energizing, and healing.

By setting an intention before the start of each run, you can also place your workout in a spiritual context. Clear intention supports you in bringing the spotlight of your conscious awareness onto a specific area of focus. When you set a conscious intention, you are letting the universe know that you are plotting a course for higher ground. You enlist the support of Spirit.

When I began my life as a runner, my intention was to become fit enough to run for 30 minutes without stopping. After 15 years of heavy smoking (40 to 60 cigarettes a day), this was no short order. Yet, supported by the power of my intention and the foundation and focus it gave my workouts, after a number of weeks I got there. I discovered the gift of resolve and strength of heart (literally and figuratively) that I had not known I possessed. This is an example of the grace available through the power of clear intention.

If you are a beginning runner, you too may want to focus your intention on supporting your new running resolution. Clear intention is also a powerful tool for established runners. You could set an intention to run with ease at an increased speed, or—conversely—to have the patience and maturity to hold yourself to a slower pace. One intention I use (a lot!) is to remember that my long-term training is better served by not treating every workout as a race!

On some days, the focus for your intention will be immediately clear and may well come from "outside" of your running life—concerns at home or a situation at work, perhaps. These are wonderful opportunities to use the regenerative and uplifting energy of your run as an avenue for grace to flow into these areas as well. By no means are intentions to be used solely in response to the negative—though they can be a powerful foundation for the increased conscious commitment needed to return to our essential, loving nature when we are out of balance.

If you are in a disagreement with a spouse or loved one, you might want to set the intention to find greater understanding for his point of view, or to find greater compassion for her situation. Perhaps there is a co-worker that you are angry with—you could set the intention to release that anger and find your way to a more neutral feeling toward that person.

There may be occasions when you are angry or disappointed with yourself—perhaps for something you have said or done. You are convinced you could have done better. In these times, you might set an intention to find forgiveness for yourself, to give yourself the gift of your own caring, and to learn from your experience.

There will be times when nothing is pressing for attention, and these days can hold the richest opportunities. I find I can open myself up for greater guidance from Spirit. I may set an intention to experience greater clarity as to what my next steps in life may be. I may set an intention to open myself more fully to Spirit's blessings. One favorite intention is to experience the unique and tender energy of gratitude at a deeper level. This is the gratitude I feel for the simple and miraculous blessings in my life—for the food on my table, for my family and friends, for the strong and healthy body that carries me on my run each day. On these days I often find myself weeping with joy as I run—I return home feeling as though the space inside of me has doubled in size.

So today, and each day before you set out for your run, make time to consciously set an intention. Take a few moments to be still and listen to what comes to heart. When setting an intention, start with these words: "My intention is to..." Focus your intention in the positive. For example, rather than saying, "It is my intention not to feel angry by the end of my run," say, "It is my intention to use my run to return to a place of joy inside." If bringing a spiritual focus into your life is new for you, a wonderful intention can be to open to the experience of a clearer connection with Spirit. Trust your own inner guidance and, above all, enjoy the process!

Through the power of your intention each day, you will open yourself to the experience of grace. When you set an intention, you are charting a clear course for where you want to go—a signpost, not just for your mind, but also for every part of your being. You are mapping a metaphysical route that gives your consciousness direction and creates a space inside of you—and in your life—where Spirit can work its magic.

2

Staying on Track

Quality: Preparation

"You have within you, right now, all that you need to accomplish your realistic goals in running. Thinking like a champion will allow you to reach that potential. Remember that all your accomplishments are the direct result of your thoughts. When you choose the right kind of thoughts, you can create the running destiny you have always wanted."
Amby Burfoot
Runner's World Complete Book Of Running

"All that we are is the result of what we have thought. The mind is everything. What we think, we become."
Buddha

"If you think it's going to rain, it will."
Clint Eastwood

Whether you run with a friend or a group, in the gym or on your own, there is one person that will always be there—you! I do most of my running on my own, as it is an opportunity for me to spend valuable time with myself in the midst of a full life. Most of the time, this is very enjoyable. I have the opportunity to appreciate my surroundings, enjoying the neighborhoods and their characters as I pass by. It can be the perfect time to seek inspiration for projects I am working on, to enjoy some time in silence and heartfelt prayer, or to simply bask in the hypnotic rhythm of my moving body.

At least, most of the time. Every now and then, I will forget to check in with who is in the driver's seat of my mind before I set out. In the middle of my workout, I'll discover that I am expending most of my energy criticizing and chastising myself. It could be anything from complaining to myself about a missed credit card payment to revisiting an old argument. The good news is that the daily discipline of my run will usually wake me up and alert me to the fact that this internal critic is at the wheel. On the days that I do not run, I can go through an entire day without noticing that I am punishing myself in this way.

In these first several chapters, we are developing a checklist together for conscious running. In the previous chapter, we talked about preparing physically for our run, and also about placing our run in a spiritual context by setting an intention. It is equally as important to take a few moments to prepare ourselves mentally for our moving meditation work. You are a multidimensional being. By preparing yourself on more than just the physical level, you will enjoy running in an entirely new way.

If setting an intention is a way for you to set a clear course for where you want to go, then one of the most powerful vehicles to help you move forward along that course, and stay on it, is an affirmation. This can be said inwardly during your run, or you may want to say it out loud, whichever fits best for you. There have been days when I have sung mine in an operatic voice as I run along the shoreline, just for the fun of it! In its own way, your affirmation will find its way into your breathing pattern and into your running rhythm.

When I began the journey of healing from my 15-year smoking habit, I would affirm repeatedly, "I am running for

8

30 minutes, easily finding my breath." Be
sounded both unnatural and untrue! At the k
only a few strides, I would be wheezing and ~~have to stop~~
frequently to walk. Nevertheless, the possibility of running
for 30 minutes and easily finding my breath sounded very
appealing. As often as I could, I got out of the house and did
the best I could—and my affirmation helped me get there
over a period of three months. When the demon of negative
self-talk started to kick in (telling me my goal was hopeless,
impossible, even dangerous), I used my affirmation to keep
my focus on the positive—to keep me moving forward
toward my objective.

This is how an affirmation works. It creates a tangible line
of energy between where you are now and where you want
to be. It moves you toward the future you desire, and it
draws your future toward you. As you repeat your
affirmation, you will begin to taste the experience of your
desired destination.

From here on, each running meditation will suggest an
affirmation that you can use, and you are also welcome to
come up with your own. If you are inspired to create your
own affirmations, make sure that they start with the words "I
am" and that they are in the present tense (i.e., they use
action words that end in "–*ing*"). Make them enthusiastic and
upbeat—this gives them power. For example, "I am feeling
fit, running strong, and living long!" or "I am caring for
myself, honoring myself and Spirit with every stride!"

Before you leave home for your run today, check in and
see what is "running" in your mind. By doing this, you can
make sure that you are not about to spend your workout
worrying, playing out negative future fantasies, or listening
to old mental tapes of arguments and negative self-talk. Take
a moment to set your intention. Then, as you run, repeat your
affirmation—allow it to become embedded in the rhythm of
your body. If you notice your mind slipping into destructive
thought patterns or random free-associated thoughts, don't
worry! This may happen a number of times during a run. Be
kind to yourself, and remember that you are developing a

new skill. If learning is to be fun (and therefore successful), then it needs to be about striving for excellence—not perfection. These are moments to bring your focus back to your affirmation, which will in turn bring your attention back to the present moment.

Once your run is completed, your affirmation does not have to be thrown into the closet along with your running shoes. Write it out and pin it up on your fridge, slip it into your wallet for the day (or longer), or stick it to the dash in your car—anywhere you can see its inspirational message.

Affirmation

I am enthusiastically opening to the loving support
and guidance of Spirit in every area of my life.

3

Warming Up

Quality: Creativity

"The will to win is nothing without the will to prepare."
Juma Ikangaa

"Running is creative."
Roger Bannister, *The Four-Minute Mile*

"A person can grow only as much as his horizon allows."
John Powell

(Today's meditation is ideal for a rest day and will need to take place at home.)

Just after my wife and I were married, she enrolled in graduate school. She found the perfect college for her studies, about a 60-mile round-trip from home. At the time, we were sharing a beautiful, battered 1976 Oldsmobile Toronado. Its hood was as large as a queen-sized bed—a very glamorous departure from the compact cars I had driven in my native England. "Luther" (as we had named our Oldsmobile) was over 20 years old and tired. He could certainly not be relied upon to make the multiple journeys to class without the possibility of breaking down. My wife suggested that we buy a new car.

I was terrified. Still young and newly married, I had never bought anything that I hadn't saved for first. A car purchase did not fit into this approach—my wife would have graduated before we had saved enough money! While I crunched the numbers and played with our budget, my wife did something that was entirely new to me. She sat down with a pile of old magazines and cut out pictures of the car she wanted, along with other inspirational words and images. Then she took a large piece of colored paper and glued onto it the pictures of the car, surrounding it with Monopoly money and words that inspired wealth. She wrote "Our New Car" at the top of the page and pinned it to the wall in the hallway.

Several weeks later, we went to the dealer and took her ideal model of car for a test drive—and later that afternoon, we drove it home! We had bought a new car. Each time I passed the car poster in our house, I smiled at her approach. Hey, I figured, whatever keeps her happy. Meanwhile, I worried about paying for it. Making car payments would stretch our finances to the limit, but we could just make it if we pulled back in some of the other areas; we were going to be cooking at home a lot more!

Three weeks after we bought the car, my wife got an unexpected new job with a substantial pay increase, along with a tuition reimbursement program that paid the majority of her tuition. A while after that, I received an unexpected inheritance from my grandmother, and the car was paid off in full—over 18 months ahead of schedule.

Now when we are looking to bring something new into our lives, while I continue to crunch numbers, I also join my wife in cutting out pictures and creating inspirational posters. There have been posters for new jobs, new investments, family, school, vacations, new business ideas and more. One of my favorites is the one I create each year for running—it's bright, expansive, and uplifting. And on the days when I feel uninspired to honor my commitment, it reminds me of the very best my running has to offer.

Today, begin to create your own unique visual bridge to your dreams. Gather together a pile of magazines, a pair of scissors, some colored pens and crayons. Start by cutting out images that fit with your running dream. Clip pictures of runners that inspire you; words and images that lift your heart; expansive landscapes; bodies that illustrate the level of fitness you are working toward; running apparel and shoes that you are drawn to. You may even want to include pictures of foods that support your commitment to leading a healthful life. I encourage you to include images of anything that is uplifting and heartfelt for you, whether or not they have a direct connection to running. Pictures and spiritual images that touch your heart as well as words, phrases, and quotations that inspire you all have a place.

One crucial ingredient is a picture of you! Take a piece of paper (I find that a 36" x 24" size offers plenty of space for bold headlines and bright pictures), and start by placing a picture of yourself in the center of the page. Then, in whichever way you are called, paste the other images all around yourself. I like to update mine each year, to keep current with my evolving dreams. Let the full force of your creativity flow! Whatever is inspirational to you has a rightful place on your creation. This is your opportunity to take part in a conscious way in making your dream a reality, and you are uniquely placed to illustrate how that looks.

Some of you may want to spend a number of days collecting materials. You may be clear right away about how your collage is going to look. Don't delay! Through creating your collage, you are sending a powerful message to your subconscious and to Spirit—I am ready to claim my dream and make it real NOW! Just begin, and allow the process to carry you forward. As the German writer and philosopher Goethe encouraged, "Whatever you can do, or dream you can, begin it. Boldness has genius, power, and magic in it."

As soon as you fully commit your energy to a project, you call on divine support—you step into a river of possibility that will carry you to the ocean of your dreams.

Once you have completed this vibrant visual bridge to your dreams, place your creation somewhere where you will see it every day: by the front door; the place where you change into your running gear or lace up your shoes; maybe on the refrigerator. I actually took mine to a copy shop, laminated it, and hung it in the shower! You could even make a smaller copy for the dashboard of your car or your computer monitor at work.

Once you have hung your magnificent living dreamscape in the chosen place, take a step back and enjoy the expansive feeling it conjures inside of you. Take a few moments to acknowledge yourself and the commitment you have shown to your heartfelt dreams. Each day when you look at it, and at yourself in the center, picture yourself living your dream— imagine it taking place right now! You have let the universe know that you are claiming your success—here and now!

Affirmation

I am claiming my success—
flexing the muscles of my divine, creative power.

4

Body Talk

Quality: Attentiveness

*"Become proficient at listening to your body
and you will eventually hear from your totality—
the complex, unique person that you are."*
George Sheehan, *Dr. Sheehan on Running*

"Listen and attend with the ear of your heart."
Saint Benedict

It has often been said that communication is the most important skill in life. When we think of communication, most of us immediately think of talking. We picture ourselves public speaking or teaching someone how to learn a new task. Yet it is the art of *listening* that is the cornerstone to cultivating clear and open communication. This applies just as powerfully to the way in which we listen to ourselves. If we are to gain access to our greatest creativity, authentic power, and joy, we must learn to listen not only to the world around us but also to the deeper places within us—our heart's desires, our soul's purpose. These are the signposts to the divine that dwells within.

As we grow as runners, we become increasingly attuned to the messages that our bodies send us, even if we may not listen to them as often as we could! If we are to become life-long runners, we must learn to listen well. If not, our bodies will let us know in clearer and clearer terms that they need our regular attention, care, and nurturing.

I am sure I am not the only runner that has pushed himself stubbornly into injury. "It's just a passing ache," I'll say, or "It's just a growing pain." And my favorite one, "I just need to run a little bit further, to get the kinks out." More subtle aches and pains are the body's early warning system—a way of bringing our attention to areas where preventive care can reap enormous dividends. While many of us experience a natural soreness as our muscles recover after a workout, persistent pain experienced while running needs to be addressed.

Our aches and pains may also be valuable information about our approach to running. Perhaps we are not spending the important time to warm up and then stretch before we set out. Perhaps our current pair of shoes has actually done much more than 300 or 400 miles and is in need of change. Maybe, just maybe, we could use a day off!

As we gain maturity and fitness in our running lives, we learn to listen not just to the "shouts" of aches and pains, but also to attune to the song our bodies have to sing. We discover our stride, and then multiple strides. Our 5k and 10k strides; our half-marathon stride; perhaps a marathon stride; and for some of you, strides beyond that. We have a stride for the flat, for grass, sand, hills (both up and down!), and for sprinting. Over months and years we develop as many strides as a painter has colors on her palette. As we immerse ourselves more consciously in our running, we begin to hear our own breath in a new way—recognizing a place where we experience being breathed as opposed to breathing.

Through running, I continue each day to deepen my ability to listen to myself in a whole new way. I have also come to recognize that mastering this practice is a lifetime journey. I am discovering that the power this skill has to offer goes beyond my running and far beyond the conversation between my body and myself. My interactions with those I care for and, just as importantly (if not more so), with those toward whom I do not feel so caring can all benefit enormously from this multilayered, heart-centered approach to listening.

I promise you this: if you do not listen to your body, it will eventually demand your attention, even if this means it has to rear up against you through injury or sickness. In the same way, *if you do not listen to the greater world around you, it too will demand your attention in more and more urgent ways.*

More often than not, when we think we are listening, we are at least partially focused on preparing our response. We might even be organizing the multiple strategies and advice we have for the person who is talking to us! When this is happening, we are not fully listening. We may even be laying the groundwork for a damaging or hurtful mis-understanding.

We may have developed the skill of listening to *what* is being said and even *how* it is being said—picking up the nuances that are not being expressed overtly. We may not, however, as yet be adept at listening to *who* is *talking—independent of what he or she is saying.* To acknowledge that the individual talking with you is an important and valuable person, regardless of that person's opinions (and regardless of your opinions about them!), is a foundational part of listening and at the core of successful communication. When I am listened to in this way, I feel truly heard, and I feel encouraged to be more candid—to share more openly with my listener and at a deeper level. Simply put, I feel safe.

Listening to someone with the ears of your heart communicates that you not only hear what is being said but you also hear the "complex, unique person" that is *behind* what is being said—the one that George Sheehan refers to in today's quote. Even if—especially if—you do not agree with or like what is being said. In my experience, there is no surer way to build trust than to listen to others in this way.

The first place to begin practicing this level of listening is with ourselves, and a great way to start is by listening to our bodies. As you prepare for your run today, if you are tempted to set out without warming up and stretching, take a moment to stop and take a breath. Listen for the voice of your own caring, encouraging you to prepare with greater diligence. Follow its suggestion!

During your run, continue to bring your awareness to your exercise as an active listener. Focus on listening to the different levels of your being. Listen to what you are listening to, and make a conscious choice to focus on the positive, on your intention for your run, and the affirmation that you are using today. Attune to your soul's song as it becomes more clearly heard in the quietness that you are creating in your run. Listen, listen, listen.

You are a multidimensional being, and through listening to yourself in this way, you can experience more fully the rich, dynamic, multifaceted being that you are. In addition, you will be better prepared to catch the gifts of inspiration, imagination, and creativity with which Spirit fills us as we create space within ourselves.

As a follow-up to today's moving meditation, hold your focus on listening to yourself as a multidimensional being throughout the rest of your day—with the same level of caring, the same fullness of attention as you have during your run. *You are not only using a whole new way of listening, you are using a new way of listening to the whole of you.* And extend this approach to those around you—listen not only to what is being said, and how it is being said, but to the divinely created being that is talking with you.

I assure you, if the one thing that you transfer from your workouts to the rest of your life is focused, attentive, and caring listening, your life can be transformed! You will gain a clearer and deeper experience of the majesty of who you truly are—for not only will you be listening, but also Spirit will be listening through you.

Affirmation

I am listening to myself and others with the ears of my heart.

5

The Chase

Quality: Expansion

*"Every day gives you an opportunity to improve.
With every run, you can try to be better.
Not just a better runner, but a better person."*
John Bingham
The Courage to Start: A Guide To Running Your Life

*"Every day ask yourself the question, 'Do I want to experience Peace of Mind
or do I want to experience Conflict?'"*
Gerald Jampolsky, *Love is Letting Go of Fear*

My own sideways introduction to running came through my passion as a hunt saboteur. I had joined a group in my hometown that was committed to stopping the practice of fox hunting by any means it could. Fox hunters are early risers, and so we had to be up at the crack of dawn, too. While I would struggle to get out of bed before nine o'clock on any other day of the week, I would willingly pull myself out of bed at five in the morning to ensure getting to the hunt in plenty of time. In my early 20s at the time, I was able to rely on the natural fitness of my body. I had never been taught to stretch before any of the sporting activities I had taken at school or college, and I wasn't about to start then.

Each weekend, I was one of thousands of people up and down the country who were doing all that they could to disrupt fox hunts. While the hunters followed the scent on horseback along with their pack of hounds, we saboteurs would spend most of our time on foot, running as fast as we could to stay ahead of the pack. We sprayed a mixture of water, lemon juice, and garlic ahead of the hunt—laying an odor on the ground powerful enough to mask the scent of the fox, confusing the hounds.

Nine times out of ten we were successful, disruptive enough to rob the hunters of the pleasure of watching a cornered fox be pulled apart by the hounds. Once in a while we would be outrun and outmaneuvered, and the fox would be caught. I, too, experienced the extra surge of power that came when I heard the scream of a trapped fox. An almost superhuman strength would come to my legs in an effort to get to the hounds before the powerful combination of training and instinct pushed them to tear the fox limb from limb. It was extremely rare to liberate a fox from the power of this final animal frenzy. What caused my heart to sink even deeper would be when a new member to the hunt, often a young child, would be initiated by having the blood of the freshly killed fox smeared on his—or her—cheeks and forehead.

I admit there was a heightened level of physical performance that was available to me through my rage. But are anger and fear really the places from which we can draw our best? Looking back, I am not sure that our tactics contributed in any way to opening a dialogue that would facilitate lasting change. On the one hand, there is the practical gain of the avoided suffering of dozens, if not hundreds, of foxes. On the other hand, I know that at the end of each day the hunters were more firmly entrenched in defending their way of life at all costs, and the saboteurs were doubly committed to undermining it in any way they could. It was not unusual for violent fights to break out between the two camps. Over the years, a handful of hunt saboteurs have been killed.

Many times in a year, I will cast my mind back to this accidental start to my running life. It is one clear, positive outcome that I can grasp from the confusion of those days. As I prepare for my runs now, I will smile as I think how I would run ten miles or more in jeans and boots without any warm-up or stretching! Now I am old enough that I have to warm-up and stretch before my run, and then cool-down and stretch at the end to ensure that I have many more running years ahead of me.

I elongate each major muscle group momentarily, then ease as it contracts briefly in its natural response, and then move into a deeper stretch. As I stretch myself physically, I wonder how I might stretch myself in other ways during my day. How can I stretch myself emotionally, and be in the world in a more balanced, open, and heart-centered way? How can I stretch myself mentally, thinking of myself and others in a more accepting and positive way? How can I stretch myself spiritually, anchoring myself within a consciousness of peace throughout the day? All these questions can be summed up in one: *How can I help to increase the sum total of loving in the world today?* ✳

If you have not included stretching as part of your workout routine up until now, then make use of today's meditation as a starting point for creating a new habit that will support you in enjoying a long and strong running life. Make sure you have warmed up (you can do this by running or walking for ten minutes or so at a very gentle pace), and then begin a light stretching routine before you set out for the body of your run. As you stretch physically, ask yourself, "What could I do in my life today to add to the sum total of loving in the world?" There is no need to look for answers at this stage; simply place the question in your awareness.

Then, as you run, ask for Spirit's guidance as you begin to move through the different layers of your being with this question. Ask yourself how you might be able to stretch emotionally, mentally, and spiritually as I indicated above.

Rather than looking for answers, listen for responses that come forward by themselves. Allow Spirit to work with the very best in you and give you guidance.

When you complete your run, and after walking for a few minutes to cool down, move into a longer period of stretching. Try not to think of stretching as an addition to your running schedule, but more as an essential part of it. As you stretch, review any responses and guidance that came to you during your run. Notice how good it feels to stretch your muscles in a focused and caring way.

This expansive feeling can be a part of your life on other levels, too, as you stretch into new ways of being. As you come to the end of your stretching, choose one of the ways that came forward for you to increase the sum total of loving in your world as a focus for your day. It can be in the way that you interact with yourself, or with another person or a situation. If more than one suggestion has come forward, make a note of them and incorporate them on other days. For today, make a point of choosing just one to act upon.

As you go forward in your running life, make sure that stretching is a non-negotiable part of your workout. When planning your day and workout schedule, include the time necessary for stretching; otherwise it can be the first thing that drops away when you are pressed for time. Each time you include stretching in your life, not just in your running but also in your overall approach to every level of life, you give yourself the opportunity to step into the very best that you are.

Affirmation

I am stretching into the very best of who I am.

6

100 Beaches

Quality: Acceptance

"My aim in life is not to run but to awaken. CONSCIOUSNESS requires
SEEING, begins with opening to what you are."
Fred Rohe, *The Zen of Running*

"God is seated in the hearts of all."
The Bhagavad-Gita

In recent years, I have done much of my running on the beach a few blocks from my home. This is a well-traveled route of between five and seven miles, depending on where I turn. I run at the water's edge; without fail, the ebb and flow of both tide and time ensures that the beach looks a little different each time I run it.

In the peak of summer, the beach looks her most manicured. Before the major holiday weekends, the city sends out trucks that comb the sand flat, evening out any dips and bumps the wind may have caused, and clearing away debris that has washed up on the shore. In the early mornings, the beach can be cool, hazy, and quiet, populated only by the occasional homeless person, or a chanting monk from the nearby monastery. On long summer evenings, she can be noisy and talkative, the boardwalk filled with runners, walkers, skaters, cyclists, and couples walking arm in arm.

In the winter months, after a passing storm, she looks disheveled and windswept, even messy. Tree trunks, seaweed, and miscellaneous flotsam and jetsam from passing ships scatter the high water mark. The air is filled with salt from the whipped-up sea. As haggard as the beach can look at these times, she feels vibrant, animated, and alive. Sometimes the wind can be blowing so hard that I wonder if she isn't trying to gift me the experience of taking flight!

No matter how the beach is, no matter what her mood, I am simply happy that she is there to welcome my feet along her shoreline, to play chicken with the rising and falling of her sea, to listen to the lap of the waves as I run at the water's edge. Correspondingly, I seem to be able to thrive in her company when no one else's will fit in my life, not even my own.

No matter what mood I am in when I arrive at the beach, she greets me just as I am—there is nothing that I need to do or be. I feel seen and accepted in a way that inspires me to see myself in a more compassionate way. Spending time in the generous, accepting presence of the beach is always healing for me.

This has been one of the most valuable lessons that I have gained from my running. I am reminded each and every time as I reach the beach that there is nothing that I need to fix in me. If I am feeling disappointed, angry, or sad, for example, the first question I ask myself is no longer, "What am I going to *do* about this?" but rather, "How am I going to *be* about this?" I can either choose to be upset with myself for feeling angry, adding judgment and recrimination to my pain, or I can choose to be with myself in a different way—to hear my sadness, and meet myself with compassion and understanding.

I can remember to breathe!

Often, as we ride the ebb and flow of life, we can become convinced that we are our actions and our feelings. We can lose sight of that part of us that has never been hurt, that has never done anything wrong, that is anchored in the knowledge that we are each unique expressions of the divine—whole and complete just as we are. And, as often as we lose sight of our own divine essence, we lose sight of it in others. Each time I return from my run along the beach, I come home with a more loving view of myself, and I am more willing to extend that loving perspective to others.

Today, as you run, look for any changes that appear on your route, and notice your response to them. Are they annoying? A disappointment? An improvement? A surprise? Notice your reaction, and then simply say to yourself, "That's interesting!" and keep moving along. As you move through your day, notice how those people in your life that you see regularly are different from yesterday, and the day before. If they seem upset, not at their best, or especially annoying, do all you can to see them through the eyes of loving. Consciously look for the divine spark that is within them. There is nothing that you have to do to fix them. When you encounter people and situations of beauty, enjoy these as fully as you can.

No matter what the mood of other people around you, focusing in this way will be beneficial for you. You may discover that just the acts of looking for and focusing upon the divinity in yourself and others will shift your experience further into the positive.

Affirmation

I am seeing myself and others through the eyes of my heart—
celebrating each Soul that I meet.

7

Running on Empty

Quality: Self-Care

"It no longer takes an injury for me to incorporate rest and recovery into my training schedule . . . rest is a component as important in my schedule as speed work or a long run."
Joan Benoit Samuelson
Winner of the first Olympic Marathon for Women
The Running Times Guide to Breakthrough Running

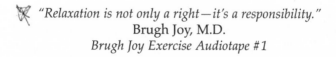 *"Relaxation is not only a right—it's a responsibility."*
Brugh Joy, M.D.
Brugh Joy Exercise Audiotape #1

It never ceases to amaze me how important it is for me to keep track of the miles I have run in my current pair of shoes. I have run in some until the heels and balls of the feet were so worn that I simply *had* to replace them. I forget that the mechanics of the shoes, the support and cushioning, begin to collapse before the outer body of the shoe wears down. Long before they look worn out, they are broken down.

I used to buy shoes in response to their looking worn out, and this meant that I often went through a few weeks of minor pulls, aches, and pains from my feet to my knees, but always below the knees—a sure sign of shoe troubles. This approach was like waiting until the bodywork on my car started to rust before changing the oil!

If we experience regular bouts of injuries and pain as runners, it can also be an indicator of a breakdown in our broader approach to taking care of ourselves. There have been times in my life when taking care of myself simply meant responding to pain. In my drinking days, I would inevitably run into problems of one sort or another. I would run out of money and not be able to get home. I would fall and hurt myself. I would wake up in the mornings with an abominable hangover. Of course, in my alcoholic thinking, I didn't go anywhere near the root cause of these problems—the drinking.

In those days, taking care of myself meant taking care of my pain. I would make sure that wherever I went, I had a few essential emergency items in my day pack: a little money for a bus or train ride home; a box of Band-Aids for any incidental cuts and grazes; and a large bottle of ibuprofen for the hangovers. I was very proud of my level of preparedness!

While the example I have shared may be a little extreme, many of us live according to a similar principle, albeit subconsciously. At best, we take care of ourselves only when we are in pain. At worst, we think that we are somehow more evolved if we are prepared for suffering. Self-care becomes a response to negative circumstances. We get sick and *then* we take care of ourselves. We pull a muscle, and *then* we slow down and take a day off. Maybe. Even then, many of us will fill ourselves with over-the-counter medications and soldier on anyway. Eventually all of us reach a point of pain when we are willing to say, "You know what? I can't go on. I need a day to get back on my feet." For many of us, it is only as a last resort that we take care of ourselves.

In a sense, the United States experienced this dynamic on a national scale after the attacks of September 11, 2001. There were a handful of days when we all lived in a very different world. In our shared pain and sadness, we took time to look each other in the eyes and really see each other, whether we "knew" each other or not. We touched our loved ones a little more frequently and made sure our friends knew that we cared for and appreciated them.

We looked for ways to support the friends and families of those who were killed that day, as well as the rescuers who worked for all of us—we felt connected in a tangible way. We lit candles and we prayed. We made new attempts to get to know those we had previously thought of only as strangers, wherever they were—at the grocery store, at the Post Office, or just passing in the street.

As a nation, we had a deeper and clearer appreciation for the preciousness of life. It took this event of immense sadness and loss for us to pause and open our eyes and hearts to what is truly of value. What will it take for us to live from a place of caring and compassion so that we will no longer need war, hunger, or catastrophe to lead us there?

In the same way that this happens on a national and international scale, it can happen on an individual scale, too. As runners, we may well only commit to taking care of ourselves when injury forces us to stay in the house for a day or two. The times we don't run are often the ones when, quite simply, we can't. Taking good care of ourselves is a powerful way to build self-trust and self-esteem. Every time we make a proactive choice to nurture ourselves, both as runners and in our wider lives, we remind ourselves that we are of intrinsic value, worthy of receiving our own attention, time, and tender loving care.

As you prepare to run today, set an intention to open to any guidance that Spirit may have for you about ways to care for yourself in a more proactive way. When I use this meditation, I take a few moments before I set out on my run to look at a picture of myself as a youngster. This helps me tune into my own loving and caring nature more directly. As I look at my younger self, and survey the journey that he has made to be where I am, my heart fills with appreciation—and with the desire to do all that I can to take care of me then, now, and the person I am yet to become.

As you run, allow your mind to wander through the landscape of what relaxes you, nurtures you, and uplifts you. It could be taking yourself out to the movies. Perhaps you would like to get a massage or a manicure. Maybe you long for time spent in prayer and meditation, a day at the beach, or an afternoon on the couch with a good book. Remember yourself when you were younger and ask, "What was nurturing and relaxing for me then? Which activities took my mind off my concerns?"

Perhaps you loved to spend the afternoon listening to a play on the radio or a book on tape. Maybe you loved riding your bicycle with no particular destination in mind. For many of us, a large piece of white paper and a handful of crayons were the gateway to hours of deep relaxation.

As a child growing up in England, I loved to listen to the cricket commentary on the radio—a game so mellow that it can take five days to play! Now, through the wonders of the Internet, I am able to take time every now and then to listen in on a game for an afternoon. Some of the commentators are still the same as when I was a child, and an afternoon spent listening to their gravel voices settles my mind and softens my heart.

As you continue through your day, notice how you treat yourself. Spending just one day consciously focused on how you treat your body can be very illuminating, and you can gain powerful insights into the way you treat yourself on other levels, too. Are you listening to the feedback that your body is giving you? Is that persistent ache best treated with another pill? Are there other areas in your life in which you mask pain rather than address its cause? Is your relationship with your body based in drama, and you only respond when things go "wrong"? Or do you proactively care for your body, resting it adequately, feeding it carefully, and honoring it with massage or some other favorite treat? Do you wait until you are on the verge of a meltdown before you eat, or are you attuned to your body's needs for replenishment? Are you getting enough sleep, or are you staying up late watching television shows that you could probably do without?

Are you allowing yourself the opportunity for rest and relaxation? Are you working through your lunch break? Rushing from errand to errand without a pause? Skipping proper meals just to keep on track? Not just physically, but mentally, too, notice how willing you are—or not—to take breaks from the thinking mind each day, from the brain that is calculating, and allow it to relax, dream, and drift. It is often in these moments, when we are willing to let go of the reins, that our most creative thoughts and inspirations come in.

Before the day is done, schedule a day off from your running within the next week and use the time for proactive self-care. Make an appointment with yourself to treat, cherish, and celebrate yourself in the relaxing and fun way that came from your moving meditation. It is by making time to step out of the everyday concerns of living that we feel even more alive!

Affirmation

I am basking in the glow of my own tender loving care.

8

Pacing

Quality: Loving Self-Discipline

"Even snails can consume continents."
James Shapiro, *Running Across America*

*"Great things are not done by impulse, but by a series
of small things brought together."*
Vincent Van Gogh

I have actually had two running lives. The first one began
in my late 20s and lasted for a little over a year. It was fueled
with the energy and raw enthusiasm that came from finding
my way out of addiction. I took up running as a way to burn
off much of the residual anger and sadness that I had
previously used drugs and alcohol to mask.

Essentially, I upgraded my addiction. Running gave me
a healthier obsession and helped to build my self-esteem. At
the end of that first year, I ran a marathon, completing it in
a great time. Less than a week later, still flushed with
success and feeling indomitable, I began training again
harder than ever. After three weeks without a day of rest, a

sudden searing pain in my hip told me something was wrong.

I continued running for a couple of days after that, but the pain was unbearable. I took a week off, ran again, but still it was painful. So I took more time off, but never enough to heal fully. I became depressed and lost my motivation. Days of not running turned into weeks, and weeks turned into months. Months became years. I channeled my energy into work and got some big promotions. I found less and less time to get back into my running. It was almost two years before I started up again, and by that stage all of the cardiovascular fitness and muscle strength that I had built up were lost. I was a beginner once again—and so began my second running life.

After almost no exercise in two years, I went out and tried to run a 35-mile week. "I've run a marathon," I told myself. "I've been able to run 35 miles a week, for months at a time. Sure, it's a while ago, but I know I'm better than all those joggers out there." I made it to the second or third day. Sore and bored with the fact that I could not run for two hours or more, I gave up once again. This was the pattern over the next several months. Sometimes I would run for a few weeks, but never longer.

Finally, I had to accept that I needed to build my fitness from the beginning—*all over again*. As part of a final year project at graduate school, I committed to return to running— and to do so *gently*. I began by running for 20 minutes, once a week; ten minutes out, ten minutes back. I did that for a month. The next month it was twice a week, and the next month three times a week. At times it was very challenging not to go further, but I held firm to my boundary of running no more than ten minutes out and ten minutes back. I would listen to the fitness czars on the radio telling me I needed to be exercising an hour a day, five or more days a week, to have any real impact on my health. I reminded myself of my unhappy experience of the previous years, and that I was building my fitness on a firm foundation while continuing to protect my body. It was OK to take time to do that.

As I started over again, I felt ashamed at what I saw as the paltry distances I was running—I was still so invested in what being a runner should look like. I got to experience firsthand the judgments that I had silently used against others in my earlier running life. Discovering the level of my own arrogance was shocking.

In the fourth month, I held at three days, but increased my run to 30 minutes each day—15 minutes out and 15 minutes back. I was beginning to feel like I was getting somewhere! I took ten months to reach a schedule of running five days a week for 45 minutes to an hour—a level of fitness I had reached in my first running life in less than three months. Yet I felt a greater sense of accomplishment this time. Rather than riding on the raw passion of recovery, I had carefully and consciously succeeded in getting back on track. Step by step—literally.

There are times when I approach the marathon of life as though I need to complete it all NOW! I rush in as though I can complete a marathon sprinting from start to finish. Whether beginning a training program or writing a book, I have discovered that breaking any project down into what I call 1k sections[1] is the most likely way that I am going to succeed. I have learned that if I take on more than is reasonable, I only succeed in sabotaging myself. When that happens, I can slip into chastising myself. From there, it is only a short walk to falling off my commitment.

Every run is comprised of manageable strides, one after the other. As a new runner, you will discover that *the best distance to run is the one that is possible.* As I know from experience, to set out to run for 20 minutes and succeed is far more satisfying (and encouraging) than to set out to run for an hour and pull up at 30 minutes. For those of you who are established runners, you have been learning to build your endurance over an extended period of time. You have

---

[1] 1k (one kilometer) is a distance that can be walked in about ten minutes or run slowly in six.

increased your long runs gradually and seen how that approach is a recipe for success.

Yet for some strange reason, when it comes to other areas of our lives, many of us try to make it to the finish line in one stride. We start a new business and expect that we'll make it onto the New York Stock Exchange within the first year. We start a new weight-training program and expect to transform into a cover model for *Muscle* magazine! In our enthusiasm to bring about change in our lives, we often force ourselves into new habits. We push ourselves relentlessly, unforgiving of anything that does not live up to our expectations. Yet it is when habits are established lovingly that they become the most deeply ingrained. When integrating new disciplines, it is our gentleness that is our greatest strength.

Today, use the time of your run to review a project you are working on. It could be in the arena of running or in some other area of your life. From the balanced perspective of your workout, consider a number of next steps for your project that are 1k sized, not marathon sized. Something that you know you can and will complete—be realistic and be gentle with yourself. You are looking for a slam dunk here. At the end of the day, when it comes time to follow through on the step, you are far better off having completed a small step than having failed to complete a huge step. Nothing breeds success like success.

If you are looking to start a new business, you could commit to making an appointment with someone you know, to hear about his experience of what did and didn't work. The 1k step would be to make the appointment. A *next* 1k step would be to go to the appointment. See how this works? If you are looking at a new training program, you could start by adding it to one day in your week, as opposed to every day. When committing to something, do yourself a big favor and set yourself up for success by choosing manageable steps.

These smaller steps may appear less glamorous, but is there more glamour in a completed step or an incomplete step? Each time we commit to something that is beyond our reach, we have a negative learning experience—and we may begin to tell ourselves we are not capable. Each time we complete a step, however small, we build trust with ourselves. We build our self–esteem *and* move closer to realizing our dreams!

Affirmation

I am experiencing consistent success
as I manifest my dreams with gentleness and ease.

9

Let Your Heart Sing

Quality: Loving

"It is an unvicious cycle; when I am happy I am running well and when I am running well I am happy . . . it is the Platonic idea of knowing thyself. Running is getting to know yourself to an extreme degree."
Ian Thompson
Marathon: What It Takes To Go The Distance

"It is the heart always that sees before the head can see."
Thomas Carlyle

Even as a young child, although I was not yet interested in running, I experienced the exhilaration of my heart beating strong and true. I particularly remember playing with my father in the pounding waves of the cold Atlantic Ocean off the north coast of France. While he stood waist deep in the surf, I sat in a small inflatable dinghy that he held onto, bow pointed into the incoming breakers. The waves were sometimes large enough that they would tumble over my father's head. To me, they were enormous! As he thrust the dinghy forward into the incoming waves, the water would break over the tiny boat, filling much of it and dousing me in cold water. I squealed with delight. I remember placing the palm of my hand on my cold chest and feeling the warmth of the deep, rhythmic pounding of my heart. I didn't need to understand the mechanics of exactly what was happening to appreciate the power of the energy that was moving inside me.

On a recent, longer training run, I began to think about the way in which my heart just keeps on beating—without my having to consciously do anything. Thousands of times, I have experienced the beating of my heart, steady and strong, as I have settled into the stride of my run, moving to the rhythm that moves me. This was something I had been taking for granted. Sure, I can keep my heart healthy by creating a lifestyle that supports it doing its job to the best of its ability. But I can't do the beating for it—much like breathing.

Our hearts keep pushing blood around our bodies, feeding every cell—pumping blood that cleanses, sustains, and mends our bodies' organs. They continue to pump even while we are sleeping, without any conscious effort on our part—this strikes me as a fantastic, and greatly overlooked, miracle. Our hearts were doing this even before we knew they existed, before we were old enough to understand what a heart was. They beat for us as young children, as babies, as new infants, and even before, as we lay in the womb. Throughout our lives, our hearts keep us nourished.

Our hearts, our physical source of life, can also be seen as a reflection of our dynamic relationship with God—the source of nourishment for our spiritual lives. Even before we understand the concept of a god, let alone experience it as a vital force in our lives, God is delivering spiritual energy to us, the very essence of our lives.

In the same way that we can support or hinder the work of our hearts, we can also make choices that support or restrict the flow of divine energy into our lives. For 15 years, I didn't just tax my heart by bingeing on drugs and alcohol. These behaviors also blurred and blunted my

consciousness—I was blocking my spiritual a
diet of negative self-talk, anger, jealousy, d
judgment. Medical institutions now accept that living in
states of stress and rage place strain on the heart in the same
way as overeating or alcohol and drug abuse. You name it—
I tried it. Finally, I had what I refer to as a "spiritual heart
attack." I found myself sitting on the sidewalk outside my
house, with my belongings scattered around me. My wife
was no longer willing to allow my resentment, selfishness,
and infidelity to be a part of her life.

In the following weeks, I came up with many reasons as
to why my life was such a mess. As I examined them further,
I saw that all the reasons were symptoms of one unavoidable
truth. I was disconnected from the source of goodness in my
life—God. I had blocked the arteries that connected me to the
source that feeds me as a spiritual being—ignored the
practices of prayer and meditation, and of spending time in
a spiritual community.

I had told myself that I didn't believe really believe in a
god, but now I began to see that I always had. In fact, I had
had many gods: booze, drugs, being right, and judgment, to
name a few. These had all been powers that I had made
paramount in my life at one time or another. Now I had the
opportunity to choose a different guiding energy in my life.

My spiritual heart attack shook me awake, and I began to
make changes. I started to approach my life with the same
renewed sense of purpose as someone who has been given a
second lease on life after a physical heart attack.

As I look back on my life thus far, I see how hard my heart
has worked to do its job of delivering life-giving energy, even
during those times when I did all I could to make that
difficult. In the same way, I also see how God has not
wavered in sending blessings my way, even as I did all that I
could to deflect and refuse them. I have come to hold my
heart and my God, the physical and spiritual sources of my
continued well-being, in a place of profound loving.

More and more I have come to understand health not only
as a physical issue but also a fundamentally spiritual one. Our

bodies are a divine gift, a miraculous vehicle to carry us through the adventures of this lifetime. As runners, we may already have a great appreciation for this due to the beautiful and uplifting experiences that we have through our running.

As you begin today's run, focus on the strength of your heart. Remind yourself of the way in which it keeps delivering exactly what you need when you need it—without you having to ask. Recognize that there are choices you can make to support the full functioning of your heart, and that through your commitment to running and regular exercise, you are making a profound difference to your overall well-being. Congratulate yourself!

Then, as you settle into your stride, as you are in the midst of experiencing your heart giving you the gift of this run, ask your heart what you can give to it. This may sound a little strange at first, and I encourage you to trust in the process of engaging in a dialogue with your heart. Speak to it as if it were another person—a running partner right there along side of you. You may want to let your heart know how much you appreciate it and the way it nourishes and sustains your body, the way it supports the joy of your running. When you think about it, many of the most memorable experiences in your life take place in the heart. The joy you feel as you run comes through the heart, as do feelings of love, gratitude, and the experience of connection with Spirit. These are all gifts of the heart. So go ahead—ask your heart what you can do for it, and then listen.

During the runs that I took throughout those months when I was separated from my wife, my heart and I talked with each other at length. My heart told me it wanted to be trusted. It wanted to be heard, and it let me know that it had a lot to say. It told me it was tired of always being overruled by my head. During many runs in shared conversation, I reconnected with my heart as the avenue through which Spirit guides me. My heart helped me make the decisions needed to reconcile with my wife. In addition, my opening heart told me that it had a dream to speak to a wider audience—that it wanted to write.

So during today's run, and throughout the rest of your day (and beyond!), take time to converse with your heart. Discover the dreams that it has in store for you!

Affirmation

I am listening to the clear and loving voice of Spirit as it speaks through my heart.

10

Drinking from the Well

Quality: Connection to Spirit

*"Running is my meditation, mind flush, cosmic telephone,
mood elevator, and spiritual communion."*
Lorraine Moller

*"Water — the ace of elements. Water dives from the clouds without parachute,
wings or safety net. Water runs over the steepest precipice and blinks not a
lash. Water is buried and rises again;
water walks on fire, and fire gets the blisters...
the ongoing odyssey of water is virtually irresistible."*
Tom Robbins, *Even Cowgirls Get The Blues*

My running is a constant reminder of the way in which Spirit expresses itself through us in infinite and unique ways. Each of us has idiosyncrasies that make our running experience our own. We have our shoe loyalties, our clothing favorites, and our particular running routes. Each time I see other runners out on the roads, I am reminded that, although we are all doing the same thing, there is no way I could mistake one runner for another.

We each have our own gait, favorite stretches, and more. What makes running different for each of us, too, is where we are running from and to—the homes, loved ones, challenges, and goals that are ours alone.

There is, however, one thing that seems to be common to all of us—we sweat! Yet I am consistently surprised by the fact that the vast majority of us are running without taking on water during our runs. Aside from the health hazard of becoming dehydrated, I have read that as little as two percent dehydration can have a negative effect on performance.

Our blood, carrying essential nutrients and cleansing our bodies, is 83% water. The muscles that carry us on our runs are 75% water.

Our brain, that amazing synchronizer of the body's functions, is 74% water. Even our bones are around 20-25% water! All in all, the average human body contains between 40 and 50 quarts of water.

I am no more likely to go out for a run without a bottle of water (or two for my long training runs) than I am to run in the road barefoot. As I replenish the liquids I lose through perspiration, I support my kidneys and liver in processing the acids and other toxins that are released into my bloodstream as I work my muscles. Water makes up the fluids that cushion my joints and muscles, and it also helps prevent muscle cramping and premature fatigue.

When I noticed what a strong reaction I had to seeing so many runners without water, I began to ask myself why? If the world around me is, perhaps, a reflection of my own inner experience, what essential item am I leaving home without on a regular basis? The answer came back *loud* and *clear*—Spirit!

In the same way that I can get through my run without water, I can also get through my days without Spirit—but it sure feels a lot harder! In fact, that is exactly what the days can be like—I am *getting through* them, as opposed to *riding upon* them.

In the same way, when I make Spirit an integral part of my day, I support my body, mind, and psyche in flushing out old energies and toxic thoughts. By taking quiet time at the start of the day to meditate, even if it is just five minutes, I can set the tone for my entire day. I touch into the place inside of me that knows that Spirit has a plan for my day and that my responsibility is to follow it and enjoy the ride.

Without a doubt, my daily run is time I can use to focus on Spirit. Running takes me there naturally—this is the cornerstone of the delight I derive from it. Whatever we can do to hold a Spirit-centered focus throughout our day will automatically improve our quality of life. We need to be taking on water throughout our day if we want to support ourselves in keeping adequately hydrated. In the same way, we need regular infusions of Spirit to ensure we raise our lives to the greatest possible level of joy.

Just as water flushes out toxins and other waste products, time spent focused in Spirit helps to flush out the frustrations, judgments, and negative self-talk that can creep into our day—before they become a dominant feature in the landscape of our lives. Just as water helps to cushion my joints and cool my muscles on the road, my connection to Spirit helps to cushion me against the jolts and overheating that everyday living can bring about!

For today's run, first make certain you take some water with you if this is not already part of your routine! At the very least, make sure that you are able to stop at water fountains on your way. Make a commitment to buy a waist pack that will allow you to carry a water bottle on your future workouts. If you are going to be running for more than an hour, I encourage you to use a pack that carries two bottles, or plan a place on your route where you can refill the one that you have.

As you run, pay special attention to the way your body responds when you take on water. Our bodies' finely tuned systems tell us when we need to take on fluids. Listen to the unique hydration gauge that your body has been blessed with—attuned to your individual needs. If you feel tight in a particular muscle, stretch and take in more water—visualize the water heading straight for that muscle, flushing out lactic acid and cleansing it with fresh blood.

Throughout your day, make it a conscious focus to replenish your internal water supply. Each time you do, also take a moment to close your eyes and reconnect to Spirit. Focus by taking three long, slow, deep breaths—while you are sitting at your desk, waiting in line at the bank, or at the store. Whether you are stuck in negative thoughts, feeling a little blue, or experiencing a physical pain, regularly reconnecting with Spirit can cleanse and renew every area of your life.

Each time we drink from the well of Spirit—the source of all things—we are reminded of who we truly are: spiritual beings, first and foremost, who are experiencing what it is to live a human life.

Affirmation

I am connecting fully with Spirit
in each moment of my life.

11

A Training Approach ... To Life

Quality: Patience

"Training is not only a means, it is also an end in itself."
George Sheehan
New York Road Runners Club Complete Book of Fitness

"It is better to light a candle than to curse the darkness."
Chinese proverb

Imagine you are watching a new baby learning to walk. She's crawling across the floor, maybe even progressing to propping herself up against a chair. Then, still getting the hang of balancing on her own, she takes a tumble. "Hey," you shout. "What's with all this falling down? That's not walking! Do it properly!" Sound ridiculous? Well, you're right, it would be. Our response to their irregular success is patience, encouragement, and a helping hand. We do not punish them. We understand and accept that falling is an integral part of learning to walk. We understand that without falling there would be no learning, no discovery of the sense of balance and steadiness.

Yet we are often unwilling to offer ourselves the same levels of understanding, compassion, and gentleness. When we begin new skills and we stumble, we chastise and punish ourselves. We even tell ourselves that there is something wrong with us. "I'm an adult, I should be able to do this. I should know this by now." I noticed that when my daughter, like many kids in the throws of learning to walk, fell on her behind, more often than not her immediate response was to laugh! If only we could remember how to enjoy the learning process in the same way—how free we could be!

As runners we have the opportunity to learn that it takes time to move from one level of fitness to the next. I remember the first day I hopped on one of the treadmills at the gym. I was fascinated by the readout that showed me how far I had run, and I figured I would head for a mile in distance. Then I was into my second mile. Somewhere around two and a half miles, I decided I wanted to make it to five.

I did make it to five. Barely. My t-shirt was sodden, my legs heavy, and it was all I could do to keep my balance as I half-stepped, half-fell off the treadmill. The inside of my thighs were rubbed raw by the cargo shorts I was wearing. The morning following my glory on the treadmill, I was even sorer—and a little disillusioned. Clearly, if I spent each day trying to run as far as I could, I was going to exhaust and probably injure myself.

When I run into challenges on levels other than the physical, my ability to remain focused on learning seems to quickly disappear. While I didn't like the fact that it would take time to build the strength and stamina to run comfortably for five miles or more, it made sense to me. And if I was not willing to listen to my own voice of reason, my body was there to remind me of what was realistic!

What if when we are upset emotionally, we were also to look at this as a learning situation, too? Perhaps we are learning how to communicate our needs and feelings more clearly. We may be learning to take greater responsibility for our actions and decisions. We are always in a position to learn how to be with ourselves and others in more caring, respectful, and compassionate ways.

From the moment we set out on our first run, and on through the accumulation of workouts, we build a running history for ourselves. As we read our magazines, join running groups, and learn from others' experiences, our depth of knowledge increases. The more we learn, the more we are able to derive a greater sense of joy from our running. We become attuned to our own learning curve. We realize that it is not realistic to add too much mileage in a short space of time. We discover that if we increase our long runs by, say, ten percent a month, we can absorb the challenge of greater distance with a pleasant degree of ease. *We give ourselves permission to learn.*

Through this learning process, we are developing a foundational skill that can have transformational effects in all areas of our lives. In this school of life, we constantly find ourselves in new situations. Unexpected challenges can come up on a daily basis, potentially throwing us off balance. If we can approach these with an understanding that life, too, is a learning process, we can change our experience for the better. This is a radical change in approach—to see that learning is not just a part of life, but *it is the very purpose of life.* We are here on this earth to learn and grow, and through that growth, we move toward a clearer experience of ourselves and of God.

It is what we learn that takes us deeper into our joy, and into love. Most of us accept that when we leave this world, we will not be taking with us the material goods that we have accumulated. My sense is that we will, however, take with us what we have learned. For if it is learning that takes us into our love, then it is our learning that will take us home to God—not the stuff that we accumulate.

This is not to say that achievements in the physical world are without meaning or use. Far from it. It is important, though, to remember that the goals are the means, not the ends. As we move forward toward our goals in life, we encounter challenges. These, in turn, bring us opportunities for learning. If we are willing to embrace these lessons, we can experience growth.

It is the same with our running. For example, you may be headed toward a specific goal, such as running a 10k race. The day of the race arrives and you surprise yourself with an even stronger performance than you imagined possible. Somewhere between 30 minutes and an hour, the race is run; the goal is attained. What is left? All the learning. All the training, commitment, and adaptability that you called forth in yourself as you moved toward your goal.

For today's moving meditation, consider a current situation that is causing you discomfort—a pebble in the comfortable running shoe of your life! As you review the situation from within the sacred temple of your run, place it in the context of this question: *What is the opportunity here for me to learn and grow?* If you find yourself slipping into a negative attitude or replaying old arguments with regard to the situation, return to the question. Look for the learning— but look with your heart, not your head. Allow the wisdom of your heart and the grace of Spirit to bring the answers to you.

As you hold this focus for your run, remember where learning has taken you in your running life. Learning to recognize that supporting your physical fitness is a way of loving yourself—and honoring your creator. Learning that holding to a commitment one day at a time can carry you far down the road. Learning to listen to your body and respond to the messages that it sends you. Learning to find your own rhythm and breath in your stride. Whether you are a new runner or reviewing many years of running, it is your willingness to experience the process of learning that has brought you to where you are.

Finally, as you stretch, cool down, and shower, take time to acknowledge your willingness to take what you may have previously seen as "mistakes" and trade them in for learning opportunities. In this way you return to the preciousness of your own loving heart. Acknowledge yourself—you deserve it!

Engage the same approach in other areas of your life as you go about your day. If you find yourself feeling frustrated, take a breath. Consider how your willingness to learn is supporting your running—steadily increasing your ability over time. *All learning takes place this way.* Holding the image in your mind of a small child learning to walk is a powerful tool that can soften your heart. Remember how she giggles as she tumbles? Give yourself the gift of the same response!

Affirmation

I am filled with laughter and joy,
embracing every area of my life with loving patience.

12

Dream Mile

Quality: Vision

*"If you want to become the best runner you can be, start now.
Don't spend the rest of your life wondering if you can do it."*
Priscilla Welch
Masters Women's Marathon record holder

*"Shoot for the moon.
Even if you miss you will land among the stars."*
Les Brown

As runners we hold a variety of dreams. Early in our running career we may have our focus on the most powerful vision of all: getting out the door and actually running. Many new runners have specific weight release and fitness goals. As we become more established in our running lives, we can be striving for a personal best time or extending our long runs. Some of us will be preparing for an upcoming race. We may long to run in a place we have as yet only read about in magazines. On a broader scale, most of us probably hold goals of experiencing more peace in our lives, more love, and a greater sense of belonging.

No matter where we may be in our training, it is not only the running itself that is important but also how we *experience* the activity of running. For all runners, and especially for those who are running for the first time, it is essential that it be a joyful activity that adds to life in a positive way—rather than being the burden of another commitment reluctantly fulfilled. I know that there have been stages in my running life where the act of running (doing) has become more important than how I experience the run (being), and this has often made the running both physically harder and less enjoyable. More often than not, it has also been during these times that I have become injured.

Running can be approached in two ways—you get to decide which you prefer. The first can feel like running through waist-deep mud; the second can feel like you are skimming across the surface like a flat stone. The first approach is to be pushed from behind by our heads—as we tell ourselves that we ought to be running today. *We should.*

The second approach is to be pulled forward by our hearts. As we choose to focus on our aspirations, we are drawn onward by the excitement and enthusiasm that naturally come from focusing on the expansive atmosphere of our dreams. In the first instance, our critical ego works us hard, cracking the whip, and we work alone. In the second, we work in conjunction with Spirit, experiencing joy and grace. We focus all our energy on our running (which rejuvenates and replenishes us), and not on worrying and punishing ourselves with negative thoughts (which tire and disillusion us).

In all learning situations, and particularly with regard to exercise (especially for those coming to a new form of exercise for the first time), pushing ourselves from behind with insults and chastisement is a sure road to becoming disenchanted with our new commitment—and ultimately to giving up. A much more effective (and pleasurable!) way to stay inspired, enthusiastic, and on track, is to draw ourselves forward by keeping our hearts focused on our dreams.

As you lean into your dreams, three outcomes are possible. One is that you find that doors begin to open and your dreams begin to gradually become a reality. The second is that the doors do not open. You give it your very best, but things just don't seem to pan out. When this happens, be mindful of who you meet, lessons you learn, and "coincidences" that take place. You are in training—and you can be sure that Spirit has something bigger in store for you. The third option is that you lean into your dream, and it comes true—quickly. In fact, you come to see that your dream has merely been a staging post for something far grander than you could have imagined—hold onto your hat!

When I first considered the idea of running as a regular form of exercise (beyond my seasonal running as a hunt saboteur!), it was in the hope that I could finally quit smoking. I'd tried to quit a number of times and not been successful. My dream was to quit, and running helped fulfill that dream. It opened me to a level of joy that I had not experienced before in my life. I began to feel strong, and not just physically. I began to feel decisive, able to make positive changes in my life; my horizons expanded. That was my dream come true, or so I thought!

Then came running in events and completing a marathon—something I would never have imagined at the start. Spirit still had other plans, encouraging me to write from my running experience, and to my amazement a book came into being. This book. Spirit's dream was *much* bigger than I ever could have imagined as I set out for my first difficult, wheezing run. From the other end of this incredible journey, most of it would have seemed impossible. Spirit, it appears, enjoys playing in the impossible. I wonder what Spirit has in store for you?

I have heard it said that having a dream is the first step in letting the universe know that we are asking for support in creating something new in our world. This may be true. And what if the communication is actually taking place in the other direction? What if, when we dream, Spirit is saying to us, "How about this? This could be possible for you. There is a place where this is already true for you. Would you like to see it?"

For today's run, you will be looking ahead into your upcoming life as a runner! If you are still working toward a regular running routine, you will want to make sure that you are participating in some form of physical activity while you follow today's exercise. You can certainly use this meditation while walking, swimming, or on the exercise bicycle at the gym. Just make sure that your body is moving at a comfortable pace. For those of you who already have an established running schedule, choose one of your lighter training days for this meditation. This is also a great meditation to use while stretching or enjoying a session of yoga.

As you exercise, allow your heart and mind free reign to move through the expansive landscape of your imagination. Ask yourself what your running life, and also your wider life, would look like if you were to be wildly successful. Perhaps you see yourself winning the Boston Marathon, achieving a new personal best time, or wearing the latest, lightest, fastest running shoes. Possibly you live in the city and long to run in an expansive forest, among snow-capped peaks, or on a beach in Hawaii. If you are like me, they all apply! Maybe you'd like to run 10 miles in a week, or 20, or 40; or you'd be happy to make running a new constant in your life. Whatever your dream may be, continue to hold a vision of it as you exercise. Listen to how it feels inside of you. There's nothing that you have to do. Just allow your imagination (which is just another word for your direct line to Spirit!) to have its way with you.

Hold this focus as a part of the rest of your day, too. When you are in the elevator, waiting in line at the market, or drifting to sleep at night, allow the rich colors of your own imagination to paint a bright and expansive picture of your successful future. The only person who puts boundaries on your dreams is you. Dreaming is the process of being willing to recognize what is truly possible if we allow ourselves the full expression of the magnificent beings that we are. Living, *full-on living*, is then to begin taking steps to move forward and claim our dreams.

Affirmation

I am giving myself permission to dream,
embracing the divine possibilities of my life.

13

Be Your Own Hero

Quality: Self-Acknowledgment

"Where have all the heroes gone? They've gone with the simplicities and the pieties and the easy answers of another era. Our lack of heroes is an indication of the maturity of our age. A realization that every man has come into his own and has the capability of making a success out of his life. But also that this success rests with having the courage and endurance and, above all, the will to become the person you are, however peculiar that may be. Then you will be able to say, 'I have found my hero and he is me.'"

George Sheehan, *Running and Being*

"Our deepest fear is not that we are inadequate. Our deepest fear is that we are powerful beyond measure. It is our Light, not our darkness, that frightens us. We ask ourselves, 'Who am I to be brilliant, gorgeous, talented, fabulous?' Actually, who are you not to be? You are a child of God. Your playing small doesn't serve the world. There's nothing enlightened about shrinking so that other people won't feel insecure around you. You were born to make manifest the glory of God that is within you. It's not just in some of us; it's in everyone. And as we let our own Light shine, we unconsciously give other people permission to do the same. As we're liberated from our own fear, our presence automatically liberates others."

Marianne Williamson, *Return to Love*

I no longer own a television, and haven't for a number of years now—seven or eight at least. I first tried giving it up when I was in my mid-20s. I turned the cheap color TV in my studio apartment on its side and covered it with a piece of Indian cloth. For two years, it functioned as a table. Then there came along a moment in history that was greater than my pledge. I unveiled my TV and sat glued to the images transmitted live via satellite from South Africa. After 27 years in jail, Nelson Mandela was walking free from his prison cell.

He looked uncomfortable in his city suit as he walked back into a South Africa, and a world, that would need to stretch to accommodate his visionary thinking. The camera panned back from Mandela to a throng of supporters just outside the prison that danced and sang in the inimitable rhythms of Soweto township music. As I watched them celebrate, as I saw and felt their jubilation, my tears started to flow. The love that they held for this man, and the dreams of the new nation that he represented, washed over me.

When, ten years later, a group of young men came to my local church to dance the traditional dances of the South African coal miners, my reaction was the same—and stronger. Two dozen men in their 20s and 30s, the "Rishile Gumboot Dancers of Soweto," swayed and drummed their feet in century-old *isicathulo*, the golden bells on their boots ringing out as they did so. I recognized that these men had been born into, grown up in, and endured through the height of the apartheid regime. Many of their fellow countrymen and women had not survived. As they were growing up, many of their friends and family, neighbors, and community leaders had been arrested, "disappeared," or killed.

As my gaze met that of one of the dancers, the blaze of life in his eyes communicated to me the resilience of a whole nation; the determination of an entire people; the strength of heart, patience, and resolve to keep holding a focus on freedom amidst all the rigors of the long years of apartheid. All these qualities were touched inside of me; and a level of compassion, understanding, and admiration I had never experienced before flowed through my heart. My mind flashed back ten years to the image of Mandela as he had walked free from prison. Right there in the church I began to cry, and I again let my tears flow freely. My wife embraced me as I shook with sobs.

The beauty that I saw in these men, and the indomitable human spirit they embodied, had thrown my heart wide open. In the days that followed, I began to ask myself, *"Why had I been so moved by this experience in particular?"* As I searched for an answer to this question, I came to understand that I saw these men as exceptional human beings—they displayed qualities that I did not see in myself. I saw them as heroes.

As runners we have our heroes, too. As a younger man in England, long before I ran myself, I was nonetheless inspired by the great middle distance runners, Steve Ovett and Sebastian Coe. Who is your favorite runner of all time? Grete Waitz, perhaps, or Steve Prefontaine? Kip Keino, Paavo Nurmi, or Joan Samuelson? Carol Lewis or Paul Tergat maybe? Or is it someone who has contributed so much to the running community—an Arthur Lydiard, Bill Bowerman, or Frank Shorter? There are so many to choose from. Perhaps there is someone in your running club or Sunday morning runners group that you admire. While the level of talent is evident in all these people, it is also the qualities that this talent is built upon that we often admire most. Endurance, perseverance, self-discipline, vision, and the strength of heart to overcome challenges—these are all attributes that carry almost hypnotic properties for us as runners.

Often, we are more willing to see certain qualities in others than we are to see them in ourselves. We need to be vigilant and willing to take responsibility for the very best in us. By not fully embracing our magnificence, we allow ourselves to remain in familiar and safe territory, which can mean living at less than our best.

Surprisingly, it can be very uncomfortable to let go of our own diminished image of ourselves. We can feel very at home in the denial of our own incredible potential, both as runners and in the wider arena of our lives. When we open our hearts to our own magnificence, we move into a clearer experience of who we truly are—spiritual beings living a human life. In this way, we begin to set free, from within, the vision that Spirit has for our lives.

As you run today, bring your awareness to someone that you admire. It may be someone that is not a runner or an athlete at all. Let your heart bring this person into focus. It could be a high school teacher, a family member, a historical figure, or a character in a novel. Whoever it is that you choose, make sure it is someone who has aroused strong, positive feelings in you: a person that you would wish to emulate. As you run, try to distill the particular qualities that you admire in them. What is it that you most appreciate in this person? Is it courage? Compassion? Do they embody selfless service? Could it be patience? It may well be a mix of a number of different traits that make up this person's way of being, but try to hone in on what it is that stands out from the blend.

Once these qualities are clear to you, you are at a point of choice—a branching in the road of your spiritual path. On the one hand, you could continue to celebrate these qualities solely in this other person. On the other hand, you could recognize that *the place inside of you where those qualities reside has been more fully awakened*. Whenever we are moved deeply by another's way of being, we have the opportunity to claim more of that way of being for ourselves. We can see our own reflection more clearly in the mirror of another's actions. Simply put, "If you can spot it, you've got it!"

As you move through your day, notice when you are touched or inspired by others. It may be by what they do or by the way that they do it. Perhaps you will notice how willing you are to see these features in others and not in yourself. We can become used to seeing ourselves in a certain way—we become stuck in a rut of our own limited perception of ourselves, choosing to project our creativity and our magnificence onto others. There is immense power available through reclaiming our inherent goodness.

For me, both in the moment that Nelson Mandela walked free from prison and as I watched the Gumboot Dancers, I was put in touch with the incredible courage, resolve, and strength of heart that had carried me through my own difficult childhood and multiple addictions. I reconnected with the place in me where the spark of life had always burned, no matter how the storm in and around me had fought to blow it out.

From this day forward, choose as often as you can to own the goodness, the *God-ness*, that you are. Claim for yourself the gift of your own magnificence. As you continue to acknowledge and honor positive qualities in others, also take a moment to remind yourself that you would not recognize those qualities in others unless they also resided in you.

Affirmation

I am honoring God, myself, and others, as I reclaim
the magnificence and inherent goodness of who I truly am.

14

Going the Distance

Quality: Faith

"Life must be lived forwards even if sometimes
it only makes sense as we look back."
Roger Bannister, *The Four-Minute Mile*

"No pessimist ever discovered the secrets of the stars,
or sailed to an uncharted land,
or opened a new horizon to the human spirit."
Helen Keller

Due to a bend in the west coast of California where I live, the beach that I run on actually faces south. This means that when I set out for my morning run, I am heading almost due east. There is something intrinsically uplifting about running toward a rising sun first thing in the morning, and I experience a sense of possibility of moving forward with my life in new and exciting ways.

In the middle of summer, the sun moves high into the sky early in the day. With the sun reflecting off both the still, summer-warmed water and the expanse of pale sand stretching before me, the scene ahead of me is heavily bleached. The heat haze plays tricks with my eyes, and the few early walkers on the shoreline shimmer like spirits at the water's edge. The landscape becomes surreal and lunar-like. My sense of distance and depth perception are weakened, and it can be tough to tell how far I have run and how far I have to go.

No matter how many times I have this experience, I am inspired again and again by the scene that greets me when I reach the marina and turn west to head for home. With the sun now behind me, all the contrast and depth comes back into my view. The water shifts in and out of the beach—a deep, almost black, blue against the khaki sand. In the distance, I can see the rounded headland and lush greenery of the Palos Verdes peninsula outlined against the deep blue of the California summer sky. In between us rises the dramatic green arch of the Vincent Thomas Bridge, which spans the entrance to the Port of Los Angeles. Nearer still, the skyline is interrupted by the enormous cranes on the dockside—living dinosaur sculptures that inspired some of George Lucas' most imaginative creations in the original trilogy of *Star Wars* movies.

Having turned in an instant from a flat, colorless, almost two-dimensional view to this deeply colorful, expansive, multidimensional landscape, I stop for a few moments, knocked back on my heels by the beauty of the world I had been moving through—and yet unaware of.

Sometimes life, like running, can be about focusing on the next step in front of us and not much more. When we look further ahead into our future, nothing seems too clearly defined. It can be exactly in these moments—when we feel called from deep inside to move in a new direction—that we can see the least about how we are going to get there.

Yet, somewhere inside of us, we recognize that, although we may be heading in what *appears* to be an impossible direction, that it is along this new path that we will discover the very best of ourselves. God plays in the impossible! When we move in the direction of our dreams, we are amazed to find that Spirit will meet us more than halfway.

Our responsibility is to move, and Spirit responds to our courage and faith.

When I stopped my drug and alcohol abuse, for a while it was hard for me to see how I was going to create a new life, new friends, and new goals. I began to set the course of my life with a new compass, a place inside of me that seemed to be focused much further ahead than I was able to see. As I followed this new feeling in my gut, my life began to improve in ways I could not have imagined. Within a year, I had met the woman who was to become my wife and lifelong partner, moved to the United States, begun a successful new job, and discovered the joy of running. All of these had been completely invisible to me—even as I was moving in their direction.

While the unknown can be intimidating territory for many of us, it can also hold the greatest opportunities to deepen our faith in Spirit and in ourselves. Today as you run, use the time to focus on an area of your life that seems uncertain. Connect with the vision inside of you that sees yourself reaching beyond that uncertainty to the place you want to be. It may be a goal in the physical world or the wish to experience a certain quality in your internal life.

During your workout today, see yourself finishing the race, meeting the time, or completing the number of days of running in the week that you wish. If your goal is more of an internal one, picture the ways in which your life will be different once you attain your goal. You may not be able to see how you will get there, and it may even seem impossible that you could. The truth is, you won't know exactly how to get there until you *are* there. Whatever the exact route, the road will be paved with faith—the faith that you have all the resources necessary inside of you to move forward. Paradoxically, you may not discover some of those gifts *until* you move forward. Put another way, the willingness to do creates the ability to do.

It has been said that we are never given anything in life that is beyond our ability to handle. When life feels overwhelming, we can cross the canyon of doubt by using the bridge of faith. As you hold the picture of how things will be, imagine a bridge connecting where you are with where you wish to be. Imagine this bridge as an arc of golden light. This bridge is your faith, your willingness to hold a vision and move in its direction—even when the way may not appear clear. It is only when you are on the other side of the bridge that you will be able to look back and understand how you made the journey to your new life. This is the very nature of faith.

As you go through your day and beyond, keep this vision of the golden bridge of faith in your mind and heart. In times when your goals seem out of reach, recognize that these are the priceless opportunities for building firm foundations for the next bridge that will take you closer to home.

When I turn and see the beauty of the peninsula come into clear view, I return home with a broader perspective on my life and a deeper appreciation of a plan for my life that is so much greater than my own. When I look back down the pathway of my life so far, I look back upon many bridges. Some are a little sturdier than others, but all are strong enough to have carried me forward. I can see clearly that there is a purpose and direction that has brought me to where I am in this moment, and I am encouraged that that support stretches off into the unseen future ahead of me.

Affirmation

Trusting in Spirit's higher purpose for my life,
I am discovering that God *is* faith in me.

15

Running Young

Quality: Playfulness

"But if the dance of the run isn't fun, then discover another dance,
because without fun the good of the run is undone,
and a suffering runner always quits sooner or later."
Fred Rohe, The Zen of Running

"There often seems to be a playfulness to wise people, as if their
equanimity has as its source this playfulness."
Edward Hoagland

I like to talk about running—both to hear from other runners about their experience and to share about the transformative effect that running has had in my life. When asked how much I run, my reply is, "Between 20 and 30 miles a week." "Wow," they often respond. "You are a serious runner." "I try not to be," I say—and I am not joking!

I have met plenty of other runners who, when they started to become serious about their running, got exactly that—serious. I've been there myself. We become so absorbed in the details of what we are doing that we lose perspective. We begin to confuse mastery with seriousness, to sacrifice joy on the altar of commitment.

Do you remember how, as a young child, an ongoing commentary ran through your mind as you would play? All too often as adults, we can be tuned into a stream of hurtful comments and put-downs that runs a loop in our minds without even so much as a commercial break! As young children, our commentary was quite different—it was dramatic, encouraging, and enthusiastic. Maybe, like me, you even spoke the commentary out loud. As I rode my bicycle up and down our street, I *was* the sheriff riding to save the town at the last minute. When I was kicking a soccer ball with my dad, I *was* the young star scoring the last goal that saved the game. When I was doing my homework, I *was* the top scientist, cracking a code that would save the planet from invasion. Crazy? Possibly. Did I have fun? Absolutely! Do you notice how kids have the get-up-and-go to play for hours and never run out of steam? It's because they are living in the natural world of their dreams—a place of boundless energy, inspiration, and joy.

Not long ago, I read James E. Shapiro's outstanding book, *Meditations from the Breakdown Lane.* It is a fascinating journal of his internal and external experience as he ran the 3,000 miles across the United States, averaging 40 miles a day—every day for 80 days. Now, this is not something I am planning to do! However, in my running recently, I have had immense fun using this as my fantasy. Even if I am running for only 20 minutes, and that's all that I have time for that day, I imagine myself somewhere on the transcontinental trail:

"...This is without doubt one of the great sporting achievements of this century. We watch now as Toby Estler, the first Englishman to run across the United States, begins to cross the George Washington Bridge. He has completed the 3,026 miles from Dillon Beach, California, in only 75 days. What a fantastic ambassador for his country. His quest has been a celebration of the human spirit..."

I return from these runs with an extra spring in my step—exultant and inspired. There have been many times when spending my run in this playful and expansive way has brought the dividend of new and creative solutions to problems that I have been stuck on for quite a while. I like to think that rather than cleanliness, it is playfulness that is next to Godliness. Whenever I hear laughter, I know that Spirit is present. When I give myself permission to experience within me the presence and innocence of a playful child, I reconnect with the God, and the good, in me.

During your run today, give yourself the gift of your own world-saving, record-breaking, death-defying commentary—from the moment the theme from *Rocky* starts playing as you leave home until you return to applause from a capacity-filled stadium. Let this gift stretch through all of your day. *Be* the world's greatest mom; *be* the chef at a five-star Paris restaurant; *be* the world's greatest lover! Play! Play! Play!

Affirmation

I am living in joy, playing into the hands of God.

16

The Trainer Within

Quality: Spiritual Fitness

*"Training enables one to set priorities. To live more fully. To be a
better person to those around you. I used to slack off for most of the
year and then cram train for specific marathons; later I would wonder
why I hadn't done better. Not a wise approach. Be sure that the goal
you set for yourself does not cause you to lose sight of this process,
this activity, this pleasure, this lifestyle choice."*
Charles Lyons, *The Quotable Marathoner*

*"Spirituality is no longer about discovering the rules;
it's about living them."*
Dr. Carolyn Myss, *Energy Anatomy*

There are as many approaches to running as there are
runners. Some swear by putting in as much mileage as
possible—150 or more miles a week! Sebastian Coe, one of
the greatest milers in history, never ran more than seven
miles in a workout and, according to him, that was six too
many! Long slow distance is the cornerstone of successful
running, say some. Long slow distance makes long slow
runners, say others. And so it goes on. In the end, the training

routine that works best for you . . . will be the one that you discover works best for you!

As many seasoned runners discover, each of us is unique in terms of what we need to focus on to get the most out of our running. When we start out in our running life, we need to draw upon the opinions and advice of those around us almost entirely—it's only natural. Then, as we build a depth of running experience, we gain greater clarity as to how we can most effectively support our own particular fitness and training goals. Somewhere along the way, we begin to listen to a voice that we come to recognize as that of our own inner trainer. It is this voice that encourages us out of the door on those cold, sleepy mornings—and to stay home when rest is the only workout that will support our long-term goals.

In our broader lives, we also have access to this inner trainer—to the place inside of us that is connected to God. In order to live a more successful and joyful life, we need to attune to this place inside of us that will lead us to greater spiritual fitness—to listen to the direction and encouragement of our internal spiritual trainer. We don't expect to improve our level of physical fitness without regular exercise. In the spiritual realm, too, with greater opportunities come greater responsibilities. To move more fully into the flow of God's giving, we also need to commit to building our spiritual fitness.

What does spiritual fitness look like? Some of the major ingredients are integrity, trust, loving, faith, and a willingness to be of service. It involves making quiet time available to ourselves to seek guidance from Spirit through prayer and to listen to the answers through meditation. You may want to consider making these activities a more significant part your life. Through your commitment to following these moving meditations, you are already embracing a new level of spiritual fitness.

You may have challenging decisions to make, to stretch into new levels of integrity and honesty with yourself, others, and God. It is not that abundance, success, and joy are a reward for a more Spirit-centered approach to life; they are simply *a natural result* of such an approach. Then, as we live our lives in a more Spirit-centered way, our prayers are not just answered—our life becomes answered prayer.

If you keep running the same distance in the same time every day, you will become very adept at running that distance at that speed. That may be the result that you are looking for. If you either want to run faster or farther, you would need to include speed or distance work in your training. Maybe add in some weight training and some hill workouts. This seems self-evident; we do what we can to move *toward* the result we are looking for. In the same way, if we are truly interested in aligning with the all-good, we need to make choices that move us toward the fullness of God's blessings.

So how do we "work out" to build our spiritual fitness? This will vary from one person to another at any given moment, and each of us knows inside what it is that we need to take care of. There may be an outstanding commitment that you have yet to honor. Perhaps there is an apology or a kind word from you that is still waiting to be shared, or a thank-you to someone—or to God—that has, as yet, gone unspoken.

As we take care of our spiritual workouts, we become able to reside at a level of greater spiritual fitness, and with that fitness comes the ability to live in an atmosphere of greater abundance. *It is as we align ourselves with our highest vision that we move into the stream of the all-good that is always here.*

As you set out to run today, set the intention to make a clearer connection with your own internal spiritual guidance, with that place inside of you that is connected with the divine. It is from this place that you will gain greater clarity as to how to move forward in your own spiritual fitness-training program. As you run, listen for places inside of you that are asking for attention—unfinished business that needs to be completed. You'll know it when you come across it, simply by the way you feel. Trust your own guidance. Make a mental note of the strongest areas. For me they tend to be broken lines of communication—with my wife, my family, friends, and myself, or with God. I find that when I take action to reopen these lines of communication, my life automatically takes a turn for the better.

A little over eight years ago, I faced just such a choice myself. Again, during one of the darkest periods in my life, running was all that kept me breathing in the midst of intense fear, shame, and sadness. A few weeks previously, my wife had discovered my ongoing affair with a woman that I had met through the Internet—a very 21st century occurrence. I had been living in a fantasy world; and while I had been lying to my wife, I had also been masterfully deceiving myself into thinking that what I was doing was acceptable.

With the discovery of my affair, my fantasy world crashed around me. I'll never forget the morning I received the phone call at work from my wife that told me she had discovered everything: the lies, the hidden phone calls, and the secret gifts and rendezvous. By the time I arrived home, my clothes were very neatly piled on the sidewalk. I was in need of a new home.

Over the next days and weeks, the only place I could find shelter from the pain was in my morning beach run. As I struggled to make sense of my life and my choices, a strong, gentle guidance came from within. I needed help and the place to find it was amongst others who had had the same experience—to find a 12-step program for sexual addiction.

This inner prompting horrified me. Even in recovery, my drug and alcohol addiction had seemed to me somewhat acceptable, even glamorous or manly, honorable scars perhaps. But sex addiction? That was for perverts and sickos, not for me. It took about six more weeks of suffering and confusion before I followed that inner prompting. When I did, I walked into a room not filled with deviants and psychopaths, but other men like me, struggling to find a new foundation for their lives. It was that room, and the choice to walk into it, that changed the course of my life for the better. I think of that choice often—especially when I return home each day to my wife and my young daughter. It was the beginning of an intensive spiritual fitness workout!

Throughout the day, ask yourself, "How can I attain a greater level of spiritual fitness in other areas of my life?" If a response comes forward into your mind and you think, "It can't be that! I could never do that!" then that is more than likely *exactly* what you need to do. I didn't say this process would necessarily be easy. If you feel comfortable in following through on the idea that comes forward, go for it! Do all that you can to continue making decisions that will support your living with integrity—aligning with the very best of who you are.

If you make just one decision today to do this, you can alter the whole direction of your life. If you continue to do this on a regular basis, change will sweep through your life, and you will be streaming along with the all-good.

Affirmation

I am supporting my spiritual fitness,
stepping into the very best of who I am.

17

Moving Forward

Quality: Commitment

"The key to making a commitment you can keep is to be realistic. It also helps if you ease your way gradually into a program that advances slowly enough to leave you eager for more rather than dreading each workout."
Alberto Salazar, *Alberto Salazar's Guide to Running*

"The moment one commits oneself, then Providence moves, too. All sorts of things occur to help that would never otherwise have occurred. A stream of events issues from the decision, raising unforeseen incidents and meetings and material assistance, which no man could have dreamt would have come his way."
Goethe

Marriage, and the commitment that it involves, used to terrify me. I feared that marriage would imprison me in some way—that I would lose my freedom. About six months after my wife and I were married, we had our first big argument. During the quarrel, there came a point when I recognized that I had reached a place that was familiar to me from previous relationships. It seemed my fears were coming true.

I walked away from the argument, changed into my running gear, and headed for the front door.

I flew out of the house and down the road, plotting to use my run as time to figure out how I would leave my marriage. In that moment, life seemed like an uphill struggle, and so I chose to run some hills. The sheer intensity of this workout always calms me. As I ran that day, a feeling grew in me that I had not experienced before. It was telling me that I was not going to leave.

I pushed even harder up the hills, trying to focus on this new feeling more intently. I was amazed to find that, yes, in some way my fears had come true—marriage was indeed taking something away from me. It was removing the knee-jerk reaction of leaving a relationship the moment that things got difficult.

I realized that, contrary to my fears, my commitment was actually liberating me. In my past relationships, when things had gotten this tough, I had simply moved onto the next one, leaving the problem behind—at least for a while. But what I also left behind were my own growth opportunities. Now, having removed the distraction of taking the easy road out, I had placed myself in a position of being more willing to give what needed to be given to make the marriage work. I needed to take responsibility for my share of the relationship "workouts," such as open communication, time for playfulness, time together as well as time alone. In running terms, I was learning how to keep my marriage fit.

When I returned from the run, calmer and more balanced, we talked it out. I am happy to report that we have just celebrated fourteen years together. Now make no mistake, this was not the last time I needed to run hills to let off steam!

It is not only in the area of relationship that commitment can seem like a dirty word! Many of us associate commitment with obligation, compulsion, and inconvenience. Yet it offers us unsurpassed opportunities to build trust with ourselves by following through on agreements that we have made. More often than not, we are willing to break commitments with ourselves more readily than those we have made with other people; yet it is exactly in this area that we can find the most leverage for transformation in our lives.

Commitment is the arena in which we align our actions with our word. Following through on our commitments is the fast track to building trust in ourselves, and this is the cornerstone for a firm foundation of self-esteem. In keeping our commitments with others, we demonstrate to them that we can be trusted to follow through on our word. As parents, teachers, and leaders in our communities, if we can model this behavior for younger adults (and children of all ages), we offer them the opportunity to find this same place of commitment inside of themselves.

As runners, we experience commitment as where the rubber meets the road (literally!). We have the opportunity to build trust with ourselves through the process of keeping our commitment to run so many miles or times per week. This can be a starting place, a reference point, from which to set a course for our lives. Our commitment to running can become a place of inspiration—an indicator of what is possible in other areas of our lives.

The key here is that you either make a commitment or you don't. You cannot be fairly committed, or even mostly committed. You are either committed or you're not. If you experience commitment as a feeling of restriction, as though you have painted yourself into a corner, then what you are experiencing is the energy of non-commitment! You may be trying to think yourself into commitment, when it needs to be made with the heart. As I discovered after I married, stepping into commitment fully carries with it feelings of liberation, relaxation, and safety. Commitment brings expansion.

For those of you who may be new to running, this is one of the greatest gifts that running has to offer. Regular running will support your building both physical fitness and trust in yourself. Your commitment to your workouts will become a beam of light that will illuminate the way forward in many areas of your life.

Today as you prepare to run, choose an important area in your life in which you would like to be moving forward. Avoid making any judgments about where you are or where you think you should be (sometimes referred to as "shoulding" on yourself); just let that area rest in your consciousness as you begin your run. As you find your rhythm and stride, begin to look for one specific step that you could take, *if you decided to*, that would move you forward in this area of your life.

The important point, at this stage, is to remember that this is an exploration of possibilities and not a commitment to action. Nor does it need to be in the area of running. Perhaps you will imagine yourself going to the hardware store to buy those shelves you have been longing to put up or balancing your checkbook. Whatever you choose to explore is just fine.

As you settle upon one possible step, allow your imagination to be filled with the rhythm and energy of your run, and picture yourself taking that step—see how it feels inside. Again, the important point to remember here is that you are just trying this on for size. You are not making a commitment here—simply exploring the idea to see if it could work for you. For example, *"I am sitting at the kitchen table at home, filling out the application for that upcoming race next month. As I fill out the form, I am feeling a surge of excitement and joy as I recognize that I am well prepared to take part in my first race."*

You can do this visualization silently inside of yourself, or (as I like to do) say it out loud as you run. As you come to the end of imagining this possible next step, listen to the cadence of your breath and the beat of your feet as they move you forward. From this place of openness, ask yourself if you are willing to commit to taking the step you have visualized. Maybe you will come to see that the action step you explore is not a fit for you—that's great, too!

Often we find out what we do want by first becoming clear about what we don't want. Now instead of uncertainty, you have clarity. You can cross that option off your list and explore others. If you have running time left, explore another possible action step, and see if it suits the situation better. Remember, *it is better not to make a commitment, than to make one and not follow through.*

When you find an action step that does fit, make sure that you give yourself a definitive timeline to accomplish it. I encourage you to stay with that one commitment during the run. If you have time left and want to explore it further, you can vision successfully completing it a second time. My experience is that I am best served by making only one new commitment during a run, and by being cautious of being carried by the enthusiasm of the run into making a slew of new commitments!

As you cool down from your workout, acknowledge yourself for making the time and having the willingness to investigate new possibilities. By simply exploring this action step, whether you decide to commit to it or not, you have already followed through on your desire to head for new horizons. This *in itself* will build the energy of change in your life.

Affirmation

I am honoring the power of my word,
keeping my agreements with myself and others.

18

Running in All Weathers

Quality: Courage

*"During the winter, you head out into the darkness for a run.
When spring comes, and the first crocus pokes up its head . . .
you know it was worthwhile."*
Nina Kuscsik
The Quotable Marathoner, edited by Charles Lyons

*"Sunshine is delicious, rain is refreshing,
wind braces us up, snow is exhilarating;
there really is no such thing as bad weather,
only different kinds of good weather."*
John Ruskin

Being a British native, moving to Southern California brought with it an enormous climate change. I have lived here for over a decade, long enough for the winter months to feel a little cold. But for the first three or four years, I wore short pants all through winter—it just never felt cold enough to do otherwise!

Certainly, I appreciate being able to run without a shirt along a sun-drenched beach and get a tan in December. Yet, there are times when I miss the more marked changes in the seasons. There is something inherently trustworthy about seasonal change; it feels natural—*right!* The monotony of Southern California weather usually overwhelms me around September, when I am expecting fall leaves and brisk air, but the sun just keeps on beating down.

Sometimes I'll close all the blinds, turn off all the lights, and lay on the floor in the darkness while I play a rainstorm CD. The experience is delicious! As the storm gathers with distant thunder and then breaks with a few heavy, individually identifiable drops, I feel an aspect of me relax in a way that it never does otherwise—an ancient and distinctly European part of me. As the sound of the rain becomes heavier and heavier, I give myself over to a relaxation that becomes meditative, cellular. The thunder moves right overhead, with rich, baritone explosions. I picture the accompanying lighting and can almost smell the cordite in the air. When the storm begins to wane and the sound of the rain stops, there are just the sporadic drips from the trees and plants. Finally, the birdsong returns, and I imagine the sun breaking through the parting clouds, and my body—no, *my being*—feels refreshed, replenished, and revitalized.

Would I want to live in a wet climate all the time? Certainly not! Just in the same way that a climate with 340 days of sunshine a year becomes boring, a perpetually wet climate would also become monotonous.   But the bad weather days add texture to my life, and I have to say that I enjoy running in the rain a great deal. On the rare occasions that there is a good downpour here at home, I do all that I can to get out and run in it. When I run in the rain, I feel like a vibrant part of my environment rather than merely someone running through it. The rain embraces me in a way that the sunshine never does. It touches me—literally. The clear skies that appear on the day after a good rainstorm are something most people have a deep appreciation for—especially my neighbors in smoggy Los Angeles. The San Gabriel Mountains—often lost behind the haze of city life—come into clear focus, their peaks glistening with fresh snow. In the driest areas, it is the rain that brings life to the desert floor, covering it with brilliant new wildflowers.

Life has its bad-weather days, too. Yet I can be a lot less open to them than I am to my rainstorm CD! I know that there is a lesson for me here. In the same way that I am prepared to enjoy the contrast, the texture, and the cleansing qualities of the wet weather, there are opportunities present, too, when life throws me a curve ball.

I have spent many hours in the past pounding the streets, trying to run off or away from difficult life situations and troubled feelings. I have yet to succeed in running *away* from anything. Sometimes the smartest thing to do is to take angry feelings for a run. We burn off their energy and come to a more balanced place, so that we can express them constructively and without harming others or ourselves. But until an issue is resolved, it will always return—floating to the surface like a cork. Running has, however, assisted me in working *through* many challenging feelings in my life.

One of the greatest qualities available to all of us as we journey through the sporadic rainstorms of life is courage. When those bad-weather days come into our lives, when all the rich textures of our shadow sides emerge, and we are buffeted by feelings of sadness, lack of worth, or jealousy— we are on the leading edge of our learning. However, many of us (especially men) have been taught that to express our deeper feelings is a sign of weakness. When our own storm clouds gather, we often respond by suppressing and hiding our stormy feelings as they near the surface. We may fear that others will think us stupid or take advantage of us in our vulnerability. So we skirt the storm, and in the short term we marvel at our ability to stay out of the rain. However, over time, we begin to dry up in the desert of our repressed feelings. The landscape of our lives becomes increasingly barren. And, as we repress our feelings, we repress not only the pain but also the joy.

As runners, we experience the aches and tenderness that come not from injury but from stretching into a new level of ability, health, and aliveness. When we increase our mileage, we experience a few days of soreness as our bodies adjust to the new commitment. Then, if we return to our previous running distance on a lighter day, we find it easier—even effortless—to cover the same distance. Voyaging into new territory brings a new level of enjoyment. Fully experiencing and expressing our feelings can be much the same. While initially we may encounter tenderness and even pain, these pass. We discover that a brighter day awaits us, and our hearts are filled with a new optimism and appreciation for life.

As you prepare to run today, bring to mind a situation that is currently causing you some upset. Perhaps something is very present for you, and you will not have to look too hard. Set the intention, as you move off, to approach your feelings as a vehicle for moving to a greater level of freedom—a doorway to an increased level of joy. Ask for Spirit to support you in exploring your feelings in a caring and understanding way. As you allow deeper expressions of feeling to move through you, both while you are running and in the broader context of your life, remember that there is nothing that you need to do with them. There is nothing to fix.

Give yourself permission to move more freely and fully in the rich scenery of your own internal landscape. Give yourself the gift of the clear skies that follow the storm.

Affirmation

I am courageously moving through
the rich and changing landscape of my feelings,
guided and protected by Spirit.

19

17 Seconds

Quality: Forgiveness

"Forgiveness is the shortest route to God."
Gerald Jampolsky
Forgiveness: The Greatest Healer of All

"Holding onto anger is like grasping a hot coal with the intention of throwing it at someone else; you are the one who gets burned."
Buddha

There have been times when my running performance has not met with my aspirations. In fact, I would say that most of the time my performance comes in a little below what I'm hoping for. When I ran my first marathon, I set the goal of finishing in 3 hours and 30 minutes. To finish in this time, I would need to run each mile ten seconds faster than I had in training, and yet I was certain that I had it in me.

That year, 1996, was the first year that the L.A. marathon used electronic tags to monitor each runner's individual performance, so I knew my time would be accurate. There was a roar from the crowd as Mohammed Ali made his way to the start line to fire the starting pistol. For a sport anchored in the qualities of resolve, courage, and strength of heart, there seemed no better choice than Ali to send us on our way.

The excitement of the event, the culmination of a year's dedication and early morning alarm calls, and the joy of striding through the streets of L.A. with tens of thousands of others lent a strength to my stride I had not experienced before. As I had trained alone that entire year, save for a handful of races, being with so many other runners was uplifting, energizing, and encouraging—especially as I seemed to be passing so many of them with ease. Suddenly, 3 hours and 30 minutes seemed very possible!

Up until that day, the farthest I had run was 20 miles, and when I passed the 20-mile marker, I still felt strong. At 23 miles, my quads and then my calves started to cramp. Occasionally, over those last three miles, I had to walk. When I came up the final hill and turned into the finishing chute, I was running. I crossed the finish line in 3 hours and 30 minutes . . . and 17 seconds.

In the weeks after the marathon, I carried those 17 seconds around with me everywhere I went. I focused on them rather than the astonishing accomplishment of finishing my first-ever marathon. I used them as an excuse to judge myself in a myriad of ways. I took every opportunity to "should" on myself! I should have trained harder or longer. I should have run more hills. I should have known more, prepared better, run faster, slower, paced myself better, started running as a kid—just think where I could be now! Over and over it went.

On the one hand, there was a year's dedication, self-discovery, commitment, and passion all culminating in a wonderful performance. On the other, those 17 seconds. The latter was winning every time! In fact, I was so frustrated with myself that I went out just three days after the race and started pounding the streets, overextending myself. Within a month, I developed an injury that took me out of running for almost two years.

A couple of months after that first marathon, still too injured to run, I was walking on the beach, trying to let go not only of those 17 seconds but now also the injury I was carrying. As I reached the turning point of my walk and began to head back, I picked out the tracks of my outbound path. The sea was pushing up toward my footprints, like a great ocean of loving lapping at my angry trail.

A few strides toward home, I stopped to pick up a particularly beautiful shell that was glistening in the morning sunrise. Just as I bent down, a gentle wave, filled with the shimmering colors of the reflected sun, moved up the beach and filled one of my earlier footprints. The water filled the shape of the footprint, running in between the imprint of the ribs on the sole, pooling in the heel, pushing up to the toe. Then, before my eyes, the sand began to soften and the shape of my shoeprint blurred, spread, and disappeared back into the beach and was gone. As I watched, my heart began to soften. I began to let go of those 17 seconds.

This is the experience of forgiveness. When we move fully into our hearts, the power of our loving will rise up to fill the holes of pain and judgment that we dig, dissolving the lies that we tell ourselves about who we are. When we reconnect with that place inside of us that is our higher Self— where there exists compassion, unconditional love, acceptance, joy, and peace—we connect with God in us. We automatically bridge the mirage of separation that is created through judgment and condemnation of ourselves and others.

Often as runners, and especially as competitive runners, we become focused on the finish line and lose sight of the journey that gets us there. We confuse who we are with what we do—with how we perform—and this can spill over into other areas of our lives. There are moments when we forget, both in anger and in enthusiasm, that as a part of our human experience there will be times when our performance will not match up to our noble expectations. Forgiveness, applied in any area of your life, will help you to re-center around who you truly are—a spiritual being who is intrinsically worthy.

As I walked home, turning the shell over in my palm, I saw that I really had no idea whether I would have run a faster time in the marathon if I trained more. I may have indeed run faster—and twisted my ankle on a rock that had been kicked out of the way by the time I got there at my slower pace! I can never know. The fact is I trained to the best of my ability at that time. I began to recognize that while running is one of the ways that I choose to *express* who I am, it is not all of who I am. I am so much more—even than that!

In letting go of those 17 seconds, and the judgments that I had made about myself based upon them, I reconnected with the feelings of joy and accomplishment that I had stifled for so long. I had completed a marathon and was proud if it! At the end of my walk home, I looked in my filing cabinet and pulled out the certificate I had received at the marathon—and that I had never quite been able to throw away. As I hung it on my office wall, I claimed completely, and for the first time, the commitment, courage, and resolve that had been birthed in that journey of completing my first marathon.

When you step out for your run today, ask for Spirit's support in truly experiencing the liberating power of forgiveness. While you run, allow a situation to come forward from your life in which you are aware that you are judging yourself. As a guide, if you find yourself thinking, "I should have . . ." this is an indication of an opportunity for forgiveness.

More than words, forgiveness is an experience, a feeling of opening and softening. To help you find that place of loving and openness, hold an image in your mind of someone that you love dearly, perhaps a child, a spouse, or your pet. Breathe! Once you have connected with the tender energy of forgiveness, it can be very powerful to go back in your heart's eye to the situation in which you have judged yourself and give yourself a long, heartfelt hug.

Keep this focus throughout your day. Whenever you notice that you are judging yourself, or if you remember a time in the past when this may have happened, take a few moments to find that place of forgiveness inside of you, and give yourself the powerful and transformational gift of your own loving.

Affirmation

I am bathed in the compassion and tender loving of my heart, forgiving myself as I remember who I truly am.

20

Trail Running

Quality: Generosity of Spirit

"Feel the flow of your dance and know you are not running
for some future reward—the reward is now!"
Fred Rohe, The Zen of Running

"Your daily life is your temple and your religion.
Whenever you enter into it, take with you your all."
Kahlil Gibran

I am always excited to travel to another part of the
country or globe, because it also means I have the
opportunity to run somewhere that is completely unfamiliar
to me. Whether I am staying a few days or more, my morning
runs will generally grow in expanding circles from the hotel
or house that I am staying in.

On a pre-Katrina visit to New Orleans several years ago,
I thrived running along the banks of the Mississippi,
sweating profusely in the humid air. I love to sweat as I run;
it feels honest, unsophisticated, and primal. My hotel was in
the French Quarter, only a couple of minutes' run from the

banks of Old Man River. I would then turn northeast and run
along the river bank, marveling at the steamboat organ, the
saxophonist that seemed to play for tips from dawn till dusk,
the rippled waters of the wide Mississippi, and the sense of
history that flowed along with its current. Music and the
river go hand in hand. The Mississippi has inspired a bevy of
blues songs, New Orleans being a point of pilgrimage for
musicians from Blind Lemon Jefferson to Janis Joplin. Only
the previous night, I had learned of the drowning in the
Mississippi in 1997 of the talented young musician Jeff
Buckley at the age of 31—another page in the life of the ever-
thickening history of the United States' longest river.

After a couple of days, my runs started to branch out
further, pushing away from the areas that predominantly
catered to tourists and into earthier parts of the town to the
east. The architecture remained the same but was more run-
down. The streets were quieter, dotted with the occasional
condemned building and wild, sprawling, overgrown
gardens. Abandoned houses and ramshackle liquor stores
loitered on street corners, and although I felt safe in the
bright sun of the late morning, I might have thought twice
before walking through this neighborhood alone after dark.

As I ran northeast along Elysian Fields (yes, really!)
Avenue, a small knot of homeless men lounging on a
discarded couch in an empty lot turned their heads to watch
me pass by, nodding in response to my enthusiastic "Good
Morning!" One of them mimicked me by getting up and
running on the spot, much to the amusement of the two
others, who slapped their knees and threw their heads back
in raucous laughter. Young children that had not made it to
school tracked my progress with wide-eyed fascination; two
youngsters in their early teens ran alongside me for a long
block, all the while looking at me rather than where they
were going, and then peeled away giggling.

Most of the locals scratched their heads as I ran by,
rivulets of sweat running down my shirtless body,
wondering why on earth I would be moving so quickly in
this heat and humidity. At nine o'clock in the morning the

temperature was in the high 80s, the humidity in the high 90s. My smile was met with the broad, gap-toothed grins of older men sitting on stoops and the playful whistles of working moms as they swept steps and storefronts and hung laundry. I kept moving forward, my Good Mornings and my smile filled with genuine affection and joy. I felt lifted by these moments of connection.

As I have run through varying neighborhoods in towns and cities all over the planet, I have focused with greater and greater resolve on my energy. From London to Calcutta, Sydney to Los Angeles, with each stride I have imagined a visible trail of clear white light stretching out behind me, spreading across the route that I have followed. Picture the vapor trail that streams from the path of a passing jet, and you'll see what I mean. As my trail of light swirls behind me it brings joy, laughter, and playfulness.

As you run today, picture a long trail of loving energy rippling in your wake. Not only is your run filled with the power of the activity itself, it is also filled with the qualities of commitment, self-care, and steadfast resolve that got you out there in the first place. Wherever you are running, you are leaving a wake of vital, life-affirming energy that will touch, uplift, inspire, and encourage all those who cross its path. Imagine this blanket of positive change settling behind you in the streets, fields, forest, path, or gym where you are running today.

Then, as you move through your day, continue to picture this divine energy flowing from you, and *through* you. Each of us is a gateway for Spirit, and as we each consciously open ourselves as a conduit we benefit too—for it blesses us on its way through.

At the end of the evening just before you go to sleep, you might like to take a few moments to review your day and notice the times when you were aware that your "trail" touched someone. Through holding this focus, you may have noticed a difference in the quality of your own experience today, not just in your workout but also as you went about the rest of your day.

Wherever you are, at home or at work, on the freeway, or visiting friends, you are an outlet of divine Love, bringing healing and positive change *simply by being there* and being who you are!

Affirmation

I am an open conduit for Spirit's healing love,
which is expressing itself through me and as me
in every moment of my life.

21

Keeping It Clean

Quality: Responsibility

"It's the effort that matters on the hard days."
Steve Jones
Running With the Legends by Michael Sandrock

*"Everyone is an athlete. The only difference is that
some of us are in training, some not."*
George Sheehan

"Liberty means responsibility."
George Bernard Shaw

Before I lived in the United States, I lived in the seaside town of Brighton, in southern England. It is a vibrant college town with a large population of squatters—people who find a way into abandoned buildings and make their home there. These buildings were often government or corporate offices that had been lying dormant for years. Faced with the choice of sleeping on the streets or squatting, the latter seemed a great choice. I remember one large multistory building in particular that had sat empty for over five years as the owner waited for the opportunity to redevelop while enjoying a sizable tax break.

One morning as I ran through a small park area in the center of town, I noticed bright flags and banners hanging from the windows, announcing a new community had moved in. Within a week, the ground floor had been transformed into a café run by volunteers from among the squatters. The café offered cheap and nutritious food to anyone who cared to stop by, housed or homeless, wealthy or poor. At the time, I was working the night shift at a local bakery. I would run along the seafront in the afternoons to fill my lungs with fresh sea air that would keep me going through the stale atmosphere of nights on the factory floor.

It quickly became part of my routine to stop in for a bowl of the day's special at the end of my run. The food was outstanding: hearty soups, homemade breads, fresh salads, naturally sweetened cakes and desserts. There were many times that I saw people come in who were clearly living on the streets and down on their luck. They would be given a seat and a bowl of food whether they could afford to pay or not. More often than not, someone in the room would step forward and pay for them.

One afternoon, after the café had been open for a couple of months, a gentleman walked in whom I had not seen before. Already, the café had its regulars and we recognized and greeted each other. The clientele was drawn from a wide pool: students from the nearby colleges as well as working men and women on their lunch breaks. Older women with purple rinses could be sharing a table with youngsters with purple Mohawks! The newcomer stopped just inside the doorway and looked over the top of his half-moon spectacles at the mixed group of people scattered among the dozen or so tables.

Shortly afterward, one of the regulars came in, a homeless man who was rarely able to pay for his meal. Once more, with no questions or admonitions, the young woman behind the counter greeted him by name and asked him how he was.

She filled a bowl with a thick lentil and vegetable soup. It was probably all he would eat that day. The gentleman in the half-moon spectacles watched this scene unfold and, after the homeless man had sat down and begun to eat his food, walked confidently up to the counter.

"You know, young lady, that you are only perpetuating his problems, not helping him." The young women smiled and without saying a word, walked from behind the counter. She gently hooked her arm in the crook of the gentleman's and walked him to the door. As they stepped outside, she turned and pointed to a small sign that hung above the entrance. It read, "Please dump your trash elsewhere." She smiled at him once more and bid him goodbye in the sweetest of voices, one that hadn't the least hint of anger in it. She turned back into the café to serve her next customer. The entire café burst into applause and the gentleman walked away shaking his head. We never saw him again.

As runners we spend much of our time in the great outdoors, relishing the splendor of the natural world around us. We are thankful for the intrinsic beauty and healing quality of nature. When we see it abused or neglected, we feel sad and even angry. Yet, along with everyone else, we may well be unknowingly dropping trash of our own throughout our day. For each time we inflict our misdirected anger or upset onto others, we are littering in our own way. When we share our unsolicited opinions and prejudices, or allow frustration in one situation to spill over into another, we are contributing to the pollution of the environment that we are in.

Taking responsibility for our own feelings is a commitment that is spiritual in nature. This is not to say that we should keep everything pent up inside of us. It means that when we have feelings that we need to work through, the opportunity is to do so *responsibly*. We can work with ourselves through journal writing, painting, or other forms of creative expression, so that we can give our feelings a voice in positive, non-destructive ways. We can talk with a friend or therapist if we feel the need for greater support. We can go for a run and get the stuck energy moving through and out of us.

The focus for today's running meditation is to recognize any opportunities for us to be more conscious of where we dump our own emotional "trash". As we take greater responsibility for the feelings that go on inside of us, regardless of the outside situation or person that *seems* to be causing them, we move from simply reacting to the world around us to responding to it in a more balanced way. The reality is, the feelings are taking place inside of us, and that is an arena that we can have dominion over—if we choose.

As you run today, allow your focus to shift to a time recently when you found yourself wanting to blame someone else for your upset feelings. As you are running, focus on the steady rhythm of your breath. If you find yourself moving back into anger, upset, or blaming, go back to focusing on your breath. See if you can shift your perspective so that you take 100% responsibility for the emotional disturbance that was going on inside of you. Not for what happened externally, as this may have been out of your control, but for the feelings that came forward inside of you. When you are willing to do this, you are moving into a position where you can effect a meaningful change in your own experience. Remind yourself that these feelings are not all of who you are. If you can relate in a caring way to the part of you that is upset, you can begin to heal that place inside.

This is a radical change from the way most us have been taught to relate to our feelings and is something that can take time to master. Each time you run, you build upon your experience, strength, and endurance until one day you surprise yourself with how far you have come. In the same way, as you begin to take greater responsibility for your feelings with each situation that arises, you will surprise yourself one day with how empowered you have become. You are to be congratulated each time you are willing to try this approach!

Affirmation

I am accepting responsibility for my own inner experience, opening the door to greater happiness.

22

Taking Flight

Quality: Adaptability

"I think of myself as somebody who has responsibility for a super powerful race car, and part of my job is to keep it pointed in the right direction. Just correct the course by a degree or two. Not a major function, but arguably an important one."
John Babington
Former US Women's Olympic Team coach

"Criticism polishes my mirror."
Rumi

I was lucky enough to be introduced to air travel at a young age. When I was eight or nine, one summer vacation I visited my grandmother at an apartment she had rented in Majorca, off the southern coast of Spain. My favorite part of the plane ride was being able to visit the flight deck and meet the captain. All the dials and lights, instrument panels and levers were fascinating to me. I felt as though I was on a spaceship. To be at the very front of the plane, looking through its diminutive windshield at the ocean of clouds below, filled me with the feeling that anything was possible.

Just before the September 11, 2001, attack on the World Trade Center, I flew from Los Angeles to New Orleans. It was the first flight I had taken in several years, and all my childhood excitement returned as I boarded the plane. We were about halfway to our destination when I could no longer resist the urge to ask a passing crewmember if I could visit the flight deck. After checking with the captain, the attendant returned a few minutes later to escort me to the front of the plane. He opened the small door that led onto the flight deck. I immediately recognized the relaxed scene that I had witnessed as a child. The crew was enjoying hot beverages, chatting among themselves, and able to turn and greet me. The autopilot was flying the plane, and the crew monitored its progress.

By the time I returned to my seat five minutes later, my mind was spinning from something the captain had said in response to one of my questions. I had shared with him how fascinated I was by the autopilot and wondered if an airplane wasn't the most accurate form of transport there was, always being perfectly on course!

Strictly speaking, the captain had replied, 99% of the time the plane is off course. As it moves forward, it is repeatedly encountering air pockets and crosswinds that push it off course. The in-flight computer checks the course setting a number of times each second against a satellite positioning system, and then makes minute adjustments. Based on this feedback, the plane is continually updating and re-plotting its course.

99% of the time the plane is off course!

Yet it makes its destination, and usually in good time.

As runners, we may experience a greater degree of boldness through our running than in other areas of our lives. We experience more of the dynamic energy that comes from taking action. We move forward, literally, each time we run, and we get a myriad of responses from our bodies. We discover if, in our enthusiasm, we are overextending ourselves, or if we are on target for gently and masterfully building our fitness and strength. We set out to run races, not knowing at the beginning quite how we will do, especially the first time. We do what we can to prepare, but until we hear the crack of the starting gun and head off on the course, we don't know what the result will be. In our running lives, we are much more like the plane: we head out in a certain direction, and then based on the feedback we get from our bodies, we reassess how we are doing and make changes in our training if necessary.

Life is just the same—we will only get feedback from our universe once we take action. It is when we take action that we engage life, and we enlist the support and cooperation of the world around us. As we lean into things, we get information back. Sometimes doors will open, and we will move forward. Sometimes they will remain closed, and we will *still* have gained ground—because we can remove that item from our list of possibilities and move forward in a new way.

When we take action we can't lose. Regardless of the outcome, we will have moved forward in our investigation of how to arrive at our chosen destination. The more we move forward, the more information we get back as to how we are progressing and how to move forward even more effectively.

Sometimes though, even before we make it into the air, we get stuck on the runway of life, taxiing back and forth, never committing to take off until we are sure that we can get to our destination without any crosswinds along the way. How often, I thought as I sat back down in my seat en route to New Orleans, had I stayed mired in fear when faced with a big decision—frightened that if I went forward I might make the "wrong" choice. How often had I decided to stay with what I knew, rather than venture into the unknown (and all the possibility it held) because I hadn't known for certain what was going to happen?

Often what keeps us stuck is our fear of the consequences of a "poor" decision. We decide that we need to figure everything out before we make the next move. We tell ourselves that we must have all our ducks in a row before we set out. Yet it is only by moving forward that we will discover the answers to many of the questions that are holding us back.

The experience of failure is a symptom of a frequent misperception—that of intertwining the results of what we do with who we are. When we keep the two separate, it is easier to see results simply as information. This information can clarify whether or not we are on course for where we want to go—just like the plane and its autopilot. When we receive feedback that we are off course, this is still *good* news—for now we have the opportunity to correct our heading and get back on course.

As you prepare to run today, set the intention to open fully to any guidance that is available to you, especially that which is in service to your moving more fully into the life you wish for. Listen for any feedback that you may have for yourself. Start by listening for any thoughts, or messages from your body, that come up around your running. Are you overstretching yourself? Are you holding back from your potential? Or are you creating a balanced and nurturing approach to your running?

There may be suggestions that come up for fine-tuning your approach to exercise, as well as to other areas of your life. Whatever comes up, simply look at the information that it contains, without demanding of yourself that you either accept or repudiate its accuracy. Just ask yourself, "Is there something here I can use to support my choices in the future?" If yes, make a mental note of it. If there isn't, let it go! You get to discern whether the feedback you receive is relevant or not.

As you go through your day, continue to stay open to feedback—both internal and external. Consciously separate the information from any wrapping that it may come in (such as anger or judgment). Listen out for guidance that can keep you on course—or that can get you back on course if you discover that you have strayed from your heading. And remember, although the plane is off course 99% of the time, it gets to its destination, and on time, too!

Affirmation

I am opening fully to divine guidance
as I journey home to God.

23

Walk; Don't Run!

Quality: Harmony

*"As an athlete, when you least expect it, you may find yourself standing on the
threshold of an accomplishment so monumental
that it strikes fear into your soul. You must stand ready, at any moment, to
face the unknown. You must be ready to walk through the wall of uncertainty."*
John Bingham, *The Courage to Start*

*"To exist is to change, to change is to mature,
to mature is to go on creating oneself endlessly."*
Henri Bergson

Early in the morning one recent New Year's Day, as on
every January 1 for more than ten years, I ran out along
the beach near my home for what is one of my favorite
workouts of the entire year. With so much of humanity
focused on the possibility of change and new beginnings,
there is a palpable sensation of promise in the fresh
winter air. A slow-moving mist and a glassy, calm sea
greeted my feet as they hit the shoreline. As I ran gently
along the water's edge, I reviewed the year that had
just ended.

It had been quite a year of completions. I had graduated from the University of Santa Monica, self-published my first book of short stories, and renewed what had been a very distant relationship with my mother. On top of these successes, I was running stronger than I had in years—the result of a more balanced approach to my training.

As I ran west with the rising sun behind me, the muffled early morning light pushed as best it could through the mist that hung over the expanse of sand in front of me. It had been several weeks since I had had the inspiration during a morning run to begin a new book, yet each time I tried to imagine myself moving forward with the project, I felt panicked and overwhelmed. It just seemed too much for me. In my mind's eye, I looked ahead to the process of writing a book much larger than anything I had written so far, and I felt as though I was looking at a hundred-mile run. Then there was the rewriting and copyediting. Then finding an agent, perhaps, and a publisher. And when on Earth was I going to find time to do this all anyway? I had been considering leaving my job to focus on this new project, but that wasn't realistic. Or was it?

The mist and fog that blurred the beach ahead of me matched the swirling uncertainty inside of me. I slipped into more and more worry and the environment around me receded. I became engulfed in a mind full of "can'ts," "shouldn'ts," and "don'ts." I was so wrapped up in my worries that I was surprised when I came upon the breakwater at the end of the beach.

A movement a few feet from the shoreline drew my eyes to the water as I turned and began my run home. About 50 feet out in the water, and slightly ahead of me, a pod of dolphins was moving parallel to the shore. My heart skipped with joy at seeing these beautiful creatures. The water was barely disturbed as they sliced in and out of the ocean.

I marveled at the magical way they propelled themselves forward so gracefully. Their effortless movement was hypnotic. As I watched the gentle rhythm of their arching backs and deep breath, I saw that theirs was a movement that could indeed carry them across vast oceans. They were an animal version of the very medium they were in. They were not *in* the water; they were expressions *of* it.

As my eyes followed their every move, I was filled with feelings of joy and freedom. "Don't worry!" their elegant loops in and out of the water said to me. "You have everything that you need to make this book happen. You <u>are</u> everything you need to make this happen." The spray of their gentle exhale soothed my worried mind. I stopped running and slowed my pace to a walk to keep level with their calm, steady progress along the shoreline.

I couldn't remember the last time I had walked along the beach; it was months if not years. While I had been so focused on the dolphins, the early morning mist had lifted. I walked parallel to the dolphins' easterly swim; their appearing and disappearing fins had the cadence of a watch. Catalina Island had emerged on the horizon from within the retreating marine layer, and I watched the morning mist swirl and dance around the palm trees as it lifted from the sloping curve of the beach road. At my feet the sand was made up of thousands of tiny shells, glistening in the amber rays of the sun. At my slower pace, the view around me was transformed into something entirely different. I had arrived in a new city on a new beach—one I had never been to before, rather than the one I had run on so many times.

Sometimes as runners we get too far ahead of ourselves; it can be in our training or in our wider lives. We worry about running a 5k before we have taken our first run. We worry about running a marathon and become so immersed in our training that we lose touch with the simple pleasures of running for its own sake. The incredible sight of the dolphins reminded me that it is important to make time to slow down once in a while—to appreciate my surroundings rather than always being focused on moving through them.

Today, instead of running for your workout, walk the same route. You may need to give yourself more time or walk a portion of your running route in the time you have available. You may find that you experience some inner resistance to this idea. That's OK; just notice it . . . and take it for a walk!

As you walk, your slower pace will allow you many opportunities for a deeper appreciation of your surroundings. The architecture, the trees and parks, the people that you encounter will all be closer at hand at a walking pace. When I am running, I rarely allow myself to stop along the way. When I am walking, I am more willing to make time to get to know my neighborhood and its people—and to get to know the gentler rhythms that move inside of me.

Don't be surprised if creative solutions to problems that have been worrying you bubble up to the surface in the quieter pulse of your walk. Remember, walking is not a crime! It is a powerful addition to any runner's toolbox and a valuable part of any runner's training log. You can stay on your feet for greater distances and extend your long runs if you walk intermittently. You'll get more energy and greater performance from your muscles. In fact, all in all, you'll get a more well-rounded workout. Walking will target the muscles in your buttocks, as well as those of your feet and shins. Walking is also a great way to begin recovery after marathons and other distance events.

Make it a conscious part of your approach to the rest of your day to take things at a slower pace. Give yourself the space to study the life around and within you at this softer rhythm. Celebrate the details and the finer artistry in each person, setting, and situation that you meet. God, it is said, is in the details.

As I walked along the beach that New Year's Day filled with the joy of my meeting with the dolphins, the project of writing a book seemed more approachable. I would start at the first chapter and take it from there. There was no need to get ahead of myself and worry about an agent and a publisher when I hadn't even written the book. I would cross those bridges when I came to them. Like the dolphins, I would move forward at a gentle pace, creating as little disturbance as possible. Steadily and surely, I would cover a distance that frenzied thinking and frantic activity could not comprehend. Did it work? Well, the answer is in your hands!

Affirmation

I am moving and living in the world
in harmony, balance, and grace.

24

Breaking Out!

Quality: Strength of Heart

"The only real failure is the failure to try."
Joan Benoit Samuelson, *Running Tide*

*"Much of your pain is the bitter potion by which
the physician within heals your sick self."*
Kahlil Gibran

A number of years ago, in what now seems to be another lifetime, I spent a short time in prison. During my 20s, I was very active in the arena of campus politics in England. One of the myriad demonstrations that I attended erupted into violence, and during a fight with police I was arrested. I was sentenced to spend three months in London's Wormwood Scrubs prison. Thus began a journey that was to change my life in dramatic ways.

Although this is now over 15 years ago, there are many times each year when I marvel at the contrast between six weeks of time here in the "outside" world and six weeks inside a prison. I was fortunate to be assigned a job in the prison laundry that got me out of the restrictive space of my cell and allowed me the considerable bonus of clean clothes every day! Still, the majority of my time was spent locked in my cell, and I resolved to spend it reading the collected works of George Orwell. I discovered that there is a limit to how long one can spend reading in a day, and my gaze would often fall upon the barred window of the cell. If I pressed my head right up to the bars, I could just see the green edge of a large open space and park beyond the outer prison wall.

One afternoon, I was reading in my cell when my attention was drawn to the window. I could hear a great deal of activity coming from the expanse of the park, of which I was able to see just the one small corner. I could hear workmen shouting back and forth and what sounded like construction. Whatever was going on, none of it was visible from my limited view. The next afternoon I returned from my shift in the prison laundry and settled on my bed for a nap. I awoke to the arrival of the evening meal at my cell door. I collected my metal tray of food but left it untouched as my attention was again pulled to the now darkening square of the evening sky framed by the small barred opening of the window.

Even before I reached the window, I smelled the fairground and its mingled scents of sweet cotton candy, popcorn, and hot dogs. Music from the amusement rides wafted in erratically with the changing breezes that swirled around the buttressed prison buildings. I pushed my head to the bars, my temples throbbing as they were pinched tight between the bars, and I was just able to see one half of a Ferris wheel as it made the downward part of its clockwise journey. I closed my eyes to fill in the rest of the unseen picture in my mind. In that moment, buoyed by children's gleeful screams and the music of the fairground, I made a pact with myself—that once I got out of prison I would put every day of my life to the greatest use possible. I resolved that I would lay my head on the pillow at the end of each day knowing that I had made the most valuable use of my life.

Right there, in the midst of my prison experience, I understood the preciousness of my life, and the gift of this realization was to propel me onto a path of transformation.

As runners, we encounter our own particular breed of challenges. There are the life commitments that snap at our heels, threatening to impinge on our running time. From time to time, we experience illness that can lay us low and keep us from our running. There are few of us who have not wrestled with the difficult experience of injury. In a broader context, we each have challenges that come forward in our everyday lives, and among these can be some of our darkest moments.

It can be all too easy to look at difficult situations as something to "get through," or even as areas to be avoided all together—"let sleeping dogs lie" was a rule for many of us as we grew up. There is far more leverage to be gained from looking at them from the viewpoint of, "What is the hidden opportunity here?" As runners we develop enormous resolve, and we can draw upon this resolve to approach difficult areas in our lives as cunningly disguised gifts—even if it sometimes appears that these opportunities are a little clumsily wrapped! If we are able to shift how we look at any given situation, we will often experience a shift in our attitude. Once our attitude shifts, we open up once again to receive divine inspiration.

Before you leave the house today for your run, pick a situation in your life that you find troubling. This will be the focus for the transformative power of your running experience today. Set an intention to see this situation with new eyes and with the eyes of your heart. The only guideline here is not to think about the problem as you are running. Avoid going over the details in your mind again as you run. Rather, let the following question be the context within which you will explore your run today: *What is the opportunity for me that is embedded in this situation?*

Choose a route that you are familiar with, so that you will be running toward an established turning point. Now, run toward the turning point using a <u>completely new route</u>. Get there using streets that you do not usually run. If you are out in more natural surroundings, run a trail that you have never run before. If you are used to running on a treadmill at the gym, hop on an exercise bike instead!

As you are moving along this new route, notice and enjoy what is around you: the different buildings, storefronts, and people in the neighborhood. There may be new sounds and smells. The surface under your feet may feel different. If you are in the gym, notice how different it feels to be seated on a bike rather than on the treadmill.

As you approach your workout today from this new perspective, you may well find that new ways of looking at the challenging situation will come to you. Just by shifting your perspective, just by approaching it from a new angle, innovative and creative responses can naturally arise. Insanity has been very humorously (and very accurately!) defined as doing the same thing over and over again while expecting a different result. As you run, pay attention to what "just happens" to pop into your mind. Through experiencing the renewed sense of purpose that can come from changing the route of your workout, you support your mind in getting the same message: *Let's try a different approach here!*

Spending time in prison is certainly an experience that I would not want to repeat—a dark time in my life. Yet prison also offered me an incredible blessing; it anchored inside of me the preciousness of my life and an unwavering resolve to make the most of each day that I can. It is the darkest soil that is often the most fertile, if we choose to see it that way.

Affirmation

I am trusting in God's plan for my life, gratefully opening to and accepting the blessings contained in all my experiences.

25

60 Minutes

Quality: Dominion

"Every hour, every morning, every afternoon was a different world and a different self that sought to run through it."
James Shapiro, *Running Across America*

"You must be the change you wish to see in the world."
Gandhi

"Seize the hour."
Sophocles

As we move more and more deeply into the "communication" age, we are bombarded with ways to stay in contact with each other—even as we are losing the ability to stay *connected* to ourselves. As we develop more tools to maximize every minute of the day, to use every moment just to keep up with our to-do list, we are in danger of leaving less and less time to focus on how we are *being*. Our doing involves more and more rushing, forcing, and demanding. We come to the end of each day, month, and year wondering why it is that we feel so dissatisfied and tired.

One of the greatest gifts I receive through running is that I get to leave all that behind for an hour each day. I have 60 minutes to be with myself, my dreams, and with Spirit. I never cease to be amazed by the transformation that can take place within the single hour of my regular run. Whether I have used these 60 minutes either to exercise hard and come back feeling the relaxed, calm tiredness of hard-worked muscles, or I have used the run for a meditation to help me gain clarity, I return each time feeling cleansed, renewed, and inspired, many times in surprising and unexpected ways.

Often my first activity upon returning home is to rush to a pad and pen so I can write down the inspiration and ideas that have come to me as I run. I can step out of the door a raging maniac and return as gentle as a lamb. Even when, in my righteousness, I have sworn to hold onto anger, often the run dissipates it and I experience the blessings of grace and release. My commitment to running proves itself over and over as a commitment to the best in me.

In times of challenge, it is a vehicle for taking dominion over my thoughts and feelings—a way to rebalance and reconnect. One hour and I come back feeling as though I have had a major tune-up. I can't get that much work done on my car in that amount of time! And I know I am not the only one—many of the runners I speak to share the same experience—60 minutes that can be creative, productive, *and* healing all in one go. Talk about multitasking!

During one such run, I started to think of the way in which life is organized for many of us between work and play. We live in a world where most of us have become accustomed to spending the majority of each year, month, and day holding on and enduring as best we can until we reach the pay-off of having time to do what we really want to do—to be who we really want to be. The dominant paradigm, from my perspective, goes much like this:

Fifty-two weeks in the year: fifty for work, two for pleasure.

Seven days in the week: five for work, two for pleasure.

Twenty-four hours in a working day: How many for pleasure? Four? Two? Perhaps only one.

It is said that the world around us is a mirror of our own internal landscape. If I have learned that it is "normal" to spend 70 to 90% of each day, week, and year at work, what is that telling me about what is going on inside of me? If my years and days are portioned out in this way, I began to wonder, what does an individual hour look like? What proportion of each hour do I spend in worry, frustration, and fretfulness, and what proportion do I spend in a place of peace, playfulness, and loving?

I decided to do the best I could to listen to myself throughout several days. I was amazed to discover that YES, I spent a large part, if not the majority, of each day battling with thoughts of unworthiness, criticism of myself and others, and anger at not living the life I truly wanted to live. There were certainly moments of caring, of feeling connected to my fellow humans, and of loving. But they were undoubtedly a series of unconnected moments in a sea of otherness.

In 12-step programs, I had learned to take one day at a time. Now I resolved to take one *hour* at a time. For the duration of each hour during the day, I would attempt to hold a focus on a particular quality. For 60 minutes I would do my best to be peace—to respond to my inner and outer world from a place of peacefulness. For the next 60 minutes I would do all that I could to hold a place of compassion inside of me, and so on. I began this a little over a year ago, and I have yet to make 60 minutes of unbroken focus! Nevertheless, this practice has radically changed my living experience. Large parts of each hour remain anchored in the energy of positivity and willingness—a willingness to take dominion over my personal experience.

As we take dominion over our thoughts and feelings, we can begin to move into a different world, one that is predominantly peaceful, loving, and creative—a world that is Spirit-filled. It is already there for us, but we need to be vigilant to stay there. It has been said that it takes only one choice to break the cycle of positivity in our lives. It takes recurring choices, one after the other, to maintain the same cycle. The price of freedom is eternal vigilance. Through holding this hourly focus, we can support ourselves in being vigilant about the place inside of us from which we step out to meet the world.

By holding a qualitative focus through each hour of a day, we give ourselves the opportunity to reconnect with the transformation that we experience in our running. We make a shift from reacting to and joining the often-chaotic world around us, to creating our own internal environment—no matter where we are. We support ourselves in making decisions and taking action from a place inside of us that is rooted in the very best of who we are—the place that is connected with Spirit.

So as you run today, notice the change that takes place in you during the time of your run. Observe how your willingness to take dominion in your life through your running calms your body, eases your mind, and frees your soul. Recognize and celebrate the many gifts that this focused time gives you, and set the intention *during your run* to carry this transformative focus into the rest of your day.

Then, for each hour during the day, select a quality to focus upon such as peace, wisdom, appreciation, forgiveness, or acceptance. You could choose any of the qualities from other chapters in this book. If you suddenly realize that you have been daydreaming about your lottery winnings, or whether you'll make it to the movies on time tonight, don't worry! This is inevitable; just take a moment to take a breath, and gently bring yourself back into a conscious focus.

For now, just try this for today. Then, if you feel called to carry this practice forward into one day each week, or perhaps more, go for it! Each and every individual hour that you choose to anchor in a positive quality transforms not just your experience but also that of those around you. You are contributing to an increase in the sum total of positivity in the world.

Affirmation

Moment to moment, I am meeting my world,
inside and out, with loving positivity.

26

Opening Up

Quality: Openness

*"The aim is to move with the greatest possible freedom
toward the realization of the best within us."*
Roger Bannister, *The Four-Minute Mile*

*"Be prepared at all times for the gifts of God
and be ready at all times for new ones.
For God is a thousand times more ready to give than we are."*
Meister Eckhart

The beach where I run most often has a clear view
of both the Ports of Long Beach and Los Angeles. Millions
of tons of goods move through them each year. Almost
every day the horizon will be dotted with three or
four container ships making their way into the port to
deliver their goods. I will smile to myself as I remember
learning to sail in the Mediterranean as a young boy,
and how my teacher taught me a little phrase to remember
which side of the boat is port and which is starboard. *"I left
the port last night,"* he encouraged me, and I have never
forgotten it.

From time to time as I run on the beach, I have noticed the shipping lanes become crowded with ten or more ships and tankers standing idle, waiting to get into port. For some reason or other, the port will not be receiving goods. Perhaps they are short staffed, or in a dispute of some kind. Just recently there were upwards of 15 ships outside the port entrance for days on end. It was not that the goods were not there to be landed, rather that the port was not open or willing to receive them.

What a powerful image for all of us! Many of us are constantly wishing for more in our lives: more love and joy, a deeper sense of fulfillment, greater financial security, definitely more time to run!

We can wonder sometimes if Spirit is ever going to get to our delivery of wealth and happiness.

It is as though we are waiting for the day when God will decide that it is time for our ship to come in. Yet the truth is that our ship is idling out there in the bay right now, and the captain is wondering why the port is closed! God will not give you any more than it is giving you right now. God *cannot* give you more, for God is always giving. Our part of the deal is to open to what is already given. There is an infinite supply of love, abundance, health, compassion, patience, wealth, and more coming our way in every moment of our lives. We have to consciously and actively choose to welcome it.

We can make a great start by setting a clear intention to open to receiving more of Spirit's blessings in our lives. Our intention will give us direction. Then we need to take action to move toward our goal. Many of us talk about being ready for more, while we do everything that we can to block it from getting to us. We cannot receive from the flow of Spirit's gifts if we continue to behave in the same ways that have brought us the experience of mediocrity. Even as we are complaining that our ship has not come in, we are adding to the blockade outside the entrance to the port.

We make receiving very difficult for ourselves, blocking its channel into our lives with busyness, anger, and resentment. We wonder why we are not experiencing the love that we long for while we fill up every minute of our day with work and worry. Where is the room for it? We talk about wanting to feel more connected with the world around us, and then spend our days alone in our cars on crowded freeways, wordlessly rubbing shoulders with each other in the supermarket checkout line, or silently guarding the television.

In order to receive, we need to make space for receiving. Notice how this happens—when we make space for one thing in our lives, Spirit will bless us with more than what we ask for. As runners we learn that, in order to open to receive the gift of increased health, we need to make space for that to happen—we create space for our running. We discover pretty quickly that improved health is not the only gift that comes into the space we create. We are blessed with peace of mind, a sense of achievement, and a greater experience of balance in our lives. We learn that to make the most of our running, we need to remove any obstacles that may stand in the way.

In the beginning we remove the greatest obstacles. We leave our cigarettes and our fatty diets behind. We commit a specific block of time each day for our running—a time that becomes sacred. We leave behind our cell phones and work worries. The longer we have been running, the more skilled we become at removing the more subtle impediments to our complete enjoyment of running. We begin to leave behind the concepts of *should, must,* and *ought to,* so that the space we have created through running is as open as possible. Spirit moves into this space that we create with greater health, inspirational ideas, and an overall sense of well-being.

Before you run today, set an intention to open to divine inspiration and to receive guidance from Spirit. Then, as you run, be conscious of the physical space that you are running in. Absorb the details of the environment you are moving through. Listen to the space that you create with your breath, expanding and filling your lungs with life-bringing oxygen. Notice the space that you create in your mind as the rhythm of your affirmation quiets your thoughts. Recognize the feeling of expansion that fills your heart as you recommit to yourself once again through your running.

As you continue on your run, begin to focus on one area in your life in which you would like to experience more of something. It can be a quality, such as love, patience, or wisdom. It can be a new goal, such as completing a project or learning a new skill. It can be a desire for greater financial wealth or meeting a life partner. It can be anything that you want, but focus on just one.

Now, as you run, ask yourself each of these questions: "What can I do to open to receiving this in my life? How can I create a space for this to arrive in my life?" Focus not on *looking* for answers to these questions, but on *listening* for them. Listen to any responses that come up inside of you. You have set the intention to be open to Spirit's guidance and may be surprised by the thoughts that pop up. You may be guided to obstacles that you can remove to create more space. You may be guided to new activities that will create the space for your wishes to come true.

Each day, even as you are experiencing the space that you have created with your running and the benefits that come with that, be open to being open to more!

Affirmation

I am opening to the infinite gifts of Spirit,
creating space for God's love and divine inspiration
in every area of my life.

27

The Turning Point

Quality: Choice

"Success is 90 percent physical and 10 percent mental.
But never underestimate the power of that 10 percent."
Tom Fleming in *Joan Samuelson's Running For Women*

"The last of the human freedoms:
to choose one's attitude in any given set of circumstances,
to choose one's own way."
Viktor Frankl, concentration camp survivor
Man's Search for Meaning

It was a straight out and back course along the sea front: my first race, a 10K in Escondido, California. As I set out along the dockside route, I was very nervous, wondering if I would be the slowest person in the race, if I would even make it to the finish. I even had a negative fantasy that I would be the last one to return, with a light truck behind me picking up the marker cones as I passed them. Of course, the race was filled with people of wide-ranging abilities, and there were those that passed me on the way out and, to my delight, there were some that I was passing, too!

I had passed perhaps four or five people when I discovered a new strategy of worry . . . what if I were running too fast and ran out of steam before the end of the course? Then, as I looked ahead and saw the halfway point where the course made a 180° loop, a distinct shift took place inside of me. I still remember it very clearly. As I saw the turn come nearer, the tables laid out with sports drinks, I connected with the place inside of me that knew I was going to make it to the end of the course, and all the fears and worries fell away in an instant.

As I made the turn, I felt as though I was starting a new race, with fresh legs, and I stepped up my pace noticeably. I no longer worried that I was going too fast. I felt attuned to my body, recognized my race pace for the first time, and settled into a new stride and relaxed breathing pattern. I passed other runners all the way back to the finish line. I had hoped that I would come in under an hour and was amazed to see the finish-line clock moving through the 48th minute as I crossed the line. I was overjoyed, and I knew that I still had plenty left inside. The race had not only shown me that my training and daily runs were paying off, but I also moved to a new level of confidence—the horizon of what was possible for me expanded considerably. As I stretched out after the race, I remember talking animatedly with my wife, believing for the first time that I could run a marathon.

One of my favorite daily running routes is also an out-and-back course. From my house to the breakwater at the end of a nearby peninsula and back gives me an even hour's running. This run is so well known to me and to my body that I don't need to wear a watch. I can run free and unencumbered. Running shorts, shoes, socks, and a small bottle of water tucked into the rear waistband of my shorts, and that's it. This particular stretch of beach is one long straight line, and I can see the point in the distance where I will turn for home from the very start.

This is a great run for me to take when I am looking to make a change in my life. More often than not, what I need is a change in my outlook. Whether there is a project I am working on or a meeting that I am preparing for, I find that I can spend a lot of time in my head telling myself how things are not going to work out. Perhaps I am preparing for an upcoming race and feel uncertain about how I will perform. And there are plenty of times when I am stuck in self-righteousness, holding onto an argument and not willing to get off my position. It could be with someone at work, with my wife, a friend—or even my cat!

As I run out along the beach toward the breakwater, I listen to that part of me that is running the loop of negative fantasy while keeping my eyes focused on the turning point of the breakwater up ahead. As the breakwater nears, I prepare myself for letting go of the old tape that is running in my head. The physical action of turning away from the direction I am thinking in, and turning for home, reminds me that I have the opportunity to consciously choose my attitude in any given moment. I am not saying that it will always be easy. The choice, however, is always there.

As runners, we all know the uplifting feeling that comes when we reach the halfway marker and turn for home. I have always joked that, for marathon runners, 13 is a beautiful and lucky number. It means we are reaching halfway and about to head for the finishing line!

While you are running today, focus on an area in your life that you are looking to make a change in, and run an out-and-back course. You may not even know how you are going to make the change you are looking for, or how you could ever let go of the feeling that you are holding onto. The great thing is, you don't need to! You may be very surprised by what comes into your mind as you turn and head for home. As you focus on the turning point at the halfway mark of your run, focus on the *possibility of change* rather than what that change has to look like.

In that first 10k race, when I touched into that place inside where I believed I could complete the race, all my fears and worries fell away, and the level of my performance increased dramatically—as well as my level of enjoyment. This paradigm applies in any area of life. The answers to all our life challenges reside inside of us already, yet we often mask them with layers of fear, negative fantasies, and righteousness that make those answers difficult to connect with. It is when we consciously choose to change our attitude and approach to a challenging situation that the resolution often appears.

As you go about the rest of your day, carry the image in your mind of the turning point on your run. Hold the picture in your mind. Whether it's a particular street corner, a lamppost, a tree in the forest, a lifeguard station on the beach, or a certain house or store. As you go through your day, you may become more aware of other choice points in your day: choices between staying in old habitual ways of being, and moving into a place of greater loving, acceptance, patience, and understanding.

Over an extended period of time, you may notice that these choice points become increasingly numerous. They will move closer and closer together in your day, until you can experience every moment as an opportunity to choose into your loving at a deeper level, re-committing to your own health, happiness, and joy. Every time you make these life-affirming choices, you also create an atmosphere around you that encourages others to do the same. Over time, *you can become the turning point.*

Affirmation

I *am* a turning point,
consciously choosing in this and every moment
to remain in a place of loving—
expressing Spirit's divine plan of peace.

28

Traveling Light

Quality: Letting Go!

"Running turns any open place into my chapel."
Dean Ottati, *The Runner and the Path*

*"God does not ask anything else of you except that you let yourself go
and let God be God in you."*
Meister Eckhart

Millions of people have come to the United States searching for a new life, and I am one of them. I arrived with little and hoped for a lot. I brought with me dreams of starting again—of wiping the slate clean and beginning anew. To my mind, this air of possibility is what lends the United States its pervasive and very attractive sense of opportunity. When I moved from England almost 15 years ago, I left behind a lot more than just friends and family. I left behind old patterns of addiction and old beliefs about what was possible for my life. I arrived knowing that I would no longer need to wade through the skeletons of my past in order to forge a new future for myself. As my plane left

English soil, I felt the sensation of old hurts and stories falling away. When I landed in the U.S., I felt ten pounds lighter!

One of the most attractive aspects for me about running has always been the absence of clutter required to take part in it. Aside from minimal clothing, a good pair of shoes, and a water container, there is no other required gear. No special protective layers, no sticks, bats, or racquets, and no ball or puck to keep track of. I don't need another person to get the game going. No expensive gear, no traveling, no membership or parking fees, and no schedules to match with someone else. Put on the shoes, step out the door, and away I go, running unencumbered.

Appearances can be deceiving. Sometimes I come to realize that I am not running as light as I think. I'll be ten minutes into my run and notice that I am thinking about a work project or a credit card payment that is due next week. This doesn't just happen when I am running either. Some days I can be dragging around a metaphorical bag full of worry and concern, and I feel its weight on my shoulders, wearing me down and sapping my energy.

The poet David Whyte jokes wryly that the reason we leave our car windows cracked open in the parking lot at work is not to keep them cool, but rather so that the 80% of ourselves that we leave behind when we go into work can still breathe! We dream of our lives being so much more, but there always seems to be something holding us back. We tell ourselves that for any one of a number of reasons outside of our control (the economy / not enough time / fill in the blank), we don't experience the level of fulfillment in our lives that we hope for—but it is often what *we are holding onto* that holds us back.

We wonder why our energy is low. Why we feel as though we are laden down, dragging around some mysterious unseen weight. I often think that is why we have become so obsessed as a culture with losing weight—it is the one arena where we receive guidance, support, and practical tips on how to let go. Yet what we are really trying to release is the old energy, past commitments, relationships, agreements, judgments, and hurts that no longer play a supportive role in our present lives. Everybody is looking to let go of something—we focus on losing weight because it's the easiest thing to see.

We hold onto rules and beliefs that are rooted in other people's standards. We hold onto the weight of old hurts. We hold onto secrets, memories, and relationships that no longer serve us. We bind ourselves to old agreements and promises that need to be renegotiated or declared complete. Even sadness, bitterness, and resentment become so familiar that it can be intimidating to let them go. We build around them, and they become the fulcrum upon which our lives are balanced.

I like to think of "Letting Go" as short for "Letting God". When we let go of trying to take outright control of our lives, our secrets, and our dreams, and hand over the reins to God, we will always get more than we bargained for. The fact is, whatever we may have (and are frightened of losing) is just the beginning of God's plan for our life. There is so much more available to us if we are willing to make room.

Before you prepare for your run today, turn your attention to something that you would like to let go of. It could be an attitude, a judgment of yourself or someone else, a way of being, or a fear of some kind. It could be an old relationship or behavior that simply no longer serves your highest good. It could be a secret that you have held out of shame or a sense of duty that you no longer wish to carry. It can be anything that you feel is holding you back from the joy that you wish for. The options, it seems, are almost endless! Whatever it is, hold it in your mind's eye; focus on it as you prepare to set out, for you are not going to have it for much longer. When I do this, I often clench my fists as tightly I can, to give myself the physical sensation of holding on and the energy that it requires.

As you step out of the door, set the intention to release this matter for the last time—to give it to God. Choose a route that takes you into some undeveloped space such as a park, open field, or beach. If you have no space available, a parking lot will work. Once you are in the open space, and before you turn for home, stop for a few moments. Picture yourself taking out a balloon and a piece of paper naming what it is that you want to let go of. Take a moment to center yourself in your heart, and picture yourself pushing the piece of paper (and the associated situation along with it!) inside the balloon. See yourself filling the balloon with the air that you have taken in during the expansive activity of running, tying it off—and letting it go! You can also mime this activity, energizing your thoughts with physical expression.

As you imagine yourself letting the balloon go, say out loud, "I release this to Spirit. I free myself once and for all from . . ." Finish the sentence with whatever applies. If you have been clenching your fists, now is the time to unfurl them. You may even notice that, initially, it hurts more to let them relax, just as it can sometimes initially feel more painful to let go of a long-held hurt, one that has become an old friend, than it does to hold onto it.

The power and clarity of your intention to release this situation magically lift the balloon higher and higher. In your heart and mind, watch the balloon float away, smaller and smaller, until it sails out of sight. Feel your heart expand as love moves in to fill the space created by what you have let go. You will be returning home a different, lighter person. You will be arriving in a new land!

Keep your run in mind throughout your day. You could find that this experience may encourage other old energies to the surface that you might like to let go of. Right where you are, you can visualize them lifting from you, sailing high and away in the same way as your balloon. And, remember, this meditation, like all the meditations in this book, can be used more than once!

Affirmation

I am letting go and letting God,
living in divine grace.

29

Food for Thought

Quality: Gratitude

"When I finish a run, every part of me is smiling."
Jeff Galloway, *Jeff Galloway's Training Journal*

*"If the only prayer you say in your entire life is 'Thank You,'
that would suffice."*
Meister Eckhart

When I was fresh out of high school, I hitchhiked and backpacked for six months around Australia. It is a vast expanse of land, an island so large it also qualifies as a continent, and especially so to me having grown up in the comparatively diminutive corner of England.

Part of my odyssey required traveling from Adelaide in Southern Australia to Perth in Western Australia. This involved crossing an enormous featureless plateau, the Nullarbor Plain. "Nullarbor" is from the Latin, meaning "without trees," and the name is accurate. When the time came to make this stretch of my journey, I had already successfully hitchhiked around most of the country. But I still felt intimidated by the immensity of the Nullarbor. The thousand-mile stretch of road that lies between Adelaide and Perth boasts only ten roadhouses (gas stations), and only a handful of those have a tiny settlement attached to them. There is a lot of hot, empty space!

A couple of short rides got me to the outskirts of Adelaide city, and after a wait of three to four hours, a huge "roadtrain" pulled over offering a ride most of the way to Perth. I climbed up into the cab, excited to be getting my first ride in one of Australia's unique multiple-trailer, transcontinental trucks—it was in excess of 150 feet in length! Before long, we were passing the sign that announced the official start of the treeless desert. My generously springed seat bounced me clear into the air each time we hit a rut in the road, which was often. There was another truck in front of us, and the two drivers chatted occasionally over the CB radio. They were both on a bonus system: the faster they got to their destination, the better they were paid. They had set out from Sydney and had been driving for 48 hours without a break.

At one point, as we rumbled along the deserted highway, the truck in front veered off the blacktop and began to roll across the parched, hard desert floor. The driver next to me called over the CB radio, but there was no response. He tugged long and hard on a chain hanging between my seat and his, which released the full force of the air horn. The leading truck turned sharply as the driver woke up from an unplanned sleep and swerved back onto the road. "That's why we always cross Nullarbor in twos," laughed the ruddy-faced trucker next to me.

Two-thirds of the way across the plain, we reached an isolated turn-off. The trucks were heading south to Esperance, and I was heading east to Perth. I have never been in a more deserted place in my life; I may as well have been on the moon. I climbed down from my comfortable aerie in the cab and into the sweltering desert. I watched the trucks disappear down the road away from me. I turned a slow circle as I looked at the landscape surrounding me.

Nothing. Some distant mountains, in the direction I needed to go, and nothing else. No sign of life. Except for the resident flies, which were excited by my appearance in this area devoid of any other people, cattle, or any kind of life. The flies clamored at my mouth, nose, and ears. Their persistency threw me into a rage. I ran up and down the road aimlessly swatting and screaming at the air around me. I dreamed of the cold beer that I would have when I reached Perth—in an air-conditioned bar with a screen door to keep the flies out!

Absorbed in my daydream, I patted my back pocket for my wallet, but the pocket was empty. I searched through by backpack—nothing. During one of the many resounding bumps during my ride in the spring-loaded seat in the truck, my wallet must have fallen out. I was still 300 miles from my destination, surrounded by desert, and night was approaching. Not only did I have no money, but the credit cards that would have given me access to money were also gone. I was barely 18 and 20,000 miles from home. In the early 1980s, e-mail was rare and there was certainly no overnight credit card replacement. I was in quite a fix.

Just as the last rays of the sun were slipping over the horizon, a car returning from a business convention (traveling in the opposite direction to where I needed to go) pulled over alongside me. The driver was concerned about my spending the night in the desert. I told him what had happened. He turned around and drove me the six hours to my destination in Perth! As I watched the desert blur into small settlements and then the suburbs on our way into Perth, my stomach tightened with fear and hunger. We arrived late on a Friday evening. Being a stranger to the city himself, my ride dropped me off at a St. Vincent de Paul shelter for the homeless, not knowing what else to do.

I made a collect call home and arranged for my credit cards to be replaced—but the local banks were already closed for the weekend, and the following Monday was a bank holiday. So for the intervening three days I stayed at the shelter. After sleepless nights spent in a dormitory with 20 odorous men suffering from the full gamut of respiratory diseases, the mornings came early. We had to be out of the shelter by 6:30 a.m. and were not able to return until late afternoon. I was given a sheet of paper that listed other organizations that offered free food services during the day. That first morning, I sat on a park bench and located the addresses with the help of my guidebook. The only location offering food during the day was a church community center on the other side of town—a steady two- to three-hour walk.

Each day, I must have walked ten miles or more in the hot sun, focused on answering the demands of my stomach. I walked past restaurants and fast food places that I would ordinarily have been able to walk into and order whatever I wanted. I passed people picnicking in parks on their lunch breaks, and kids spilling out of candy stores after school. I looked longingly at hotel entrances, imagining their clean white sheets and comfortable beds. I thought of food constantly, dreaming of what I would order and where I would eat once I got some money in my pocket.

The food that I ate those three days was often bland, washed down with insipid, sweet tea, but it was some of the most welcome food I have ever eaten. I came to see my eating habits in a whole new light during those days. How I had taken for granted the fact that I could eat what, and when, I wanted! My teenage eyes no longer ogled at the women that passed me in the street, but at the food they were snacking on!

I was outside the bank an hour before it opened that Tuesday morning. Minutes after I had cash in my hand, I was sitting in a nearby restaurant looking at a plate of buttermilk pancakes and a strawberry milkshake. I just sat and looked at the plate, watched the fresh warm maple syrup soak into the pancakes, and the condensation run down the side of my milkshake glass. After shoveling the first half of the meal into my mouth, I slowed and began to savor each bite. Food never tasted so good. Now I remember that morning before many of my meals.

We have a great deal to be thankful for, yet sometimes the turmoil and demands of our everyday living can close us off to the simple and immediate miracles with which we are blessed. We can become so focused on what it is that we want to attain in our worldly life, that we become accustomed to overlooking the blessings that are already very present in our life. As runners, we can become so focused on our next race or goal time, that we can lose sight of what we have already—the sanctity of our running and the healing and respite that it offers. Yes, our daily run is the rich reward of our perseverance and commitment to consistent training. But it is also a result of being blessed with fit, adaptable, and willing (most of the time!) bodies.

As new runners, we can become frustrated that we are not attaining the level of fitness that we want at the speed we would like. We lose sight of the fact that we have made it out of the door for another day, and that our bodies are supporting us in moving toward greater fitness. Our bodies are smart. If we are progressing slower than we imagined we would, it can be because our bodies are aware that we need to move into a new form of exercise gently in order to avoid injury.

Today, pay special attention to the simple beauty that surrounds you as you run. Keep your eyes peeled for the miracles that are laid out before you. Perhaps it is a flower poking up through the asphalt on a busy street or the smile of a passer-by. Appreciate your body as it carries you forward with each step, and remember the gift of the home that you stepped out from and will return to. Listen to the gift of your next breath.

The miracle of a human lifetime and the opportunities for loving and learning that are contained within it—that is what we woke up to this morning. After that, everything is a bonus! Let this be the focus of your run today, and I encourage you to anchor yourself in this energy of gratitude for as much of your day as you can—and beyond.

Affirmation

I am grateful for the gift of life and for all its many blessings—
both seen and unseen.

30

In the Flow

Quality: Abundance

"Training is like putting money in the bank. You deposit money, and then you can take it out. When you train, you deposit your daily miles. The more training you put in, the more money you have in the bank. But you can only expect results based on the training you put in."
Fred Lebow
The New York Road Runners Club Complete Book of Running and Fitness

"I keep the telephone of my mind open to peace, harmony, health, love, and abundance. Then, whenever doubt, anxiety or fear try to call me, they keep getting a busy signal—and soon forget my number."
Edith Armstrong

One of the most enjoyable aspects of running a familiar route over a number of years is that I come to recognize the other people that I share it with. There are surprisingly few people that run along the shoreline where I do. Most of the runners and walkers choose to stay on the concrete boardwalk, far from the lapping waves. Playing tag with the incoming tide, I pass a regular group of fishermen that stand along the shoreline. When the fish are not biting, the men talk animatedly among themselves, enjoying each other, their arms outstretched, no doubt telling tales of great catches. They are mostly older men from the Vietnamese community, and we have neither a common language nor sport. But we do share a love of the outdoors and the beach. My waves of greeting are always met with nods and broad, genuine smiles.

I passed by them, month after month, strung out along the beach, their long waterproof pants enabling them to get a few yards further out into the sea. I noticed that from time to time a cry would go up, and all of them would rapidly reel in their lines and run along the beach. I tried to see what had caused the sudden uproar but could make nothing out in the sea. I wondered if this were some kind of competition, in which they could only fish one spot for a certain amount of time. Although I had seen this happen over a number of months, there was no way that I would interrupt my run to see what was going on. I simply wouldn't allow a break in my routine!

One day, resting a strained calf muscle and choosing to walk for a few days rather than run, I heard the familiar cry go up—here was my chance to understand! I stopped where I was. The fishermen were running toward me, some of them pointing out into the water. I scanned the water for jumping fish. I looked in the sky for the circling and diving pelicans that are always a sure sign of a school of fish. I saw nothing. Standing still, I followed their outstretched arms and began to make out the faintest of shadows on the water. I looked up to see the cloud, but there was no cloud. About 15 yards out from the beach, the shadow moved parallel to the shoreline. I had to focus intently to keep from losing sight of it in the shifting waves. The shadow was not *on* the water but *in* it. To the casual eye, the school of fish under the surface created such a small change in the surface color of the water as to be unnoticeable. The galloping fishermen came to a sliding halt, some of them casting their lines while still running! Sure enough, within a matter of minutes, laughing joyously, they were pulling in dozens of fish.

To the casual eye, life can often seem empty of the very things we are looking for. I don't just mean the material goods but also the relationships, the fulfillment, and the creative expression that we long for. How is it, we ask, that some people seem to be able to just cast their line into the sea of life and pull out what they want, while others struggle just to get what they need?

Like the fishermen who had become trained to see the subtle movement of fish under the water, I, too, had been able to focus on them when I took the time to slow down. Often we need to ease back from the busyness of our lives to see what has already been given to us by Spirit, waiting to be reeled in. We may discover that while we are working so feverishly for what we want, we are missing out on the gifts that we already have. In many ways, we need to learn to see what is already there—learn to see the shape and outline of our own joy, success, and wealth as it moves in the calmer water below the disturbed surface of our frantic living. Simply by shifting our focus to a consciousness of abundance, we can bring more prosperity into our lives.

Don't get me wrong. I am not saying that there isn't work involved here! The fishermen on the shoreline do all they can to put themselves in the best place to catch the fish, and they are poised to move if they need to. They show up time and time again, regardless of whether or not the day before brought them the catch they were hoping for. It is their preparedness, constancy, and willingness to cast their line— to show up with an attitude of joy each day—that puts them close to the catch. Spirit does the fine-tuning.

We can all take steps to move ourselves closer to the catch. We need to be willing to let go of what we think abundance ought to look like. There is more than just the one route you have planned to get to where you want to b~
Be open to what is offered from God. While you
wishing for a long-awaited raise at work, Spirit may

different job waiting for you elsewhere—one that will give you the rewards and success you are destined for—if only you would be open to seeing it.

Before you set out on your run today, ask for Spirit's guidance in clarifying what your next steps may be that would move you more into the flow of abundance. Then, take a moment to focus on an activity in your life that makes you feel wonderfully opulent. An excellent indicator to look for is that you felt peaceful and carefree while you were doing it. For me, returning from a glorious run and then lying in a deep, hot bath, complete with bubbles, and reading a good book is when I feel wealthy, and royally so. You might simply focus on the expansive joy of your run.

Take some conscious time on your run to reacquaint yourself with what abundance feels like. Notice the full feeling in your heart as you find your stride and your concerns fall away. Appreciate the unique way in which you see the world you are running in. Connect with your heartfelt appreciation of your friends and loved ones. Bathe in the rich multitude of blessings that you have already been given.

Several times throughout your day, pause to see where you are in relation to this feeling of abundance, for this feeling is an energetic magnet that will draw greater and greater abundance to you. Focus on it, tune into it, and become familiar with it. If you have wandered from it, take a moment to visualize the fishermen on the beach. Remind yourself of their consistent willingness to show up, to find enjoyment even in the times of waiting. Reconnect with the image you chose to focus on during your run and the spacious feeling that it brought forward in you. This is the feeling that tells you that you are on the beach, with the waves of prosperity lapping at your toes. It is only a question of time before the catch will come into view.

Affirmation

I am living in the divine flow of the all-good—
abundance is my natural state of being!

31

Emergency Run

Quality: Peace

"So as my run ends I am back in my body. The energy I felt at the beginning of the run gradually filling my mind and soul, gradually creating a unity, a wholeness, a peak feeling of being at one with myself and the universe. What they call 'in zen,' 'satori.'"
George Sheehan, *Running and Being*

"No man can think clearly when his fists are clenched."
George Nathan

The focus of my running has gradually shifted from being a place of refuge *from* myself, to being a place of deepening the connection *with* myself—and with Spirit. There are still occasions, though, when my daily run is a time for me to seek sanctuary from things that aren't going as well as I would like them to. As I run out along the beach with my stride powered by strong feelings, I push a little deeper into the sand. I wonder, sometimes, if it's not the extra weight of the worries that I am carrying. This is certainly not my most efficient or effective stride. And that's OK; sometimes just moving my body, getting out there and circulating the blood, can help to shift me out of the frustration I am immersed in.

As runners we have a great amount of mental strength at our disposal. We develop the discipline to get out each day for our run, even when it could be all too easy to let it slide. We build the strength to run longer, working with the mind to overcome the physical trials of distance running. We learn to persuade the body it has one more step to take when it thinks otherwise. A strong mind is indeed a powerful asset to any runner. But when, in our more human moments, we are at sea in an ocean of strong feelings, we can use our strong mind to push ourselves deeper into righteous indignation. In these moments, when we confuse willfulness with willingness, our mind can be our greatest handicap.

On one of those irate days when I was pounding along the water's edge, I looked out at a line of tankers heading for the Port of Los Angeles and saw another powerful metaphor for my anger and frustration. When I am fully immersed in my righteousness, my feelings are like an enormous freighter steaming forward at full speed, laden with a full cargo of rage, and God help anything or anyone that gets in the way! The oceangoing tankers can take many miles to turn around, and my feelings can be just the same way. It can take me quite a while to change course, even after I have realized that I need to. My first step is usually to get out for a run.

It is in our minds that we perpetuate anger and upset—justifying, rationalizing, and excusing. Sometimes the powerful muscle of the mind that we have created through our running can work against us. It latches onto the glowing embers of angry thoughts and fans them into flames, and sometimes into an inferno. In these moments, our first point of business is to bring ourselves back into our bodies—and our running is a powerful tool that can be used for just that purpose. Whether you are in need of an emergency run or not, today's workout is an opportunity to practice and experience the focus of bringing ourselves back into our body, back into our breath, and back into the present moment. Then, when we really need it, this avenue back to our center is available to us at a moment's notice.

As you set out for your run, ask for Spirit's assistance in finding greater peace and set your intention to come into balance. From the outset, focus on your breath. When we are angry, we tend to breathe less deeply, so keep returning to your breath. Fill not only your lungs but your abdomen, too, drawing life-giving, cleansing oxygen into your body.

As you continue, focus on connecting with, and listening to, the different areas of your body. Start by paying attention to the beat of your feet as they strike the ground. Notice the way your flexible foot rolls from heel to toe with each stride. When we are in the midst of very strong feelings, we tend to run up on our toes. Make sure that you are starting each stride with your heel, and rolling through the arch of your foot, onto the ball, and pushing off. As you feel the entirety of your foot in each step, feel the muscles in your calves and shins contracting and releasing as they push you forward. Listen to the power and courage in your legs as they propel you along. Feel the strong anchor of your hips stabilizing you. Feel your chest and abdomen as they move in and out, filling your lungs and fueling your workout. Make certain you bring the air all the way into your abdomen, loosening muscles that can often get tight when we are holding onto anger. Listen to the way your body celebrates as you refresh and replenish it with regular doses of water.

Marvel at the light swing of your arms, effortlessly balancing you as you run. From time to time, allow your wrists to relax fully, so that your hands and fingers flop back and forth as you stride along, as if you were shaking water from them. This will allow more tension to be freed, and you will automatically feel your shoulders release. Every now and then, allow your hands to drop down by your waist so that your arms are fully extended and shake out your hands some more.

Listen for the joy in your face as the breeze touches it, as the sun warms it. Be amazed by the laughter in your hair as the wind brushes through it. Notice where you are looking—

when we are stuck in our heads and over-thinking, our gaze often drops to the ground at our feet. Make a conscious effort to look up and around you; this will extend your frame of reference and begin to shift you into a more expansive mindscape.

Remember, it's not just you that is running but your body as well! Much of the deeper peace that is available through running is accessed by making time to really be with ourselves—to enjoy listening to the rhythm of our breath and to the song of our body as it carries us along. It is as we reconnect with our bodies that we will start to feel that oceangoing tanker of upset beginning to slow down and change course.

As you go through the rest of your day, make a conscious effort to listen to your body, and watch out for any tension that may be building up. Many of us spend hours sitting at desks in front of computers. Taking a few moments to check in with your body will support you in coming away from a day's work more relaxed and energized. If you do notice yourself responding to a person or situation with anger, use the same process as you used during your run to relax and re-center. Take a couple of minutes, a number of times a day, and do a once-over on your body. Starting with your feet, scan your way through your whole body, breathing into, shaking out, and relaxing any places that seem tense. One thing is certain—you are much more likely to be successful and effective in your world when you are coming from a place of balance and peace.

Affirmation

I am balanced and at peace—in body, mind, heart, and spirit.

32

Changing Lanes

Quality: Encouragement

"I sometimes think that running has given me a glimpse of the greatest freedom a man can ever know, because it results in the simultaneous liberation of both body and mind."
Roger Bannister, *The Four-Minute Mile*

"If you constantly think of illness, you eventually become ill; if you believe yourself to be beautiful, you become so."
Shakti Gawain, *Creative Visualization*

One of the most challenging aspects of moving to California from my home country of England was leaving behind my friends and family. A number of years after my move, my father—by this stage well into his 80s—became suddenly incapacitated. An eye operation to remove a cataract had been unsuccessful, resulting in a debilitating loss of sight. It became clear that it was no longer safe for my father to continue living on his own. I knew that this necessary move from independent to supported living could be one of the greatest challenges that our relationship would face.

Being so far from him had been a constant concern for me since I had moved to the States. Now that voice inside of me, the one that told me I was a bad son, inconsiderate, selfish, and uncaring, was dominating my thoughts. It was having a field day, and I was buying into every word it said.

I flew back and forth between Los Angeles and London to help my father through his move while honoring my graduate school commitments. I am still very thankful for the incredible support and love that his neighbors and friends showed him while I was away.

During my first visit, we calculated that an assisted living community that he had his heart set on was indeed within his financial means. I began the process of cleaning his home from top to bottom in preparation for sale. Then came the task of choosing a real estate agent and putting the house on the market—both new ground for me. We interviewed a number of financial advisors and chose one who would manage the funds that came from the sale of the house—new to me again. On the second visit, I helped my father go through a home, garage, and attic filled with 80 years of living. Although the one bedroom apartment that he was going to move into allowed him to keep his favorite pieces of furniture, clearly he would not be able to take the majority of his things with him. We began the very challenging process of deciding what to keep and what to donate or sell.

As we went through trunks filled with photographs dating back to the late 1800s, I found out more about my family history in one week than I had in the whole of my life. With the move only three days away, I had to encourage him to make many quick and difficult decisions as to what to keep and what to let go. I was certainly not as patient as I would like to have been, and from time to time tempers flared.

Finally the day of the move came. Although the house was not yet sold, I encouraged my father to trust that a buyer would come forward (my encouragement was as much for me as him!). He moved in the morning, and in the afternoon a house clearing company came to take away the final items.

As the sun set that evening, I walked around the empty home. Just my sleeping bag remained in the bedroom my father had always kept for me. The rest of the house was empty. The house I had left each day in my teens to commute to my first job. The *home* I had fled to for shelter and love in the midst of drug and alcohol addiction—and which had welcomed me unconditionally.

That night I struggled to get to sleep. I worried about whether I had done the right thing. A voice inside my head told me that I ought to move back from the States and take care of him myself. It told me that my father had only moved to keep me happy. I tossed and turned. I tried to distract myself by listening to the small radio but was soon frustrated by its insistent joyfulness.

My running shoes called to me. At 3 a.m. I got up, put them on, and stepped out into the cold nighttime air. My father's home was in a quiet suburban area on the outskirts of London. At three in the morning it was still and silent. I breathed a deep lungful of cold, moist, foggy air. The silence was a sharp contrast to my noisy thoughts. I was stuck on a track of negative self-talk, a dark loop of negative fantasies.

Running through a sleeping city is an incredible experience. I could feel the peace and tranquility rising from the hushed houses. Nothing stirred. No pedestrians and no cars. It was still too early for deliveries—and too late for revelers. Absolute quiet. I ran a loop through the neighborhood of about a mile and a half in length, staying close to my father's home. I ran in the center of the deserted road, which was bathed in the mist-softened glow of the streetlights. I ran the circuit once and began to feel my body relax a little. I ran it again. I peeled off my top layer as I warmed up, and ran the circuit again.

I completed the third loop and watched the now familiar houses slip by as I moved into the fourth circuit. Halfway around the fourth loop, a realization came to me in a flash— a sure sign of a gift from Spirit. Here I was running a loop, staying in familiar territory—fearful of taking a different route in case I got lost—and I was doing the same thing in my head. I was staying with the familiar voice of my inner critic, running the old tapes of self-criticism, worry, and self-judgment over and over again.

"It's time for a new approach," I said to myself, and took a turn onto a new street, asking Spirit to guide me home safely. I was no more than a hundred yards along this unknown street, when two wild foxes scampered into the road ahead of me: one full grown, the other a youngster. All three of us stopped, about 20 feet apart. Their reflective eyes flashed at me. I smiled and said a gentle hello. I noticed how calm I felt all of a sudden. As I looked at the foxes, I saw my father and me, moving peacefully and safely in the tranquility and stillness—and I knew that my father was at peace with the decision that we had made. Then I saw, too, that the older guiding fox was Spirit, letting me know that it was walking beside me, watching over and supporting me in taking new and courageous steps.

As the foxes held my gaze, I started to think about my willingness to journey back and forth between California and London. I looked at the level of mastery I had shown in taking on the new tasks of selling the house, seeking investment advice, going through the house, finding movers at short notice, and the love and encouragement that I had shown my father almost without fault. Almost. And almost was OK. I was not trying to be perfect, simply striving for excellence. I really *was* doing my best. The foxes sniffed the air and moved on into a garden to my left. The voice of criticism in my head fell silent.

Negative self-talk can become a habit, and even an addiction. We may spend much of our waking hours listening to an internal dialogue of fear, worry, and judgment. It takes conscious effort to take out this tape of critical dialogue and replace it with a more uplifting and encouraging conversation with ourselves. Making this choice places our lives against a more life-affirming background, sustaining our ability to attract and experience more positive outcomes in our lives.

For your run today, choose a route that is a loop. See if you can use the running track at a local college or school, if there's one available in your area. If not, map out a circuit around a park, through your neighborhood, or around the block where you live. As you move round this circuit, listen for one of the negative loops of thought that runs in your head. It might be one about your running, telling you that you are not fit, fast, or strong enough. It could be one from work perhaps, telling you that you are not worth that promotion or raise. It could be one from the world of advertising, telling you that you are not rich, pretty, thin, or young enough. Listen to it fully, to how tedious, judgmental, and draining it is. Listen to what you are telling yourself, to what you are accepting as fact rather than fiction—for fiction is what it really is!

When you have had quite enough of this, simply take your run off into a new direction. Break away from the circuit you are running—step out of the loop of self-criticism, leaving the cycle of negativity to run and amuse itself. As you move off in a different direction, you can say, "I am taking a new and positive approach." Explore what you would rather be hearing instead. If you were to talk to yourself with loving encouragement, what would that sound like? Give yourself permission to be buoyed up by the power of your own creative, positive thinking. Be your own greatest fan!

In my experience, my inner critic can lurk in my mind like Cato, Inspector Clouseau's sidekick in the *Pink Panther* film series. Just when I least expect it, it can leap out at me and throw my life into turmoil.

As you go through your day, continue to keep an inner ear open for other tapes of negative self-talk that may begin to play. Sometimes they can start out quietly in the background, unnoticed. Before we realize it, they become the only tunes that are playing. When you notice this happening, remember how you stepped off the circular route of your run, and replay that moment in your mind's eye. Say to yourself again, "I am taking a new and positive approach!"

Each time you step out of a rut of negative self-talk, it becomes a road less traveled and you start to journey through life on a route of positive, uplifting, and creative thought—this is the gateway to a life filled with positivity and joy.

Affirmation

I am supporting myself with constant, loving encouragement.

33

Finishing Strong

Quality: Independence

"In the greater game we strive not for winning, but to extend our personal boundaries of who we are and what we can be, not as much to become faster as to become more, not to punish but to enjoy, not to beat someone else, but to become the best we can be, not to destroy others, but to create ourselves in motion as a celebration of our creaturehood. True excellence is achieved only in playing the greater game."
Lorraine Muller in *Boston Marathon*
by Tom Derderian

*"Don't bother just to be better
than your contemporaries or predecessors.
Try to be better than yourself."*
William Faulkner

There are many starting and finishing lines in a runner's life. There are the obvious ones that lie at the beginning and end of any race that we run. Then there is the starting line that we cross each time we set out for a workout, which transforms into a finishing line when we return. Our workouts are a sacred daily pilgrimage—they change us.

Sometimes we are transformed in clearly identifiable ways—we experience a particular insight or attain a new level of performance. Many times we return home changed in ways that are more subtle and that build over time. We look back one day and realize we are happier, healthier, and hold a broader vision for our lives than ever before.

I think what draws many of us to running is the experience of freedom that we can have as we move. One of the greatest joys of running for me is the freedom I experience from the fact that most of my finishing lines are of my own making—I have a large degree of control as to whether I reach them or not. Whether I attain the distance or time I am trying for largely depends on the level of my own commitment and the consistency of my training. As a running enthusiast, even in races, I am running primarily against myself.

Life, however, can be very different! I can find myself in many situations when the finishing line can seem largely under someone else's control—and it may be constantly moving, too! Whether I find myself in the midst of a contract negotiation, applying for a new position, or trying to complete a seemingly ever-expanding project at home or work, there are often so many variables that I can begin to feel defeated even before the "race" is run.

This shifting finishing line that is under others' control presents me with some of the most frustrating experiences of all. Then a friend of mine related a story that offered me an entirely new approach.

He shared with me how he had been embroiled in a lengthy lawsuit. At no stage could he get a clear sense of whether he would win or lose. This became increasingly frustrating and wore upon him. The worry that he might lose the case, and the ensuing financial consequences, began to have an effect on his health. The case looked as though it could stretch out for many more months. Then, something changed.

He told me, "I asked myself, 'What is within my sphere of influence, regardless of what is going on in the case?' I realized that the only area I really had any control over was me. So I resolved to approach the case with the very highest level of courtesy, integrity, and honesty that I could muster. Regardless of how the other parties in the case were going to behave (and they had already shown that they were more than capable of acting unpleasantly), I was going to be courteous. I knew that those choices and options were within my domain, and so that's what I did. In that way, I knew that whichever way the case went, I would know that I had won on my own terms—that I had stayed anchored in the very best of who I can be, independent of the external result."

His story illustrates how he chose to move his frame of reference from a number of external finishing lines (winning the case, outwitting his opponent, proving to the judge that he was "right"), to internal ones—acting with as much integrity and kindness as he could, regardless of what was going on around him. Whichever way the case went, he set a course for his own finishing line and arrived there strong and fresh.

From the moment he made this shift in approach, his experience of the trial changed dramatically. He began to sleep better, and the case no longer negatively impacted his health. Ultimately, the case was decided in his favor! Was it a coincidence that he also won his lawsuit? I don't think so. When we commit to the very best of who we can be, and especially when we are inundated with invitations to sink to lesser ways of being and continue to choose otherwise, Spirit has a way of taking care of us.

Today, when you set out for your run, set an intention not only for how you want to experience your workout, but how you want to live the entire day. This and every run is an opportunity for you to mark out the course for your whole day—and to set your own finishing line. Set the parameters of what a successful day would look like within your own dominion. It could be to move through the day with greater compassion toward others. It could be to use your finances with greater discernment. It could be to be microscopically honest throughout the day. The possibilities are endless—as are the opportunities.

When we shift our frame of reference from the external to the internal, our experience of life no longer depends on the opinions and actions of others—we become truly independent. And it is when we live from the very best of who we are that we truly come home to ourselves and to our God.

Affirmation

With Spirit as my partner,
I am living the very highest vision for my life.

34

Desert Run

Quality: Self-Appreciation

*"You are a special person. Reward yourself with self-praise
as you achieve each interim goal..."*
Hal Higdon, *Marathon: The Ultimate Training Guide*

*"It was part of the constant pleasure of the desert,
the way in which it never fails to offer subtle surprises and
rewards. With so much taken away, other things emerge with extra keenness."*
James Shapiro, *Running Across America*

*"Nothing but stillness can remain when hearts are full
of their own sweetness, bodies of their loveliness."*
William Butler Yeats
The Tower (1928) *"Meditations in Time of Civil War"*

Recently I had the opportunity to spend a few days at a
cabin in the Mojave Desert just on the Nevada side of
the California/Nevada border. Hand built by its first
owner, the cabin sits on a hillside, lifted from the desert
floor by its foundation of mine tailings. From its vantage

point, I could see the glow of the nighttime lights in Las Vegas, nearly 50 miles away, and on a clear day, across the distant Interstate, past the mountains to the town of Nipton on the horizon.

It simply was not practical, or safe, to run in the desert itself. A multitude of different cacti would tear at anyone moving faster than at a very cautious and attentive pace. Then there were snakes to watch out for, too! My hosts recommended that I run down the dirt track from the cabin to the main road and back again, a round-trip distance of about six miles. While this was shorter than my regular daily run, taking into account the heat and the increase in altitude, it seemed a sensible option.

I ran early enough to avoid the worst of the heat. The dirt road was uneven and dusty. At almost every bend, wild rabbits scurried off the path to hide in the expanse of cactus. I remembered enough from the animal tracking classes I had taken at college to know that the scat I passed had been left by bobcats. I allowed my feet to make as much noise as possible to announce my arrival to any rattlesnakes that were moving slow in the cooler morning air. Every now and then, I would reach into my waist pack and check that the snakebite kit was still there.

At each of the intersections I crossed that led to the numerous disused mines, I would stop and scratch a large arrow into the dirt with a stone to remind me which was my way back. This was certainly a different experience of running than my safe beachfront runs back home. I felt extremely vulnerable in this unfamiliar environment. No proper road, no accessible phone, no neighbors. My hosts knew that if I was much more than an hour, they ought to come looking for me. The nervous energy that I was expending made the run a little harder, but I felt alive in a new and immediate way.

I reached the road, amazed to hear how noisy it was. From the cabin, the road was inaudible, an artery of sporadic lights in the nighttime that cut through the vast black emptiness of the desert floor. As I ran back and the sun rose higher, my lungs started to sear a little in the dry heat. I was pleased and relieved to arrive back at the cabin safe and sound. My hosts were filled with praise for my run, both for the distance covered and the time taken to complete it. It seemed nothing unusual to me.

I went out onto the patio area at the front of the cabin to stretch. In the distance, I could see the road I had just run to and it looked far away. I could no longer hear its noise, and even the big Interstate trucks looked like toys. I realized that I had never before been able to see the entire length of one of my runs from start to finish. I noticed a number of the landmarks I had passed: the green mound of tailings to the west, the windmill of the water pump, and the home of the closest neighbor, a little over three miles away. With so much taken away from the environment I was used to, I could see my accomplishment more clearly. Six miles is a good distance.

When we remain focused on moving forward in our lives, looking to stretch and grow, embracing our spiritual growth as a lifelong commitment, it can be easy to forget to take time to look back at how far we have come. As we shift from one level of learning to the next, we become forward-focused, eager to see what Spirit has in store for us and the gifts we are to discover in ourselves as we meet the next challenge in our lives.

As we develop depth in our running, and look forward to running longer, faster, and stronger, we can lose sight of the simple and powerful qualities that we have birthed in ourselves. Our running first becomes regular, then a habit, and then routine—an expected part of our lives that in no way seems unusual. The willingness, strength of heart, resourcefulness, patience, courage, and consistent commitment that are the cornerstones of our running can become so familiar to us that we do not see them anymore.

It is a vital and empowering experience to take stock from time to time of who and where we are. Yes, it is important to maintain a clear, forward focus in life. And it can also be when we look back across the previous months and years of

our lives' journeys—and see just how far we have come—
that we will appreciate not only how many blessings have
been given to us but also the blessings that *we* are.

As you are running today, let your focus be one of
appreciation for who you are—no one else does you quite
like you do! Immerse yourself in appreciating and
acknowledging yourself, not only for the physical
strength and commitment that enables you to run as far as
you do but also for the choices you make—the person
you are consistently choosing to be—that have brought
you to this very point. Take time to appreciate the positive
impact that running has played in this change. Each
and every single time you honor your commitment to
running, you are affirming that you are precious,
important, and worthy!

I don't think any of us can get too much appreciation!
While it can be rewarding to experience acknowledgment
from others, it is when we develop the ability to honor,
celebrate, and value ourselves—when we become more
internally rather than externally referenced—that we
develop a powerful and supportive skill that fills our lives
with the glow of self-loving. If we make time in our lives to
appreciate ourselves, then we develop a friend that we can
always count on to encourage, inspire, and support us—
ourselves!

During the rest of the day, make a conscious attempt to
appreciate the distinctive way that you choose to move in the
world—the unique way God is expressing itself in the
universe as you.

After my trip to the desert, I returned home with a
broader perspective on my life and a deeper appreciation of
who I am as a runner, a husband, a friend, and a human
being. Take time to appreciate yourself, and the magnificence
of who you are will also come into clearer focus!

Affirmation

I am appreciating the magnificence of who I truly am.

35

Rinse and Repeat

Quality: Protection

"I run into being and becoming and having been. Into feeling and seeing and hearing. Into all those senses by which I know the world that God made, and me in it. Into understanding why a Being whose reason to exist is 'to be' should have made me into His image."
George Sheehan, *Running and Being*

"Prayer does not change God, but it changes him who prays."
Søren Kierkegaard

I am a big fan of the bathtub—a remnant of my European heritage perhaps! I have been known to soak my tired muscles for an hour or more, particularly on an evening after a long and challenging morning run. But immediately after getting back from a workout, nothing beats the combination of elation and relaxation that a hot, refreshing shower offers. It's one of the images I use to keep me going during hard training runs.

I stand under the streaming water, allowing the satisfaction of another honored commitment to my running (and thus to myself) fill my being. Relaxing into the pleasant blend of tiredness and exhilaration, I scan my entire body and make note of any areas that may need special attention: ice, massage, or the focus of extra stretching.

In the glow of my completed workout, I am especially attuned to the deep level of gratitude I have for the blessings of continued good health and physical strength. I have a deep appreciation for the miracle of my body and the pleasure, balance, and insight it affords me through running. While in the past I have taken for granted the fact that I return home in one piece day after day, I have since transformed my shower into a time to anchor in my gratitude for my safe return home, untouched by injury, dogs, or cars.

I imagine the water that is falling onto my body to be a waterfall of golden-white healing light, the light of Spirit, and I repeat out loud a laminated Body Blessing[2] that hangs in my shower. It reads as follows:

Loving Creator,

Bare and warm in your presence, I acknowledge the miracle of my body.

Every day you bless my feet, toes, and toenails.
You bless my ankles, my calves, knees, thighs, and hips.
You bless all the muscles, tendons, bones, and nerves throughout my body.

You bless my sex and all the ways my body expresses both masculine and feminine energies.

You bless my back and spine, my abs, chest, and butt.
You bless the natural landscape of my entire body: its curves, creases, moles, wrinkles, and veins.
You love and bless all of my physical uniqueness.

---

[2] Available at www.body-blessing.com

You bless my heart and lungs.
You bless my blood and all the good things it carries.
You bless all my internal organs and systems, as they function fully
and support each other in harmony.
Each and every cell of my body is filled with your healing light.

You bless my shoulders and arms.
You bless my elbows, wrists, hands, fingers, and fingernails.

You bless my neck, throat, and voice.

You bless my eyes and my ears.
You bless my nose and sinuses, my mouth and teeth.
You bless my face and all my skin.
You bless my brain, my head, and my hair.
You bless my Spirit.

I am deeply grateful for the Earthly life my physical body gives me
today and every day, and for the joy I receive through running.
And as I make peace with myself, I know I am contributing to peace
in our world.

And so it is!

And so I let it be!

As I move through this blessing, I envision each part of my body—both internal and external—being bathed in the healing and protective energy of Spirit. At the same time, I imagine the me that lives inside the vehicle of my body being swathed in the safety of this energy. My thoughts, my feelings, my dreams and aspirations, I place all of these into this light. By the end of this blessing, I am filled with profound gratitude for the amazing gift that is my body and with a clearer connection with the divine being that my body carries in the world—me!

As I see myself at the center of this stream of light and love, I feel safer and more at ease. As a result, I am more empowered to deal masterfully with all the experiences that are part of daily living, whatever they may be.

As you run today, imagine yourself bathed in a shower (or cloud, or bubble, or whatever works with your imagination!) of golden-white light. As children, we often had imaginary powers, such as cloaks that made us invisible or protected us from bullets, or evil spells. As adults, we may not feel we need protection from the same forces (unless we live in a major city!). Nevertheless, consciously making time to surround ourselves in the light of Spirit can help us keep our balance when others are losing theirs. As a runner, I will take any help I can get to keep me fit and injury-free and out of the path of crazy dogs and drivers!

When you return from your run, use your time in the shower to envision yourself being bathed in this light. You can use the blessing I have used above, and you may want to develop your own that addresses your particular needs. Remind yourself that this light is available to you wherever you are. Throughout your day, you can imagine this light surrounding you, supporting you, and energizing you. Whenever life throws me an unexpected curve ball, one of the most powerful tools available to me is to ask for Spirit's assistance and light.

Affirmation

I am filled, surrounded, and protected
with the healing light of Spirit.

*"All that you want to be, you already are.
All you have to do is move your awareness
and recognize the reality of your own Soul."*

John-Roger
Chancellor, University of Santa Monica

Qualities and Affirmations

Preparation
I am enthusiastically opening to the loving support
and guidance of Spirit in every area of my life.

Creativity
I am claiming my success—
flexing the muscles of my divine, creative power.

Attentiveness
I am listening to myself and others with the ears of my heart.

Expansion
I am stretching into the very best of who I am.

Acceptance
I am seeing myself and others through the eyes of my heart—
celebrating each Soul that I meet.

Self-Care
I am basking in the glow of my own tender loving care.

Loving Self-Discipline
I am experiencing consistent success
as I manifest my dreams with gentleness and ease.

Loving
I am listening to the clear and loving voice of Spirit
as it speaks through my heart.

Connection to Spirit
I am connecting fully with Spirit in each moment of my life.

Patience
I am filled with laughter and joy,
embracing every area of my life with loving patience.

Vision
I am giving myself permission to dream,
embracing the divine possibilities of my life.

Self-Acknowledgment
I am honoring God, myself, and others, as I reclaim
the magnificence and inherent goodness of who I truly am.

Faith
Trusting in Spirit's higher purpose for my life,
I am discovering that God *is* faith in me.

Playfulness
I am living in joy, playing into the hands of God.

Spiritual Fitness
I am supporting my spiritual fitness,
stepping into the very best of who I am.

Commitment
I am honoring the power of my word,
keeping my agreements with myself and others.

Courage
I am courageously moving
through the rich and changing landscape of my feelings,
guided and protected by Spirit.

Forgiveness
I am bathed in the compassion and tender loving of my heart,
forgiving myself as I remember who I truly am.

Generosity of Spirit
I am an open conduit for Spirit's healing love,
which is expressing itself through me and as me
in every moment of my life.

Responsibility
I am accepting responsibility for my own inner experience,
opening the door to greater happiness.

Adaptability
I am opening fully to divine guidance
as I journey home to God.

Harmony
I am moving and living in the world in harmony, balance, and grace.

Strength of Heart
I am trusting in God's plan for my life, gratefully opening to
and accepting the blessings contained in all my experiences.

Dominion
Moment to moment, I am meeting my world,
inside and out, with loving positivity.

Openness
I am opening to the infinite gifts of Spirit, creating space for
God's love and divine inspiration in every area of my life.

Choice
I *am* a turning point, consciously choosing in this and every moment to
remain in a place of loving—expressing Spirit's divine plan of peace.

Letting Go!
I am letting go and letting God, living in divine grace.

Gratitude
I am grateful for the gift of life and for all its many blessings—
both seen and unseen.

Abundance
I am living in the divine flow of the all-good—
abundance is my natural state of being!

Peace
I am balanced and at peace—in body, mind, heart, and spirit.

Encouragement
I am supporting myself with constant, loving encouragement.

Independence
With Spirit as my partner,
I am living the very highest vision for my life.

Self-Appreciation
I am appreciating the magnificence of who I truly am.

Protection
I am filled, surrounded, and protected
with the healing light of Spirit.

WEB SITES FOR QUOTES

http://www.boulderbodywork.com/bios/index.html

http://www.whatquote.com/quotes/Clint-Eastwood/12086-If-you-think-it-s-go.htm

http://www.racingtheplanet.com/resources/

http://archive.thenorthernecho.co.uk/2002/8/11/124961.html

http://www.quotegarden.com/confidence.html

http://www.georgesheehan.com/essays/essay1.html

http://www.quotelady.com/authors/author-j.html

http://www.devinesports.com/Article.7+M547b7a742bd.0.html?&cHash=71fa48ad1e

http://en.thinkexist.com/quotes/priscilla—welch/

http://www.whatquote.com/quotes/Les-Brown/376-Shoot-for-the-moon--.htm

http://www.cybernation.com/quotationcenter/quoteshow.php?id=28356

http://www.positiveatheism.org/hist/quotes/quote-h1.htm

http://www.goethesociety.org/pages/quotescom.html

http://www.agingfabulous.com/sunshine-is-delicious/

http://www.ohiorunner.com/Running—Quotes.aspx

http://www.rrca.org/coaching/ch3.html

http://www.whatquote.com/quotes/Henri-Louis-Bergson/18435-To-exist-is-to-chang.htm

http://www.lovely.clara.net/cocreation.html

http://www.anvari.org/fortune/Quotations—3/347.html

http://www.dailycelebrations.com/092599.htm

http://www.schipul.com/en/q/?1081

About the Author

After traveling extensively in Europe, Asia, Australia, Southern Africa, and North America over the course of ten years, Toby Estler moved to the United States from his native England in 1994, amidst virulent rumors of an expulsion personally demanded by then Prime Minister Margaret Thatcher. He does all that he can to perpetuate those rumors.

Since landing in the United States, he has grown up and become a husband, father, author, poet, seminar leader, and life coach. He holds a Master's Degree in Spiritual Psychology from the University of Santa Monica and is a member of the Los Angeles Poets and Writers Collective. He also makes a truly remarkable leek and potato soup.

One of the millions of runners that head out each day in search of peace, meaning, and inspiration, he can currently be found running along the beaches, rivers, trails, and roads of Southern California, where he lives with his wife Teresa and daughter Hayden.

Blending well over a decade's management and leader-ship experience in sales and marketing with the additional strengths and qualities developed through running (as well as some very particular skills learned at Her Majesty's pleasure in Britain's Wormwood Scrubs Prison), Estler now offers inspirational life coaching to individuals and groups in both personal and business settings.

You can enjoy daily uplifting quotes, additional running and exercise meditations, as well as thoughtful, inspirational reflections at his website: www.runninghomeonline.com. To share your experience of using the material in this book, request information about his coaching and seminar availability, or to receive his leek and potato soup recipe, you can e-mail him at runninghome@earthlink.net.

ROBERT D. REED PUBLISHERS ORDER FORM

Call in your order for fast service and quantity discounts

(541) 347- 9882

OR order on-line at **www.rdrpublishers.com** using PayPal.

OR order by mail: Make a copy of this form; enclose payment information:

Robert D. Reed Publishers

1380 Face Rock Drive, Bandon, OR 97411

Send indicated books to:

Name _____

Address _____

City _____State _____Zip _____

Phone _____Fax _____Cell_____

E-Mail _____

Payment by check or credit card *(All major credit cards are accepted.)*

Name on card _____

Card Number _____

Exp. Date_____Last 3-Digit number on back of card_____

Note: Shipping is $3.50 1st book + $1 for each additional book.   Qty.

Running Home: 35 Moving Meditations for Runners
by Toby Estler . . . .$14.95   _____

The Small Business Millionaire
by Steve Chandler & Sam Beckford . . . .$11.95   _____

The Joy of Selling
by Steve Chandler. . . . .$11.95   _____

Ten Commitments to Your Success
by Steve Chandler. . . . .$11.95   _____

Customer Astonishment: 10 Secrets to World-Class Customer Care
by Darby Checketts. . . . .$14.95   _____

LifeForce: A Dynamic Plan for Health, Vitality, and Weight Loss
By Jeffrey S. McCombs, D.C.. . . . .$11.95   _____

Other book title(s) from website:

_____ $ _____

_____ $ _____